A SMALL-TOWN WESTERN FF ROMANCE

Greta Rose West

COPYRIGHT

PUNK
ROSE

PRESS

ALSO BY GRETA ROSE WEST

Wild Heart: Welcome to Wisper

Subscribe to the newsletter for this short introduction into the Cade Ranch world and for extra goodies and scenes. Sign up at gretarosewest.com.

THE CADE RANCH SERIES IN ORDER

BURNED

BROKEN

BUSTED

BRAVED

BLINDED

THE WISPER DREAMS SERIES IN ORDER

RIVERS BETWEEN US

STORMS INSIDE US

MOUNTAINS DIVIDE US

LIGHT BETRAYS US

MIDNIGHT SURROUNDS US

ACKNOWLEDGMENTS

Book 9. Mind blown.

Here comes a bunch of thanks!

To Sean and Wyatt, love you. This next year is gonna be a whirlwind, but I've never been more excited. Even if I'm still too young to be a Gma, Wyatt, thanks for making me one!

And to my little Westie, who has just come into my life, but oh boy, did you make an entrance! Granny G is always on your side. Don't read this book! Or any of my books. Ever.

Thank you, Peter Senftleben. I don't know any more ways to tell you how lucky I am and how grateful I feel to have found you. If my lips could reach all the way to NYC, I'd kiss ya. Although, you'd probably hate that. So I'd wave from afar and blow kisses. How's that? Mwah, mwah, mwah!

Joanne Machin, I appreciate you more than you can know. You always say, "feel free to ignore this suggestion if you hate it," but I never hate your suggestions. I rarely dislike them! Just about every sentence I write is made better by your work. Thank you.

Chelsey and Natalia, I needed some outside input for this book. Thank you for giving it. You didn't know it, but when we met, you became inspiration I didn't know I wanted. Thanks for reading this book way before it was polished to a shine. I hope I didn't shock you too badly when I dumped you in the middle of a spicy love story out in the sticks of Wyoming, and in the middle of a series, no less! And thanks to Teewow for introducing us. Drinks are on me next time!

Oh, and Natalia, to answer your question, no, I've never taken a dip in the lady pond, but there's a little bend in the river of my brain. It leads to the lady pond, and no man could ever brave its rapids! ;p

Thanks to Elle King for her song "America's Sweetheart". It's Abey's song and I jammed out so hard in my car for a month straight! Also, to Brandi Carlile, you and the stunning lilt and fall of your voice inspire me pretty much every day.

If you follow me on social media, you've probably seen posts and stories about my overzealous love of bears, and how at my writing retreat in Asheville this past summer, I met and fell in love with a group of indie romance authors. We made friends with a black bear, and we've become a little tribe, and now there isn't a day that goes by when we don't laugh or lift each other up. We help each other with many of the gazillions of things we have to do to write, release, and promote our books. Sometimes, one of us has something really exciting to celebrate, and our DMs become a party! Or sometimes we get spitting mad about something, and I'm so thankful that I can go to any one of these women, and they will support and encourage me. Thank you and I love you, RAWR. You are my safe space. ;)

A huge shoutout goes to the ladies in the Wisperites Unite Facebook group who helped me name Red's store. I can't even remember what I called it before I asked for input from the group, but whatever it was, it was awful. Thanks to Lissanne, Darcy & JD, Kimberly, Laurie, Lucinda, Jeanie, Geri, Tessie, Pamela, Michelle, Nikki, Penny, Cori, and Jo Ann. The Red Wild Outdoors was a mash-up of a few of your suggestions, and I LOVE it! Thanks for always being engaged with the stuff I post, and for supporting me in this whirlwind author thing I'm doing! xoxo

And last but never least: Thank you, ARC team!!

Thanks for always hyping my books. Sometimes I get discouraged or frustrated, like when someone leaves a nasty review or sends me a passive-aggressive email about the word "ain't," but then I get a message from one of you, telling me how much you love one of my characters or how you wish you could move to Wisper. It's then that I remember how to keep going and why I should. Thank you. Thank you from the bottom of my heart. Thank you.

To Chelsey & Natalia:
A love like yours should be in every book!

https://www.thetrevorproject.org
https://www.matthewshepard.org

CHAPTER ONE

ABEY

IF YOU LOVE SOMEONE, set them free.

Could I apply that to myself? Or how 'bout this: if our lives have been made up of a series of moments in time filled with love and chaos and wonder, would anyone mind if I deleted a minute? Just one. Specifically, this one...

"So, are you butch?" my date asked, looking at my chest, right at tit level, as she unfolded a paper napkin and placed it over her mini skirt-covered lap. "Or soft butch? Is that why you got involved in law enforcement?" Finally, and for the first time since the hostess had led us to our table and we'd sat, Kayla's eyes lifted to mine.

I stared down at my outfit, a loose-fitting red and black flannel and black skinny jeans. Was I giving off that vibe? A butch vibe? Just 'cause I'd worn a flannel shirt? What kind of question was that? Who didn't wear flannel? There was literally nothing more comfy, and mine was thin and soft. I spent forty bucks on the damn thing. It was probably the most expensive piece of clothing I owned.

"Sorry?"

We'd been in this restaurant in downtown Jackson for three minutes, and already, I regretted coming on this date.

The couple at the table next to ours clinked their tiny ceramic teacups in a toast, but other than that, the buzz of conversation around us was low. I peeked left and right. The topic of my sexuality wasn't one I wanted broadcasted. I mean, obviously, I was gay. I was on a date with a chick, for shit's sake, but c'mon.

She shrugged. "I didn't mean anything by it. I just meant, like, who are you?"

She hadn't meant anything by it? It could mean so *many* things. And how did my flannel shirt have anything to do with who I was or my job as a deputy for the Teton County Sheriff's Department? Hadn't she noticed the almost see-through black lace tank underneath? I'd left the flannel's buttons open so she would. My boobs were practically screaming to get out of the damn thing.

I would admit, no one would refer to me as the foremost expert on lesbian lingo, but I was pretty sure there weren't a lot of "butch" women walking around with their chests on display.

But my rack wasn't the thing I'd hoped my date would notice about me.

Unfortunately, it was usually the thing women did notice, which was exactly the reason this was my first date in over two years. I didn't want a hookup. I wanted more. Who didn't?

Who didn't want love?

"Uh, I don't really know how to answer that question."

I was just me. Just Abey. Why did she feel the need to categorize me? And now my date had me wondering if there was a website somewhere out there that listed all the different types of lesbians. Could somebody clue me in? Sitting across from an extremely feminine woman, with her flowing dark hair, a face full of makeup, and long pink fingernails, I frowned in confusion as it dawned on me that I was pretty clue*less*. Was what I wore a comment on the kind of women I was supposed to want? Did that transfer over to the bedroom?

"But what do you like, Abby?"

Her mispronunciation of my name burrowed into the back of my brain, like an itch. I scratched the back of my head, trying to dig it out with my fingernail. It didn't work. I kept my nails short for my job. Convenience wasn't often found when trying to load bullets into a gun with long daggers superglued to the ends of one's fingers.

"Do you like femme girls, masculine girls—what's your preference?"

"Um," I mumbled, unsticking the one-page laminated menu from the table in the new Italian/Tibetan fusion restaurant in Jackson, Wyoming, the one that was supposed to be "to die for," but was more like "might kill me by salmonella poisoning." They should've served the complimentary tea with a side of hand sanitizer. The whole place was like a sticky, garlic-y hole in the wall.

Who drinks hot tea in the middle of summer anyway? Then again, who wears flannel in this weather? Did it mean I *was* butch?

"My name is *Abey*," I clarified, trying not to seem bitchy, but jeez.

The whole conversation was making me uncomfortable, and she knew my damn name. We talked about it when she called me last night. She'd even commented that it was unusual. Was it too much to expect my date to pronounce my name correctly? Seriously, who was the "manlier" person in this scenario?

"It's not hard," I said. "It's the first two letters of the

alphabet: AB. Or if, like, you're standin' in front of a beehive, and one bee flies out, you'd say, 'Oh look, there's a bee.'"

She blinked once, but there appeared to be no recognition anywhere within her brain.

"That's me," I sang in a cutesy voice, "a bee," and I wiggled my fingers above our table. She didn't laugh, so I continued. "And I prefer *women*. I also prefer steak and potatoes." If this chick wanted good food, we should've gone to José's Diner back in Wisper.

Except I was the one who'd suggested going to Jackson. The city's busy summer tourism made for better anonymity. I wouldn't have been comfortable going on a date in Wisper. Too many prying eyes. But there were more than enough good restaurants in Jackson, and none of them had ever made me worry about food poisoning.

My date, cute Kayla, frowned in further confusion. We'd been set up by a friend of a friend who was friends with my friends, who I might've already decided to arrest.

Looking up from the menu and into her eyes that were lined with false lashes, all I saw was a watery blue void. Best to cut and run now. "You seem, uh, nice, Kayla, but I dunno if this is me." I dropped the menu, and it stuck right back to the spot I'd just peeled it off of.

Kayla smiled, but it seemed fake, which made me question why she'd even wanted to go on this date in the first place. It wasn't my freakin' idea. We'd barely spoken in her car on the way to the restaurant, and what we did say felt forced and awkward.

"Okay." She watched me wiping my hands on my thighs as I carefully tried to avoid getting the sticky yuck on my hat in my lap. "Would you like to go somewhere else?"

One point for her. She could read the room. Maybe the night was salvageable. Maybe cute Kayla could be my person. I looked up and unleashed on her what those terrible friends called "the full Abey experience." I flashed her the biggest smile I could. "Yeah? You wanna get outta here, find somewhere we can share a big ol' steak?"

She made a disgusted face, shaking her head. "You want to share food? And actually, I don't eat meat."

Aaand nope. "Welp"—I popped my lips—"I don't really like food without it."

"Is that a metaphor for, like, your sexuality? Are you bi or maybe just questioning?"

"Huh? A metaphor?" I didn't mean to do it, but a snort escaped me. "No. I just like steak. Beef, really, all kinds. I'm not real particular." I felt the need to explain further because she was looking at me like she didn't understand English. "Y'know, like, hamburger, meatloaf, chili?"

Now she was gaping at me like I'd grown two extra heads, and that was when I knew for sure I needed to get out of this ridiculous restaurant and run for the hills. I wasn't the richest person in the world, but I stood and pulled a fifty from my pocket. I set it on the table next to the drink I hadn't touched. "Sorry. Drinks are on me, but I, uh—"

She blinked two more times in confusion. Had she never been dumped before? Probably not. She was beautiful, if you went for the perfect, no-hair-out-of-place thing, but c'mon. We clearly weren't compatible. Had about zero things in common. Wasn't that obvious at this point? According to her, in her saltine-beige Hyundai on the way here, cute Kayla's hobbies were shopping and making TikTok videos. She couldn't be more opposite of me if she tried. I liked getting dirty, hiking and mudding, and I got the feeling that if she got a speck of dust on her shirt, she'd scream.

I wanted something different. Was that so wrong?

"I gotta go."

"Are you sure?" she asked, grabbing my hand as I tried to make my escape. Now, she was batting her spider-leg eyelashes at me and stroking the inside of my wrist with her middle finger. "I mean, we could go straight for the good stuff, if you want."

"The good stuff?"

"Sex," she said, pursing her lips, and the corners tilted up a little.

Yikes. That had been a little too loud for my liking. I looked around, but it didn't seem like anyone had heard her. No one scoffed or made the sign of the cross over their chest. It was what my mama would've done, even though she wasn't anywhere near Catholic. In my opinion, she wasn't even a good Christian sometimes. Not that I was an expert on church. I hadn't stepped foot in one since the ninth grade.

"You're really sexy," Kayla said, looking at my chest again. "We could go back to my place."

Ah. And here was why she'd agreed to the date. I wasn't opposed to some good ol' strings-free down and dirty, though it wasn't my usual MO. But then again, I didn't really have an MO. But then she blinked again, and I felt the urge to swat at her eyes with a rolled-up newspaper.

I pulled my arm from her grasp carefully. I didn't want to be rude, but her come-on was giving me the heebie-jeebies. "No, thank you. Sorry for wastin' your time. Have a good night."

I almost ran out the door. I snatched my phone from my back pocket as I went, and as soon as I cleared the building, I popped my hat back on my head. The hat I wore every day. The same one everybody in my life who loved me didn't seem to have a problem with, but this chick, cute Kayla, had been eyeing like it offended her personally. Jackson, Wyoming was the wrong place for her if a Stetson wasn't in her fashion vocabulary. Besides, I had Instagram. Cowboy hats were all the rage with the trendy women set these days. Mine had become a little more worn-in and sweat-stained than the hats girls like Kayla wore on IG, but the point was, I liked my damn hat!

I called Sam, and as soon as she answered, I scolded her. "You and Juneau made me come on this date, so you better put your butt in a car and come get my dumb ass."

"Oh no," she said. "It's not going well?"

"Ain't goin' at all. Just come get me."

She winced in my ear, sucking in air through her teeth. "I can't, Abey. I'm so sorry. The kids and I are babysitting for Carly tonight. They didn't leave me a car seat for little Donny, and Frank's working your shift."

Dammit. "I'll call a cab."

"Don't be ridiculous. It's way too far. That would cost a fortune."

True. "I'll call Juneau."

"She's out of town. Remember? She has that conference thing this weekend. Why don't you try Phil or Cal?"

"I'm not callin' those two old biddies. Neither one of 'em should be drivin', 'specially not after dark." Groaning, I looked up at the sky, cursing my friends silently. Oh, book club would be hearing about this. They were the assholettes who'd arranged this date. "Alright. I'll figure it out. Bye."

"Abey, can't you call the station—"

I hung up. I felt terrible about it. It wasn't like me, but I'd apologize when I saw Sam at the library tomorrow.

No, I couldn't call the station, not the one in Wisper, 'cause, like she'd said, her husband Frank had taken my shift tonight, and my boss had gotten stuck at headquarters here in Jackson. There'd been some kind of HR nightmare at the main Jackson station. I wasn't sure of the particulars, but I knew Carey had his hands full. I didn't want to make his night worse. No, my co-workers had enough to deal with without me calling them with my drama.

The rest of the guys from HQ had sticks up their butts about me being a deputy, y'know, 'cause I was a woman and all—God forbid—but I knew Carey'd paid for it over the years, so I stayed out of their way when I could. Which meant I wouldn't call any other station in Teton County either.

Fine.

Clicking my screen two more times, I called the one person on the planet I *really* didn't want to, rubbing at an annoying twinge I had begun to feel that festered an inch below my sternum.

"Mama?"

"What, Abey? My show's on. I can't talk."

In this age of digital streaming, she couldn't just press the pause button?

"Ah, yeah, I know. It's Saturday night, but I need a ride. I'm in Jackson."

She took a drag from her cigarette; I heard the inhale and the sizzle of the paper burning at the end. "Call Frank."

"Can't. He's workin' my shift."

"Why's he doin' your job for you, Abey?"

"I, uh, I had a… date."

"Girl, you know that ain't what Jesus wants."

The twinge turned into a full-blown ache. I rubbed harder.

"Yeah, Mama. I know you think that, but I still need a ride. If it makes you feel any better, the date was a bust."

"Hm." That one syllable told me everything I needed to know about how my own mother viewed my sexuality. Besides the judgmental looks and the comments she some-times made that I was hurting Jesus' feelings because that was what her pastor was always spouting, she never made a peep about the fact that I was gay. Since Daddy died, she avoided the subject like the plague.

Breathing through my nose, I closed my eyes, tapping on my chest now. Damn near beating on it. "Y'know what? Never mind. Thanks anyway." I hung up.

Shit. Shit. Shit. This would be the last time I let somebody convince me not to drive my own damn truck on a date.

I didn't want to call my brother. He had so much on his plate. My niece was probably already in bed, and Bax had to get up before the sun every morning. The last thing he needed was to be awoken on a Saturday night and reminded that he was alone with no one to take out on a date since his wife Candy had died. My brother was still heartbroken, and I'd walk across the entire Teton range before I bugged him.

I had two other brothers. One lived too far away, and the other one might as well have. Dixon was about as reliable as a piece of toast.

When I turned to pop a squat on the curb to download Lyft, I caught a glimpse of a possibility. A sexy but argumentative possibility.

Devona Mescal.

Devo.

It wasn't unusual to run into someone from my hometown in the city. Wisper was still severely lacking in entertainment and food options, although, if José from the diner heard me say that, he'd chase me down the street and threaten to paddle me with his spatula. His chili was the best I'd ever tasted, but a girl could only eat so much chili. But my point was, variety was the spice of life. Right? Wasn't that the saying?

"Last ditch effort," I said to the summer moon, and a shooting star zipped in front of it. Maybe that was a good sign?

If this didn't work, I'd be spending half my next paycheck on a ride.

I held my breath as I approached the one person from my hometown who didn't automatically smile when she saw me.

I really didn't like asking people I barely knew for help. Offering the help—easy peasy. Asking for it was a whole other thing. And maybe I worried a little about how Devo might turn me down when I begged her for a ride. She wasn't exactly known for holding her tongue, and I felt pretty confident that tongue was loaded with all kinds of things she might feel the need to spit at me.

But if she wasn't the sexiest woman I'd ever seen, I was a liar.

I hadn't known she was gay until the day I arrested her the first time. I'd figured she might be since she worked at the community center and it had become a safe haven for LGBTQ kids, but I hadn't had confirmation until that morning. As I slapped cuffs on her wrists for organizing a protest without a permit, parking in front of a fire hydrant, and mouthing off to the sheriff, her anger was delectably adorable. Her cheeks had turned red as a rose, and she huffed and puffed all the way across the street to the station. She hadn't really been "in custody," but she'd pissed off Carey that day with all her backtalking, and he thought she could use a little time to cool off.

She wore cutoffs that day, too, and I remembered the way her short but shapely legs had filled them out. But besides the physical attraction I felt toward her, she'd managed to mesmerize me a little with the way she was always up in arms about something. It was endearing. And admirable.

Not like me. I had a lot of opinions, but I kept them to myself. I was too afraid to be judged for going against the grain.

But not Devo. No siree.

And now that I'd spotted her, I really hoped she'd say yes when I asked for a ride because I was excited to be trapped in her truck with her. I wanted to know what injustice or wrong-doing she was all jazzed about these days. I just wanted to listen to her talk.

There was something about the passion in her voice when she got all hot and bothered about the issues she believed so passionately in. She was a loud, big presence for such a little lady. Secretly, I always loved getting called over to Ace's House. Not that I was glad for whatever incident I'd had to respond to, but Devo was usually present. If I was being honest with myself, I always got a little excited to see her and hear her huffing and puffing again.

Tonight, Devo appeared to be picking up her dinner from Punky's, the best pizza place in Jackson. She held a pie box in the air in one hand like she was about to serve it to a table of diners. Hopefully, that meant she was headed back to Wisper, which was also my destination. Or she might've been headed home to Barton, but she'd have to pass through Wisper to get there. Either way, it was in my direction.

I winced silently but straightened my shoulders as I walked closer. Somehow, approaching her felt like walking toward a guillotine.

"Hey, Devo." Throwing her a limp wave when she turned at the sound of her name, I kept my pace toward her truck parked across the street from the awful restaurant Cute Kayla had taken me to. Apparently, Kayla had decided to stay for the ambiance 'cause I hadn't noticed her leave after I did. "It's Abey Lee. Remember me?"

Devo rolled her eyes. I saw it eight car lengths away before she turned to slide the pizza box into her front seat. I also noticed that she'd tucked her hair behind one ear, her tits were little and high, even without a bra, which she had definitely not worn tonight, and her hips swayed in a seductive manner when she moved. They looked soft and wide.

Well, I didn't know if they were soft, but I could imagine wrapping my hands around them. Bet they'd feel soft then.

She turned back toward me, and when she spoke, the annoyance in her voice rang loud and clear. I was definitely not her favorite person. "You've arrested me twice. What do you think?" She looked me up and down, her eyes lingering just a few seconds too long on my legs, and she crossed her arms over her thin blue tank top. Her skin looked light brown and velvety.

I stopped ten feet in front of her. I wanted to touch her, just to see if she'd be as warm as I imagined.

"There somethin' I can help you with, *Deputy*?"

"Um, yeah, actually. I kinda need… a ride. And I was thinkin', since you're here and I'm here, and we're both goin' back to Wisper…"

Devo snorted, then blew a raspberry. The way her face pinched up was freaking hilarious, but I figured laughing at her probably wouldn't help my cause.

"You were thinkin' that, were ya? No, I can't give you a ride. I'm workin' tonight. I can't just pick people up and chauffer them around."

Pointing to her cutoffs and flip-flops, I asked, "You're workin'? That your uniform then?"

She rolled her eyes again.

A long, awkward silence stretched between us, but she didn't look away or make any move to get in her truck and leave. Her eyes shifted back to my legs in my jeans, and I watched how her full lips pursed.

It was a standoff, a deadlock, a duel of sorts at high noon or, well, maybe more like eight at night.

I could shoot a beer can off a fencepost from fifty yards away on a bad day, but I'd never been good at fighting, so I figured I best do the thing I knew she was waiting for, but I kicked the curb in front of me three times hard before I did it.

Resting my boot on the cracked hunk of concrete, I slid my hands into my back pockets and leaned forward a little. Devo tracked the movement, then her eyes snapped back to mine.

"I'm sorry I handcuffed you, Devo. Twice. And I'm sorry I laughed when you fell on your ass when you tried to be cool and jump the cuffs."

"Seriously?" she squeaked. "*That's* your apology?"

"Well now, I was just doin' my job, y'know?"

She growled at me!

"But I *am* sorry, Devo. Truly. And if you would be so kind, please can I catch a ride?"

I thought I could see her resolve slipping. She relaxed her defensive stance and dropped her arms to her sides, and right then, the burn in my chest disappeared. Maybe I could win her over. Maybe I could entice her onto Team Good Ol' Abey Lee.

"Fine," she grumbled and turned toward her truck, fumbling her keys in her hand and sassing me under her breath.

CHAPTER TWO

DEVO

DEPUTY LEE GRABBED the passenger-side door handle and yanked it open, then jumped into my truck. I swore I caught a whiff of honey when her hair fell over her shoulder. Under her brown cowboy hat, she'd worn it down, which was unusual. Normally, she kept it tied back in a tight pony at the base of her neck.

I hadn't tried very hard to hide my annoyance when she begged me for a ride. I'd been starving all day, so I'd changed after work and driven straight for Punky G's. Extra cheese pizzas with extra pineapples could put me in a happy food coma any day of the week, and bonus if it came from Punky's. I couldn't wait to get home to eat the pie currently resting on the deputy's lap. Okay, fine, so I had been planning to devour a couple pieces on the way home, but now with her beside me, I wouldn't, because I would most likely embarrass myself by sounding like a pig rooting through mud for a rotten tomato as I scarfed down a piece or four.

Plus, I really wanted to check on the little green pepper plant I'd potted and nurtured. Two months of babying it and no peppers yet. Hopefully, it wasn't still in the throes of death. I'd watered it, sung to it, and set it in the sunniest spot in the backyard. What more could the damn thing want from me? Was one tiny green pepper I could put in a salad for my mom so much to ask?

But Deputy Lee had caught me in a lie. It was a little white one. Big deal. Did she plan on locking me up for that too? Obviously, I wasn't working—my shorts barely covered my thighs. Truth be told, I was still mad at her for almost arresting me. Twice. But I knew if I said no to her, my boss would hear about it, and Theo wanted the community center I helped run, Ace's House, to have a good working relationship with the sheriff's office.

Fine. Whatever.

"Thanks," Deputy Lee said, a little bit out of breath from jogging to catch up with me before I drove off and left her stranded. "And before you start in on me, lemme say again, I'm sorry."

"You were right, Deputy Lee," I said grudgingly, keeping my eyes on the congested traffic around Town Square as I backed out of my parking space and we joined the barely moving queue. The people offering horse-drawn carriage rides to tourists were one block ahead of us, stopping the flow of cars and casting downtown in a red brake-light glow. "You were just doin' your job. Besides, Theo says I have to be nice to you. Where's your sheriff-y truck?"

Snapping her seatbelt into place, she chuckled and said, "At my house. And just call me Abey, please."

"Okay, Abey, how'd you get to town if you didn't drive?"

"My date picked me up."

I glanced at her out of the corner of my eye. I refused to look directly at her because then I'd see how attractive she was, and I would *not* bow down to that fact, even inside my own head. If I looked at her, I couldn't stay mad at her. "You wore that dumb hat on a date? With a *woman*?"

Still reeling from learning that, in fact, I was not the lone lesbian in Wisper like I'd thought, my jaw had dropped to the floor of the sheriff's station when Abey told me she was gay after she arrested me the first time. She'd even looked proud of making me speechless.

That was almost a year ago, and I'd spent the last twelve months trying not to notice her. Just 'cause we were both lesbians in the same small town where there were no others did *not* mean we had to hook up.

"What in the world is wrong with this hat?" She flicked the underside of the brim with two fingers. "I wear it every day at work, and nobody ever kicks up a stink. It ain't like I wore it inside the restaurant."

"It's dumb," I said, staring straight out the windshield, still working hard not to look in her direction. I definitely hadn't noticed how it really *wasn't* dumb, and in the right light, the shadows from the hat made her eyes seem to glow with a blue light that could've come straight out of some poem about the starry cosmos.

"Well, thanks for that. My ol' granddaddy gave it to me 'fore he died."

"Really?" I squeaked, finally turning her way a little. *Shit.* "I'm sorry. But you're… You're prettier without it."

Okay, fine. She was gorgeous, her naturally highlighted blond hair and tan skin absolutely flawless. And that was to say nothing of those eyes. Neverendingly deep, beautiful pools of blue that lit up like happiness itself when she smiled. Which she did a lot. She was funny and sarcastic, and had we not been "frenemies," I would have been charmed by both.

"I was just kiddin'," she admitted with a not-at-all-cute, throaty chuckle. "Sorry, that was kinda mean. Bought it out at

Bob's Feed and Tack." Tipping the hat up with another touch of her index finger, she turned in her seat toward me. "But you think I'm pretty?"

I shrugged one shoulder. "You're the only other gay woman in Wisper, or Barton, for that matter. Can you blame me for checkin' you out?" Like, literally every single day. I rolled my eyes at myself and immediately hoped she hadn't noticed.

"I thought you were just tryin' to figure a way to set me on fire. Wait, you know we're not the only two, right?"

"No, I didn't know that. Who?"

This time, she shrugged. "Not my place to say. But I will tell you"—she wiggled the same two fingers she'd flicked her hat with in the air—"there's two, and they're both considerably older than you and me."

I lost the fight I'd been having with myself not to stare at her. "Really?"

"Yup." She smiled so big when I finally gave her my full attention. Jeez. Her smile was bright and electric, and an errant thought flitted through my head: *what would it feel like to have that smile aimed at me every day?*

I shook it off with a little shudder. "Okay. I respect that, but that's cool. So then you're still the only other lesbian in town, at least the only one around my age." Like we had our own little club.

"How old are you?" she asked.

"Twenty-seven. Almost twenty-eight. I'm surprised you don't remember that from arrestin' me. Twice." I harrumphed. "How old are you?"

She laughed, biting the inside of her pale pink lip to hide a smirk, like maybe she was lying and she had remembered but was trying to act innocent. "You're a young *thang*. I'm thirty-two. And you were never under arrest. Not technically. Not yet."

Quickly looking away, I could already feel her charms working their magic on me, and I wasn't ready to like her yet. *Dammit.* But somebody needed to clue my subconscious into that stubborn fact.

Plus, she was totally checking me out. I could feel her eyes on me as we made our way to the highway through town, and it wasn't the first time.

And fine, I'd checked her out too. She had legs for days. She was at least half a foot taller than me, with an athletic build. She was strong but thin. I wondered if she worked out to stay in shape for her job. Or maybe she had just been born naturally perfect.

I'd seen her in action several times, not including the two times she'd hauled me to the station. Which was why I still held a grudge. Okay, fine, so I didn't have a permit when I tried to hold a gay rights protest in front of the sporting goods store owned by the local jerkoff curmudgeon, Red Graves, and she did warn us that morning not to block the fire hydrant. Technically, she could have just issued a fine, but then I went and ran my mouth. Apparently, calling the sheriff a "good ol' boy suck-up" was grounds for arrest. He never charged me formally. Mostly, he used it as a "time-out" for the loud-mouth contrarian I was proud to be.

Only in Wisper, Wyoming.

But the second time was one-hundred-percent unjustified. That jackass Red made it his mission to catch me in front of his store every time I walked past, just to argue with me and cause problems. He called me a carpet muncher, so I socked him one. I couldn't reach his face, so I punched him in the gut. And then Abey was there, appearing out of nowhere to slap cuffs around my wrists, and she threw me in the same holding cell she'd stuck me in the first time.

Another time-out. But whatever. Red deserved it.

But every time I ran into her in town, I remembered the two times she'd had her hands on my shoulders as she led me to jail. There was no way for me to forget because she was always stopping by my job. Her boss thought she was a better choice to help us deal with the troubled teenagers and the few women who'd come to Ace's House to escape bad home situations or abusive marriages.

I couldn't complain about Abey then. She *was* helpful, and I knew it had to be more comfortable for the women to talk to her than it would've been for them to talk to Sheriff Michaels or Deputy Sims 'cause they were both extremely male. Frank Sims was like a big boulder that patrolled Wisper in his truck, oozing testosterone out of his manly pores.

Abey was the better choice in those situations by a mile, and she really did have a beautiful soul, always ready and willing to help people in need. She'd volunteered more than once to help out with some of the fundraisers we'd held over the last couple of years.

It was annoying, in a super sweet, totally endearing way.

And her smile itself? Drop-dead gorgeous. Her lips were the softest shade of pink I'd ever seen, like the lightest pink peony petal.

And behind her friendly eyes and the lazy tilt of her lips, there was a ferociousness inside her. But she never let it out. At least not that I'd ever seen. She could joke with the raunchiest of men, she never seemed to be in a serious mood, and she made light of things in hard situations if it wasn't inappropriate.

Maybe that was how she dealt with difficult things, by trying to lighten the darkness they often brought.

The sexiest thing about her, though, was her belief in and passion for justice. I kind of felt bad that I had been on the wrong end of that conviction a couple times.

We had that in common, though my belief in justice was what paid her salary. It was why I kept getting locked up. So far, I hadn't gotten into too much trouble, and nobody'd pressed charges. Although, if I pushed my luck much further, I wasn't sure my boss would have my back. He was still mad at me for punching a fellow Wisper business owner. And it didn't help that The Red Wild Outdoors sat directly across Main Street from Ace's House.

"So why didn't your date drive you home?" I asked, hoping she'd keep talking and I wouldn't keep thinking about the color of her eyes, or her hair, or how I wanted to know what it would feel like to swipe my thumb slowly over that perfectly pink bottom lip.

"Well, probably 'cause I ran outta there quicker than a cat in a dog storm."

I laughed. I couldn't help myself. "Why?"

"Well, first, she pronounced my name wrong even though we had a whole conversation over the phone about it. And second, she was wearin' these fake eyelashes. It was all I could see when I looked at her, like big ol' spiders were takin' over her eyes."

I snorted. I could picture it, a tarantula over each eye, its legs dangling down. "How did she pronounce your name?"

"She called me Abby."

"That happens to me too. When people see my full name, spelled D-E-V-O-N-A, they assume it sounds like 'Dev-vona' instead of '*Dee*-vona'. Pretty common mistake. And then instead of Dee-vo, they call me 'Dev-vo'." I rolled my eyes. Who would go by the name 'Dev-vo'?

Abey nodded. "It's annoyin'. I didn't think it was too much for me to expect her to get that right."

Huh. Something we had in common. Go figure.

"My friend Millie wears fake lashes," I said, "but hers are subtle."

"Yeah, my sister-in-law used to wear 'em, too, when she and my brother would go out dancin'. Sometimes, when I'd stop by the house in the mornin', they'd be stuck to her cheek like some weird spiny bug."

A giggle slipped through my lips, and I had to admit, "You're funny."

"Been accused of worse," she said, smiling, and relaxed back against the seat. It felt like such an odd thing to see her loosening up around me when, not even an hour ago, I'd been convinced I hated her guts. But from what little I knew about her, that was just Abey, and feeling her relax beside me made me feel more at ease too.

I still felt her eyes on me, though, as we took the turn onto Route 20 and drove into the darkness. Silence had descended between us, but it felt like she wanted to talk.

Finally, in a soft tone of voice I'd never heard from her before, she said, "Can I ask you somethin'?"

"Yeah, I guess," I answered warily. Were we the kind of friends who talked like this, like we were familiar? Definitely not.

"It's... I dunno. Sensitive? It's lesbian stuff."

I hadn't meant to laugh again, but I couldn't remember anyone ever phrasing a question like that. "Lesbian 'stuff'?"

"Never mind."

"No. I'm sorry." That was rude of me. It was clear she wanted to ask a serious question. "Please, ask me."

"Okay." She fidgeted a little. I felt the movements under the dingy cloth upholstery covering my truck's long bench seat, but then she stilled. She removed her hat and rested her hands over it on top of the pizza box on her lap. While I tried really hard not to notice how her hair cascaded down her back and how static inside the truck drew it to stick to the seatback, she asked, "What exactly does 'butch' mean?"

"What?" Wasn't that Lesbian 101? She didn't know that already?

"Am I… that? Do I dress butch? I wear flannel a lot. I didn't know I wasn't supposed to. When you look at me, is that what you see?"

"Why're you askin' me this?"

She hesitated, and there was so much vulnerability in that pause.

"No," I said to ease the uncomfortable air surrounding her whole body that was pulsing out around her in waves. "I mean, I don't really know the official definition of the word butch, but in my view, it's a lesbian who prefers to present in a more masculine manner than feminine." I risked a quick glance in her direction and saw her deep in thought, her eyebrows pinched together and a frown on her lips. "You know? Like women who might wear their hair in a guy's type of hairstyle, or maybe they wear clothes that are traditionally more masculine. Maybe clothes that don't accentuate the female parts of a woman's body. A butch lesbian is more masculine than feminine."

I shook my head. "You *definitely* don't fit that description, and it has nothing to do with you wearing flannel. Everyone wears flannel."

No matter how hard I tried, I couldn't stop my eyes from finding their way between her thighs. Every time I looked her way, my eyes caught on her legs in her sexy, hip-hugging jeans. That wasn't what I considered "butch."

In fact, I considered myself more on the "butch" spectrum

than Abey was. She wore her hair in a severe style for work, but like tonight, it was loose and gorgeous. Definitely feminine. She'd grown it out over the last year. She used to wear it the same length as me, maybe a little longer than my messy bob, probably for her job, but now, every time I saw her in town, it had grown longer.

"Actually," I said, "the flannel looks really good on you. It brings out the highlights in your hair." I nodded to her shirt. "And *that* flannel fits you well, in a feminine way." I'd already imagined running my hands underneath so I could wrap them around her hips to pull her closer for a kiss.

Great, Devo. Way to be supportive of a fellow lesbian. Imagining mauling her with your tongue is not *support.*

"But does that mean… If I were butch, would that mean that I think like a man? Like I see myself as a man?"

"No, not necessarily. Some women might, but it's not a prerequisite. Abey, LGBTQ is a spectrum. You fall on that spectrum wherever you choose to. There is no parameter you're required to meet to be butch or not butch."

She nodded but didn't say anything.

"You are who you are," I said. "Whoever you want to be."

Had she never had friends she could talk to about this? What about her family? I talked to my mom about everything.

"Yeah, but…" she hedged. "Does it mean that I'm supposed to be with a certain type of woman?"

"No. Absolutely not."

Still, I could tell she felt uncomfortable, so I thought for a moment. Maybe I could find a better way to help her understand.

"Take me, for example," I said. "I consider myself to be smack-dab in the middle of the spectrum. I'm one-hundred-percent gay. There's no in between for me. I'm only attracted to women, but all kinds of women. My last long-term relationship was with a woman who's extremely feminine, but then Dede, remember her? The bartender at Manny's?"

"Yeah. She moved away, right?"

"Yeah, she did, about a year ago, I think, but we hooked up a few times before she left, and she's more butch than anyone I've ever dated. Definitely more than you."

"So then what kind of lesbian am I?"

"You tell me. How do you see yourself? What do you prefer in a partner?"

"I… I've never really had a partner."

"Oh. Well, if you imagine yourself with your ideal partner, who do you see?"

She blushed. I didn't even have to look at her to know. I felt it. The temperature inside my truck rose twenty degrees. Or so it felt. The truck was an old piece of shit. It didn't have air conditioning. I could've rolled down my window to cool things down, but then the fast rush of the air from the highway would've drowned out the sound of her voice, and the intimacy of this conversation dictated that she needed to be heard and understood.

"It's okay," I said. "You don't have to tell me. But I guess it's somethin' for you to consider, in case you ever decide you want to… find someone."

"I do," she whispered. "I really want that." She took a deep breath and blew it out loudly, effectively ending that part of our conversation. She never brought it up again. "What about you?"

"Me?"

"What're you lookin' for?"

"Oh, I dunno. Same as everybody else, I guess. Someone to love. Someone to share my life with. You know, the usual."

"Yeah."

Time flew while we talked, and it surprised me how

easily the conversation flowed. When we pulled into Wisper, she asked, "Could you drop me at my house, please? It's over on Third Street."

"Sure."

"Thanks. Where do you live?"

"With my mom. In Barton. I know, it's lame," I said. "But she's all alone, you know?" My next question surprised me, but I really wanted to know. "Do you go on dates often?"

"No," she said. "Not really. Which explains my clueless-ness. You?"

"Not at all."

"Hm." She nodded.

My admission probably hadn't surprised her. It wasn't like lesbians paraded around small-town Wisper, Wyoming, hanging out by the hardware store, yelling, "Hey, girl, hey!"

Her vulnerability had softened me toward her, and suddenly, the sweet scent of her hair in my truck and the familiar way she felt sitting next to me, even though she never had before, were drawing me to her. All of my senses focused on her, how she breathed and moved. Every little noise she made had me dying to know the thoughts in her head.

"But I would," I said, and I caught the tender skin on the inside of my bottom lip between my teeth. *Devo, no! Just no.*

I couldn't help wondering about her. Where did she go for sex? She'd said "not really," but did that mean she did date occasionally? The curiosity was killing me, and I had no idea where it had come from. Probably because she looked hot as hell, with her tight jeans and silky lace tank under her flannel and her boobs dying to spill out. Besides the racy undershirt, her outfit was also very Abey. If she wasn't dressed in her work uniform, she wore jeans and a flannel, but sometimes, she'd tie the flannel in a knot at her hip. Tonight, the stark red and black from her shirt made her hair look an even lighter blond. My eyes kept going to her hair.

Like now as I glanced her way again, I noticed how the natural highlights weaved throughout the darker yellow strands, and the baby hairs closer to her face seemed almost white and so curly. They were adorable, and so was the dimple deepening on the side of her cheek. I'd never noticed a dimple before.

"I mean," I hedged, trying to gauge her reaction to the direction of the conversation, "if there were more opportunities. But you know—there aren't."

She nodded. "Don't I know it."

The energy in the truck shifted. I held my breath for way too long before it all came out in a gush, and I heard myself say, "Theo says there's places in Boston where guys can go to… to meet other guys, if, like, they wanna hook up."

She looked at me. I felt her quizzical gaze on the side of my face. "Oh yeah?"

My next sentence came out really fast. "Yeah, and everyone there already knows no one's lookin' for a long-term thing. Just sex."

"Hm. Sounds handy." She laughed. "In more ways than one."

I laughed too. She was just so damn charming, but I caught myself. This was weird, right? Why all of a sudden was I nervous around her?

"You okay there?" she asked, cocking her head and watching how my smile turned into a wince.

But I'd never really given her a fair chance. I'd been pissed when she threw me in the clink, and then my anger at her was all I'd really been able to see. But tonight was the first time I'd ever noticed that there seemed to be a lot more to her.

Obviously, there was, and I was interested. And attracted. Like, a lot.

"Yeah." I laughed, but it sounded like I was choking. What the hell was I doing? But I kept going. "It's just, well, I've never heard about a place like that for women. At least, not around here. Have you?"

My hands tightened around the steering wheel. Oh man, I was fucking this up big time, and she probably had no idea the direction my thoughts had gone in.

"Sure haven't."

Come on, Deputy Lee. Grab a thread here. Did she really have no idea why I'd just said what I'd said? I gave it one last good shot. "If there were a place, would you… go there?"

"Dunno," she mused, but then she turned in her seat, facing me and looking right at me.

I kept my eyes on the road, but a funny, tightening feeling seemed to be taking over the space where my heart usually beat at a leisurely pace.

Finally, she was picking up what I'd just thrown down.

Or I thought she was.

She sounded almost surprised when she asked, "You would?"

And now, like an idiot, I shrugged. "Maybe, as long as I wasn't in a relationship at the time."

Her voice came out all husky and sexy. "*I'm* not in a relationship, Devo," she said. "Are you?"

Oh, she'd totally gotten it.

"No, but I hooked up with Dede Vasquez a couple times. I already said that. Sorry." Could she hear how my voice had started to shake? Nervousness rushed through me like wildfire. And why on earth was I bringing up the last woman I'd banged? Like, for real? *What is wrong with you?*

Finally, I looked at her. We were stopped at a light in the

middle of downtown Wisper. There was zero traffic, so when the light turned green, we sat there, just staring at each other.

Her eyes flashed cobalt before she said, "Um, Devo, you probably don't know this about me, but I'm not usually one to mince words. So, are you hittin' on me? I mean, is that what this is? You wanna have sex?"

My face had to be the color of a dark red cherry, and a warmth flooded my lower half. It zipped and zinged all the way down to my toes in my dollar-store flip-flops. My skin felt like it had caught fire, and I held my breath again, hoping like hell she wanted it too.

This night couldn't have taken a more surprising turn if I'd dreamed it up myself.

Could she tell I hadn't worn a bra tonight? She probably could, especially 'cause the seatbelt across my chest was making my breasts more noticeable, pushing them out on either side of the wide strap. I still felt her eyes on me, and I swore I could feel them zero in on the tips of my nipples, which, of course, were trying to poke through my tank top.

"Maybe," I whispered.

A soft huff of breath escaped her mouth. "I won't handcuff you, unless you're into that sorta thing."

I smiled. I really tried not to, but I lost the fight with my lips, and they lifted up. "Promise?"

She smirked, and a slew of images of the two of us pressed together flooded my mind—fingers wet, seeking hidden-away places, tongues hot and demanding.

I looked away. My breath quickened, and my heart must've thought I was running a marathon. *Oh God, if we do make out, I'll be all sweaty!*

I'd envisioned this, had thought about it many times when I'd seen her out around town or at the sheriff's station.

Abey had a light about her, and I was drawn to it. It was finally a relief to admit it to myself.

I'd been working at Ace's House long enough to know that people didn't gossip about her. No one outwardly questioned her sexuality, which was a little odd since our small town seemed focused on the subject these days. The opening of the pro-LGBTQIA+ community center saw to that. But Abey's name never came up, even though I knew for a fact that some of her friends knew she was gay. But maybe the rest of Wisper had no clue.

So, if she was attracted to me, too, would she act on it? Or would it be too dangerous for her if anyone found out? I hadn't considered that before I'd begun this outrageous conversation, in the middle of town, in my truck with her lithe legs only two feet from mine on the bench seat.

What would she do if I reached over and slid my hand up her thigh?

When I dared to look at her again, I noticed her breathing had sped up a little too. So maybe this wasn't at all one-sided.

"I live half a mile from here," she said, her voice coming out all breathy and low. So maybe she was attracted to me, too, or maybe my pheromones or the sexual charge in the truck were messing with the sound of her voice. Or was it all in my head?

I nodded, turning back to watch the light intently. When it blinked back to green, I tapped the gas pedal, but the truck lurched forward. "Shit."

She laughed at me, and her tone became a little teasing. "This is an interestin' turn of events, I have to say."

Once more, I looked at her and noticed the smirk was still firmly in place, but I saw something else. It was in her eyes.

Hunger.

"You sure about this?" she asked.

I breathed, "Yes." And now my heart *pounded* against my ribs. My fingers flexed on the steering wheel. I wanted to touch her.

"Okay then," she said easily, relaxing back against the seat again. "I can't wait to taste you."

The truck swerved to the side of the road, and my foot slipped off the gas pedal. "Oh my God."

So then, not *all* in my head.

CHAPTER THREE

ABEY

"IT'S BEEN A WHILE FOR ME," Devo said as we climbed side by side up my stairs. I hadn't touched her yet, but I was aching to. "I mean, the last time was before Dede moved away. A year."

"That's okay. It's been a while for me too." When we got to the top, I tucked an unruly flip of hair behind her ear and smiled at her.

Her hair was the thing. She kept it cut to her chin, and it was sexy as hell and black as midnight. That one stubborn strand was always popping out of place, and she had an adorable ducktail at the back of her neck she couldn't seem to get rid of no matter how many haircuts she got. Every single time I saw her in town, I searched for it.

"But I figure it's like ridin' a bike," I said. It had only been one lock of her hair between my fingers, but just that tiny bit of contact had my hands shaking. I tried to hide it while I unlocked my front door.

"Yeah," she said kind of breathlessly as I looked at her over my shoulder again. I couldn't stop looking at her. How crazy was it that I'd started the night with my first date in I couldn't remember how long, and now, instead, Devo stood on my doorstep, nervously waiting for me to touch her?

I turned the doorknob, trying to remember if I'd picked up my dirty clothes and thrown them in the hamper before I'd left for the worst date ever. I hadn't prepared for anyone to come home with me. I wasn't expecting it.

Didn't look like my neighbors were home. Their cars weren't parked in the driveway below my garage apartment, and I was glad for that. If Devo'd let me make her come, she could moan and scream all she liked without anybody knowing what we'd gotten up to.

She followed me inside, and I flicked on my tiny living room's light, dropping my keys in the ceramic bowl Frank's foster daughter, Nic, had painted for me by the door. "So, um, yeah. This is where I live. It's small, but it's only me, so…"

"It's nice," she said. "I live with my mom still. I already said that."

"I'm not broke," I rushed to say. I lived meagerly, but that was on purpose. "I mean, I make okay money, but I help my family out sometimes. And what I don't use, I save. I'd like to buy my own house. Get me some land. Just a little bit. Maybe get some animals." Why was I rambling?

"Me too." And now she was blabbing a mile a minute, just like me. "I mean, I've been savin' for a house too. My mom and I rent. I really lucked into my job at the center. Theo's amazing, and I'm pretty sure he pays me way more than he should. And, actually, I wouldn't mind havin' a horse. We used to have one when I was a kid in New Mexico."

She took a big breath and held it, looking around my front room. The kitchen was squished into the corner and only had a two-burner stove, but I rarely cooked. Diner takeout was my gourmet meal of choice most nights.

"You nervous?" I asked, turning to face her and dipping my head a little to put myself in her eyeline.

"So nervous," she whispered when her eyes met mine.

I pressed my lips together, trying not to grin, trying not to show just how much I liked this side of her. The uncertainty in her eyes and the small smile growing there was a hell of a lot different than the scowl I had gotten used to seeing when she and I had reason to be near each other.

Backing up to my couch, I sat and patted the cushion next to me, trying to exude confidence and authority, but I was pretty sure my insides were shaking. Maybe we could talk first and she could relax. "C'mere."

But instead of sitting next to me, she climbed over my legs and straddled me. Just like Cute Kayla had said, "going straight for the good stuff." Tentatively, I wrapped my hands around Devo's hips, slipping my fingers through her belt loops as she centered her core above mine.

Her pink tongue swiped out to wet her lips. "You're not nervous?"

Looking up at her, I couldn't take my eyes away from the sheen across those plump lips. "Sure I am, but more than that, I'm so turned on by you."

"You are?"

"Yeah," I whispered, unbuttoning her shorts. I pulled the zipper down slowly. It sounded so loud in my quiet apartment. "Have been since the first time I arrested you."

She gulped.

"Devo, if this is too fast, just say it. I-I don't wanna read the signals wrong. I don't usually do stuff like this."

It was fast, but wasn't that what she wanted? A hookup? Wasn't that what the whole convoluted conversation in her truck had been about? I hadn't been lying; I'd never brought someone home with me for a quick fuck before.

But something about Devo and the way she was looking at me made me think that, if I'd said no, I would've regretted it forever.

It was a one-time thing. It had to be. My job made it so I couldn't make a habit of these kinds of meetings. Like a hole in the head, all I needed was the residents of Wisper saying to each other, "Did you know Deputy Lee is a lesbian?" It would distract people, which would make it harder for me to do my job well.

"No." She straightened her shoulders. "It's just that, besides Dede—who, let's be honest, everybody knew was a 'fuck and run' kinda girl—the last time I was with a woman, it was someone I was in a relationship with. It didn't end well. She really hurt me." She blushed, her light-brown cheeks deepening to a dusky rose color. "Maybe I made it sound like I was used to this… this kind of thing, but I'm not."

"I'm sorry," I said, feeling a stab of anger for whoever Devo's ex was.

She'd mentioned living on a reservation in New Mexico tonight, but I'd already known that about her. I'd never forgotten any of her personal information. How could I? She'd lived a pretty interesting life, and maybe I'd become a little smitten with her. It was probably just attraction, but I'd heard her once telling someone at Ace's House about her childhood.

And I thought I remembered something about her ex-girl-friend. Did she live close? Would they get back together? Looking in Devo's eyes, I saw goodness there. I couldn't understand why anyone would ever hurt her.

"But you got me beat. Like I said, I've never actually had a real relationship. Not a serious one."

She frowned. "Why not?"

"Dunno." I shrugged, my shoulders lifting her hands with the movement, and she gripped them harder, like she was afraid she'd fall off my lap. She didn't need to worry. My hold on her hips grew stronger by the second. If I hadn't left fingerprint bruises there, I would've been surprised. "I have to be careful 'cause of my job." I took a steadying breath. That was the last subject I wanted to talk about now. "Never mind. Story for another time."

Touching her stomach tentatively, I flattened my hand on her skin and turned it, pushing beneath the waistband of her shorts and her underwear while I leaned closer. Her belly was so cute, with a soft little pudge beneath her navel. I traced it with my thumb, and my heart raced as I slipped my fingers between her thighs and lifted up till I felt the wetness I couldn't wait to taste. I couldn't seem to look away from her deep brown eyes. Nervousness flashed in them, but I also saw need and want.

"Don't *you* hurt me," she said on a breath. "Promise me."

"Deal," was my reply right before I pulled her down to my mouth with my other fist on the back of her head, tangling that sexy black hair in my fingers, begging for her to come closer.

But I wouldn't promise anything. I never made them. They were too easy to break, and when a promise had been broken, well…

Nothing in the world felt worse.

It seemed like Devo's nerves flew right out the window then. She dug her knees into the couch cushions beside my thighs, lifting up above me so I had better access to her pussy, and I took advantage and slipped the pad of my thumb over her clit.

She moaned loudly, and breath forced its way out of my mouth all choppy, but I closed my eyes, trying to find calm inside, trying to imprint this night in my mind, to concentrate on what she felt like, what touching her skin felt like, and what kissing my fantasy made me feel. She'd barely touched me yet, but touching her was ecstasy.

She was soft and warm beneath my hands. Her body had give, but she felt delicate somehow, like I might break her. I knew I wouldn't, but the thought made every smooth glide of my fingertips across her skin exciting.

I'd already licked her lip gloss away. It tasted like cherries jubilee ice cream. Her lips were swollen and wet, and I wanted to bite them. They left trails of her saliva over my lips, and she kissed me like she'd die if she didn't, like she couldn't help herself from plunging her tongue in my mouth over and over. I thought *I* might die and wither away if she stopped. The moment felt velvet and electric. Devo's slow and languid tongue stroking against mine made me chase more of the hot, wet pressure. She made me desperate to kiss her deeper.

I already knew I could get addicted to this—to the way kissing her made me feel. Somehow, confidence flowed through me, and I didn't feel so nervous anymore.

Her eyelids fluttered, eyelashes batting lightly over her cheeks, like she was surprised at how good our kiss was. It hadn't surprised me. I'd known since I saw her carrying her pizza tonight that I wanted to kiss her, and all it took was one look in her eyes to know it would be good.

The pizza had been forgotten on the seat of her truck, but we could zap it in the microwave later.

The kiss was so good that I'd forgotten where my hand still was. I tilted my head, kissing her harder, trying to wipe her surprise away with my tongue and my hand as I added a second finger to the rubbing I was giving her between her legs. She was soaked already, and that fact made *me* wetter. I felt it welling and leaking, my own arousal dampened the insides of my thighs, and the warmth made me moan too.

When she pulled her shirt over her head, she was bare beneath it, like I'd thought. She could get away with it 'cause she was so tiny, but she wasn't too skinny. Devo had some meat on her bones, and she was confident about it, about her body. It made me want her more.

"You're beautiful," I whispered, locking my eyes on hers, and she gasped as I lowered my head and licked a nipple into my mouth, feeling the other hard bud with the back of my free hand. Her breasts were pretty, small but full, teardrop-shaped perfection.

She was pumping her hips now, pressing down on my fingers, making them rub her right where she wanted, and she whispered my name, "Abey."

Just those two syllables coming out of her mouth made my heart beat even faster. "You comin' already?"

"I'm close. It feels too good. God, your fingers."

Oh. Well then, by all means, let me show you what else I can do.

Next thing I knew, she was on her back on the floor, knees bent, feet planted on the carpet, and her underwear and cutoffs were in a pile next to my boots. I could barely remember the frantic rush to get her clothes off. I still had on my jeans, but she'd popped open my fly, and the anticipation of her hands on me down there was a heady feeling.

She rested one leg up on the couch, and the other she spread wide for me. I rubbed my hands up and down the insides of her thighs, inching closer to her pussy each time with my thumbs, teasing her a little.

She watched me, and the sexy smile lifting her lips made my nipples ache.

Lowering down between her legs, finally, I dove in, driving my hands under her ass cheeks, bringing her body to my mouth like my very own platter of heaven, and she groaned and her head lolled to the side as I ate her out. She reached for me, her hands closing over fistfuls of my hair, pulling and pushing me to work her harder with my tongue.

Her pussy was pretty, too, the light brown color of her lips contrasting against the deeper pink of her clit. God, she tasted good, even better than she smelled. She was salty and sweet, and… bare. She'd shaved, and I *liked* it. I liked that I could see how wet I made her, *loved* feeling her labia rub against my mouth and chin.

I slid two fingers inside her finally, completely mesmerized by the way her body sucked me in, the way she drew my fingers into her warm heat like it was exactly where they belonged. I curved them, searching for the spot I knew was there, and when I found it, I pressed the pads of my fingers against it while I flattened my tongue against her clit, and then I rubbed her with it, swallowing the taste of her down my throat and reaching up to cup her breast in my other hand.

I palmed her breast, squeezing and massaging and rolling her nipple between my thumb and finger, pinching a little. Her breast was as soft as rose petals, and it jiggled in my hold as the rest of her body twitched and moved to the rhythm of my tongue and fingers.

Her head lolled to the other side. "So. Good. So… so… ohh."

I was soaked, and the hot, wet spot between my thighs made me wild. I rolled my hips over and over, dying for her to get me off, too, seeking invisible pressure to make me come with her. The seam of my jeans was doing a pretty good job on its own. My pussy swelled and pulsed.

"Oh, God," she panted, hopefully feeling that intense crescendo building up inside her.

She pulled her hands out of my hair and gripped her knees, lifting them to her chest, opening her legs wider, digging her fingernails into her own skin. She bared her whole body to me. Offered it up. She showed me everything.

No one had ever done that for me before.

"Yes!" she cried out as I added a third finger, feeling the tight fit and the way her wetness allowed them to glide smoothly. She was silky soft inside. "Oh God, you're really good at that."

I couldn't help myself. I shoved my free hand down my jeans and rubbed hard in my own wetness she'd caused. I wasn't even sure I'd need the friction. Just hearing her and watching her ready to come apart had my whole body lathered and about to explode. That had never happened before either, not without some serious clitoral stimulation.

She stopped moving. "What're you doin'?"

"I wanna come with you," I said. "You make me ache."

"No." She sat up. I pulled my fingers from her body, and she pushed me gently away, moving up onto her knees in front of me. "*I* will make you come."

"What's it matter who makes who come?"

She laughed. Her soft puff of breath washed across my face, and her eyebrows dipped down in confusion. "'Cause that's the fun part?"

"Oh."

She swallowed. "Get naked."

"Um, okay," I said, and I lifted up onto my knees too. "I have a bed, y'know."

Shaking her head slowly, she kissed me quickly and licked the taste of herself off my lips, and then she speared me with a smile so seductive, my breath caught in my throat.

When Devo smiled, she was transcendently beautiful.

She reached forward with both hands, easing my flannel down my arms. Quiet blanketed my apartment, but the living room light was still on. It was a sobering moment, like one of those things you think you should mark in your memory, but I didn't know why.

We weren't friends. This would only be a one-time thing.

Funny how I had already begun trying to come up with reasons to repeat it. Excuses to get my mouth on her again.

Bunching her fingers below the hem of my tank top, she pushed up and gasped lightly when her eyes landed on my stomach, but she moaned when she saw my breasts, and I helped her by lifting the shirt over my head. My plain nude-colored bra was too small, and I didn't have time to do girly shit like go shopping for lacy bras, so my boobs spilled out the sides a little.

Her eyes zeroed in on them. They glazed over a little, her mouth going slack. She liked my tits. A lot, if the look on her face was any indication. Maybe I didn't mind *her* checking out my rack. Cute Kayla who?

She inched closer on her knees, and I felt the heat from her body on mine right before she pressed her breasts against my chest, reaching around my back to undo my bra clasp. Curiosity and innocence flashed in her eyes, even though we were in the middle of doing something the exact opposite.

She said, "We can make each other come."

I dug my teeth into my bottom lip and tried not to moan. I liked the sound of that.

As she gazed up at me, she was confident. Sexy. She knew what she wanted. And she knew how to get it.

I liked that too. *A lot.*

Pulling my bra straps down my arms, she tugged it away from my body and let it fall to the floor.

And then it was *on.*

She didn't wait for me to remove my jeans. Her wet mouth closed around my nipple. She massaged it with her tongue, smashing her face against my breast, rubbing her cheek against it. Pinching it between her teeth, she pulled hard with her tongue and lips, and when she reached between my jeans and belly, breath rushed from my mouth and I gasped.

I wanted my pants off. I didn't want her hand to find any resistance, but that first touch of her fingertips pressing on me, skin on skin, searching lower, finding the place that needed her most, made desire *throb* inside me, and the thought flitted from my head.

The need within me pulsed and ached as she pushed even lower, and when she felt my pubic hair, she closed her eyes, inhaling slowly and cupping me with a possessive hand. Like my pussy was hers. Like she owned it. Like she would decide where this night was going to go, when she would allow me to beg and writhe for her to give me more.

My chest heaved with breath, making her chase my tit with her mouth. She *really* didn't want to let go. But then she did, and she moved to the left side.

It was silly since she'd just sucked my other nipple until it felt like a direct connection to my clit. I hadn't thought anything could feel more sensitive, but when her mouth closed around my right nipple, a sharp stab of heat pulsed inside me. I tried to grind my thighs together to ease some of the ache, but she shook her head no, using her hand as a barrier, locking my legs apart.

She made me smile, this bossy, dominant Devo. Well, she

was always kind of bossy, but I loved that she was being that way with me here, above the Carringtons' garage, in the middle of Wisper, alone, just her and me. There wasn't anyone around for her to argue with, to fight.

She could just be herself, and her confidence made me want her even more.

How much could one person want another before they broke?

She'd asked me in the truck who my perfect person would be, what they'd be like.

Didn't she know? She was my perfect person.

No one had ever made me feel the way Devo Mescal made me feel. If a relationship with her looked at all like how sex with her did, she would be my perfect partner.

A perfect push and pull existed between us. We both gave, and we both took in tandem.

I groaned and pushed my hips forward, trying to ride her hand. She wouldn't let me, but I was desperate for more. But that was part of the give and take, because the desperation felt amazing. The ache inside me doubled in intensity just thinking about how she might touch me next.

No doubt she could feel how wet I was for her, and when she released my nipple and kissed my neck, licking her way up to my mouth, I tilted my head, captured her mouth with mine, and let my tongue lead me wherever it wanted. I let myself get lost in her.

I hadn't been lost in a long time. Maybe I'd never been. Maybe I'd never *allowed* myself to get lost.

But I liked being lost inside Devo. It was hot but light and… good. Which was a revelation to me, since every time I'd had sex with someone, it had felt like I'd been doing something wrong, something bad, even though I knew logically I wasn't.

The need building for her between my legs felt like it would catch fire. I was burning for her now. I begged, "Devo, *please*."

And then she began to rub.

Slipping two fingers between my pussy lips, she groaned into my mouth, a low rolling of her vocal chords that I felt all the way down to my toes, and I lost all sense.

I lost control. Nothing else mattered but her body on mine.

My eyes rolled closed, and I swayed on my knees, pumping my hips to find release on her hand. It was like her fingers had been made for my body; they knew just where to touch, how much pressure I needed, and what would make me wild.

I moaned, and my head tipped back. I felt my hair, loose and swaying, sweeping my low back as I rolled my hips, trying to fuck her hand.

"Yes," she urged, and my legs opened wider for her.

My thighs shook as they tried to hold me up, and I ground my body harder against hers. I wanted to learn her movements so I could get what I needed from her. She liked me taking what I wanted from her body. It was made clear by her moans.

But the nerves had fled from both of us. There were no inhibitions anymore.

This wasn't my first rodeo. I'd had sex before, but never like this. All of my experiences had felt shallow, and the only thing I remembered about any of them was that I had felt like one of those old horse rides for kids outside the grocery store, where you put your fifty cents in and it took you around for a ride.

That was all they had been, rides. And not very good ones.

But now, feeling how Devo touched me, how she knew just what to do, I knew she had a lot more experience than I did. I was five years older than her. It should've been the opposite, but seeing the heat in her eyes, feeling it on my skin, knowing she was watching me and she liked what she saw—she washed away all my insecurities.

Her free hand found its way into my hair at the back of my head. She twisted her fingers until she had a good grip, and she pulled me face to face with her again, whispering, "You are the sexiest woman I have ever been with."

She pulled my mouth back to hers, and when I reached between her legs again, she was *dripping* wet, and she whimpered at the contact. She swayed on her knees too.

It gave me confidence, and I deepened our kiss and lowered my body so I could reach up inside her with my fingers and beg her to come as I rubbed her slippery clit with the pad of my thumb.

I wanted to give her the best orgasm of her life.

"Yeah," she whispered, leaning her head on my shoulder so she could reach between my legs easier. "I like that."

"So good," I breathed.

She nodded, turning her head and leaning her forehead against my cheek. Did she wash her hair with rosewater? She smelled so good.

She thrust her hips forward, seeking more pressure, and I did the same, losing myself in the sensations of her fingers stroking through my wetness slowly but firmly. She spread my lips apart with two fingers, rubbing with her middle finger, swirling circles around my clit with a whisper-soft touch. It was a tease, and it was working.

We were both so wet, I could hear it, the slipping and sucking sounds we made inside each other. It didn't take long then, and I was breathing like a first-time runner. There wasn't a damn thing I could've done about it, though, because she was making me insane. I'd never been so close to coming for so long a time before.

It felt amazing, the orgasm building up inside me, getting ready to break me into pieces, but it was like my body was waiting for hers, buzzing, trembling deliciously, and biding its time so we could explode together.

I tried to kiss her, but she whimpered again and disconnected her tongue from mine. She didn't move her mouth away, and it was the hottest thing I'd ever felt, to breathe into each other and fuck each other silly with just our fingers.

"I'm comin'," she said, gasping. "Oh yeah. Abey!"

"You go, girl," I whispered, rubbing harder and licking into her mouth again.

Reaching around her back, I pulled her closer with one hand, crushing my body to hers. My breasts pushed under hers, her nipples dug into my chest, and the drunk way her eyes dropped to watch them rubbing together was so fucking hot—her mouth open, breath coming out in the sweetest moans.

I couldn't hold back anymore. How many times had I gotten myself off to images in my mind of this exact scenario? Too many. And now that it was coming true, my entire body felt like it was hurtling toward the orgasm of all orgasms.

She froze and called out, "Yeah, Abey. Yes!" Her whole body hummed with satisfaction, and she lurched forward till she was draped over me.

We fell backward, and the fall was like nothing I'd ever felt before. It increased the pleasure inside me times a thousand. Everything tightened and clenched, and when I was flat on the floor, legs splayed beneath hers, Devo dropped between them, pulling my jeans down just far enough.

Before I even knew what was happening, she latched onto my clit with her hot lips and tongue, her fingers still pumping inside me, and the ends of her hair tickled my thighs as she licked me to ecstasy and back. I gripped her head between my hands, letting my fingers get lost in her hair, trying to control her mouth on me, but she wasn't having it.

She was in control.

When her other hand hovered over my nipple, her palm flat and careful, I felt every degree of her body heat as she lowered it millimeter by millimeter. Barely touching, she rubbed in a rigid circle above my breast, making my nipple as hard as ice as it peaked and reached for her while her tongue worked fucking magic between my legs.

She ate my pussy, lapping and sucking and swallowing my cum down her throat, and I writhed beneath her mouth.

Finally, her hand melted against my breast. Her warm palm covered and surrounded it, and my nipple slipped in the crook between two fingers.

Looking down between my thighs, I watched her mouth on me, her pink tongue working hard and fast to make me come as she squeezed the two fingers together, pinching my nipple between them, and I broke apart. Shattered like glass at her expert touch.

Devo sucked my clit into her mouth at just the right moment, still licking quickly with the tip of her tongue, and my entire body became galvanic and full. I felt one-hundred-percent present in the moment. It was a place I'd never been before.

My back arched, my toes curled, and my head rolled back on the floor. I opened my mouth to let out the scream that had been building inside me, but I clamped it shut at the last second. I held the scream inside, and I breathed my release silently, like I usually did.

'Cause when all the action you got was from your own damn hand, and your family and the people around you had been telling you that you were a sinner your whole life for wanting exactly what you currently had in those hands…

Well, you tended to be quiet when you came.

CHAPTER FOUR

ABEY

One Month Later…

"You want the job or don'tcha?"

My boss stared at me, his auburn eyebrows raised, waiting for me to finally give him an answer. I did want the job, but it wasn't so black and white.

The Wisper sheriff's station ran like a well-oiled machine, so Carey wanted to spend more time in Jackson and other much needier parts of Teton County, and that meant there needed to be somebody in Wisper who knew what the hell they were doing.

Apparently, he thought that person was me.

Acting Sheriff? Me? Was he high?

I fiddled with his name plate on his desk in his office and said, "I think I want it, boss, but… I dunno. Y'know?"

"Abey, just make a damn decision."

I picked up the name plate, flipped it around in a circle in my hand, then set it down again. "Why aren't you offerin' this to Frank? He's way more organized than me."

"Yeah, he is, but Frank's got a lot goin' on in his personal life. He's here, but his mind is at home with Sam and the kids. It's what he wants. Besides, you've been my right-hand man now for years. I want *you* to take the job."

"Okay, well, I mean, can you just give me, like, maybe a week to think about it?"

"I've given you a month already!" he argued. "What's the holdup? It ain't like you to waffle back and forth."

"It's just that I'm… y'know. I'm a *woman*."

Would anyone even listen to me? That was kind of an important factor to be weighed here. The sheriff needed to be someone with authority, someone with clout who held the respect of the people.

He rolled his eyes. "You don't say?"

"C'mon, Carey. It doesn't bother *you*, but you know it'll bother a lot of other people."

"Like who?"

"Like some of the other deputies."

"Frank's the only guy you see on a regular basis, so who cares? Let me deal with any pushback. That's part of *my* job."

"Yeah, I guess, but you know there's a lot of people, residents of Wisper, who won't like to see a woman in charge." Like my mama.

"And you care about that all of a sudden? What's really goin' on here, Abey? These things have never held you back before. Why now?"

My daddy's voice boomed through my head. *"How dare you? You tryin' to shame your family? How could you do this to your poor mama? I raised you better than this."*

"I dunno. I guess it's just that the LGBTQ thing hasn't

ever been a part of the conversation around here, but with Ace's House openin' up and more and more people talkin' about it, it's bound to be an issue. I don't wanna make your job harder."

Carey was the only person I'd ever confided in about my sexuality. It had never been an issue with him. He didn't see me any differently than he did Frank or Shelley. We were coworkers and friends. Period.

"Abey, can you handle it?"

And my voice was louder than my daddy's on this subject. "You know I can."

"Yeah, I do," Carey said. "I got faith in you. That's why I'm offerin' this to you. So. Again. You want the job or not?"

"I think so?"

"Good. I'm takin' that as a yes. No backsies. You got one week to prepare while I get ready. I'll be back and forth sometimes, so it won't be like you're on your own, and Frank and Shelley will be here to help you. You know that. I'm also sendin' you a couple new deputies. Dan is a new hire. He's a little stiff, but he was military. I'm hopin' he'll relax quickly. And Roxanne is an old pro. She started out at the Corner Junction station, and then she moved up to the park. She's had to deal with all kinds of calls. She knows her shit. Actually, she reminds me a little of you. So you'll have even more help than we usually do around here. How's that sound?"

"Good, I guess. But you really think hirin' another woman will help matters?"

"Just wait till you see her," he said. "If anybody has a problem once they get an eyeful, they'll keep it to themselves. I can promise you that." He snickered and swiped his coffee tumbler off his desk to take a big chug.

"Okay." I hoped to hell he was right.

I had to hope the people of Wisper could see me as an authority. What if they couldn't? What if, because I was a woman—who, surprise, was also gay—I'd create more of an opportunity for trouble? I didn't want to cause anyone trouble. I only wanted to help.

My mama didn't think I could. She didn't believe in me. She thought people like me were the problem with the world.

And things had been coming to a head around these parts lately. It seemed small-town Wyoming was catching up with the rest of the world. The townsfolk gossiped like teenage girls behind closed doors about everything under the sun. That was nothing new, but it used to be that nobody spoke out in the open about who was gay or who wasn't.

Yeah, those days had died. It was all anybody could talk about now, and I didn't want to be the focus of that gossip. How would that help me in my job?

I was pretty sure it wouldn't.

And just because they all gossiped about it did not mean they all accepted it. Some did, and some could be more than supportive, but not all.

Which was exactly the mission Devo had tasked herself with—to make every single person in Teton County love gay people—and it was the reason she kept ending up at my station.

Not that I was complaining about it. Quite the opposite, actually, though I'd never tell her that.

And speaking of, I heard someone approaching down the hallway behind me. The sound of Devo's footsteps had become a familiar and welcome addition to my workdays, and I would never forget the quiet sound of her scoffs.

I could hear her breathing, and the sound sent goosechills all the way down to my toes.

There hadn't been one single night in the last month when I hadn't thought about the time Devo and I had made each other come.

Without turning, I asked, "What now, Devo?"

But there'd been plenty of days I wished I could forget, particularly the days she'd stormed in, demanding that I arrest Red Graves, everyone's favorite local asshole.

This time, she waited outside Carey's office door, tapping her little foot impatiently, waiting for me, probably so she could complain about Red again.

Memories of her feet in a pair of my socks and her sexy legs resting across my naked body while we ate cold pizza on my couch that night had my body heating up, and I could feel beads of sweat collect at the back of my neck.

Carey lifted his eyebrows and nudged me out his door, then kicked it shut with his boot. *Thanks for the help, boss.*

My recollection of that night was a red-hot memory in my mind. My hands twitched to reach out and touch Devo the way I had a month ago. It was hard now not to stare at the crotch of her jeans and imagine what was underneath—that smooth, wet, *shaved* skin…

She narrowed her eyes at me when we were face to face, but I stood more than a head taller, so she had to look up. "For the last time," she said, "are you gonna do somethin' about Red Graves or not? He's up to no good again. How many times do I have to report him?"

Looking at her face and the evocative curve of her full bottom lip was my new favorite thing to do. She was beautiful, but the opportunity to gaze down upon her was usually present 'cause I was about to tell her no or put her in cuffs, which, historically, made her mad, but man, did the indignation make her even sexier! Her deep, earthy brown eyes held nothing back.

"I told you. I can't do anything until the man breaks a law. You know this. He's not hurtin' anybody—"

Her face flashed with frustration, and she plonked her fists on her hips and cocked her head, giving me a glare that could've taken down a grizzly all on its own.

"He's not hurtin' anybody *physically*," I amended, "and I can't arrest him for bein' a dick. Wish I could."

I walked away. I had to, or I'd kiss her again. I bet she had no idea how adorable she was when she got angry.

She scoffed and followed, her short legs scrambling to keep up. "Have you seen the bullshit hangin' in his front window?"

"Not today," I said, looking at her again. Her face was like a drug. I stopped walking. It was too difficult to keep going and stare at her at the same time without tripping myself.

My gaze lingered on the side of her mouth as she sneered and laughed indignantly, and then it moved to the high planes of her flushed cheeks and then the edges of her eyelashes and how they flared out at the ends like a faerie's wings.

"Oh, well, go have yourself a look." She shook her head. "I don't get it. Why aren't you offended? He's openly hostile toward everyone. Doesn't it piss you off?"

"Yeah, it does," I said, knowing full well how much I was frustrating her, "but it's not my job to get offended every time some old coot makes a shitty comment. Until he lays hands on someone or breaks a law, there is *nothin'* I can do about it."

"Whatever." She rolled her eyes. "I thought I'd have an ally in this. I thought you'd be on my side."

"Devo, I am on your side. It ain't like I don't hear this shit every day in my personal life. My own mama thinks I'm personally offendin' the Almighty. She says I'm hurtin' Jesus' feelin's every time I have"—looking behind me and then toward the front of the station, I made sure no one was around to hear me—"'impure thoughts' about a woman. But as much as I'd like to handcuff her and duct tape her mouth shut, I can't. Just like I can't do to Red. I'm sorry. Besides, I'm not convinced his behavior has anything to do with Ace's House or anti-LGBTQ stuff."

She scoffed. "Right."

I really was sorry. I could see the hurt and disappointment in her eyes, and making her feel that way ate at me, but there really was nothing I could do.

She crossed her arms over her chest, and I had to concentrate really hard not to notice how that made her breasts push up and forward, like she was aiming them right at me.

"I heard you've been offered a promotion but that you're thinkin' about turnin' it down."

"Where'd you hear that?" Who the fuck was blabbing about that? Could nothing stay private in this town? It was Shelley. I knew it was. Freaking busybody.

"Around. Why would you turn it down? If the sheriff was a woman—a *gay* woman—don't you think that might make a difference around here?"

I shrugged. I'd had the same thought, but I'd also had the thought that it could cause all kinds of trouble, which was why I hadn't taken the job yet. Not officially. "That ain't anybody's business. Now, go on about your day."

She shook her head again and turned to walk away.

I watched her go, trying not to notice how her hips swung from side to side and her ass cheeks jiggled in her jeans. "And Devo?"

"Yeah? What?" she snapped without turning around.

"Don't you go eggin' Red on. *You* I have no problem handcuffin'. Hear me?"

When she turned finally, I couldn't hide my smile. She had to know how sexy the thought was to me. And she had to know that, despite the fact that I couldn't do fuck all about Red Graves, I loved her tenacity—her fight. 'Course, that particular personality trait had landed her in a jail cell a couple times already, but nobody had pressed charges, and her boss usually bailed her out of trouble.

Did she know that no matter how many times I tried not to, I still remembered every pulsing second of the orgasm she'd given me? I remembered every thrust of her fingers inside me and her mouth on my body. And did she know that five times a day I looked at my phone and wanted to call her?

She narrowed her eyes at me, then spun around and stormed out of the hallway, huffing and puffing the whole way. Her hair was so cute the way it flicked out in all kinds of directions, and I wanted so badly to lick beneath the little ducktail on the back of her neck.

"So," Frank nudged when I got back to my desk and plopped into my chair as the front door slammed shut behind Devo, almost hitting her in her sexy ass. Her jeans were the luckiest motherfuckers on the planet.

My chair spun toward Frank, but I stopped the rotation with my boot, trying not to watch Devo out of the corner of my eye through the big front windows as she stomped down the sidewalk toward Ace's House. At least she hadn't gone straight back to The Red Wild Outdoors across the street.

Focus on your job, Abey.

I needed food. Specifically, I needed some chili from José's Diner. It always made me feel better. "So what?" I said.

"You takin' the job or not?"

"Y'know, technically, it's not a real position. I mean, it's just an actin' sheriff thing. A *temporary* thing."

"Yeah," he said, "but you never know what possibility it might open up."

"I guess."

"Why aren't you more excited about this? I figured bein' in charge would make you giddy. You're always tryin' to boss me and Carey around."

"No, I'm not," I said, hand to my chest in mock-offended style.

"Right," Frank said. "Whatever you say. Well, I think you should do it. Besides, if you don't, Carey will have to bring in some outsider, and you know that's gonna put Shelley in a tizzy. You don't want that, do ya? All hell will break loose around here."

He was right though. Our receptionist wasn't one to welcome newcomers easily. I was a little concerned about the new deputies, and I hadn't even met them yet.

I looked at my partner. "Why're you tryin' to push me into this? You're not mad Carey didn't offer you the job?"

"Nope. I'm happy for you. You should be happy for you too. I've got Sam, Murph, and Nic waitin' at home for me." Frank was a goner for his new foster daughter. She'd been with them a year already. I couldn't believe how fast time had flown by since then. "I don't want any job that keeps me here late doin' paperwork. I get enough calls in the middle of the night. Besides, we've got plans this fall. I'm takin' my family up to the Pacific Northwest to camp and fish when the kids have fall break. I'm so dang excited about it. Did I tell you we bought a camper?"

"Yeah, you did. Like seventeen times. It's real fancy, la di da, and it's even got a bidet. So now the image of you straddlin' some fancy toilet with a stream of water shootin' up in the air to wash the shit off your asshole is all I can see when I look at you."

Frank laughed. The idiot laughed! What the hell was wrong with the man? Before he settled down with Samantha and their kids, nothing made him smile and laugh the way he did now. He was like a different guy.

"It's a hairy affair," I said, making a "yuck" face, but then I laughed too. Man, it made me happy to see my friend so blissed out.

"Well," he said as he composed himself, wiping tears of laughter away from his eye, "whatever you decide, I got your back."

"Thanks, partner. Right back atcha."

He nodded, then unlocked his desk drawer and grabbed his gun, fitting it into his holster on his hip as he walked to the door. "See you tomorrow then. Oh, Abey?"

"Yeah?" I said, with my phone halfway to my ear to call José.

If I asked real nice, he'd deliver an extra-large cup of chili right to my truck, with little soup crackers, shredded cheddar cheese, and extra chopped onions. I kept a spoon in my center console for just such an occasion. Truly, I didn't mind doing fifty extra burpees every morning if I got to eat it at least three times a week, and I *hated* burpees, which said everything a person needed to know about José's chili.

"Looks like you got your hands full already today."

"Huh?"

"Look," he said, and he motioned with a nod out our front door. "Think you better get your butt on across the street. If I'm not wrong, the assistant director for Ace's House and old Red Graves are goin' at it again."

"Dammit, Devo," I muttered under my breath.

I shoved my phone in my back pocket and patted my vest, making sure my cuffs were still attached. I hadn't meant I wanted to handcuff her today! Not in any official capacity, though, if she wasn't always causing a ruckus, I wouldn't have minded binding her wrists for some other way less official reason.

Why'd she have to go and make things so damn hard?

CHAPTER FIVE

DEVO

"DEVO, YOU'RE KILLING ME HERE," Theo said. "This is the third time you've landed yourself behind bars. I can't keep turning the other cheek."

My exasperated boss hung his head, and I chose not to tell him I'd spotted a new patch of gray hairs on the top. Yeah, not the right moment at all. Personally, I thought the gray was cute. His boyfriend was gaga for it. Brady said they made Theo all the more regal, but Theo did *not* agree, so yeah. Kept my mouth shut.

"What're you sayin'?" I faced him fully and looked up at him with my hands on my hips. It was a little embarrassing that there were iron bars between us, but my boss and I had always seen eye to eye, even though we came from completely different walks of life. "Are you firin' me?"

He rubbed two fingers over his forehead, digging them into the skin, probably trying to rub away his frustration.

If he did fire my ass, he had good reason, but seriously, how could everyone expect me to stand around when people I cared about were being treated so unfairly? I couldn't do it!

"No. I'm not firing you. *Yet*. But Devo, you cannot keep

getting in trouble like this. We're supposed to be upstanding members of the community. What will people think?"

I scoffed but instantly felt bad about it. "Maybe they'll think I'm fightin' for their rights. That's all I'm doin', you know."

"I know you *think* that's what you're doing. But Devo, you committed a real crime today. I have no doubt Mr. Graves will press charges. How's that going to help your cause?"

"My cause? Mine? Isn't it your cause too?"

He stared at me through the cell door. I'd never seen him so angry.

"No, Devo. This is on you. Breaking someone's storefront window because you're mad about a product they're selling is your cross to bear. Don't you even try to put this on Ace's House. We can't be connected to that kind of activity. In fact, if you are charged with a crime and you end up in front of a judge, that's what you had better say. Or you *will* lose your job."

Kicking my shoe against the cell door, I nodded. He was right. I knew he was. And I didn't want to bring negativity to Ace's House or to Theo. He'd done so much good in the community already in the short time we'd been open, and I was grateful for my job. Truly, I had been since the day he hired me.

But I was also pissed off. The rest of Wisper seemed to accept Ace's House. They could see the good we'd been doing, even if we were still "those homosexuals" to a lot of people, but not Red Graves. He made it his mission every day to offend me or Theo, the people who came to Ace's House seeking help, and sometimes he even disrespected Abey right to her face. A freakin' cop!

And still, she did nothing, even when he told her he didn't

have to do what she said when she'd ordered him to put out the burning rainbow flag he'd lit with a Zippo last week in the middle of downtown. It was just a small promotional window cling someone had stuck to his store's front window. I didn't even think it had anything to do with the gay community, but Red hadn't cared. He was convinced I'd been the one to put it there, so he set it on fire.

And when she tried to talk to him, he told Abey he wasn't taking orders from "someone like her." He'd meant because she was a woman, or maybe he knew she was a gay woman.

But whatever the reason, it was rude and condescending and disrespectful. He wouldn't move a muscle until Abey called Sheriff Michaels on her radio, and then when the big man stomped across the street to give Red the evil eye, he finally stepped on the burning plastic, then turned heel and slammed his doors closed behind him.

Was it wrong of me to chuck a brick through his window just because he was intolerant and sold bullshit anti-gay T-shirts?

Okay, fine, yeah, it was. But what should I have done? God, that man infuriated me! I'd never met someone who offended me so deeply just by breathing and by the disgusted look in his eyes every time I interacted with him.

What had I or anybody else ever done to him to make him so mean?

"I'll ask Brady to stop by here on his way home. Hopefully, he can help you untangle this mess, but Devo, please don't make this harder than it needs to be. Don't make me have to fire you. I don't know what I would do without you. Ace's House can't thrive without you. Please?"

Aw man, I couldn't take it when he said things like that. "I'm sorry. I just get so *mad*."

"I know. And I understand. I really do. But there are

better ways to handle your anger. I think you know that already."

"Yeah," I admitted as Abey poked her head in the room of shame, the one usually reserved for drunk idiots who needed to sober up and, apparently, me. She handed Theo a bottle of water to hand to me, and she flashed me a pity smile. She'd warned me.

I crossed my arms over my chest and narrowed my eyes, and she tossed a granola bar through the cell door, right at my head.

"Thanks a lot."

"You're welcome," she said with a grin, and she ducked back out of the room.

Theo flashed me a pitying look, too, as he passed the water bottle through the cell bars. "I have to go. Some of the workers from the resort in Jackson are coming today."

"They are? Why?"

"They're getting ready to strike, and they're using Ace's House as a place to meet beforehand. I told you about it last week. If you weren't always trying to make trouble where there doesn't have to be any, maybe you would've remembered." I winced audibly as he looked at his phone. *Shit.* I'd completely forgotten. "They'll be here any minute. And there's a girl who's been coming in with some of the summer kids, but I have a bad feeling about her. I want to keep an eye on her."

"What do you mean? You think she's in trouble? Dangerous?"

"Not dangerous, no, but I don't know. It's just a feeling."

"Yeah, but your 'just a feeling' was spot on with Murphy."

Theo had called Abey's partner, Deputy Sims, and thankfully, he'd figured out Murphy's secret. They'd gotten to him just in time, before he'd died out on the streets, alone, starving, and freezing two winters ago, and now, Murph was officially Frank's son. He and his wife had adopted Murph as soon as they could get the adoption through the court system.

"I'm keeping my eye on the situation, but I could really use the backup." He raised his eyebrows at me.

"I know," I said as dejectedly as I could and scuffed my shoe against the cell door again.

Dammit. I felt awful for putting him in this position. And I felt *really* bad that I'd forgotten about the strikers. Was he right that I caused problems where there didn't need to be any?

No. I loved Theo. He was more than a boss. He was a treasured friend, had been since the day we met, but he was wrong.

Standing up to injustice was *always* the right thing to do.

"I've got to go. I'll talk to you later if I have time."

"Wait. You're just gonna leave me in here?"

"Yeah." He scoffed. "I am. Maybe you can use the time to think about how you'd like to conduct yourself in the future *if* Brady can get you out of this. And that's a big if."

"Fine," I whined, but it felt really shitty to frustrate him like this. He had a lot going on in his life with grad school and running the center, and that was besides all the people at Ace's House every day and all the fires he had to put out with them.

But did no one besides me care about the big jerking redneck across the street?!

When he was gone, Abey came back into the holding room. Seriously, the place was a dump. The two small cells were so old and weak, I probably could've pried the door open with my fingers. I didn't though. It wouldn't have earned me much goodwill with the Sheriff's Department, with Theo, Red Graves, or Abey.

And… okay, fine. I didn't want to make her mad or make her job harder either. She had kind of been all I could think about this past month. Her and her long fingers and her hot mouth and the way she looked up my body when she was between my legs, the heat in her eyes…

But the point was that we hadn't really talked since then, not about what had happened between us or if we were going to do it again. Or if maybe we wanted to go out for dinner? Or… I had no idea. Something? Anything!

I just wanted to be around her when we didn't have to talk about the illegal things I had done or when I wasn't locked in handcuffs. Maybe it was why we hadn't talked. Maybe her need to uphold justice was the thing that had kept us apart.

But crazy things happened to my body when I remembered that night. Heat and moisture welled between my legs, my nipples would harden to the point of pain, and if I wasn't panting harder than a bear in a summer drought, then I wasn't remembering it right. Like now, even though I was behind bars.

And she didn't even try to make it easy on me. Her work shirt was unbuttoned because the sheriff's station was like a sauna, and I could see the hint of her curved waist beneath her white tank top underneath. The flare of her hips was like a siren's call, and even her worn work boots were sexy.

Ughhh.

My dirty mind went straight to imagining pushing under that tank top, lifting up to caress the undersides of her breasts while my tongue was in her mouth. God, her breasts. I bet she didn't have any clue just how mouthwatering they were, and how sexy they looked, spread across her chest when she lay flat on her back for me on the floor, with my mouth between her—

Gah! Snap out of it!

"Got yourself in a pickle this time, didn't ya?" she said. She was trying to hold in a silent chuckle, but she hadn't hid it very well.

I didn't reply. What could I say that wouldn't embarrass me further?

"Alright, well, the sheriff says I can release you on your own recognizance. You ain't gonna run, are you?" She eyed me, narrowing her gorgeous, bright blue eyes in mock suspicion.

"No."

"Good. Step back."

I held my wrists together, like a prisoner in a maximum-security ward, and took two steps back from the door, waiting for the warden to cuff me for transport.

"Funny," she said. She opened the door and hooked the cell keys to a clip on her belt. "You're free to go. But Devo, stay away from Red. In fact, you might just go on home and hunker down there until you can talk to your lawyer."

I rolled my eyes. "Fine."

Turning, she lifted my bag from the stainless-steel table behind her, then handed it to me.

I rolled my eyes again. I couldn't help it! The smug smirk on her face irritated me to no end. I wanted to wipe it away with my lips. I swiped my stuff from her hands, trying with all my might not to remember how they'd felt on the insides of my thighs, when the tips of her fingers grazed my wrist.

When I turned away from her to get the hell out of the station and the mortifying situation I'd put myself in—again —she whispered, "I thought about you last night."

I stopped in the doorway.

Wh-wh-what? By now, I'd figured my proclivity toward lawlessness had turned her way off.

"Yeah," she said, "I think about that night a lot."

"How nice for you." I winced. That wasn't at all what I wanted to say, but the fact that she wouldn't do anything about Red was pissing me off more and more.

Seriously, did she not see how this affected her own life? My life? Everyone's lives? People like Red Graves were the problem with our country. Sure, you could have a difference of opinion. I'd even be fine with him hating gay people, but when he went out of his way to be cruel and to cause pain to innocent people, well, *that* I just could not stand for.

But those thoughts were completely at war with the memories of her hands and tongue all over my naked body, warm as they caressed my skin, sliding into my—

"You ever think about it?"

"Nope," I lied, and I dashed from the room, down the hallway, out of the station, and all the way home, like the good little lawbreaker I was.

Stupid wilting mums.

Weren't they supposed to be late-summer/fall flowers? They'd died the day after I'd bought them, which was three days ago!

"Mom, I'm home," I called when I walked through the door to our little two-bedroom house on the outskirts of Barton, purposefully ignoring the dying plants on the porch. It usually took about twenty minutes to get home from Ace's House in the summer, but if there was snow on the mountain roads, it could take an hour or more. "We really need to switch out this lock. My key got stuck again."

"Then don't lock the door," my mom called from her bedroom. "I think your mums are dead."

This was the house we'd lived in since we moved up from Solo, New Mexico, except for the year I'd lived with my ex-girlfriend over in Idaho. Before that, I'd lived with my parents and my brother and sister near my mom's family on the Mescalero Reservation. My mom and dad had both been raised there, but when I was sixteen, my dad had taken a job near Barton at a horse ranch, which he'd quickly lost.

He died a year later, and I hadn't really missed him since. He'd never been a supportive dad. Or husband. I could still remember the relief we'd all felt when he was gone, when his debts and the fights he always seemed to get into couldn't make my mom's anxiety go berserk anymore.

Maybe it was a harsh thing to admit that I didn't miss him, even just to myself, but he'd always been a miserable person. He took it out on my mom and my brother and sister and me. The fact that he'd never been physically abusive didn't endear him to his family. The lack of his positive presence in our lives and the daily strife he'd caused had been painful enough.

The memory I had from seven or eight years old of my brother and sister standing on either side of me, holding my hands, gripping them painfully while we watched and listened to our dad scream and rage at our mom in our old kitchen because she wouldn't give him her paycheck had made an impact on me. We'd needed groceries, but my dad had wanted the money for gambling or beer or whatever else he'd considered more important than feeding his children, and I remembered wondering if my mom had ever even loved him. And if she had, why?

When I was thirteen, I came home from school one day and told my parents I was gay. I could still see the look on my dad's face when he rolled his eyes, shook his head, and walked out of the house.

My mom, on the other hand, celebrated with me. She baked me a cake.

"Yeah, I can see that the mums are dead," I said, walking through the living room toward the hallway, "and Mom, I told you, it's not safe for you to be out here by yourself without at least lockin' the door."

"That's what you keep sayin', Devil, but we've lived here for years and never had a problem. And I keep the windows open, so what difference does it make anyway?"

"Good point." Leaning against the door jamb outside her bedroom, I looked past her shoulders at the photograph that had been hanging near her workspace since the day we moved in. Before that, the carefully framed image had hung in our living room. She said she'd found it at a flea market a year or two after I had been born. It kind of surprised me that it had lasted all these years; it was the only piece of art that survived our move from New Mexico to Barton. "But I wish you wouldn't. We have that brand-new air conditioner. Why don't you use it?"

She loved that picture. At least once a day, she'd pause in front of it to sip her coffee and admire the way the photographer had captured a mountain stream swollen with water that flowed and cascaded over fallen trees and river rocks of varying shades of browns, lilacs, and moss greens. The water itself glistened in all shades of blue, deepening and lightening where the sun gave its light or stole it away. Fir trees lined the edges of the small waterway, protecting it as it carved out its place in the world through the passage of time.

Mom said she'd never seen anything so beautiful, had never had such a visceral connection to an image. Sometimes, I'd even catch her touching the protective glass with the tips of her fingers, as if she could gauge the temperature of the water through the photo, could soak up the oxygen held within, and it would make her breathing easier.

When things had gotten bad with my dad, she'd spend hours gazing at that photo, like just the look of it soothed and comforted her.

I'd searched and searched but couldn't find who the photographer was. All we had was a vague location where the photograph had been taken. The words "Holly Lake Trail" had been scribbled on the back left-corner edge of the picture. I had hoped to find prints of the photo I could've had made into a blanket for her or coasters or something so she could see it everywhere, could wrap herself up in this thing she loved so much.

But I'd had no luck. The photographer was a ghost. The person was probably long dead. And there was more than one Holly Lake in the world, one right here in Wyoming, up in the Tetons, in fact, but my mom had found the image when we still lived in New Mexico, so it was more likely a lake down there somewhere. And I wasn't about to go trekking through the mountains to try to find it anyway. Yeah, not my style at all. I was more of a TV and potato chips kind of girl. I did drive up there, though, but the Bridger-Teton National Forest was huge. There was no way I could find one bend in a stream from twenty-something years ago, if it was even in Wyoming.

"How was work?" she asked, and she adjusted her table fan so it was aimed right at her face. She followed my line of sight to the photo and ignored the air-conditioning subject or any subject that had anything to do with me spending my money on her, as usual.

She could be so old-school. Apart from the super-fancy sewing machine I'd bought her with my first paycheck from my assistant director gig at Ace's House, she hated any kind of upgrades I tried to make to our little home. Our landlord was lazy, so we'd learned to do any repairs ourselves.

My mom had taken care of our family pretty much by herself for years, and that was while having to survive through all my dad's crap. She deserved to live in a nice place, whether she liked it or not. This house, while full of good memories after my dad passed, was kind of a dump. I had plans to buy her a nice house. Even if I got married someday or lived with someone, I'd bring my mom with. She deserved to be taken care of.

"It was… fine," I lied. I sighed and dropped my bag on the seat of the armchair next to the door, then took a step inside the room and plopped down on it.

"Devona!"

"What? It's *my* bag. It's not like I sat on your stuff. Ow, my keys are diggin' into my butt." I adjusted them and burrowed further back into the chair with my legs hanging over the arm.

"Serves you right, and why're you lyin' to me?" she accused, tightening her lips around the end of the thread between her teeth and narrowing her eyes at me over the top of her reading glasses. She didn't use them to read, but she couldn't thread a needle without them.

"I'm not lyin'."

"BS. And why're you home so early? I didn't expect you till six or seven. Theo give you the afternoon off?"

"Somethin' like that."

She speared me with a look. "Devona Leona Mescal. What'd you do?"

I scoffed. "Nothin'!"

"Oh, Devil, the admission of guilt is in the sound of your

voice." She turned back to her machine. "When you lie, you squeak like a prairie dog. What did you do?"

"I'm just havin' trouble with that old jackass across the street again."

"Oh," she said, threading her needle, then adjusted a piece of fabric underneath and turned the handwheel on the side of the sewing machine. "The man who runs the outdoor store?"

"Yeah. It's a hikin' store. Or a gun store. Whatever. I dunno. He sells bullshit if you ask me."

"Mm." She loaded her orange spool of thread onto the little spinner thing on the top of the machine.

This time, it looked like she was working on some tribal tunics. She sold them at powwows and festivals around the area. But my favorite thing she made was her traditional Apache moccasins. They were so dang comfy, and handy, too, if I needed to run out to get the mail, 'cause they had leather soles that were soft but thick so the gravel driveway didn't hurt my feet. Each pair was beautiful, with custom colors and beaded designs her customers requested.

She even had an Etsy store to sell her stuff, but her day job was lunch lady at the Barton elementary school, which had a whopping total of thirty-seven students last year. Middle and high schoolers got bussed down to Corner Junction for classes 'cause Barton was too small in population for the county to provide us our own schools. Corner Junction wasn't much bigger, but two state highways intersected there, so it made sense to put schools there. Wisper was closer, but the roads in winter got a lot worse to drive than the road down to Corner.

It occurred to me that if the opposite had been true, I probably would've met Abey when we were teenagers, assuming she had gone to school in Wisper—I didn't know,

I'd never asked her—and it had me wondering what could've come of that.

"Anyway," I went on, shaking the thought from my head, "this time, that old jerk put a T-shirt in his front window that's so offensive. It was the last straw, Mom. I'm tellin' you."

"Again, I ask: What. Did. You. Do?"

Looking down at my purple "Equal rights for all doesn't mean less rights for you. It's not pie" T-shirt, I picked away imaginary pilling from the well-washed fabric as I admitted, "I… I, maybe, sorta, might've thrown a brick through his window."

She spun her chair, gasping. "Devona!"

I winced. "I know. It was stupid."

She was glaring at me now. "Did you get fired?"

"No. Not yet. But Theo's so mad at me. I feel awful."

Taking off her glasses, she closed her eyes and pinched the bridge of her nose with two fingers.

I loved my mom's hands. They were strong, her fingers long and thin. They were nimble, but no matter the task, they could do it. I'd always admired her strength. She had always been the backbone of our family. She was still, even though my sister and brother were grown and living in different states. I was the oldest, and the problem child, if this conversation was any indication.

"Girl, you better grow up, and quick." She stood, abandoning her project and swiping her "Liluye's Custom Crafts" coffee mug from her sewing table. "How could you, Devo? You know the position that puts Theo in, right?"

I followed her to the kitchen, pulling an island stool from under the counter to sit on. I tucked my knees to my chest and crossed my feet like I was a kid again, balancing on my butt, waiting for her to serve me a frybread taco on a paper plate like she used to. "I know. Don't you think I feel awful? And… there's more."

"What more?" she asked, turning in front of the open fridge door to glower at me.

"I kinda… got arrested again."

"Oh, Devona." She hung her head and shook it slowly.

"This time, Theo thinks Red might press charges." My phone buzzed in my back pocket. "Hang on. This might be my lawyer."

"Oh," she groaned. "So now we're the kinda people who have lawyers?"

She turned back to pull out the leftover fried chicken I'd brought home after the potluck at Ace's House yesterday, and I answered my cell. She liked to feed the crunchy breading to our neighbor's chickens. Was that the healthiest snack for a chicken?

"Hi, Brady."

"How's my little window breaker this afternoon?" he asked, punctuating his sentence with a chuckle.

I groaned.

He laughed again. "Look, I know Theo's pissed, but don't worry. He'd never let you go. And I already talked to Red. He's pretty pissed, too, but if you pay to replace the window and the merchandise you damaged when you hurled a brick through it, he said he'll consider not sendin' you up the river."

"Does he have to apologize for using derogatory language about lesbians? And does 'merchandise' include the wildly offensive T-shirt hanging in his window?"

"I wouldn't hold my breath for an apology, and yep. Plus a whole rack of the damn things. Some of the shirts got ripped when the shards of the glass from the window were embedded into the fabric, so that's clearly your fault."

"No," I said. "I'm not payin' for that stuff. Sorry, Brady. I know you're tryin' to help, but no way."

"Don't say sorry to me. It's *you* you're hurtin' if you don't reimburse him."

"I'll pay for the window, but I'm not payin' for any anti-LGBTQ crap. Those shirts imply that the letters stand for liberty, guns, and beer!"

"I saw the shirts, Devo. And you're right, They're flat-out rude, but he has the right to sell 'em, and if you don't pay the damages, you may end up owin' an even bigger fine if this goes to court. You might even have to do some jail time."

Everything stopped. Everything became still and quiet, like the wind had stopped running outside the kitchen window, and it even felt like the earth had stopped rotating. I thought I might throw up. "Jail?"

My mom gasped, spinning on a foot, her hands full of greasy, half deboned chicken, and speared me with a look so full of judgment, I was afraid I was about to be grounded or pummeled.

"Jail," Brady confirmed. "We might be able to avoid it, but with the other two infractions on your record, I can't guarantee it. Depends on the judge we get."

I jumped off the stool, knocking it over. "I can't go to jail, Brady! I'm already a lesbian, which means the head bitch who runs the joint won't be able to convert me and finger me in front of the guards to prove her dominance. She'll kill me!"

"Devona!"

"Sorry, Mom." I winced. Had I really just said that in front of my mother?

"Well," Brady said in my ear, "there's an image I'll never get outta my head. Lemme see what I can do. I'll call you tomorrow."

CHAPTER SIX

ABEY

WHEN I WALKED into The Red Wild Outdoors, Wisper's local go-to for all things hunting, camping, and hiking, Red was standing in the middle of the store with a scowl on his face and a broom in his hand.

"Howdy, Red," I said, but I saw the shirt Devo had been going on about on a rack to my left. They came in red or navy blue and had the capital letters LGBT in bright white at the top on the front side of the shirt, and underneath, it said, "Liberty, Guns, Beer, and TRUTH."

Dammit, Red. That really was offensive, like he couldn't stand for gay people to claim the letters LGBT. They had to stand for something redneck-ish too. It struck me as funny, though, that whoever had designed the shirt left off the Q. Couldn't come up with a clever enough alternative?

I fought the urge to roll my eyes and tried to keep my opinion off my face. "Everything okay in here?"

Scowling at me, he griped, "Define okay."

Red looked tired, not like he'd had a rough night's sleep —or maybe he had—but he always gave the impression that he was tired of life. The deep, dark wrinkles around his eyes told me so, as did the way the corners of his mouth always turned down, even when he tried to smile, which didn't happen often.

His short gray hair had thinned so much on the top of his head that I could see his scalp shining through the few hairs he still had left under the store's bright florescent lights, but it was still plenty thick and bushy in the back.

The guy had been in Wisper his whole life, except for when he'd served in the military in his younger days. The Navy, if I remembered right. He never talked about his service though.

He was a loner by choice, but he attended a weekly poker game with some of the other old timers, and even they complained about his gruff attitude on occasion. He was divorced, and the rest of his family lived in other parts of Wyoming, some up in Montana.

"You need help boardin' up that window till you can get it replaced?"

"No. I don't need your help. You even know how to hold a hammer, woman?"

"Red, why you gotta be such a dick?"

"What? How dare you talk to me like that?"

Ah, shit. I hadn't meant to say it out loud. But c'mon. "Look, I'm sorry, but are you really surprised after the crap you been pullin' lately?"

"You got some nerve. Me? You're tryin' to make *me* out to be the bad guy now?" He shook his head and let the broom fall. It clacked loudly against the tile floor when it hit the ground.

"Yes, you," I said, following him as he marched through the maze of T-shirt racks, shelves full of Yeti tumblers, and stacks of fishing hats with handmade lures pinned to them, until he was standing behind his sales counter. I stood in front of it, hands on my hips. And oh joy, he'd even had the LGBT thing printed on stickers. I picked one up from the pile of them he'd stacked in front of his cash register and held it high for him to see. "Ace's House is right across the street."

He shrugged. "What do I care about Ace's House?"

The cowbell on one of the doors jangled when somebody else entered the store. It was Brian Nichols, a local ranch hand and friend of Red's.

Red nodded at him. "Brian."

Mr. Nichols tipped his hat at me but spoke to Red. "How you doin', ol' man? Heard about your window. Just wanted to check in on ya. Make sure we don't need to get a posse together to go teach the vandal a lesson."

Red grinned at me manically, raising his eyebrows in defiance.

I shook my head. "You better be jokin'."

"'Course I was," Mr. Nichols said.

"I'm not," Red replied.

I sighed. "Nobody's puttin' a posse together. Nobody's doin' anything. You hear me?"

"You ain't the sheriff, missy," Red said.

Not yet. He was bound to have a coronary when I did become acting sheriff.

"Nope, but the sheriff would agree with me, and if you doubt me, go 'head and give him a call. Let's see how pleased he is with you for interruptin' his busy day when he finds out I told you but you didn't listen."

Mr. Nichols laughed awkwardly and slid his hands into the front pockets of his jeans. "We're just havin' some fun, Deputy. Who broke the window, anyway?"

Red growled. "That little b—*troublemaker* who works across the road."

"Dammit, Red."

"What?" he argued. "I said troublemaker. I didn't say bitch."

"You're a piece of work, you know that?" I said, completely exasperated. "Can't you back off just a little? Y'know, if you played it right, you could actually sell to the people you been tryin' to offend. I thought you were a *smart* business owner."

"I don't need no rabble-rousers comin' in here. The business I do with normal people suits me just fine. Besides, you ever heard of the right to free speech?"

"Yeah, I heard about it," I said. "Which is what allows me to tell you that sometimes, you're downright insufferable."

But there wasn't anything I could do about it. I turned to go.

Mr. Nichols bristled beside me. He smiled when I looked at him, though, and I saw kindness in his eyes. I knew he could see both sides of the issue. His kid had come out as transgender a couple years ago. He didn't love it when his only child chopped off all his hair and asked to be called Oscar instead of Olivia. He loved his kid, so he was trying to accept Oscar's transition, but he wouldn't have chosen it if he'd had a choice. Hell, a couple years ago, he *would've* rounded up a posse.

But there were still a lot of other people around town who'd buy the offending T-shirt. I wouldn't have been surprised if it was Red's bestseller.

Devo thought Red was the ultimate redneck—and who could blame her with the show Red seemed to like to put on —but she didn't know that he'd donated to Brian's son's crowdfunding campaign to help pay for his top operation.

Actually, no one knew that besides me. And Red wasn't aware that I knew. I had just happened to be standing behind him when he donated to the website on his phone after he'd seen a poster about it tacked up to the bulletin board at the station before the Fourth of July festivities last July. Red had come in to complain about out-of-towners parking illegally in front of his store.

I had no clue why Red was acting like such a twat towards Devo. I wasn't even sure if Red knew why, but somewhere deep inside the old fucker lived a good friend and a helpful member of our community. I was 78 percent sure of it.

Flashing Mr. Nichols a knowing smile, I turned, headed toward the door, and said, "Have a good rest of your day. Don't forget I offered to help with the window when the arthritis in your shoulders has you cryin'."

I let the door slam shut behind me, and I wasn't even sorry.

"You got my medicine?" my mama called when she heard me on her porch, struggling to open the screen door with my hands full of groceries and her monthly medications from the pharmacy. The pharmacy bag felt heavier than the shit from the Food Mart.

"Yeah, Mama. Got it right here," I mumbled. "You could say thanks, but you ain't gonna, are ya?"

"Put it on the table," she said when I entered her kitchen.

Her dirty dishes were in a gross pile in the sink, and her trash can was overflowing with no bag. Dammit. *She* wasn't gonna clean up the freakin' mess, not with all her aches and pains.

Since my dad died seven years ago, Mervella Lee, my mama, had been living in the trailer park east of town. My oldest brother took over running the farm we'd grown up on, but Mama's health and her general crankiness stopped her from working anymore. She hadn't really wanted anything to do with the farm after my dad passed anyway.

The Lee Family Fleece farm had never been a thriving business. My other brothers and I had tried to convince Bax to sell the land—it was worth a pretty penny—but he could be just as headstrong as our dad, so ten miles down the road from Mama's trailer, he was currently struggling with the same flailing business my dad had failed to make a success. My other two brothers were no help, and I had my job with the county.

Raising sheep had definitely never been my idea of a career choice, but it didn't matter anyway because me running the farm had never even been an option since my dad had believed women couldn't raise sheep. Or run businesses. Had he never heard of Oprah? But I was pretty sure he'd meant *gay* women. Why he'd thought that had anything to do with farming, I had no idea.

Bax wasn't an intolerant dick, though, so at least there was that. Mama still maintained that she didn't care about any of it. But if he did sell, the money could set her and Bax up for the rest of their lives, could put my niece Athena through college. I had to give my brother credit though. He'd done his best to continue the Lee family legacy, whatever that was. Our dad had left us without much to be proud of. Besides, if Bax sold, we all knew our brother Dixon would piss away any money he got from the sale.

Bax had offered for Mama to live with him, Athena, and Candy before she passed, but Mama had said no. She didn't want to "be in the way." Instead, she'd used her part of my dad's life insurance payout to buy this trailer.

If I never had to have another conversation about any of it, that would suit me just fine, but if Bax ever did sell, I'd miss the land. I'd miss riding it. I'd miss all the memories of me and my three brothers exploring it as kids.

Those memories were all I had left of our dad before he basically disowned me. Before who I was made him hate me.

"Mama, why ain't there a bag in the bin?"

"I ran out."

"Why didn't you text me so I could add it to the list? I just came from the damn store. You knew I was goin'."

"Don't get smart with me, young lady," she griped.

"I'm thirty-two freakin' years old, Mama."

"You're still younger than me, and I'm your mother, so you should treat me with respect."

"Oh." I laughed. "You mean like how you treat *me* with respect?"

In her hoarse smoker's voice, she grumbled, "Watch it."

"Whatever. Make sure all the meds are right, 'cause I gotta work second shift today. I need to get back."

Swiping the bag from the table where I'd set it, she dug through it. "Why's Carey makin' you work such long hours?"

"He's not *makin'* me do anything. I offered. We've got two new deputies comin' to Wisper, and they're gonna need trainin'. I gotta show 'em how we do things, but before they get here, I need to get some stuff sorted."

"You see?" she said. "I told you a woman don't belong in a position of power like that, and now he has to go and hire more people to cover your behind."

Oh my God. Lord, I'm begging here. Give. Me. Strength. You know what? No.

"Well, Mama, you were wrong. He hired more deputies 'cause he plans to spend more time at the main station, so he's puttin' me in charge of Wisper. How you like them apples?"

"Now why'd he go and do a thing like that?"

Her verbal dig was like a slap to the face. I stumbled back a step but then caught and steadied myself. "'Cause I'm damn *good* at my job."

"Do you have to put a cuss word in every sentence you say?"

Shit, if the word "damn" bothered her so much, she'd hate to hear the way I talked around my friends. Dropping my hat on the table, I pulled my hair out of the ponytail it had been in at the back of my neck, then redid it so it was tidier. Damn thing wouldn't stay in its elastic holder no matter how many times I pulled it tighter. "Why's it so hard for you to believe I'm good at what I do? Can't you see how much I love it?"

"Well, now I know you love it." She offered a rare smile and walked behind me to pull the few strands of hair I'd missed from under the collar of my work shirt. "Lemme do it."

She pulled the ponytail out again and worked on making it nicer, and I thought, *This woman is nothing if not miserable.*

Her smiles were few and far between, and the truth was that she'd never admit to me being proficient at my job because she didn't believe it was right for a woman to hold any kind of authority. Like a lot of people, it was the way she had been raised. It was my daddy's opinion when he was alive. She would never have argued with him, and she didn't feel the need to change now. She all but threw a fit during the last presidential election when there were no less than three women running. It had never made sense to me. She *was* a woman, for shit's sake, but she'd be the first to tell you it wasn't right.

After she'd fixed my hair, she patted my shoulder and walked around the table to grab the bag of medicine. "In my day, we didn't have lady deputies or sheriffs. It's just a little unorthodox."

My eyes bugged out of my head while I tried for the millionth time to understand the nonsense coming out of her mouth. "What century do you live in?"

"Huh?"

Pick your battles, Abey. "Never mind."

She looked in the bag again, picking up each bottle of medication and checking the label like I'd trained her to do, because before April Cunningham took over running Wisper's pharmacy, Abel Jameson was the pharmacist, and he was eighty-five and well into the throes of dementia before his family had made him retire. Mama's blood pressure medication had been mixed up with some little kid's ADHD meds. That had been a fun trip to the hospital.

"I get my social security check Wednesday," she said. "You wanna take me out to Idaho Falls? I need new shoes, and I s'pose I'll take you to lunch, too, to that steak place you like so good."

"I'm gonna be workin' a lot. Can't Bax take you? I don't know if I'll get a day off this week."

"Your brother's a busy man, Abey. You know that. He's got his hands full with Athena and the farm."

I had a big soft spot for my twelve-year-old niece, so I didn't argue. Since we'd lost Candy, Bax and Athena had been having a hell of a time, especially Athena, and living on a stinky farm with my big dumb brother, the poor kid needed a break every now and then. The least I could do was keep her ornery grandma away from her when I could.

"Okay, well, how 'bout Dixon? He lost his job, didn't he? He should have plenty of free time."

Too bad my other brother, Brand, the only successful

member of our family besides me, lived too far away to be any help. Lucky fucker.

"My baby boy's goin' through somethin'. You know he's got the depression, and you oughta be more considerate of his situation. Besides, they done took his truck away. Hauled it right outta his driveway."

"Who did? His truck was stolen? Why didn't he call me?"

"No. It was them foreclosure people. You know," she said with a wave of her hand, dismissing the fact that her "baby boy" was an irresponsible fuckup.

And for the record, *I* was her damn baby! I was the youngest. Out of the four of us, Dixon was the third in line for the white-trash throne, and Baxter was the oldest. Brand was the second-born, and he'd hightailed it out of Wisper the second he graduated high school. We didn't see him but once or twice a year, if we were lucky. His construction company in Sheridan kept him just busy enough that he didn't get roped into coming home very often. He'd even offered to build a second house on the farm for Mama to live in, but she'd refused that too.

She was actively trying to be miserable. There could be no other explanation.

"You mean his truck was repossessed?"

"Yeah, that's what I said, ain't it?"

"Well, that's great," I muttered while I unloaded the totes of groceries onto her counter, after I'd reorganized all her dirty dishes. I had no clue where they'd all come from, but she had a substantial collection of well-worn plastic cups with kids' cartoons on them. Maybe she'd picked them up at a thrift store. "Can you just order your shoes online? I don't think I'll have time to take you all the way out to Idaho Falls, maybe not till next month."

"No. I gotta try 'em on, and you know that shippin' fee all them online stores charge is a racket."

"Oh my God, Mama. I'll pay the damn shippin' fee."

"Abey Juniper Lee! Don't you take the Lord's name in vain. How many times I gotta tell you?"

CHAPTER SEVEN

DEVO

"JUDGE PINE WANTS you and Red to work this out between yourselves," Brady said when he called me in my truck on my way to work Saturday morning. Theo was still angry with me, but at least he wasn't fuming anymore. Smoke had stopped pouring out of his ears. At least, I hoped it had.

"What does that mean? When did you talk to a judge?" I turned my radio down, muting the sound of some seriously soothing folk rock playing on the little indie FM station out of Jackson, and tapped the button on my phone to put Brady on speaker. "I didn't know I had a judge already."

My Chevy pickup was old as hell, so it didn't have Bluetooth capabilities, but I bought one of those magnetic phone holders and stuck it to my dash so I wouldn't get a ticket for breaking Wyoming's "distracted driving" law.

"Well, you do, but not officially. I talked to the Honorary Devlin Pine last night after Red threatened again to file formal charges against you. Didn't you get my text? And I think it means Judge Pine doesn't wanna deal with you two. He was the judge the last time somebody took Red to court."

"No, I didn't see your text. Sorry. I was runnin' late this

mornin'. And who took Red to court?"

"His ex-wife. It's been years, but Judge Pine remembers it, and not fondly."

"Oh. Well, I don't blame the judge or Red's poor ex-wife. The man is absolutely insufferable."

I waved out my window to Kari Whiteriver as she walked with her two kids down the side of the road. Barton had a park, but the seesaws had been broken for two years. The metal slide sat in direct sunlight, so it burned your butt if you slid down the thing. I still remembered my little brother, Avi, screaming as he slid down when we were teenagers. He'd worn shorts that day and got a big red burn on the backs of his thighs. The park still had a sandbox, though, and I figured that was where Kari and her kids were headed at seven in the morning. A local carpenter had built it under a big quaking aspen tree, so unlike the slide, the sandbox was nice and shaded from the warm early-morning sun.

"Since I'm a mediator for the Teton County court system, I expect he wants me to figure it out. And I've got a plan, but you aren't gonna like it."

Uh-oh. "What plan?"

"Well, we could try to talk it out first, but I got the feelin' after my conversation with Red last night that isn't gonna be super productive, so instead, you and he are gonna trade places."

"Trade. Places." I said the words, hoping they'd make better sense if I said them slowly, but it didn't work. "What in the world does that mean?"

"It means, startin' Monday, Red's gonna do your job, and you're gonna do his. For a week. Maybe if y'all get a better understandin' of what the other's life is like, then maybe you won't continue to go at each other like a couple of rabid dogs."

"You cannot be serious. You want him to do *my* job? The job in which he will encounter gay, lesbian, and transgender people? Poor people, homeless people? No," I said. "Think of somethin' else, Brady, 'cause that's just askin' for trouble. I can't even imagine the things he'd say to 'em."

"You want this guy to understand, don't you?"

"Well, yeah. If he could just see how great some of these people are, he wouldn't be such a jerk."

"So," Brady went on, "is there a better way to accomplish that? Think about it. He'll see the things they're up against. He'll have to help 'em with all kinds of things. He'll see the heartbreak they face and the difficulties. And I know you don't wanna hear this, but I think you may have Red pegged as somethin' he's not. For what it's worth."

Yeah, right.

But he did have a point, although I had no idea how he would accomplish the task of talking Red into this cocka-mamie plan of his, especially 'cause Brady himself was gay and not shy about that fact. Everyone in town knew Brady and Theo were shacking up in the attic apartment right across the street from Red's store. It wasn't too long ago they had been the talk of town, but most people had gotten used to it by now and had adjusted.

"Besides," he said, "Theo will be there, and I'll ask Frank or Abey to stop by to check on things when I'm not there. Make sure nobody strangles Red."

"Okay, but you have to talk to him about how he speaks to people. I won't agree unless you promise me that you and Theo will talk to him before he interacts with anyone. This is supposed to be a safe place. Red's attitude could make it unsafe *real* quick."

"I promise."

I was kind of bummed that I wouldn't be there to see

Abey in action, but grudgingly, I had to admit that Brady was right that something needed to be done about the animosity between Red and me. "But what about me? You want me to run his store? And why would Red agree to this?"

"You have retail experience, right?" he asked.

"A little, yeah." I'd worked in fast food and had learned how to do the cash register, and I'd been the checkout girl at the bait and tackle shack in Barton for two summers after my dad died, when I took any job I could find to help my mom pay the rent. How hard could selling rude T-shirts and bear spray really be?

"And Red will agree to it because Judge Pine is threatenin' to charge you both with contempt if you don't."

I sighed. Great. Just great. "Okay. I'm trustin' you, if you really think this'll work."

"You still gotta pay for the window and the shirts."

I rolled my eyes. "Fine."

"Okay. I'm headed over to Red's place now. I'll let you know what he says."

When I pulled up in the alley behind Ace's House and parked, our head of maintenance, Vern, was out there, breaking down cardboard boxes and trying to fit them into our already full dumpster.

He smirked when I got out of my truck. "Heard you chucked a rock through Red's front window."

"It was a brick," I said, yanking my bag from the tangle it was in on the passenger seat. The long strap had gotten stuck on the metal seatbelt clip when I'd dumped it into my truck in my rush to not be late to work and piss Theo off further. "But yeah, you heard right."

He raised an eyebrow and adjusted his Ace's House baseball cap. "Should I ask?"

"Please don't. I'm so mad at myself for doin' it. And Theo's pissed."

"Oh yeah," Vern said. "I heard that loud and clear when I got here a little while ago. Why do you think I'm out here? He was yellin' at Brady on the phone. They never fight."

"That's probably 'cause Brady told him about his genius plan to have me and Red switch jobs next week, which means you guys will have the pleasure of workin' with that old jackass."

But if it kept me out of jail, I was all for it.

"Ah, Red's harmless," Vern said. "And don't worry. I'll keep an eye on things, and you know Theo would never let him do anything to hurt anybody."

"I know. Thanks, Vern. It's just that some of these kids are confused and fragile. You know? What if he says somethin' stupid and they believe him?"

"They won't, Devo, 'cause you'll be back, and all they have to do is look at you, at how you live your life. You're a good person." He chuckled. "You know, when you're not breakin' people's windows."

I shrugged. I tried to be a good person. Had my recent lawbreaking stricken it from my record?

"Thanks. You want coffee? I think I'll run over to Coffee Shot and get Theo his favorite. Maybe I can get ahead of his bad mood."

"Naw, thanks though. I'm tryin' to cut down on caffeine. I've been workin' out, and I'm changin' up my diet." He lifted his arms and flexed his biceps. He'd worn his usual white tank over jeans, and I could see the difference already. He'd really been paying attention to his appearance lately, which was night and day from when I'd first met him. I would've even gone so far as to say that Vern was handsome, and I'd even noticed a couple of tourists ogling his backside last week at the farmers market.

Backing away, I whistled. "Lookin' good!"

"Aw shucks," he said, red-faced, and I giggled.

Vern was an odd guy, but he'd turned out to be one of the nicest people I'd ever worked with. No matter the task, he was always willing to help or get his hands dirty. I'd known he was a good person and a hard worker the first time we met. Everyone thought I was nuts for trusting him, but I knew all he needed was a chance and someone to rely on him, someone who valued his opinion. He found that in Theo, and in me, and now, Vern was a different guy. He took pride in Ace's House, and it showed in his job.

If someone like Vern could change his mind when he'd spent most of his life around crude, intolerant people, why couldn't Red do the same? Or was everyone else right that Red wasn't really homophobic and I was just blind to the truth?

"Alright. See you in a bit."

"That you will," he said as he turned and pulled his boxcutter from the loop on his jeans, then twirled it in a circle in his hand. "You surely will."

———

I made my way across Main Street and stepped over the threshold into Coffee Shot, and as a gust of really cold air conditioning rushed at me, cheers erupted from the customers. People smiled at me and clapped.

"What?" I said, stopping in my tracks and looking around, confused.

"It's about time somebody put Red in his place," Finn

Cade, one of Wisper's resident horse ranchers, said. He tossed a wink my way and smirked.

"Yeah," Aubrey said, laughing. "He deserved it, but don't do that to my window, okay?" She owned the only bookstore in Wisper, Your Local Bookie, and was a member of Wisper's romance book club.

Abey belonged to that club. I'd seen her going into the library for their meetings. Thinking about that had me wondering just what they got up to at their meetings. How detailed did they get when they discussed the sex scenes from the books they read? Imagining Abey reading raunchy dialogue out loud made me blush a little.

I shook the thought from my head. "It was wrong. I shouldn't have done it."

Walt, the owner of Coffee Shot, handed me my favorite, an iced double shot cappuccino. "Saw you comin'. It's on the house." He winked and smiled, but it didn't surprise me that he wasn't voicing his praise for my misdeeds. He probably didn't want to risk people talking badly about him or his business, but the feisty smile on his lips said it all.

No one liked Red. He really was a jerk, not just to me but to most people. He was rude to just about everybody he encountered. Men, women, even children. But nobody seemed to know why. What had happened to the guy that had turned him into such an outright dick?

"Well," I said, "thanks, guys, but still, it wasn't my finest moment. And my boss is *not* happy. I'm gonna need his favorite drink, too, Walt."

He nodded and got to work making Theo's large iced mocha latte. Hopefully, a little caffeine pick-me-up would pull a smile out of my frustrated friend.

"Red pressin' charges?" Finn asked as he stood and placed his empty cup in the dirty-mug bin behind him.

Walt had been experimenting with serving coffee in reusable ceramic mugs instead of unrecyclable disposable cups with the wax coating lining the insides. It worked well if you stayed at Coffee Shot while you drank your hot coffee, but if you needed it to go, it was kind of problematic. Trying to get Wisper's residents to bring in their own reusable coffee mugs or tumblers was proving to be a headache.

"He wants to, but Brady's tryin' to convince him to work it out with me. I have to pay for the window, of course, but he wants Red and me to switch jobs for a week. Brady thinks that'll change Red's mind about Ace's House. I guess he thinks it'll make us understand each other better or somethin'."

Finn chuckled doubtfully. "That's one theory."

"You don't think it'll work?"

He shook his head and lifted his black cowboy hat from the table. "Hey, Walt, whip me up an iced chai tea latte to go, would ya, please? If Aislinn finds out I was here and didn't get her tea, I'm in for it. Charge me for a new tumbler." Looking back at me while he fixed the hat over his long blond hair, he mused, "I wonder if Red has it in him to change the way he thinks. He's been mean a long time."

"Maybe Brady's right though," Aubrey said. "Nobody knows why Red is the way he is, so maybe somethin' will shake loose while he's at Ace's House. You never know. Here," she added as she stood, and she handed me a wrapped chocolate chip muffin. "For your good deeds."

"Thanks," I said and smiled. "Really, you guys." I looked around the coffee shop, at Finn and Aubrey, but there were more people sitting at the coffee shop tables, smiling up at me, some whose names I didn't even know. "Thanks for the support."

CHAPTER EIGHT

ABEY

WALKING into The Red Wild Outdoors Monday morning to make absolutely sure Red didn't need help—though, as cranky as he had been lately, I knew it was probably a wasted effort—my boots squeaked, and I stopped on a dime when I saw Devo behind the counter.

A devil's smile crossed her lips. I wasn't sure if it was because it was me walking in or because I'd found her doing something… naughty?

I narrowed my eyes. "What're you doin' here? Where's Red?"

"He's at Ace's House. I'm workin' here today." She shrugged like it was no big deal. "Nobody told you?"

"No. What the hell?"

"We traded jobs for a few days," she said as she walked around the counter. A black and white flannel was tied around her hips, and she wore a fitted, white T-shirt, cutoff khaki shorts, and clunky brown hiking boots.

She looked hot. Normally, she wore jeans or pants. Except for the night we'd made each other come. She'd worn shorts that night too. I would never forget them or how they'd fit her, so snug on her hips.

"Like what you see?" she asked, probably 'cause she'd noticed me drinking her in.

"I do," I said. I couldn't lie.

Touching the tip of her tongue to the bottom of her two front teeth, she tilted her head. "Thanks."

Shaking my head, I tried to clear it. It wouldn't do to be thinking about her body, not while I was on the job, but then she turned to adjust some hiking hip packs on a display table to her right, and my clear mind became all kinds of fuzzy.

Jesus. The backs of her thighs called to me. I wanted to feel them, wanted to run my hands up and down the smooth skin. Her legs looked strong but not overly muscular, and I remembered how soft they'd been when my face was between them. And right then, it became my mission to get her on her hands and knees so I could lie beneath her and drag her pussy to my mouth, licking her most sensitive flesh while I held those legs open with my hands wrapped around her luscious thighs. She could go down on me at the same time.

Scraping my teeth over my bottom lip slowly while I imagined her in my bed, I was lost in a pussy-fueled fantasy, but she coughed and said my name.

"Hello-o-o?"

My eyes flicked up to hers. "What?"

Crossing her arms beneath her perfect, high tits, she knew what I was thinking. It was evident from the smirk on her face. "I asked why you're here. You haven't said yet."

I cleared my throat. "Right. Uh, I just wanted to check in on Red. I didn't get a chance yester—"

"Check on *him*?" She threw up her hands. "Why? Why

are you so concerned about that freakin' asshole? Why aren't you checkin' in on me?"

"Well, 'cause you're the one who broke the law, and you don't have arthritis."

"Who cares? I don't get it. He's outright hostile to me, to you. To everyone! I hate him."

"I know who he is, Devo," I said. "But he's also my neighbor and a resident of Wisper, so therefore, I check in on him just like I would any other person in this situation."

"Correction. Every person except *me*."

Was I right that this was less of a "things should be equal" thing and more of a "my feelings are hurt" thing? The little glint in her eyes and the way her beautiful mouth turned down into the smallest hint of a frown told me it was.

"You have a family and friends, co-workers. You have support. Red doesn't." Still, I felt bad, because she was right.

"That's his own fault."

Lifting my shoulder, I said, "Maybe. There's some stuff you probably don't know about him though."

"Why does everyone keep sayin' that?" She cocked a hip and planted her hand on it, and I watched how her thigh muscle jiggled a little as she turned her foot out. It was sexy. "Like what? I'd like to know what's so *great* about Red Graves. What do you know that I don't?"

"Ain't my place to say," I said, lifting my eyes back up to hers.

She scoffed. "It's pretty ironic, you defendin' the man who would be utterly disgusted at the way you're lookin' at me right now."

"I'm not defendin' him, but Devo, this is my job. Okay? I love my job. I'm good at my job. And sometimes, I don't get a say in the things I have to do. Sometimes, I have to deal with people I'd rather not. I can hoot and holler about it all I want, but I still gotta do it, and in cases like Red's, it's easy to see it's not so black-and-white."

I walked further into the store and stood right in front of her. "I suspect Brady put you and Red up to this *Freaky Friday* stuff, hopin' y'all might learn a thing or two, so maybe instead of accusin' me of betrayin' you, you could try to get somethin' out of the experience."

"Whatever," she said.

I took off my hat, held it in front of my chest like a white flag, and took one more step toward her. I *had* been thinking about her. I did want to check in with her, but I didn't know if she wanted that. "*Are* you okay? I think about you a lot. But I don't know where the line is, y'know?"

She blinked and stepped closer to me too. "What line?"

"The line that tells me if I'm comin' on too strong, or if I'm mixin' my duties as a deputy with how I should act as your… friend, or like someone who—"

In a quiet voice, she asked, "Someone who what?"

"Someone who likes you."

Both of her dark eyebrows pitched up, and I wanted to trace them with my fingertip.

"You like me?"

I nodded, feeling kind of shy now that I was saying it out loud. "Yeah. You know, when you're not bein' a pain in my ass."

"Fine," she said, all exasperated with me suddenly, and she threw her hands up in the air again. "I will admit that I think about you too. Okay? About that… night, but this is me, Abey. I *am* a pain in the ass. It's part of my—"

Something came over me then, and I needed her in my arms. She'd finally admitted the pull between us wasn't a one-sided thing. As I stomped toward her, I looked behind me, out the door, making sure no one could see what I was about to do. Red had boarded up the window, so that was a plus.

"What're you doin'?"

Resting my hands over hers still on her hips, I steered her backward to the long checkout counter, then lifted her up and plopped her sexy ass on top of it. I looked up at her above me and said, "Kiss me." I worked my body between her legs, loving how it felt when she wrapped them around my waist.

"Why?" she asked, looking in my eyes as her boots dug into my ass cheeks over my ugly, brown polyester work pants.

"Why kiss me?"

"Yeah. You sure you wanna kiss a pain-in-the-ass felon?"

I laughed under my breath. "You're not a felon. At least not yet."

She pulled me closer with her arms around my shoulders, inspecting my face, her brown eyes roving all over me. I liked how it felt to have her attention on me when she wasn't yelling at me or frustrated with me. Well, maybe she was a little.

"I like you too," she whispered. "We were good together."

"Yeah," I said kind of breathlessly, remembering when she'd had her hand between my legs. But as much as I thought about her body, I couldn't get the memory of snuggling with her on my couch out of my head. The memory of holding her. Of her holding me. Of the way it had felt when she'd dragged her fingertip up the inside of my arm slowly as she told me about growing up in New Mexico. "I felt somethin' that night. It was different than anything I've felt before."

"Me too, but maybe it was just 'cause we were so caught up."

"No," I said, tucking that unruly, curly flip of hair

behind her ear. It was like that one lock of hair had a mind of its own. Today, it had curved out away from her face, like a hook constantly and determinedly trying to draw my eyes to the edge of her mouth. "I don't think that's all it was."

"How can you know?"

"S'pose I can't," I said, "unless you kiss me again. Then I'll know for sure."

The cowbell on the front door jangled, and I froze.

No one could see me like this. I shouldn't have taken the chance.

Releasing her, I stepped back, and Devo, noticing the wince on my face, slid down from the counter. She adjusted her shorts and walked behind the register as a man entered the store.

"Hi," Devo said to him. "Welcome to The Red Wild Outdoors." Then she muttered to herself, "God, that's a stupid name. Sounds like a conservative river rafting company." She cleared her throat and adjusted her frown to a toothy smile. "What can I help you with today?"

"Who're you?" Artie Crane asked, removing his cap and running a hand through his short brown hair. He had a big bulge of nicotine gum tucked inside his right cheek. He'd been trying to quit chew for a year at least.

"I'm Devo. I'm fillin' in for Red today."

"Red didn't say nothin' 'bout a woman workin' here."

"Uh, no, he wouldn't have." Devo tucked that adorable lock of hair behind her ear again, but it popped right back out. "This is a new… arrangement. But I'm here to help."

He looked her up and down and laughed. "Whatcha know about ammo? 'Cause that's what I need."

She pinched the lock of hair between two fingers and then yanked it behind her ear nervously. "Um, ammo?"

"Ammunition," I whispered, trying to help. "He means bullets."

He glanced at me in greeting. "Deputy."

"Hey there, Crane," I said, righting my holster around my hips. I wanted to re-tuck my shirt into my uniform pants so it was straight, but how obvious would that have looked? Did he know how close I had just been to sticking my tongue down Devo's throat? "How's the family?"

He nodded and looked back at Devo. "They're fine, but they're gonna need some food in their bellies come winter, so I need me some ammo."

Devo's face fell. "Why do you need bullets to feed your family?"

Crane laughed. "You do know what ammunition is, right?" He threw his hands in the air, turning toward me. "She for real?"

"Crane's a hunter," I said. "He hunts deer and elk. He needs ammo—bullets—because he'd like to go huntin'."

"Of course I know what it is," she said, rolling her eyes, but then she pegged Crane with a thoughtful frown. "But why can't you just go buy meat at the Food Mart?"

"That's not how this works, missy. I got all the necessary licenses and permits. I got my tags. The season starts in a couple weeks. I just need ammo. You gonna sell it to me, or do I gotta go find Red and tell him you can't do the job?"

"No!" Devo rushed to say. "Nope. I can help you. Um—" She looked around the store until her eyes landed on about a hundred different brands and types of boxes of ammunition under a glass case lining the south wall. She walked there slowly and lifted the lid. "These look nice. The green box is kinda cool." She picked up a box of birdshot and held it up in the air. "Will these work?"

"Sure," Crane said, "if I was huntin' quail. That's twelve-gauge birdshot for a shotgun. I need the big-game ammo for a rifle. One shelf down and three to your left. Blue box. The Federal thirty-aught-sixes, 180 grain. Gimme three boxes. You see the little elk head on the side?"

Turning the box in her hand to inspect it, Devo nodded. "Aw. He's cute."

Now, Crane rolled his eyes. "For future reference, if you're not sure what kind you need, you can check that. You'll see an animal or a target for target practice, but most hunters will already know what they need."

"Okay. Thanks." When she had them on the counter by the register, she knocked one of the boxes to the floor with her elbow and then bent to pick it up, but she whacked her forehead on the edge of the counter and yelped, "Ow!" If she hadn't been so completely out of her comfort zone, it would've been funny.

Crane looked at me, shaking his head in exasperation. "Where is Red?"

"Well…" I hesitated. "Red's across the street at Ace's House."

"And why the hell is he over there?"

Devo interrupted, rubbing the sore spot on her head with the heel of her hand, "He's doin' my job, and I'm doin' his. It's not a big deal."

Crane looked her up and down. "You the one broke his window?"

She blushed as she rang up Crane's ammo. I liked the way the pink color made her eyes seem brighter. "Maybe. That'll be $127.98. Holy crap! For bullets?"

"Yes, little girl. These are premium rounds, then you got your state tax, huntin' tax, ammo tax. These bullets ain't no joke."

She lifted one box and studied it, then dropped it into a

plastic bag with the other two. "Yeah, but that much money for these tiny little boxes? That seems extreme."

"They'd be a lot more anywhere else. Red keeps his prices as low as he can. Oh, and he gives me a veteran discount. Make sure you put that in." He pointed at the cash register. "Twenty percent."

Devo looked at me, questioning the discount, and I nodded. I knew for a fact that Red treated his veteran customers really well. He also donated to the Wounded Warrior fund every year, and he gave out coupons for any soldier who attended group meetings at the veteran's center in Jackson.

"Hm. Well, I can't say for sure if this is the right solution to that mess, but I also can't disagree Red might need a push to be kinder sometimes." He peered down at Devo. "But you won't be breakin' any more windows, will ya? That ain't gonna help your cause."

She had enough humility to say, "No, sir."

"That's good then." She adjusted his price on the register, and he handed her two one-hundred dollar bills, but before she put them in the drawer, he added, "Don't you wanna mark those with that pen Red uses? Gotta make sure they're not counterfeit."

I tried to help again. "If the mark is yellow or gold, it's legit. If it's dark or black, it's a fake."

I was standing right there. He better not have given her counterfeit bills. But I knew he hadn't. Artie Crane was a fair and honest man, if not a little rough around his edges.

"Okay." Devo searched around the register and found the pen he was talking about. She held it up to look at it in a better light. "Cool." She popped the cap off and drew a line on each bill. After she'd made sure they weren't fake, she counted out Crane's change and dropped a paper receipt into the bag. "Thank you, and you have yourself a nice day."

Crane laughed and shook his head. "And you do the same."

"See ya, Crane," I said, and he waved me off as he left the store with a black Red Wild bag dangling from between two fingers.

As soon as the doors shut behind him, Devo's eyes narrowed, and she came around the counter toward me. "What was that about?"

"What?"

"Are you not out?"

"I-I'm not *in*." I winced. That wasn't really an explanation. "I think a lot of people know I'm gay, but no one brings it up. And I guess I don't like to make a show of it, y'know?"

"'Make a show of it'? What does *that* mean?"

I thought before I spoke, not that it helped me explain much. "There's a lot of… well, in my line of work, there are a lot of people who don't agree with… same-sex… Um, y'know. Lesbianism." God, I hated that word. "So I keep it to myself. Guess I'm just tryin' to make things easier for Carey and Frank."

Devo scoffed under her breath. "Easier for them? Or do you mean for you?"

"Yeah, it makes things easier for me, too, I guess."

She shook her head, clearly not buying it.

"Look," I said, "it's hard enough bein' a woman in this job. Addin' gay on top of it, well, that's just askin' for trouble."

Her face fell. "I thought you were braver than that."

What? *Seriously?* "You're judgin' me?"

"No, no, I—"

"Yeah, you are. I expected better of you. I thought *you* were an ally."

"Wait," she called after me as I turned to go.

I was getting mad. She had no fucking clue about the things I had to deal with. How every single law enforcement officer in our jurisdiction looked at me like they didn't think I could perform the duties of my job because of what was or wasn't between my legs.

"I gotta go," I said.

I was angry she'd said it. And hurt. The little spot in the middle of my chest burned. I rubbed at it over my shirt, trying to make the burn recede, but I should've known better. It never did. And funny, I suddenly realized it was the same feeling I got when something my mama said, or something she didn't say, hurt. It put the same uncomfortable pinch there.

"I need to check on Red, make sure he isn't ruinin' anybody's life, or some kid ain't shovin' his head in a toilet."

"I'm sorry," she said, and I heard her boots squeak on the tile floor when she stopped following me. "Really, Abey. Please forgive me."

"Never mind." I tried not to sound hurt. But I was. "Anyway, I gotta go."

CHAPTER NINE

DEVO

DAMMIT. I shouldn't have said that.

Abey was right. I *had* judged her. And I had no right to.

If I were being honest with myself, though, I guess I'd hoped she was out. If we dated, things would be so much easier if we both were. But we weren't dating. We were barely friends. But she was also right that people around here tended to treat you differently if they knew you were gay. Most people were more accepting nowadays than they used to be, especially in the last few years, but still, if you were gay, you were "other."

Maybe I didn't know what she'd been through to get to where she was in a male-dominated job, but it wasn't difficult to imagine just how hard it could've been. I felt like a heel for questioning her. Me, the super-woke lesbian who worked at an LGBTQ safe house.

Devo the devil strikes again.

My mom was the most supportive parent I'd ever heard of. My dad had been something else entirely, but his opinion had never really mattered to me. I guess I got lucky that way. But I couldn't imagine having to live and work around people who thought your very identity was wrong, who disagreed with you even being in the field you loved working in.

While I thought about ways to apologize—I could show up at her apartment with cookies, but I didn't even know if she liked cookies, or any baked goods, for that matter—I heard a noise in the back of the store. It sounded like someone ransacking boxes in the storeroom.

I tiptoed to the curtain Red had hung from the doorframe behind the register and listened. The stupid curtain had a picture printed on it of some big, brawny, bearded dude crouched down next to a beautiful elk with an antler rack the size of my truck and a bullet hole in its chest. The poor thing had blood coming out of its mouth.

Had an animal gotten into the back room? Did I leave the back door open when I came in this morning? If there was a raccoon or something back there, it'd make a big freaking mess, and then I'd get charged for the damage. Red had already cussed me up and down when he handed over his keys this morning. He had zero faith that I wouldn't burn his business down in the matter of a week.

That was fine. I had even less faith in his ability to be supportive and kind to people at Ace's House.

I grabbed the broom next to the door and aimed it out in front of me, then swiped the curtain aside and jumped into the back room. "Who's there?"

Bent over what looked like a box of freeze-dried macaroni and cheese packets, a man dug through the box next to it, and it looked like I'd scared him nice and good as he straightened and stumbled backward.

He yelped. "Shit on my dick!"

He held his arms up in the air like I'd pointed a gun at him instead of a household cleaning implement. It then occurred to me that maybe I should've found an actual gun to

use. God knew there were bound to be some in this patriar-
chal, Old Spice-smelling, man-fest store.

A laugh exploded out of me. "What did you just say?"
The whole situation was hilarious. I mean, what was I even
doing in this stupid place? "What're you doin' back here? Are
you stealin' from Red Graves?"

"Sorry," he said, wincing and trying not to laugh. "It just
came out. You really scared me."

The burglar was at least a foot taller than me, with brown
hair and a matching 'stache and beard. He looked like one of
Red's usual customers, probably an elk killer himself or
maybe a hiker. We got a fair few of those in Wisper.

"No, I ain't stealin'," he said. "Well, okay, maybe that's
not the whole truth. Technically, I s'pose I am stealin' since I
don't plan on payin' for this shirt, but Red's my uncle, so it
doesn't exactly count." He stepped closer, tripping over
another box on the floor. Its lid was nowhere to be found, and
I saw at least two dozen photo albums in there probably filled
with more dead animal pics.

"No," I said, still aiming the broom at him, "I'm pretty
sure it still counts."

He chuckled and held up a black shirt with bold red font
that said, "Kill it Red Wild Style." "Uncle Red likes us to
wear 'em when we work for him."

"He's really your uncle?" *Ugh! What a stupid tagline.*

"Yeah. His brother's my dad. Or my dad's his brother,
or… well, you get the gist."

"So why didn't you come in the front door?" I asked,
realizing I must've forgotten to lock the back door. Oops.

He stepped around the box in front of him and touched
the end of the broom, but I didn't lower it. I didn't know this
joker. He could be lying.

"'Cause the shirts are back here. They have been since I

was a kid. I used to work for my uncle when I'd come down on the weekends in high school." Hanging the T-shirt over his forearm, he pulled his phone from his back pocket. "Here," he said. "I have a voicemail from him." He tapped the screen a few times, and then Red's rude, growly voice filled the storeroom:

"Yeah, Ryder, this is your Uncle Red. I need you to come work the store for a couple days. There's some rude girlie gonna be there fillin' in for me, but she don't know shit about sellin' sportin' goods. She probably doesn't know how to work a register. I need you to keep an eye on things for me. I'll be across the damn street at the community center. Don't ask, and don't tell your pappy a damn thing. But get your ass to the store tomorrow mornin'. Nine a.m."

"God, he's such a dick! I do too know how to work a register, and I'm not some 'girlie.'"

Ryder laughed. "Sounds like you know my uncle, alright."

I rolled my eyes. "You don't need to stay, Ryder. I've got things covered."

"Everybody calls me Rye," he said, "and are you sure, 'cause it's almost deer season. There's bound to be some guys comin' in for ammo and new guns. I can help with that."

"You can?"

"Yep."

Relief filled every cell in my body. I'd barely made it through the sale of bullets. How the hell was I supposed to know anything about guns? "Thank you. That'd be great."

He pulled the animal murder T-shirt over his head, then wiggled out of the blue one underneath that he'd been wearing, tossing it behind him onto the box of mac and cheese as he followed me back into the main part of the store.

Rye's rock-hard pecs stretched the shirt. He had a boy-like charm, I could already tell, but he oozed manliness, and the veins on his forearms looked like they were ready to pop off his skin. I was sure he'd fit right in at Red Wild.

"There's women's shirts in that box, too, and," he said, catching on quickly, "some say 'Hike it Red Wild Style,' instead of 'Kill,' if you like that better." He stopped dead in his tracks when he saw the big, boarded-up Main Street window. "Whoa! What happened here?"

"Don't ask," I groaned.

"Uh, okay, but you know I could walk outside and ask the first person I saw, and they'd tell me."

"Fine! I broke the damn window. That's why I'm stuck in this stupid store. My lawyer said the judge wants Red and me to work through our differences on our own time, and he thought me workin' here was a good idea, and Red's workin' my job as assistant director of Ace's House. It's the dumbest thing I've ever heard of, and I think all this stuff"—I motioned to all the hiking and hunting crap with a flick of my hand—"is stupid, but here I am." I held my arms out wide. *Just shoot me now.*

I couldn't take a whole week of this.

"Alright, alright, I get it. You are diametrically opposed to huntin'," Rye said with a wry smile. "It's not so bad though. Most of the stuff Red sells is pretty harmless. It's mostly just outdoor stuff and T-shirts. You know, that kinda thing."

"Oh yeah," I said. "I know about the damn *T-shirts*."

"Okay, that's a bit of an extreme reaction. What's so bad about 'em?"

"Never mind." I didn't really want to get into it and risk making the only person willing to help me at the moment uncomfortable. Then again, what was the saying? The truth will set you free? "But your uncle's a jerk, and I really don't wanna be here. I've already had to sell bullets. It made me feel violated." I pointed behind him at the dead elk curtain. "And what's with that curtain? It's so inappropriate!"

He turned to see what I was pointing at and then laughed at me. "It's not inappropriate for this store. That's a prized bull elk. It inspires the hunters when they come in. That's the kinda kill they're all hopin' for."

"Ugh."

He laughed again, his easygoing demeanor making me want to punch him in the solar plexus. So were his honey-brown curls. He kept swiping them off his forehead, pushing them up and away from his face. "What's your name, anyway?"

"Oh, right, sorry. It's Devo."

"Devo? That's an odd name for a girl."

"Why does everyone keep callin' me that? I'm twenty-seven years old. I'm a *woman*."

"Yeah." He chuckled. "But you're about the size of a peanut. Sorry. Didn't mean to offend."

"It's fine," I said, finally realizing that Rye could give me the answers to all my questions. "Hey, so maybe you can help me understand. Why's Red such a jerk? Abey said there's stuff I don't know about him. I got the feelin' she meant he'd been through somethin' and that's the reason he's an utter jackass."

Rye sat on the stool behind the cash register and flipped through a gun inventory book on the counter. "You know Abey? How's she doin'? How's her mama?"

"I know her, yes. I haven't met her mom though. But Abey's fine, I think. She was just here."

"Cool," he said. "I haven't seen her in a couple years. Last time I came to town, she'd just made deputy, so maybe it's been a few more than a couple. We used to go muddin' together. Me, Abey, her brother, Bax, and some of our friends."

"Muddin'? Abey?" My eyes drifted to the side as I tried to imagine her crouched over the handlebars of some bulky four-wheeler, racing guys up a mountain. Yeah, that really did check out. I could see it.

"Yeah, you know, four-wheelin' through the mud. It's fun as hell."

I hadn't known Abey was into that kind of thing, but I supposed there was a lot I didn't know about her.

"Anyway, dunno what you mean about Red. Who specifically has he been mean to? Besides humanity."

"He's been givin' us a hard time. There's a lot of LGBTQIA+ people who come to Ace's House, and Red seems to have an issue with us."

"Ohh. Well, that doesn't surprise me. I'm sorry you have to deal with that, but it's probably nothin' you did."

"Okay, well then, who did? And *what* did they do?"

Rye's eyes strayed from mine. He'd seen something through the front door windows. He stared hard at whoever had just walked by, and then he popped off the stool and jogged toward them. "Was that Aubrey? Uh, the, well, you know, the woman who owns the bookstore down the street?"

Stepping beside him, I looked out the window, too, and saw the sway of Aubrey's strawberry blond waves as she walked toward her store. "Yeah. That's her. Why?"

He backed away from the door and looked at the floor. Easygoing changed to closed up in an instant.

"How do you know her?"

"I used to know her late husband," he said, "before he passed. He was my older brother's best friend." He shook his head, and I got the feeling he was trying to shake a thought away. "Anyway, Red's wife, my aunt Connie, she left Red.

My cousin, Junior, went with her when she left, and Red's never been the same. The rumor was that she left him for a woman."

"Was it true?"

"Dunno. Besides when Red calls to ask me to help him here at the store, I don't really talk to him much. He's a lot older than my dad. They're not very close. I'll ask though. I doubt they sit around talkin' about how they feel, but he might know somethin'." Suddenly, a wry smile broke across his face. "I'd give my left n—" He coughed, still smirking. "I'd pay a lotta money to see him workin' over at the community center."

"It's killin' me! All I can think about is what he's sayin' to those young people."

"Aw, I wouldn't worry about it," he said. "Red's a prick, sure, but he's harmless. He wouldn't really hurt anybody."

"Yeah, but he probably won't help them either."

And those people *needed* help, which was the real reason I was worried.

CHAPTER TEN

ABEY

THE NEW DEPUTIES, Dan and Roxanne, were like Olive Oyl and Popeye, if Popeye were five foot eight and Olive Oyl was a flippin' giant. Jesus! She had to be over six feet tall if she was an inch. They bickered like siblings, and I was already fed up with the both of them.

"Just follow me and observe today," I said. "Wisper's a small town, and you're not from here. It may take a little while for people to warm up to you."

"I don't really need people to warm up to me, ma'am," Dan said. "I can do my job without bein' involved in the town gossip."

I snorted to myself. *Go ahead and tell yourself that. Let's see how well you do.*

"Oh, that's right," Roxanne said, "'cause Dan here's the best kept secret in all of Wyoming, ain't that right, big man? Nobody can do a better job than he can." They'd just met hours before, and she was already annoyed with him. She rolled her eyes, and I could see the strain on her face with the effort of holding back and not jackhammering him into the ground with her fist like a nail in wood.

"Can it, both of you," I scolded as we walked up the stairs to Ace's House, still in a mood from my conversation with Devo yesterday.

That stupid burn in my chest was back full force. She thought I hid my sexuality just to make things easier on me, like it was a cop-out? The whole conversation festered inside me like a splinter under my damn fingernail, if my fingernail was my whole body and the splinter was missile sized.

A buzz of activity filled the community center when we walked in at nine in the morning. Sounds of laughter and people talking danced in the air, and when Theo zipped out of his office and out the back door to hurry after whoever had just slammed it, I got the feeling we'd stepped into a mess.

Theo's partner, Brady, saw me, though, and made his way leisurely from the gymnasium on my left. "Mornin'. Everything okay?"

"Yeah," I said, "just checkin' in. I spoke to Devo. She said R—"

The man in question, Red Graves, came marching down the hallway, with three teenagers following him, looking pissed as all get-out, with their fists in the air and common teenage indignation on their faces.

A preschool-aged little girl with kinky red hair had attached her body to Red's left leg, and he dragged her like my daddy used to do with me, but there was no smile on Red's face. It didn't seem like he liked the game she wanted to play. In fact, he looked terrified. Good on him though. He had more energy for an old timer than I'd given him credit for.

"That is so rude!" one of the teenagers who'd been following Red was saying.

"Yeah!" Her friend nodded and crossed her arms over her chest. "Where do you get off?"

I kind of felt bad for the guy. He seemed to be getting it from all sides today. "You okay there, Red?" I asked, trying not to laugh at the horrified look on his face.

"No! Deputy, I'm beggin' you, call the judge! Tell him I did what he asked." He stopped in the middle of the hallway as another preschooler came running at him. The little guy jumped on Red's back, latching his arms around Red's neck in a strangle hold. Red's eyes found mine, and he pleaded above the chatter of the teenagers and the squealing of the little kids, "Please!"

Roxanne stepped forward, pulling her whistle from the side pocket of her vest, and she blew into it. Everyone froze and covered their ears so the high-pitched noise didn't rupture their eardrums. But then she bellowed, "Knock it off!"

The boy released the death grip he'd had on Red's neck and slid down Red's back to the floor. He landed on his butt on the hard wood, and a tremble began in his chin. His lower lip popped forward, he opened his mouth, and a wail filled the whole three-story building. I would've been surprised if Shelley hadn't heard it next door at the station.

Roxanne winced, flapping her arms out in front of her toward the boy. "No. Don't do that. No, no, no. Don't cry!"

The kid cried harder.

Dan snickered beside me, and Roxanne threw her elbow back at him. As tall as she was, it almost hit him in the face, but he saw it coming and tried to move out of the way. Instead, it landed with an audible crack to his throat. He dropped to his knees, clutching at it, gasping for air.

This was the help Carey had promised me? *Jeez.*

Roxanne winced. "Shit. Sorry."

"Tell *him* sorry," I said, rolling my eyes. I held out my hand for Dan to grab onto so I could pull him up, but he shook his head and lifted himself on wobbly legs. Roxanne rolled her eyes. She didn't seem too concerned about her new partner.

"She said 'shit,'" the little girl announced, looking up at Red from where she was still attached to his leg, like a koala on a eucalyptus tree.

Theo returned from wherever he'd gone out back, taking in an eyeful of the shitshow. "Anna, Tucker, you know you're not supposed to be down here. Did you sneak out of story time again?"

Anna nodded, and Tucker shook his head vigorously.

"Go upstairs, please," Theo admonished. He pulled his phone from his pants pocket and called someone. "Are you missing two four-year-olds?" he asked the person at the end of the line. "Yes, they're on their way up now."

The gang of teens slunk slowly away, looking guilty as they retreated to the gym while trying not to make eye contact with the three deputies watching them. And then they turned and fled.

"Now, please, Anna," Theo said. "Tucker, this is your yellow warning. If you get one more, you won't be allowed to go to the park after lunch."

"Okay," Tucker conceded. He wiped the tears off his face, leaving a streak of snot above his lip as he scrambled to his knees and stood.

Theo groaned. "Come on. Let's go get you cleaned up first." He held out his hands, and Tucker and Anna grabbed hold of them. "Is everything okay, Deputy? Do you need me?"

"No," I said, looking back to check on Dan. His eyes were watering like crazy, but he was breathing. "I think we're fine. This is Deputy Fitts and Deputy Draven. I just wanted to introduce 'em and check on y'all. You might see 'em around."

"Okay," Theo said. "Thanks. Sorry. I've got to deal with these two."

Roxanne nodded, giving Theo a *pshaw* kind of look with a wave of her hand and blushing as she gave him a once-over.

"No problem," I said.

Theo called over his shoulder, "Sorry, Brady. See you at home later. Have a good day, babe." Theo looked down at Tucker, who was now picking his nose, and at the long, slimy ribbon of snot attached to his finger as he pulled it out of his nostril. "I hope yours turns out better than mine."

I watched Red's face as the couple said their goodbyes, hoping for Red to act supportively so that, in my head, he'd redeem himself from the carpet-munching comment Devo had told me he'd made. She had me quietly questioning him. But Red didn't react like someone who thought gay men living together was wrong or disgusting. He rolled his eyes, but I thought it might've been a "this is an annoying public display of affection" look more than anything else.

I hoped.

Man, but I was jealous. Jealous that Theo and Brady didn't fear that public display like I would've. What would it feel like to live like that? To know that no matter who was around, no matter who saw you, that you felt confident in yourself and in your relationship enough not to have to care what people thought?

Could that be all it came down to? A choice? Was it that easy? Could I just *choose* not to give a shit what anybody thought of me?

"Thank you, love." Brady cringed at the snot and the grossed-out look on Theo's face, and then to me, he said, "I'm off to help my mom out at the reservation. I hope nobody burns the place down while I'm gone." He shook his head as he left.

It was hard to gauge Dan's reaction to Theo and Brady. His face never seemed to change from the serious, stern law enforcement look he had now.

Roxanne, on the other hand, was easier to read than a book. Disappointment flashed in her eyes, and maybe a little jealousy, too, when she realized Theo and Brady were a couple. Had they not been, she would've had it bad for Theo. Even now as she watched him walk away, she sighed.

"C'mon, Red," I said, taking in an eyeful of the man. He'd never been such a mess. "Let's grab some fresh air."

Red's shoulders slumped, but he followed when I turned and headed back through the open front doors.

When the four of us were standing in the sunshine, Roxanne and Dan both popped their Oakleys over their eyes, and I rolled mine. They had a lot to learn about our small town. Walking around looking like they were in the National Guard wouldn't get them very far with the people of Wisper.

"You gonna make it through the week, Red?"

"What in the world was that judge thinkin'?" he grumbled. "All that Devo girl does around here is babysit a bunch of entitled brats. What good's it gonna do me to be here?"

I tried not to scoff. "Entitled?"

"Yeah. Those jerks stomp around here, bullyin' me because I sell guns. One of 'em said she was gonna call PETA on me."

"Red," I said, shaking my head. "Those kids aren't entitled. They're young, and they probably have a lot to learn about the world, but they're not at the community center 'cause their parents are off on a cruise in the Caribbean. Some of these kids are homeless, or they spend time here 'cause their home situations are unbearable. You're just an excuse for them to exercise their normal teenage muscles. You can't take offense or get mad."

Red had the good sense to look embarrassed about what he'd said.

"And the little kids are here in the *free* daycare program 'cause their parents work hard jobs that don't pay shit. They can't afford regular daycare, and technically, it's still summer. School doesn't start till next week. They've got nowhere else to go. Now, I dunno what the judge intended, but I'm bettin' there's somethin' you can figure out to be helpful while you're here."

He grumbled again, this time incoherently.

"This here's Deputy Fitts," I said, motioning to my gargantuan shadow. "And this is Deputy Draven. This is their first shift in Wisper, and I really don't wanna have to make Fitts arrest your ass. Get it together, huh?"

Roxanne shifted on her feet, probably dreading having to do what I'd just threatened. Red was a grump of epic proportions.

Red growled at me, didn't even acknowledge the new deputies, and disappeared back inside.

I looked up to the heavens, hoping for some divine intervention where Red was concerned, and then turned to go, motioning with a wave of my arm for Roxanne and Dan to follow, but I heard Sam's voice calling me from inside and stopped.

"Wait!"

Turning, I smiled at the town's librarian and one of the best friends I'd ever had as she shuffled quickly toward me in her flowery skirt and "Books are my happy place" T-shirt. She was like the sister I'd always wanted, really. "What's up, Sam?"

She stepped out onto the front stoop and shielded her eyes from the sun with her hand. "You didn't call me back last night."

"Oh, right. Sorry," I said. "I had a lot on my mind."

"Yeah, I know, which is why you should've called me back. Plus, Murph had one of his nightmares. I was kind of stressed."

"I'm sorry." I reached for her other hand gripping the strap of the fabric tote bag she'd slung over her shoulder and squeezed. "Is he okay?"

"Yeah. It wasn't a bad one, but you know how I worry."

"What's the therapist say about it?"

"She thinks it's his way of dealing with all the trauma he went through when he and his mom were homeless. All that anxiety and the unknown. But she wants us to talk about it. Demystify it, you know? Make it normal and comfortable for him to open up. I think it's working."

"Good," I said. Murphy was like a nephew to me. I hated to think about him struggling. "Sam, this is Deputy Fitts and Deputy Draven. They're new." To Dan and Roxanne, I said, "Sam's married to Deputy Sims, who y'all met this mornin'."

"Oh, hi," Sam said. "I heard we were getting some fresh blood. I hope you're settling in okay." She smiled at Dan and Roxanne. Roxanne smiled back, extending her hand for Sam to shake, but Dan only nodded.

"Nice to meet you, ma'am," Roxanne said.

Sam chuckled. "Please, just call me Sam. Nice to meet you too. I'm sorry to run, but I need to get back. I just came to make some copies. The copy machine at the library's broken." She hefted her bag higher on her shoulder. "But Abey, you're coming to book club, right?"

"Uh, I dunno. Not sure if I'll have time today. I'll try."

"Try hard," she said. "We're starting a new book this week. It's a fantasy romance."

"What, like with fairies and elves and all that bullshit?"

Sam scoffed. "Yes, and it's really good, so you better not back out."

"I won't," I admitted.

I'd never do that to her, but I really wasn't looking forward to reading about made-up creatures. I liked the real-life romances better, even if they were between a man and a woman.

Out of all the books we'd read since starting book club, my favorite had been a male-female hockey romance. Now there was a legitimate sport, with broken bones, blood, and fist fights. It made me want to go to a game. I hadn't been since my daddy had taken me to see the Yellowstone Quake at the University of Wyoming when I was a girl.

"A book club?" Roxanne asked.

"Yeah," Sam said. "You're welcome to join, Deputy. It's a good time to do it, too, since we're starting a new book. You like to read?"

"Love it," Roxanne said.

"What kind of books?"

I could feel Roxanne stiffen beside me, and behind her sunglasses, she side-eyed Dan. "Fiction," was all she said.

Sam nodded. She understood Roxanne's hesitance. Some people still referred to the romance genre as "lady porn," but as I had learned in the last year, it was so much more than just steamy sex scenes.

Even as a gay woman reading straight romance, it could be empowering. And sometimes, I even felt like I'd learned to voice what I wanted out of life better from reading the stories Sam assigned every month. We hadn't read a lesbian romance yet, even though I bugged her about it as often as I could, but Sam told me she was still searching for the right one to fit the overall book-club group. We had some picky members. Little did Sam know, a couple of those ladies would probably love a lesbian romance, no matter which one Sam ended up choosing. I'd already read a few on my own and loved them. It was the coolest thing to read about a character that represented who I was on the inside.

"Join us then," she told Roxanne. "You can meet a bunch of local women, and we always have a good time."

"Thank you."

"Sorry, Deputy—what's your first name?" Sam asked Dan.

"Daniel Draven, ma'am," he said, finally shaking Sam's hand.

"Nice to meet you. I was saying sorry, we don't have a book club yet that men can join because a few of the women have requested that the romance book club stay a man-free zone. I've been trying to talk Frank into starting one, but yeah, that'll *never* happen."

"Not much of a reader anyway, ma'am," Dan said.

She nodded, smiling at his brusqueness. "Alright, well, I'll see *you* two later, right, at book club?"

I rolled my eyes but smiled at her. "Yeah, yeah. We'll be there."

Sam swooped in to kiss my cheek. "Drag her butt to the library, Deputy!" she called over her shoulder to Roxanne, and she hopped down the steps on her way back to the library.

"Pretty relaxed work atmosphere 'round here," Dan said.

I had the feeling he'd meant for it to sound like an observation, but it sounded more like a criticism to me.

CHAPTER ELEVEN

ABEY

"Yo!" Sam yelled. "Jeez. If I didn't know any better, I'd think none of you had ever met a new person before. Everybody, sit down!"

The book club ladies fawned over Roxanne, and she did her best not to react and to follow all the introductions.

"You're so tall. I bet guys love that," Carly said, looking up at Roxanne from her much shorter height.

"Uh, you'd be surprised," Roxanne replied.

"Where you from?" asked Billie.

"Choctaw."

"Where is that?" asked Aislinn, standing next to Billie, holding onto her arm for guidance.

"Oklahoma. It's a really small town."

Aislinn laughed in her uppity way. "Wisper is really small."

"Yeah." Roxanne looked like a deer in headlights amidst all the attention.

"Back off, ladies," I said. "Let the poor woman breathe. Roxanne, have a seat. Don't mind them."

"*Everybody* sit," Sam said again, exasperated.

"Roxanne and I might have to head out early, Sam. Sorry, but things are kinda busy today. I still have a lot to show her. We're on our lunch break, but if we get a call, we'll have to pop off."

"No problem," Sam said.

Everyone took their usual seats while Billie led Aislinn to hers, but the questions kept coming.

"What kind of romance do you like?" Aislinn asked.

"Um, all kinds, I guess," Roxanne answered. She watched while Billie fussed over Aislinn, making sure Aislinn's purse was within her reach on the floor.

No matter how many ranch hands and other employees Aislinn oversaw at her job out at Cade Ranch as the head of their office team, Billie would always see her as a little sister. If you knew what a loud personality Billie could be, it was kind of sweet, but then, Aislinn had been visually impaired for a long time, and it was obvious she didn't need anyone's help. She seemed to tolerate it from Billie, though, for the most part.

"You don't have a favorite sub-genre?" Aislinn asked, swatting at Billie. "Sit down, would you? I'm fine."

Billie swatted back and stuck her tongue out at Aislinn, knowing she couldn't see it, but then Billie took her seat and lounged back into it like she was at home.

"*I* don't have a favorite sub-genre," I said, and Roxanne smiled at me, probably grateful for the backup when faced with a pack of snarling busybodies.

"So, Roxi," Billie started, "what's your story?"

"I don't really have a story," Roxanne said. "Like I said, I'm from Oklahoma, but I've been livin' and workin' in Wyoming for several years now. I was assigned to Yellowstone after trainin' at the Corner Junction station. Sheriff Michaels asked me to make the move to help Sheriff Lee."

"Sheriff Lee?" Aubrey said, wiggling her eyebrows in my direction. "Fancy, fancy."

"Oh, please." I flicked a hand in a circle around the room. "Don't act like y'all haven't been talkin' about my promotion this whole time. I already know it's the subject of gossip."

"Yeah," Sam said, sitting in the chair next to mine. "But *you* haven't said a word. Why's that?"

"'Cause it's not a big deal."

"Well," Phil said, "congratulations all the same. We're happy to know you'll be the one lookin' after us. And Roxanne, Yellowstone?" She and Cal took their usual seats together next to Roxanne. "I bet that was interestin'. All those tourists. I'm Phil, by the way."

"Phil?" Roxanne asked, no doubt trying to decide if she'd heard the name right.

"Philomena," Billie supplied. "And that's Cal next to her. I'm Billie by the way, and this is Ace."

Cal raised a hand, wiggling her fingers. "Hello."

Carly leaned forward on the other side of the circle with baby Donny in her arms. The kid could sleep through the apocalypse. "I'm Carly, and this little bundle is Donny." She nodded to the rest of the group as they got situated in their chairs. "That's Aubrey, Daisy, Juneau, and you already know Abey."

Roxanne followed as Carly introduced everyone, then asked sheepishly, "Who's Abey?"

I raised my hand in the air, then took off my hat and rested it in my lap. "That'd be me."

Roxanne blushed and removed her hat, too, but hers was a county ballcap. This was the first time I'd seen her without it. Her hair was a light-brown color, and it fell just past her shoulders, but she'd worn it pulled back in a low pony like I usually did. There wasn't a lot you could do with long hair if you wore a hat at work, and now that mine had grown longer, if we went on a call, I had to have it up and away from my face in a bun so it was un-pullable. Drunk idiots *loved* to pull hair. People were used to seeing me in a hat, though, so I never bothered doing anything cute with my hair anymore.

Roxanne seemed extremely confident on the job, but get her around a group of gossiping women, and she was shy as a rabbit. She winced when she realized she hadn't known my first name, probably scared to piss off her new boss.

Shit. That was me. *I* was her new boss. Weird.

"It's cool," I said. "Don't think I told you my first name."

"Yeah," Billie interrupted, "but what we *really* wanna know is, are you married? Dating? And if so, what's their name?"

Subtle, Billie. Really freaking subtle.

Cal tsked. "Billie!"

"What, Cal? Tell me you weren't wondering the same damn thing."

Cal looked at her long plum-painted fingernails, then her eyes rolled up toward the ceiling.

"Uh," Roxanne said, scanning the faces all looking at her, "I'm not married. Never have been. I'm almost forty, so that's kinda sad, but I'm not datin' either."

"Aw, well, you just haven't found the right person yet," Carly said, smirking at me. "But if you were to meet someone here in Wisper, you could invite them to the dance."

Jeez, these women! They were relentless. I knew they were all hinting at me. They were just as biased as everyone else around here, even if they didn't mean anything harmful by it. Roxanne looked like someone people might assume to be a lesbian, probably 'cause of her stature, her hat and sunglasses, and 'cause of the plain look of her face without makeup. But I already knew from her reaction to Theo that she liked men. But even if she was bisexual, no, I would not be dating my new subordinate. I rolled my eyes and shook my head at my friends.

I'd already read them all the riot act for the awful date they'd set me up on earlier in the summer. I wouldn't be taking their suggestions for potential dates ever again.

Besides, I'd already found someone. We had some stuff to figure out, but I had hope Devo and I could get there. Maybe I was getting ahead of myself, but I would not be clueing these loudmouths in on it. Except maybe for Sam. I'd told her about sleeping with Devo after the night we shared, but I hadn't yet told her things had kind of been heating up again.

More memories of the night we'd spent together flooded my mind, and my cheeks got hot when I remembered the taste of Devo's—

Roxanne looked at me. "What dance?"

"Ignore her," I said, trying to stop thinking about Devo and hoping I hadn't moaned out loud.

I shook my head at Carly, clearly disapproving of her matchmaking efforts, but she didn't even have the decency to look chastised. She shrugged and smirked, and little Donny startled in his sleep and threw his tiny arms out to the sides. She cooed to him softly until he cuddled back into the crook of her arm.

"We have a festival every year at the start of fall," I explained. "Ace's House sponsors it, and this year, there's a dance. There'll be live music and a big dance floor in the center of town. You'll probably have to work it."

"Yeah," Sam said, "'cause you know there's bound to be trouble. Somebody will get stupid."

"You're right about that," Phil added. "We haven't had a big macho man fight in town since Doug Morris went to prison. We're due."

"And guess who gets to plan it," Aislinn complained. "That's right. Me."

"You work at Ace's House, Aislinn?" Roxanne asked.

"No. I live and work at Cade Ranch. I run the office. But my brother is the director of Ace's House, and he's hopeless with that kind of stuff if I'm not helping him."

"Don't listen to her," Billie said. "He organized it the last two years, but it gets bigger every year, and Theo knows how uptight and obsessive Ace can be, so he's putting her to work."

"Yes, that's right," Aislinn said, "and already things are getting out of control. Do you know how much work goes into shutting down an entire downtown area? Plus, there's the food and town-wide decorations. What the hell do I know about all that stuff? But Theo's in his last year of graduate school now, plus running the center. He's really stressed out."

Yeah, and it probably didn't help that his assistant director kept landing herself in my jail.

"I told you I'd help, Aislinn," Sam said.

"Yeah," Billie added, "and you know Evvie and I will help, too, Ace. Complain some more, why don'tcha."

Aislinn crossed her arms, but she conceded. "I know. Thank you. Oh, and Abey," she said, turning her body in the direction of my voice, "you and I should sit down soon. We'll have to block off roads that day so no one parks on Main where we're going to set up the dance tent. I'll need you to decide the boundaries."

My first thought was, *Why are you asking me?* But then I remembered that I was in charge. "Sure thing." Guess it would be up to me now to enforce things like that.

"Oh, Theo?" Roxanne asked. "I think I met him this mornin'."

"You did," I confirmed. "Theo is Aislinn's brother. And

the other guy you met at the center, the one with long black hair?"

Roxanne nodded, and that look I'd seen on her face earlier appeared again, after her hope about Theo being single had been dashed.

"That's Brady," Aislinn said, "his man."

"Oh."

I smiled apologetically. "Brady is Theo's partner. They live above the center in the attic apartment."

"Right," Roxanne said, and she deflated and slumped back in her chair.

"What does *that* mean?" Aislinn asked, though it sounded more like an accusation. She was ready to jump down the throat of anybody who dared to criticize her brother or Brady.

"Nothin'!" Roxanne said. "It's just that, I mean, if someone asked me to imagine the perfect guy, I'm pretty sure I'd conjure up your brother. It's too bad he—"

"You got something against gay people, Roxi?" Billie asked, slinging her legs over the arm of her chair. "Too bad he what?"

Roxanne straightened in her chair. "No. I do not. In fact, to answer your earlier question, MM is my favorite sub-genre of romance. It's hot. I was only gonna say that it's too bad he doesn't have a straight twin brother. If he did, I'd be in love."

Billie relaxed and laughed.

Carly squealed, and our resident romance author, Juneau Moonlight, clapped her hands together.

"Ooo, now she's fitting in around here. G'on, girl. We all loved the MM book we read last month." Juneau wiggled her eyebrows in Cal's direction. "Even Cal!"

Cal shrugged, and Roxanne laughed.

It seemed like Roxanne had caught on that we were a pretty inclusive group and had relaxed. She had no idea just *how* inclusive. "Alright," she said, "well, if Theo and Brady are taken, and there's no evil twin ready to sweep me off my feet, who else you got for me? This ol' girl's been in a bit of a dry spell, and I need to break free."

Cal tsked again at the impropriety, and Phil laughed. "Give us some time," she said. "We'll think of someone."

"Guys, are we ever going to talk about books?" Sam almost whined her question, holding up a dark-red hardcover book with lots of swirls on the front and dramatic gold lettering, but she should've known better by now. Roxanne was fresh meat.

"You're about my age," Aubrey said and winked. She was a few years older than Roxanne's "almost forty." "Let's do lunch. I can give you the lowdown on the available guys in town. But be prepared—there aren't many. Where you stayin'?"

"I've been rentin' a place on the outskirts of Jackson, but I'd like to find a place here. I drive enough on the job. I don't wanna have to drive back and forth, 'specially in the winter."

"What about you, Abey?" Daisy asked, joining the conversation finally. She'd been watching me quietly, but I had no clue why.

"What about me?" I asked innocently, turning my hat in my lap. No matter how I fixed it, it felt like it would fall right to the floor.

Daisy arched a brow, smoothing some loose hair up into the bun on the back of her head. She was on her lunch break too. Her husband, my favorite, chili-making Wisperite, José, pushed her to take the hour off every time we had book club, even though lunchtime always got busy at the café. The man would walk on water for her. Even Daisy admitted he was too sweet on her sometimes. "Have you started seeing someone?"

"No," I said, trying to quell the tightening in the pit of my stomach, even though every single woman in the room knew I was gay and each one supported me. Still, my dad's voice sounded loud in my head, and it weaved through the anxiety I always felt when the subject of my love life came up.

"This ain't how a member of my family should be behavin'. You brought shame on this family. It's bad enough, you wantin' to be a cop."

"Why do you ask?"

"No reason," Daisy said easily, lounging back in her orange and green tweed armchair. She planted her hands on the arms and drummed her fingers over the threadbare fabric as she crossed her legs and bounced her white sneaker in a measured rhythm. She'd forgotten to leave her black José's Café apron at work, so now, I focused on the logo instead of looking her in the eye. "It's just that I might have, ahem, seen you in Red Wild with a certain community center employee."

She grinned, and I tried my damnedest to look unaffected.

"Abey!" Sam yelped at me. "Why didn't you tell me?"

Dammit. I should've said something to her. She knew I liked Devo. We told each other everything, usually, but this was a tricky subject. If it was more than just a hookup, it was tricky.

"Listen," I said, scooting forward in my chair. My hat tried to tumble to the floor, but I caught it just in time. "There's nothin' goin' on. She's… cute, but y'all know I can't do anything about it. I've got my job. She's got hers. It wouldn't be the right thing."

"What?!"

Oh man. Now I'd gone and done it. The whole room erupted.

"That's bullshit," Billie said. "What're you scared of?"

"There's nothing wrong with it," Daisy added. "Luuk's

the town vet, and no one has a problem with him and my son Kevin. Or if they do, they better not say it to my face!"

"If it's meant to be, it'll be," Phil chimed in.

Cal was quiet. She probably agreed with me, although I knew for a fact she didn't have a problem with same-sex relationships. I peeked at her out of the corner of my eye, wondering if she felt a similar panic like the one still swirling around in my stomach. And that damn burn was back, right behind my chest bone, throbbing again.

Cal knew that I knew about her recent secret admission to the LGBTQ community, but we hadn't talked about it. Phil, on the other hand, wanted to shout it from the rooftops. She told me so when I'd caught them kissing in Phil's truck during a rainstorm one afternoon not too long ago. She'd parked in a parking lot, but she must've accidentally bumped her hazards button, 'cause I'd seen them flashing and had pulled over to make sure she was okay. I'd never seen Cal so embarrassed, even when we read the BDSM book in book club, but I promised them I would never out them.

If they'd found love with each other, I would be the last person to judge or gossip about it.

Watching them together discreetly, I thought, *It's funny how polar opposite they are,* as Cal tried her best to look as heterosexual as she could, whatever that looked like, and Phil gazed at Cal, smiling with all the love in the world in her eyes.

I kind of understood. Devo was all I could think about, day or night. I'd even dreamed about her, about kissing her and holding her hand. I probably looked like Phil did now when people caught me daydreaming.

But taking her to the dance and dancing with her in front of the whole town? That wasn't real life. I couldn't do that. I still felt queasy and like my chest might catch fire when I thought about how I'd practically jumped away from her when Crane had come into Red Wild.

I was kicking myself for my reaction. I was so mad at myself for accusing her of judging me. She wasn't wrong. I had acted like a coward. And I knew my dad was judging me from the pits of Hell itself.

The truth was that I judged myself.

When I finally made eye contact with Sam, her forehead crumpled. She was sad and hurt, and I felt like a total douche canoe for not telling my best friend how much I really liked Devo.

While I prepared to tell everybody to shut the hell up before I arrested all their gossiping asses, I whispered, "Sorry," to Sam. She shrugged, and I rubbed my knuckles in a circle over the burn, hoping it would go away.

CHAPTER TWELVE

DEVO

"How's it going over at Red's place?" Theo asked when he called me at lunchtime.

"It's goin'," I said. "How're things over there?"

"I need you back here. Can you please learn something from this and put it behind you?"

"I'm not sure what I'm s'posed to be learnin'," I mumbled and sighed into my phone. "I'm tryin', Theo. I promise. What's wrong?"

"Nothing's wrong, exactly, but nothing is right either. Red is… God, that man is an asshole."

"Ha! I told you!"

"I never argued that point, Devo, but him being here and you being there is really messing things up. I've had to add all your phone calls and meetings onto my list. Brady's trying to help, but you know he has two other jobs. I even asked Vern to make some of your calls, but Calysta from Great Goods hung up on him."

I grimaced. Man, was I glad Theo couldn't see my face. "What'd he say to her?"

"I have no idea. I prepped him and basically told him

what to say, but leaving him to handle it alone was my mistake because when I walked into your office at the tail end of the call, I could've sworn I heard him telling her how sexy her voice was. I tried calling her back because we really need to get our order in for all the essentials—toilet paper, hand towels, hand soap, you know?"

"Yeah."

It wasn't the end of the world. We could run to Costco in Idaho Falls for all that stuff, but Theo lived life by the book. Since he'd gotten sober, he stuck to a schedule and made spreadsheets for everything. It helped him tame the chaos, and all I was doing was adding to that chaos.

"I've left her two messages, but she hasn't called back yet."

Ooo. That didn't sound good. "Text me her number," I said. "It's on my list, the one I taped inside my desk drawer. I'm just sittin' here. I can call her."

Hopefully, she'd answer, but Calysta worked from home. She had three young kids and was a single mom, so in the summer, sometimes she'd only work half days because she was on a never-ending quest to find things to do to entertain them.

"Thanks."

"I'm really sorry, Theo. Truly, I am."

"I know you are. I know you feel bad, but the problem is, sorry's not really going to cut it. I need action from you, Devo. Do you understand that? This isn't high school. It's not a cute little protest downtown about some perceived slight you think you feel. This is a big deal. If, God forbid, you have to spend time in jail, I'm thoroughly screwed."

Perceived slight? Really? Did he have my back at all? But I said, "I know. I get it. I'll do better."

"Thank you. I have to go. Red's supposed to be watching

the daycare kids, but they're like little sharks. They can smell the fresh blood in the water. Last time I walked by there, they had him pinned to the wall."

"Where's Lacy? Isn't it her job to watch them?"

"She's in your office, trying to get the rest of the orders in. Hopefully, no one will hang up on her."

When we ended our call, I dropped my head onto the checkout counter. I felt like a grade-A jerk for putting Theo in the awful position he now found himself in.

I really was a devil, wasn't I?

"Everything alright?" Rye asked when I set my phone next to the cash register and sighed heavily.

"Yeah," I said, sitting upright again. "Just a little hiccup at Ace's House."

"Red causin' trouble?"

"Nothin' too bad so far, but my boss is stressed."

"Devo, you could go back to work. I can handle the store."

"Thank you, but no. That wouldn't be right. If the judge found out I didn't fulfill my end of this thing, he might throw me in jail."

Rye winced. "I feel bad we're just sittin' here though."

"Yeah. What can we do to help Red?" That was the point of this whole thing, right? I was supposed to be helping Red even though I couldn't stand him. "I've already cleaned. There was an inch of dust on every surface in this place. I tidied up all the displays, but what else?"

I'd also packed up the extremely expensive leftover "I hate gay people" shirts and tried to hide the evidence deep in the bowels of the storeroom under other boxes that looked like they hadn't been touched since 1974. And for my efforts, I knocked over an old tripod, then tripped and fell on it, breaking off one of its legs, and it tried to stab me in the thigh. Whatever. I could buy Red a new one if he really needed it, but I doubted he did. The tripod looked older than the rest of the junk in the back room and had been covered in cobwebs. Whatever Red used it for, it probably wasn't even compatible with modern technology.

Rye thought for a minute, chewing on the end of a ball-point pen with Red's slogan "Hike it Red Wild Style."

It reminded me how dumb the slogan was, but it got me thinking about style.

Red had none.

I looked around the store. I had no idea when Red had opened it, but the customer-facing part looked like it hadn't been updated or reorganized in a decade at least. The place was a scrambled mess. He sold clothing for different outdoor activities, but the racks were spread out everywhere. There should've been a designated clothing section, just like there should've been a designated camping section, a fishing section, and a gun section. I could've done without the last, but still. It seemed stupid to me that the guns were displayed on one wall and the bullets were in a case all the way at the other end of the store. That made no sense. When people walked into The Red Wild Outdoors looking to spend their hard-earned money, they needed to be able to find things easily.

I could help with that, and the fact that it might make Red mad if I rearranged his store only spurred me on and got my organizational juices flowing faster.

Abey walked into the shop at 4:45.

Rye and I had been working all afternoon on our restructuring plan, and we hadn't had any customers since lunchtime, so both our heads popped up when the bell on the door clanked and jingled.

"Abey Lee!" A wolfish grin broke out over Rye's face, and he took three big strides across the store to hug her, lift her straight off the floor, and twirl her in a circle. "How you doin', baby girl? It's so good to see you."

"Rye!" She grunted, trying not to smile and holding onto her hat. "Put my ass down. I'm packin' two guns, not to mention a Taser and pepper spray."

"Oh, ho, ho, you're the big woman on campus." He set her on her feet, and she glanced at me over her shoulder. She tried not to smile, but Rye had a way about him.

I was kind of surprised all the single ladies in town hadn't stopped in to flirt with Rye. The two female tourists who had come into Red Wild and shown an interest in the rugged, good-looking sporting goods salesman, with a smile I knew could make panties melt all over town, had been shot down quickly. He had been polite, but it was easy to see his interest was elsewhere.

Interestingly, he watched every time Aubrey George walked past Red Wild on her way to work, sometimes during her lunch breaks, and every evening on her way home. He never asked about her or said anything, apart from his first day here, but each time, I watched the way his whole face lit up. He still hadn't talked to her, though, at least not that I'd noticed. There had to be history there. I didn't know what it could be, but I bet it was juicy. It wasn't my business, though, unless he brought it up.

Besides, I had my own shit to figure out.

Finally, Abey gave up the fight. She grinned at Rye, and her brilliant smile and the color blooming across her pale cheeks caused a reaction in all my secret spots. They warmed and tingled, but then I remembered what I'd said to her the last time I'd seen her and what she'd accused me of.

Her attention was pulled back to Rye when he slung an arm over her shoulders, and she punched him playfully in the ribs. "What're you doin' here?"

"Just came to help," he said.

"I haven't seen you in forever. How's your dad?"

"He's good. He's old, but he's still workin' the ranch. He'll never die. He's got plenty of help this year, so I was able to come help Uncle Red." Rye made a face. There was more to that story too. He seemed fine about helping his uncle, so maybe the look of grumpiness had been about his dad or their ranch.

Abey laughed, and it was the softest thing I'd ever heard come out of her mouth, like the warm ringing of a windchime in the afternoon sun. "Tell him I said hello, will ya?"

I'd always thought she was hot, since the first time I'd seen her, before I even knew she was a lesbian, but in the moment, with that rosy blush spreading across her cheeks, making her blue eyes sparkle, she was beautiful.

Absolutely stunning.

Even though I knew how tall she was, I marveled at her height every time I saw her. Probably 'cause I was about the same height as a fifth grader. I was obsessed with the color of her hair too. Having naturally black hair all my life, I'd always been a little jealous of blonds. Jealous of the variation of color in her subtle highlights. Her white-blond curls made me want to twirl them around my finger, but she wore a hat so much that it tamped down the curls and turned them into subtle waves. But when it was hot and humid like today, those shorter wisps framing her face curled and twisted underneath the brim of her hat. I'd never seen anything more adorable.

Her hair had grown a bit since our night together, but every time I'd seen her since, I had been complaining about Red or whatever else and hadn't noticed. Today, it fell down her back to her shoulder blades. She hadn't pulled it back into the low ponytail she usually wore.

No. Today, her hair lay loose, free, and gorgeous.

She pulled the hat off, shook her hair out a little, and ran her fingers through it, and I wanted to touch her, just to know if the blush on her cheeks made her skin warm. I wanted to see if it spread beneath her work shirt, wanted to follow it with my tongue. How far down did it go?

Looking back up into her eyes, I wanted to kiss her. Who cared if she wasn't out? I mean, did I really?

"Devo." She nodded in greeting finally, pressing her lips together, and Rye looked at me, then back at Abey. She cleared her throat, and it was the first time I noticed the long column of her neck. It was sexy and smooth, and logically, I knew it led down to cleavage, but she'd never let it show when she was working.

It didn't stop me from imagining moving my lips over the soft skin there and lower, taking in an eyeful, and hopefully handfuls, of her ample breasts. Just seeing them hidden beneath her shirt, and probably a restrictive sports bra, turned me on.

"Well, c'mon in," he told her. "We've been workin' on a few things for Red since Devo's stuck here in Red Wild purgatory. Wanna see?"

"Yeah," she answered, but she was looking at me, probably wondering what the look on my face was about.

Sex. It was about sex. Yeah, yeah, so I was a breast woman. What of it? And Abey's boobs were the things of dreams. Her whole body was a strong, tall, cool drink of water. She was a water goddess, and I was landlocked, dying of thirst in the desert, waiting for her to quench me all over.

"Here," I said, clearing my throat and trying to blink away the lust she'd caused as she came closer with Rye on her heels. He was genuinely happy to see her. I pushed the piece of paper I'd been sketching my plan on out in front of me. "We're reorganizin' this place."

"Ah, shit, Abey," Rye interrupted, running his hand through his hair, pulling Abey's attention away from me, and like a jealous, lovesick teenager, I wanted to stomp on his foot. "How's your brother? I haven't talked to him in a long time. I called him when Candy passed, but he never called back, and there was some shit goin' on with my dad, so I forgot to call again. I'm so sorry for y'all's loss."

"Thanks," she said softly. "It's been hard on him." She breathed deeply and let it out in a loud sigh. "He's... hangin' in there, y'know? Athena, their daughter, is strugglin' though. It's heartbreakin', but she puts on a good show."

I hadn't known Abey had lost her sister-in-law. Hadn't even heard through the grapevine. The sad look on Abey's face broke my heart, and now it was all I could do not to reach out to pull her to me so I could hug her sadness away. She tried to smile it away. She couldn't let anyone know how she really felt. It just wasn't her style.

"He still have the same number?" Rye asked. "I'll give him a call, see if he wants to get a beer some night while I'm here."

"Yeah, same number. I bet he'd like that. How long you here for?"

"Oh, I dunno. A week or two maybe. Or lemme put it this way: I'll stay as long as I can put up with Uncle Red. His house ain't the relaxin' oasis you probably think it is."

She laughed, then turned back to me, looking right in my

eyes for a few seconds, and for the first time, I saw the struggle inside her. It was a rare, open moment, but then her gaze dropped to the piece of paper in my hand. She looked back up. "Looks good. Red know you're doin' this for him?"

"No," I said. "And please don't tell him. Rye wants to surprise him."

She bit her lip. "I hate to rain on your parade, but do you really think Red will keep this up? He's not usually one for decorations and nice-lookin' displays." She looked around the room at the mess we'd made, pulling shelves and racks of clothing to the middle of the store so we could clean underneath them before we made new displays.

I couldn't help the evil glint I could feel forming in my eyes. Yeah, yeah, so I was supposed to be helping Red somehow, but I already knew Red would be pissed at anything I did to better his store just because it had been my idea.

The knowledge filled me with glee.

"This place has needed a makeover since 1992," Rye said, "but you never know. Red might love it."

Abey couldn't take her eyes away from mine for some reason, and then finally, she said, "Um, Devo, could I talk to you? In private?"

Rye took the hint. "Hey, you girls talk. I, um, need to run across the street anyway, talk to Uncle Red. I think he mentioned some deliveries he's got comin' in. Better sort that out."

He left without another word, and as soon as the door clicked closed, Abey leaned across the counter. She dropped her hat on the wood top and kissed me. One small peck on the lips.

"What was that for?" I asked, bewildered, and I licked her kiss into my mouth with the tip of my tongue.

"I just needed to do it," she said with a sly smile. "At

book club today, I lied about you, and it made me feel sick to my stomach. I thought a kiss might make it go away."

"I didn't know about your sister-in-law. I'm so sorry, Abey."

She kissed me again gently, then whispered, "Thank you."

"Wait. You lied? Why? And I can't believe you're in Sam's smutty book club."

"Why not? She's my best friend," she said. "What's the big deal? Anyway, someone saw us together in here the other day, before Crane stopped in, and the girls were talkin' about it today, askin' if there was somethin' goin' on between us. I said no, and all I've been able to think about since is that you were right to accuse me. I may be out to my family and a few friends, but I'm not *out* out, and I lied to make things easier on myself. I'm sorry for gettin' mad at you."

"Thank you, but I was wrong to call you out about it. It's not my business. Your life is not my life. I don't know the things you have to face in your job every day. I'm sorry." I twisted my lips nervously, then asked, "But *is* there somethin' goin' on between us?"

She shrugged, and a tiny smile brightened her face. "Do you want there to be?"

"Well… Yes. But that would mean we'd need to go on a date." Narrowing my eyes, I was trying to deduce how she'd react to what I was about to say. She hadn't reacted to my date comment. "Are you… available to do that? I mean, you practically jumped away from me when you thought someone might see. Where would we go?"

"I'd love to take you out," she said. "But you're right. I can't be loud about it 'cause of my job, but we could do somethin' quiet."

"Quiet? Do you mean secret?"

She shook her head, and little pieces of her hair stuck to

the side of her mouth. She hooked a finger beneath them and swiped them away. "I'd like to take you to do somethin' fun. And Rye's got me thinkin' about my niece. I haven't had a lot of time off work lately, but she's been buggin' me to go four-wheelin'. I mean, if you don't mind her taggin' along? Well, actually, it would be more like we were invitin' ourselves since my four-wheeler's out at my brother's place, but it's the property we all grew up on. Bax took it over when my dad passed. He's been tryin' to run it, but then Candy died. Anyway, it's my favorite thing to do, four-wheelin', so I thought you might like to come with me, and I'd love for you to meet Athena. She's my favorite human." She puffed her cheeks out with a breath, then released it. "That was a really long sentence, huh?"

"Yes." But she'd just asked me out, and she'd forgiven me for being such a judgmental jerk. I couldn't stop grinning.

"Yeah, it was a long sentence, or yeah, you'll go with me?" Her pink lips pursed into a smirk. "The type of ridin' we like to do can get pretty muddy."

"Both."

"Really? You don't mind gettin' dirty?"

"With you?" Didn't she know? "Dirty's all I wanna be."

CHAPTER THIRTEEN

ABEY

"YOU BETTER BE on your best behavior, Mama. You hear me?"

Mama rolled her eyes as she closed her fridge, and the compressor started its telltale whine. It was the same old beast that had sat lonely in our garage out at the farm since I was fifteen years old, until Mama made Bax drag it to her trailer.

"I'm serious. This is serious. I really like this woman." Under my breath, I mumbled, "The one time you wanna venture out into society in seven years, and it's on my freakin' date?"

"What kinda name is Devo anyway?"

"It's short for Devona."

I stopped her from packing the ham sandwiches she'd made into my little plastic cooler with my hand on her shoulder, and she turned to look at me. "Please, Mama? And would you mind packin' a PB&J too? In case she doesn't eat meat."

"Fine."

"Thank you."

My brother had agreed to let Athena come with Devo and

me out on the four-wheelers, but his permission came on the condition that he would come too. And of course he'd told Mama what we were doing, so she'd invited herself. Bax must really have been in the slop not to realize what a mess he'd made for me.

Bringing my churchy, homophobic mother on a date with two lesbians, my brother, and a preteen was just about the furthest thing from fun I could've conjured up. I was already trying to think of ways to shut her up in case she started talking about brimstone and hellfire or how Athena should abstain from sexual intercourse or even kissing a boy until she was thirty and married with three kids.

But here we were. And Devo was on her way over to pick us up. She had actually been excited when I told her Mama wanted to come with us. She said if there was a better way for her to get to know me, she'd love for me to tell her one.

I'd already met Devo's mama when she'd been at the center one day, helping the latchkey kids after school in the craft room, although that was back when Devo had still been angry at me for arresting her the first time. But her mama was a beautiful woman, and it had been easy to see where all Devo's spunk had come from, not to mention her shiny, gorgeous black hair and her lose-yourself-in-'em dark brown eyes.

I heard Devo's truck as she turned onto the short gravel drive outside Mama's trailer. *Way to make an impression, Abey. Ask your date to pick you and your mom up at the trailer park.* I rolled my eyes at myself, feeling my heart speed up and my cheeks turn an embarrassing shade of red.

"You gonna get the door for her or just stand there like an imbecile?"

I huffed an exasperated breath at Mama and then breathed in loudly through my nose, smoothing my hands down my tank and shorts. Devo hadn't seen me in anything other than the deputy-brown puke color I had to wear for work since that one night—the night she'd blown my mind.

Mama turned away to finish packing the cooler. "You look fine."

"Gee, thanks." *What a ringing endorsement.*

I'd given up on the hope that the trailer didn't smell like stale cigarettes, but I knew Devo wouldn't judge me for my mama's vices. I'd tried to cover it up with heather-scented air freshener, but that just made the stench smell like a flowery ashtray, which might've been worse.

When I finally opened the door, Devo gasped. "Oh! You look like America."

I laughed. Couldn't have stopped myself for anything. "What?"

Her eyes traveled down to my bare legs. "Blue jean shorts, a red tank top, and white high-tops?"

"Oh, well, I…" Looking down at myself, too, I realized I must've looked like a Fourth of July pinup girl, though my Converse tennies were beat up, dirt stained, and probably ten years old. Mama had even French braided my hair on both sides of my head like I was six, but it was better this way. Kept it out of my eyes while I was riding. "Thanks?"

"I like it," Devo said, smiling up at me and looking as pretty as any woman had a right to. She was a vision, standing in the little bit of sun shining on Mama's porch, with her midnight hair sticking out all wonky like it liked to do.

Mama yelled, "You're lettin' all the bought air out!"

"Come in." I smiled. I couldn't back out now. I was committed to this disaster in the making. "We're almost ready."

"What's your family do?" Mama asked Devo.

We'd driven out further north of the trailer park and were about to turn off the highway onto old Fish Creek Road. Our family farm was just another couple miles from here.

"My brother and sister moved away a few years ago," Devo said. "It's just me and my mom now, but she's the lunch lady at Barton Elementary. In her downtime, she sews and knits and makes all kinds of crafts she sells on her Etsy store. *That's* the job she loves."

"Oh," Mama said in a tone indicating she was surprised at what Devo had said. "I worked the lunch line here at the high school when my kids were young."

"That's cool," Devo said as she took the turn. "Did you like doin' that?"

Mama snorted. "Did I like servin' a bunch of snot-nosed teenagers? No. I did not." She jabbed her thumb toward me. "I had enough of that, dealin' with her and her brothers."

Devo laughed but tried to cover it with a cough. I wished she wouldn't. I liked the sound of her laugh. It was breathy.

"You'll learn real quick that my mama doesn't pull any punches. Right, Ma? You say whatcha think." Except for when it had to do with me and how I'd disgraced our whole family. *That* she never made a peep about, not once, except to tell me Jesus was disappointed in my "life choices." But to this day, we had never sat down to talk about it. I'd tried, but she always came up with ways to steer the conversation elsewhere.

"Yes, I do. And I raised you to do the same."

"You did."

Devo's lips curved up, and she peeked at me for a second. "I like that about Abey. My mom raised us the same way. My dad wasn't really around when he was alive, so she was pretty much a single mom most of my life."

I'd sat between them while Devo drove, and to make things even more awkward, I kept remembering the shooting star I'd seen the night Devo had given me a ride home and how the air in the truck between us had crackled with... *something*. I couldn't stop picturing the way she'd bitten her lip and her eyes had darkened as she looked at me while we'd sat silent and still at the stoplight.

And I remembered how my body had felt weightless when I came with her mouth between my legs.

Mama broke the spell 'cause she kept looking past me at Devo. I couldn't figure out why till she asked, "You Native American then?"

"Yes, ma'am," Devo answered. "Apache. I was born on the Mescalero Reservation in New Mexico. It's where my last name comes from, Mescal."

"Mm. I know it. My friend Doris married a man from there. His name was Victor. He passed recently, and Doris has been a wreck."

"I'm sorry to hear that. You should talk to my mom sometime. She might've known him."

Mama smiled. It seemed Devo was winning her over. How that could even happen, and so fast, I had no idea. Go fuckin' figure. "I might do that."

We turned onto the property I'd grown up on since the day I popped into this world, slimy and screaming, and just like it always happened, memories swarmed my head.

My daddy was everywhere on this farm.

I couldn't look anywhere without seeing him. He was in the barn, wrangling sheep to shear them or deworm them. It was so easy to picture him out in the fields or on the porch up at the old yellow house, drinking his morning coffee and contemplating the mountains in the distance, or in the equipment barn, tinkering with the four-wheelers or trying to build yet another contraption to make shearing the sheep easier. His ideas never worked, but it had been his mission in this life. Raising sheep wasn't an inexpensive endeavor, and he thought the less time he had to spend shearing would make his efforts as a whole more profitable.

Remembering him made me smile. I missed his scruffy beard and the way he would sit in his ratty recliner in the living room, with one foot up on the footrest and the other propped up on the toe of his shoe, pounding his fist in the air when he disagreed with a call the refs made during a hockey game on TV. It had been my favorite thing to do, to watch with him, to be on his team. My brothers loved it too. Our dad had been the king of the universe when we were young.

He had been our everything.

It was his words from the day I turned fifteen still living in my head rent-free that hurt, and the promise he'd made to me every day before that, the one he'd broken so easily when he'd caught me kissing Paula Dagmar in the barn.

From that point on, the man who'd promised to always love me, the one who had been so proud of "his yellow-haired angel," the father I'd looked up to my whole life, became a stranger to me.

I'd felt his disappointment and disgust in every interaction we had after that.

And it taught me that you shouldn't make promises to someone you claimed to love because there was bound to be something about them that made them unlovable.

Or made you unlovable.

Why set them up for the disappointment?

Mama was remembering my daddy too. I could tell by the way her eyes darted everywhere and from the little smile etched into the side of her mouth. Maybe she didn't remember him telling me that I was shaming our family, that I disgusted him.

That I'd never be his angel again.

Or maybe she did remember. Maybe it was how she still felt. But I knew she wanted me in her life. Still expected me to be. She may not have said it out loud, but she made it clear every time she called me to help her with something or when she'd fix my hair like she had this morning.

I held onto those things. If they were the only things she could give to let me know she loved me, then I'd hold them tight. But why did the familiar burn flare up in my chest when I thought about it?

We parked by the house and climbed out of Devo's dirty white truck to the sound of my brother whistling from the barn, trying to gain our attention. He waved when I spotted him.

"That's my brother Bax," I said as I waved back. Mama was already marching toward him. I grabbed the cooler from the truck bed and led Devo in that direction. "He's the oldest. I'm the baby."

"You are?" Devo asked. "I wouldn't have guessed that. I'm the oldest in my family."

"Oh, look at you," I joked. "All big for your britches. C'mon. I'll introduce you."

"Lil' sis, I'm glad to see you," Bax said when we stepped inside the shade of the barn. "You're just in time to help me deworm." He motioned out across the holding pen he'd rounded his ewes into.

I'd always liked how the sheep looked every spring after shearing. Their coats were clean and short and soft. Once the fleece started to grow back, it got dirtier and dirtier every day, and smellier. By this time in the year, they grossed me out. The lambs were always a hoot, though, the way they hopped and bounced around. But Bax's flock was beginning to dwindle. It had me wondering how long he'd try to keep the farm going. How long till he admitted the truth to himself.

"No, thanks," I said as I set down the cooler by my feet. "Forgot to wear my sheep-shit outfit today."

Mama tsked. "Abey."

Bax laughed, turning his friendly smile in Devo's direction. "And who's this?"

She stepped forward with her hand out. "Devo."

Bax shook it. "Devo? That's a cool name, like that band from the eighties. That where your parents got the name?"

"No." She laughed. "I've heard that before though. My name's Devona, but I like Devo better."

"Me too," he said.

Bax had a knack for making everyone feel at ease. He'd always had it, and when I was younger, I remembered being jealous of that. I was the tall, lanky closeted lesbian, the one secretly in love with all the women he and his friends used to ogle on the covers of the *Playboy* magazines they'd hidden out in their forest fort.

But Bax *lived* to make our mama uncomfortable. He stared at her, daring her to make some rude comment about me bringing a date—who was a woman.

Mama said nothing. She wouldn't. She believed wholeheartedly that as the eldest son, and with my dad gone, Bax was in charge. She'd do anything he said, and she would never criticize him. Not out loud anyway.

"We brought sandwiches and chips for lunch," she said innocently, looking around the barn. "Where's my granddaughter?"

"Athena will be down in a minute. When she found out Aunt Abey was comin', she had to pull out her muddin' outfit." He grinned at Devo. "I hope you came prepared to wreck those clothes." He nodded at her khaki shorts and white T-shirt, chuckling. "You shouldn't have worn white."

"Devo loves to get dirty," I said, then realized how it sounded. "She's not afraid of a little mud. Are ya?"

"Not at all," she said with pink cheeks just as Athena came skidding into the barn. She threw herself at me and wrapped me up in a tight hug.

"Hey," I said, hugging her back. "How you been, girl?"

"Better now you're here," she whispered, looking up at me. God, I ached for her. To lose your mama at such a young age? I wouldn't have survived that.

I tugged on her light-brown pigtail. "Good. Missed you."

"Missed you too." She peeked at Devo. "Is that your girlfriend?"

My face caught fire, and Mama grumbled.

Athena flashed her a sour look. "Granny, get over it already."

Mama smiled at her. "Where's *my* hug, wiggle worm?"

"Right here," Athena said, stepping away from me to hug her grumpy grandma.

Mama pulled on the same pigtail I'd just tugged at till it slipped out of its elastic band, then she redid it so it was even with the other one. Poor Bax was hopeless with ponytails and braids even though Mama had given him how-to lessons. "Hear you caused some trouble with your friends last week."

"So!" Athena blinked and looked at Devo. She wasn't even trying to hide the change of subject. "Who's ready to kick up some mud?"

CHAPTER FOURTEEN

ABEY

BAX CONVINCED Mama to come with us even though she said she'd prefer to stay and clean the farmhouse, so we all rode out into the sunshine on our ATVs. She was in too much discomfort from her arthritis to clean her own place, but she'd hurt and twist herself up like a pretzel for Bax and Athena. Case in point: riding four-wheelers.

Hashtag: Priorities.

Mama rode behind Bax on his old black beast, clutching at his shoulders for dear life, but he went slow, following behind Devo and me on my blue mud baby, and Athena led the charge on her own new four-wheeler. She was proud of that thing. Bax told me Athena washed and waxed the pink monstrosity once a week.

"Are you sure you're not gonna crash this thing?" Devo was a nervous wreck behind me, and the anxiety had her tugging hard on the loops on the waistband of my shorts, so I kept jumping little bumps on the dirt trail so she'd have to hold on tighter. It was a beginner-level trail though. She was never in danger.

"Positive," I called over my shoulder, trying to make my

voice louder than the buzz of the engine. "I know this land like the back of my hand, and I can drive this thing better than I can drive my truck."

"Okay," she said. "If you say so. But can you sit down? You're givin' me a heart attack!"

I sat, and Devo wrapped her arms around me, twisting her fingers around my tank top over my stomach. Her body was warm against mine, and she glued her front to my back, nestling her head against my shoulder to block the wind on her face. Why had I waited so long to sit? She could've been holding onto me the whole time!

Athena goosed her thumb throttle to propel herself further in front of us. She was still pissed her dad wouldn't let her install a twist throttle, like the one he'd been riding since boyhood. But like me, Bax had been riding since we were three feet tall, so he had years more experience than she did, and everyone knew thumb throttles were way safer than the old twisters. Athena was just stubborn, but I reminded her every time she whined about it that I rode a thumb-throttle quad, too, and that usually appeased her a little.

"Are you sure she should be drivin' that thing?" Devo was terrified but trying to act cool. She was failing, and it was cute as hell.

"She's an old pro. Besides, this is nothin'. It's pretty flat land. You'd probably lose your lunch if you saw the terrain we ride sometimes. Almost flipped this baby couple months ago," I tossed over my shoulder, patting my wrapped handlebars. I had my riding gloves on for better grip, but with Devo and my mama in tow, we wouldn't go for difficult terrain.

"Flipped it? Like, upside down?"

Laughing, I revved my throttle, too, and caught up with Athena just as she slowed to a stop in the meadow by our lake.

We parked, and Devo said, "Wow," as I helped her off my quad. The only other sound I heard in the little clearing beside the lake was the cheery, robotic twitter of Western meadowlarks flitting through the air and a big black raven squawking nearby in the safety of the trees. "This place is great."

I looked around at the little finger of the forest reaching out at the bottom of the mountain I'd been riding up my whole life. Still water glistened on the lake under the warm September sun until a fish jumped and disturbed the reflection of the forest on the glassy surface.

The shiny memory I could see of me in a glittery, pink bathing suit, squealing and jumping off my daddy's shoulders into the lake when I was seven, dissolved in front of my eyes.

I nodded at Devo's comment, tucking my riding gloves into my back pocket and breathing in the spruce and pine, the clean air, and the fresh dirt we'd just turned up. A more beautiful place did not exist in the world.

"Abey, come get the cooler," my brother said as he helped Mama down from his ATV.

This ride was easy compared to some we'd tackled, but it was the only one we'd ever convinced Mama to come along on. She was terrified too. But now that we were out here, I was glad she'd come. It was good for her to get out of her damn trailer. I still couldn't understand why she'd wanted to move there.

But now, with the memories of my dad swarming my head, I had a feeling the choices Mama had made since he died had to do with the memories crashing through her head, too, of the life we'd lived as a family. She could be a real pain in the ass. We disagreed about pretty much everything, but she was still my mama. I loved her, and I wished she'd live more. I wanted her to find happiness again.

I hoped my dad would've wanted that for her. He may not have loved me like he'd promised, but he'd loved her, and she deserved it.

Devo wandered toward the lake, shielding her eyes from the sun's glare with her hand as she looked around, and I grabbed the cooler, set it down on a fluffy patch of grass, and pulled a couple cold water bottles out.

When I handed one to her, she smiled, cracked it open, and took a long drink. Drops of water dribbled down her chin, and she swallowed and laughed, so I swiped them away with my fingers, looking at the wet spot on her T-shirt where they'd dripped.

"That was fun," she said.

"Yeah. I love it. I've been so busy with work, I haven't had a lot of time to get out here, but this is my happy place."

She nodded toward Athena, taking another sip. "She's a spitfire, huh?"

"She is. Takes after her auntie." I winked. "C'mon. You hungry?"

"Yeah. Starvin'. What's for lunch?"

The only time I could find to take Devo out was on this impromptu lunch date. It wasn't ideal, but any time I could spend with her made me feel happy, and she seemed to be having a good time.

"Mama made ham sandwiches, but we have PB&J if you don't eat meat."

"Why wouldn't I eat meat? Ham and cheese is my fave. Is it American cheese, or are you one of those fancy cheddar cheese people?" She bumped her shoulder against my arm.

Smiling big, I said, "Girl, American cheese every day of the week and twice on Sundays."

"Score!" She giggled. "When we were really broke, we'd eat cheese and generic white bread sandwiches every day for lunch and dinner, unless my mom had time to make fry bread. Then, we'd eat cheese and fry bread tacos 'cause we couldn't afford meat. We had a lot of those days after we moved here. Then my dad died, and things got even harder financially. My mom worked more jobs than I can remember to try to pay the bills."

"Ooo, I love fry bread with a little cinnamon and honey. So good. You ever had mutton?" Devo made a face, and I breathed a laugh. "When things got tight around here, that's what we had to look forward to for dinner every night. Used to cry myself to sleep 'cause my daddy slaughtered my favorite sheep for us to eat. Pistachio was his name. God, I still miss that stupid animal."

Devo took hold of my hand as we headed back toward the others. I'd never brought a date home before—I couldn't even have imagined doing it five years ago—so having her here felt kind of foreign, but it also felt nice. I loved my family, and Devo was the kind of woman I would've been proud to show off to my daddy, had things been different.

If I was different. If he had been. If the world was different.

My brother's eyes flicked to our joined hands. He looked at Mama quickly, but she was still busy opening a bag of sour cream and onion potato chips and setting paper towels out for us on the picnic blanket Bax had set down.

We sat, and Athena started in on her investigation after she noticed Devo holding my hand, but I let go before Mama noticed. "How'd you and Aunt Abey meet?"

"Oh, well, how did we meet?" Devo asked me with a hint of a smile on her lips.

I smiled back. I didn't think anyone on the planet could keep a straight face when her lips lifted and her face lit up like that. She looked beautiful out here in my favorite place. "At Ace's House."

"Oh, right," she said. "That's where I work. When my boss was renovatin' the place, I heard about it, and I went there to beg for a job."

"It's next door to the station, right?" Bax asked. "I don't get to town much."

Devo nodded. "Yeah."

Mama handed me two ham sandwiches, and I passed one to Devo and bent my knees so I could angle my body in her direction as she talked.

She took the sandwich and wrapped her napkin around it like a holder, then took a huge bite. "Thank you for this," she said with a full mouth.

"You're welcome," Mama said, like she was surprised at being thanked, though I knew I'd thanked her more than once for making lunch. But what could it hurt to tell her again?

"Thanks, Mama."

She smirked at me and shrugged a little.

"Thanks, Granny," Athena said.

"Yeah, Mama. What would we do without ya?" Bax flashed her his most ass-kissing grin. He ate half his sandwich in one bite, then mumbled, "I'll take that PB&J unless somebody else wants it."

She didn't even wait for us to answer. "Here you go, son," she said, handing it to him and then patting his hand like he was seven instead of thirty-seven. What a suck-up.

He took it from her with a grin, shoved the rest of his ham sammy in his mouth, then unwrapped the PB&J from its plastic covering and didn't even wait till he finished chewing before he ate half of that.

"Gross, dude. Ham, cheese, peanut butter, and jelly in one bite?" I shuddered, and he lifted one shoulder in a shrug.

"So," Athena said, "I heard you threw a brick through the window at Red Wild."

Devo choked on the sip of water she'd just taken. "Um" —she coughed to clear her throat—"I did. It wasn't the smartest thing I've ever done."

"And I heard Aunt Abey arrested you, so isn't this, like, a conflict of interest, you goin' on a date with her?"

"How do you even know what that means?"

Athena rolled her eyes at me quite dramatically. "Aunt Abey, I'm almost thirteen."

"Oh, right."

"I hadn't thought about it like that," Devo said. She looked at me. "Is it?"

"Maybe? If I couldn't be counted on to haul your ass to jail if the judge ordered it, but I think we both know I'd do it. And Carey or Frank would if I didn't."

"Great," Devo said.

"At least they take the job seriously," Mama said. "And watch your language around Athena."

Athena rolled her eyes, but then her eyebrows drew together when she looked at Devo and cocked her head. "Why'd you do it?"

Devo's gaze rounded our little circle as she tried to decide what she wanted to say or how she should say it. "I shouldn't have done it, Athena. It was wrong. I was just really, *really* angry at Mr. Graves. More than that, though, I was so frustrated. I'd tried time and time again to talk to him. We had an argument. It wasn't our first, and I guess I got fed up with the way he treats me and the people I work with."

"What do you mean?"

Devo hesitated. I knew she probably felt uncomfortable bringing up the LGBTQ issue, especially in front of Mama, who she could probably guess didn't have the most favorable opinion about it.

I stepped in. "Some people in this life don't know how to be kind. Or maybe they know how, but they choose not to be. Sometimes Red Graves is one of those people."

"He was mean to you?" Athena asked Devo.

"Yeah."

My brother spoke, raising an eyebrow at his daughter when she looked at him. "Kinda like when you tripped Jenny Culver, Athena, and then you laughed at her when she fell. That wasn't very kind."

She scoffed. "I wasn't talkin' about me. Besides, she tripped me first, and she said we were poor and that I smell like sheep poop."

"That sucks," Bax said, and I could see the turmoil behind his eyes. What that asshole kid had said wasn't untrue, and he hated it. If I knew my brother, he was pissed at himself and he blamed himself. "She shouldn't have said that, but it's the same thing. Devo got arrested when she did what she did. Is that what *you* want?" He threw a little wince Devo's way, but she shrugged and smiled. It wasn't like she could say it hadn't happened.

"No, but Aunt Abey would never arrest me."

"Yes, I would, if you did somethin' that was against the law. If you hurt someone."

"Seriously?" Athena squeaked. "That's messed up."

CHAPTER FIFTEEN

DEVO

"You'd arrest your own niece?" Athena huffed.

Jeez. How did we land in the middle of this conversation? Not only had I dragged us down the gay rabbit hole, but now I had to figure out how to make this kid understand right from wrong. Abey's mom's discomfort about the subject was easy to read from the pinched look on her face.

She might've been coming around to the idea of Abey dating me—*maybe*—but she clearly did not like what she'd heard about me. My illegal exploits were probably the hot topic around Wisper these days. It seemed like Abey's mom knew about my misdeeds, so she'd clearly heard the rumors.

"She would do it, Athena," I said, "because Abey believes in right and wrong, and 'cause she believes in the power of the American justice system. If you do somethin' against the law, she's the person who will uphold that law. Right?" I asked Abey, and she nodded once. "It's a quality to respect about her, don'tcha think?"

I respected her for it, even though I'd never given Abey that impression. That was wrong, too, and it was something I needed her to know.

"I'm sorry I did what I did, Athena, and I have to make it right. To Mr. Graves and to Abey and myself. Maybe you could think about how you might make things up to this Jenny girl."

My little nugget of advice seemed to sit well with Abey's mom. She nodded at me, but Athena twisted her lips into a pout and crossed her arms. "Fine."

"Good," Bax said. "Now, that's enough talk about that. Wanna skip rocks? I bet I can get mine farther than yours."

"Nuh uh!" Athena jumped up and took off toward the lake.

Bax followed, but he turned back. "C'mon, Mama. Show us how it's done."

Abey's mom stood, dusting crumbs off her jeans, and followed Bax and Athena to the edge of the lake.

"Wanna go for a walk?" Abey asked me, and she held out her hand.

Reaching up, I took hold of it, and she hauled me off the ground. "Sure."

I followed when she pulled me over a crop of large boulders, crumbling rocks, and up a dirt path, and we climbed higher into thicker forest.

"I meant what I said, you know."

"I know," she said, still pulling me behind her. "C'mon."

She was surefooted, and I was a panting mess, trying to keep up with her long strides. After a little while, she noticed and slowed her pace, and we wandered off the trail. Once we were far enough away that the others couldn't see us if they looked, she led me into a secluded area beneath the huge roots of a tree on the side of the steep hill in front of us. The thick roots wound through the dirt and acted like a roof above us, and there were three large boulders framing the area. It felt like we were in a cave, except the sun blazed high above, and it lit up the tree's already changing leaves. The glow of the cottonwood's fall foliage basked Abey's face in a warm golden light.

As she backed up to the dirt wall behind her, I asked, "What's your mom's name? I just realized you didn't tell me."

She laughed. "I didn't?"

I shook my head.

Reaching for my belt loops, she pulled me against her body. "It's Mervella. Most people call her Merv, if you can believe that. My daddy used to call her Vella."

"She seems nice," I said as I fitted my hands over her hips and lifted up on my toes to reach her lips.

I thought she would kiss me, but she became still. Her face scrunched up in confusion. It was absolutely adorable. "Are you kiddin'?"

"No. Why would I joke?"

She shrugged. "She's such a grouch sometimes that I guess I don't see her as 'nice.'"

"Well, it's clear she loves you guys."

"Can we not talk about moms right now? I was puttin' all my best moves on you."

"Oh." I laughed. "Okay."

"C'mere," she said, pulling me closer, her eyes fixed on my lips. "I've wanted to kiss these lips all day."

"Really? Even though I'm a criminal?"

"Yes," she said. "And it got worse when you spilled water all over your shirt." Her eyes flicked lower, right to the still-wet spot. "I kept tryin' to imagine what was underneath."

A smile played at the edges of my mouth. "Oh, really?"

"Yes," she said again, touching her lips to mine.

"You sure you wanna be doin' this when your family is fifty yards away?"

"Fifty yards?" She laughed. "Give that to me in feet, and then I'll tell ya. Besides, it's more like two hundred, and they wouldn't dare come up here. If Mama saw us kissin', she might faint. She'll do anything to avoid that."

"Abey—"

The smile in her eyes vanished and was replaced with a fire so blue. It danced and grew darker as she said, "Kiss me, Devo. I can't wait anymore."

A quiet moan escaped me while she cradled the sides of my face and held me still, caressing the lines of my jaw softly, and then she kissed me like she needed the connection the same way she needed air to breathe.

She was a master of kisses, her lips soft and demanding, her tongue fluid and searching, and I felt like I could kiss her until the end of time.

I'd always laughed and rolled my eyes when I heard men claiming women, calling them "mine," but now I understood. I didn't want to share Abey or her lips with anyone. Could she be mine?

Could I kiss these lips forever?

"It was nice today," she whispered when we came up for air. "I've never brought anyone out to meet my family before."

"Really?"

She arched an eyebrow. "Is really the only word you know?"

"No." I giggled. "It's just that when you attempt to be sexy, it's kinda disarmin'."

Her hands slid down my neck and my back, and then she gripped my hips tight. "Really?"

I didn't dare laugh. The way she was looking at me, the lust and need I saw in her eyes, was anything but funny as she reached for my hand and slid it slowly between her legs.

"You disarm me too. Feel how wet you make me?"

I could feel it. The crotch of her cutoffs was damp, and when I smoothed my fingers up her thigh and worked them beneath her underwear, her pussy was slick and hot.

"Oh," she breathed and she moaned.

It was a heady thing to know my hands had elicited the sound from inside her.

I wanted more.

Unbuttoning her shorts, I dragged them down with her undies to her ankles and untied one shoe, smiling at her red and white reindeer socks as I pulled her foot out.

I kneeled in front of her and gripped her bare thighs with my hands, my thumbs sweeping over the soft insides. "Open."

She gasped but widened her stance as my knees touched the dirt of the forest floor, fallen leaves, and dried pine needles. They dug into my skin as I dragged my fingers up her legs slowly, loving the feel of the fine blond hair against my fingertips. Abey didn't shave her legs, but her hair was so light, there was no need.

When I fingered her and touched my tongue to her clit, she moaned again loudly. I looked up her body to watch, but she bit her lip to stop the sound.

Lust looked good on Abey Lee.

Hunger flared in her sapphire eyes as she looked down at what I was doing to her, her hair falling out of her braids in messy yellow tendrils that framed her face. God, what I wouldn't have given to pull my fingers through those braids and spread her hair out on a pillow.

I added another finger, and her eyes rolled shut, so I pumped slowly and buried my mouth between her soaked lips, licking as far down as I could and back up, applying pressure to her clit. And when I flickered my tongue over it, she whimpered and gripped my head with both hands.

I worked quickly, swallowing the salty taste of her body down my throat while applying just enough pressure to her clit with the flat of my tongue, and I pumped my fingers in and out of her soft core, over and over again. Her hips began to move to my rhythm, like my mouth was a magnet her body was drawn to.

"Yeah," she breathed. "More please."

I added a third finger, and she squeezed the crap out of my wrist with her thighs, holding my hand hostage as I finger fucked her in the forest.

Slipping beneath her tank top, I slid my other hand up to her breasts. She'd worn a sports bra so I couldn't feel the warmth and softness I craved to touch, but as I looked up at her, she dropped her head and opened her eyes again, and when I pushed up through the neckline of her T-shirt, she pulled my fingers into her mouth with her teeth, sucking and licking.

The sound of our breath echoed loudly between the boulders, and I knew she was close as her eyes drifted closed and her mouth went lax. I dragged my hand down her stomach and flattened it over her taut belly, rubbing her saliva into her skin as I increased the pace of my fingers inside her.

She threw her head back silently, and her mouth opened, but she didn't make a sound as she froze in place and fractured apart against the side of the mountain, with little bits of sunshine still peeking through the roof of the forest, casting a soft glow over her body, waking it up, and making her come alive for me.

"How was your lunch date?" Rye asked when I got back to the store.

"Good." I couldn't help the smirk on my lips, the ones his childhood friend had just been kissing.

My underwear was soaked and sticking to my thighs, but I didn't care, though it was a little uncomfortable riding back to Abey's brother's house on the back of her ATV. Luckily, her mom had decided to stay out at the farm, so I drove Abey back to her truck at her mom's house while she sat next to me in the cab of my truck. She'd leaned close to kiss my neck while her hands roamed all over me.

Her family had been oblivious to our shenanigans. At least, I hoped they had been, but it was all I could think about. There was something about her.

Something about that Abey Lee.

I knew she had been reserved because her family had been close, but there was something about the way she kept so quiet during sex, like making any sound during her orgasm was forbidden. Why did she come like that, with no sound?

I wanted to make her scream with pleasure, and I had an idea about how I might do just that.

"Oh really?" Rye said like the cat who caught the canary. "Didn't you go with her mom and Bax?" He laughed. "Uh…" He pointed to my hair and blushed. "You got a leaf there."

I patted around till I found it and yanked it out. "Whoops," I said, blushing, too, still remembering the soft feel of Abey's skin on my fingers.

"Devo. Who are you? I thought you were this innocent little—" He pressed his lips into a line and stopped himself from calling me a little girl. "Sorry. I just didn't expect you to get some on a lunch date with my best friend's little sister while his mom and daughter were there. You're a ba-a-ad girl."

"Ha ha," I said, rolling my eyes at his terrible attempt at a sheep joke. "We just kissed." It was a lie, but c'mon. Like I'd tell him the truth—that I'd tongue fucked Abey with her mom not even a half a mile away? Yeah, right. "This isn't weird? Talkin' about this with me?"

"Naw, I've known Abey was into girls for years." He shrugged.

"Really?"

He nodded. "Yeah, Bax told me when we were teenagers."

"What did he think about it?"

"It was his little sister. He was shocked at first, but he saw how she struggled with it in their family. I think it made him sad for her, and he's always been protective of her. But don't tell me too many details. I can't afford to see Abey as a sexual person. I still see her as a twelve-year-old pain in the ass who followed me and Bax around."

"Deal. And hey, keep it to yourself, okay? Abey's discreet. She has to be 'cause of her job."

That was what she'd said, but it was about more than that. It was obvious there was more to it any time Bax or Abey or their mom brought up their dad. Things got weird and uncomfortable.

Rye held up a hand. "Say no more. Besides, who'm I gonna tell?"

"Thanks for lettin' me take a little extra time. Abey said she won't have a day off for a while, but with the new deputies finally here, she could take a long lunch. It was fun."

"Welcome. You can repay the favor. I need to run an errand."

"What kind of errand?"

"I, um, I need to pay a visit to someone. I won't be long."

"Okay. Take however long you need. I'll be here," I said,

smiling like an idiot, still basking in the glow from making Abey come with my mouth and fingers. I had all kinds of ideas of things I wanted to do with her.

Now I just needed to get her alone to do them.

CHAPTER SIXTEEN

ABEY

MY RADIO WENT off at a quarter to five the next morning.

Taking a long lunch meant I'd had to work till ten last night, and man, was I dragging.

No matter how wiped I felt, I always had a hard time falling asleep after a long shift, and I had a feeling that taking the acting sheriff gig was going to see my sleep schedule destroyed and my nerves frayed. Plus, I was anxious. Carey had meetings and obligations at the main station all day today, so this would be my first shift on my own.

But I wanted it and where it could take me. Maybe the dreams I'd told Devo about weren't so far off—a house of my own, some land. The problem was that I didn't have any aspirations to be the sheriff. Running for office, campaigning? That was *so* not me. I loved my job as it was. Why did it have to change?

Looking up at the ceiling as I lay in my bed, I sighed. Everything was changing.

I just needed to push through. That was what I'd always done in the past with hard things.

So get a move on, lazy bones.

But I'd just been dreaming about Devo again, and so badly, I wanted to snuggle back into my feather pillows and catch the thread of that dream, hold on tight, and return to laughing with her in the patch of light streaking in through the little window in the holding room at the station. I laughed out loud when I realized Devo had been locked in a jail cell in my dream.

Was that a subconscious metaphor?

I shook my head. *You're an idiot, Abey, and the sheriff, at least for now, so get. Out. Of. Bed!*

Static filled up my bedroom as Shelley held the Press-To-Talk button again far longer than she needed to. She knew it would wake me up and keep me up.

Rolling to the edge of my mattress, I grabbed my hand-held radio charging in its base on my bedside table and answered her. "Yeah, Shelley. I'm up. Whatcha got for me?" The memory of what Devo had done to me in the woods still rang loudly in my mind. I couldn't stop smiling.

But then the urgency in Shelley's voice had me jumping to my feet. "Emergency at Ace's House."

I pulled on my uniform and purple and green mallard duck socks while she talked, then stuffed my feet in my boots and tied them. "What's goin' on?" Unlocking my gun safe, I armed myself quickly and located my keys.

"There's an altercation. I don't know the particulars, but I can hear some guy yellin' out in the back alley behind Ace's House."

"Lock the doors just to be safe. Who called it in?"

"Red Graves."

Shit.

"Who's fightin'?"

"Dunno, but Red reported a kid in danger."

"10-4. On my way." It didn't even occur to me that I hadn't brushed my teeth till an hour later, so it was a good thing I kept a toothbrush in my locker at the station. But at least I remembered my hat.

Silently, I raced through sleepy Wisper. I didn't know what I'd be dealing with, so I turned on my roof lights but didn't use my siren. It was only a two-minute drive from my apartment, but when I pulled up in front of Ace's House, the place looked deserted.

The outside lights weren't on, there were no lights shining in the windows, and the doors were closed. During the summer, at least one was usually left open if someone was there, even this early. Theo liked it that way so the community felt welcome to come inside any time.

Patting my vest, I made sure I had everything I needed and rechecked the safety on my gun in the holster on my hip. When I got out of my truck, I looked down the alley between the station and the center but didn't see any activity. Shelley had heard voices out back, though, so that was where I headed.

Once I got to the side of the old three-story brick building, I heard struggling. Someone grunted, and I swore I heard the *thwack thwack* of someone hitting someone else.

Navigating the gravel beneath my feet carefully so I wouldn't make a sound, I flipped the snap on my hip holster, my hand wavering over my weapon, and peeked around the back of the building by the cement loading dock that opened up into Ace's House's storage room.

What I saw put the burn back in my chest again, and it pissed me off so much that I had a hard time catching my breath.

Red scrambled on the ground, trying to get back to his feet in the parking area behind Ace's House, nursing a split lip and holding his arm gingerly, like it might've been broken. He must've just gone down, because only a few feet away, another man was yanking on a teenage girl's wrist, trying to drag her away with him.

"Sheriff's Department," I said, lacing as much authority as I could muster into my voice. "Sir, I'm gonna need you to let go of the girl." The assailant startled and threw a glare at me over his shoulder, and Red stilled. An eerie silence settled over us all, and the crisp morning air reminded me that fall would be here soon.

The man narrowed his eyes. "This is *my* kid. I'll do what I want with her."

The girl was in pain. That was clear to see as she winced and tried to pull her arm out of her father's grip, and then she sobbed silently. She had been with the group of teenagers giving Red a hard time a few days before. She seemed familiar to me because of that day, but I felt fairly certain she didn't live in Wisper, and the guy, her father if what he'd said was true, was a stranger to me. That didn't mean they hadn't moved into town recently, but if they had, I most likely would've heard about it somehow. We did get newcomers occasionally, but plenty of people lived off the grid or in remote places in Teton County, doing their best to avoid tourists and the busyness of Jackson Hole and Yellowstone. There was no way for me to know them all.

From this man's old, well-worn clothing, the scuffed, well-used look of his boots, and the anger on his face, I thought he might've been one of the latter.

"*Now*." I hadn't yet raised my weapon, but I was about to.

My hand rested on the butt, and I adjusted my grip when the jackass looked away, just in case. My stance was all business—legs spread shoulder-width apart, chin tucked, shoulders low and relaxed—but adrenaline burned through my veins like fire.

The look in the guy's eyes was… worrisome. He glanced at my gun, and then me, and then he barked a laugh. "Who's gonna make me?"

Was he serious? My badge was in clear view, my uniform and shoulder radio couldn't be mistaken for an odd fashion choice, and the gun now in my hands said everything I needed him to know. "Sheriff Lee, that's who. You think this is a toy gun?" I asked. "Let go of her now, or I'll shoot, and we can discuss this in the ER with your wrist handcuffed to your hospital bed."

The asshole laughed again. "Like I'm scared of you, girl. You prolly can't aim that pea shooter for shit. Now, this is family business. Mind your own."

Pea shooter? It was a fucking Glock. My gun could rip a new asshole right through the middle of his chest.

Discharging a firearm without a good reason was a definite no-no, but I wanted to clip this dick's ear just to get his attention. Unfortunately, that would only cause headaches and paperwork.

I had a feeling, though, that he was about to give me a reason.

"Deputy," Red whispered low, "he's armed."

Yep, I'd already clocked that. It was the main reason there was a gun in my hand. Had he not been armed, I probably would've grabbed my Taser, but a pistol hung from a belt holster on the man's hip under his unbuttoned plaid shirt.

The left chest pocket of his flannel had been ripped open,

and I could see the pasty white skin of his elbow through the hole there too. The tank he wore beneath it, over his beer belly, was off-white and stained. I prayed silently that he wouldn't touch his weapon. I prayed even harder he hadn't been drinking or wasn't the kind of person who would use that pistol on his daughter, but that didn't mean he wouldn't try to use it on me or Red if he felt threatened enough.

"You okay, Red?" I whispered, but my eyes never left the man's.

"I'm fine."

The quiet sound of Red's voice told me a great deal about the situation before I'd arrived. Red was old, but he was capable. He'd spent plenty of time in the woods. He knew how to handle himself, and he knew guns. He sold them, for shit's sake. That he had been taken down by this man and had even a little bit of fear about the man hurting the girl told me I should have a healthy dose of fear too.

I did, but I also had a big ol' dose of confidence. I knew how to handle men like this. I'd dealt with plenty in the past on the job. And I'd known one personally.

He used to be my dad.

"Last chance," I said. "Let. Her. Go."

He ignored me. "Get in the fuckin' truck, Sylvie. I ain't tellin' you again."

The girl shook her head quickly and tried to take a step away, but her father yanked again, and she yelped.

Tears poured from her eyes. "Daddy, *please*! You're hurtin' me."

He just yanked again, and she tripped forward.

"Sir, I have asked you four times now. If you won't let that girl go, I'm *going* to shoot. That's a promise. She may be your daughter, but I don't know that. I don't know you. All I know is that you're hurtin' a *child* right now, and from my estimation, you're the one who hurt this man"—I tipped my head toward Red beside me on the ground—"who I *do* know and who called 911. That's enough cause right there, buddy. If I have to put you down, it won't be sweat off *my* brow."

Dammit. I didn't really want to shoot this asshole, but he was twice my size and I was alone. Protocol dictated that Shelley had already called for backup, but they hadn't arrived yet. It wouldn't be long. I knew that, but if I waited…

If he hadn't been holding onto a child, I might've chosen to tackle this jerk. I had a few tricks up my sleeve to subdue him, but I was afraid of what he might do. Clearly, hurting her wasn't causing the guy any anxiety.

He laughed again, and disdain for a "girl" cop had him rolling his eyes as he yanked hard enough on his daughter's arm that he might've pulled her shoulder out of the socket. She screamed and begged him to let her go as he turned toward an old, rusted-out Ford truck parked behind them. Sylvie dropped to the ground in agony, and her father released the grip he'd had on her wrist.

He laid his hand over his weapon.

That wasn't his first mistake.

Sylvie's eyes slid to mine. She was terrified. She didn't think I had any chance against her bully of a father.

He began to draw his gun from its holster, and I stepped one foot back and pressed my boot into the gravel. I steadied my arm. Sylvie scrambled backward as quickly as she could with only one working arm.

Good girl.

Her father watched her, and he gripped the butt of his gun tighter.

C'mon, jackass. Don't be that guy.

I had no clue what he would do, if he would really threaten his daughter with a deadly weapon. But he was contemplating it, and that made my choice pretty easy.

"Don't say I didn't warn you," I whispered to myself as I waited the last two seconds it took for Sylvie to be a safe distance from her father. I aimed my gun at the meat on the side of his calf. The dude had tree trunks for legs. It was an easy shot. I knew I wouldn't miss.

Red flinched a little in reaction to the sound when I fired. Sylvie stiffened against the dumpster she had been trying to hide behind, and her dad jerked around in surprise. He hadn't thought I'd really do it. Shock and disbelief colored his mean face, but he hadn't been fast enough to beat my bullet. It hit his leg right where I'd aimed, and he dropped where he stood.

Sylvie clambered to her feet and rushed to Red, who was still nursing his wounds on the ground. It said a lot about her relationship with her father.

"Are you okay?" she asked Red and he grunted. I knew him well enough to know he hadn't been hurt too badly. If he had been, he would've been cursing up a storm.

The back door to the community center banged open, and Theo and Brady appeared in the doorway in their pajamas, hair all mussed and eyes blurry with sleep. I didn't look away from my perp, but I could see Theo's hair standing up out of the corner of my eye.

"Stay where you are," I said and they froze.

I hit the PTT button on my radio. "Shelley, send an ambulance to the alley behind Ace's House."

"Dispatched 'em already," she replied. "I've been watchin' y'all on the security feed. I pulled it up when I heard the commotion. That guy messed Red up proper. Frank should be there any second, and Roxanne and Dan are on their way to you now too."

"Thanks."

I didn't holster my weapon as I approached the father of the year, but he clutched at his leg as he glared up at me. Pfft. His next mistake had been underestimating my aim.

"Move and I shoot again. Capiche?"

"Fuckin' cunt," he spat up at me, and then he *literally* spat at me.

"Nice to meet you too," I said, stepping away from his loogie. "Oh, and you're under arrest."

I disarmed and cuffed him, but I was nice and didn't do it behind his back. I read him his rights and let him hold his leg and curse till the ambulance got there. He hadn't apologized to his daughter. She was still shaking and nursing her arm next to Red. They looked like twins, both of them babying their left arms with their right. Sylvie's father made sure to sling a few loogies at his daughter, too, before he was hauled off in the ambulance. Right before the paramedics closed the bay doors, he hollered, "Don't you go back home! You ain't welcome in my house anymore!"

As they drove off with the douchebag cuffed to a stretcher and Roxanne looming over him, clutching her Taser in her hand, I kneeled in front of Red and looked him over. "You okay there, old man?"

"I'll live," he grunted. The tired look in his eyes caused a pang of sadness in my gut. It didn't look like he needed to go back to bed, but more like the world had worn him out.

"What happened?" I asked both him and Sylvie.

She looked at the ground again, and Red stared at the side of her face.

"C'mon. Somebody's gotta tell me."

I would've laughed at Red's inability to say whatever the hell had been caught in his throat—it was just so unlike him not to have a mouthful—if he hadn't seemed so upset.

I concentrated on Sylvie for a minute while Red gathered himself. He stood, and I held out my arm for him to use for support. He actually took hold of it and steadied himself. I didn't make a big deal about it, but it was a big deal. Red wasn't one to reach out to anybody.

"What's your last name, Sylvie?"

"Locke."

I heard Frank arrive behind me. When I glanced over my shoulder, he was already in a huddle with Red, hopefully getting Red's side of the story.

Turning back toward Sylvie, I called behind me. "Frank?"

"Yeah, boss?"

"Will you send Dan to the hospital with Roxanne, please? I don't trust Mr. Locke farther than I can throw him."

"Done."

I heard gravel shifting under his boots as he stepped away to make the call, and I lowered myself beside Sylvie. The gravel beneath me bit into my ass cheek, but I shifted a little, and it wasn't so bad.

The danger was gone, but Sylvie still seemed scared, kind of turning in on herself, but more than that, she looked sad.

I smiled at her gently. "I'm Deputy—" I cleared my throat and changed my approach. Introducing myself as the sheriff or the acting sheriff still didn't sound right to my ears, and I doubted she cared either way. "I'm Abey. Can you tell me what happened please?"

When she looked into my eyes, I saw a lot of pain in hers. She kind of reminded me of myself when I was her age, her long, blond hair naturally wavy, and she'd twisted little braids into the ends here and there. She was innocent, a baby to my eyes, but from the feeling of disappointment and hurt radiating out all around her, I had a feeling that tonight she'd learned more about growing up than she'd ever wanted to know.

She didn't answer my question, so I asked, "Can you move your arm?"

She nodded and whispered, "I told Red not to call 911."

"Yeah, but he didn't listen. It tracks, don'tcha think? He rarely does what I want him to either."

She smiled but said nothing. Not a peep.

"Can you stand?"

She did what I asked, and we got up slowly. My ass was screaming at me now, but I tried to ignore it, because Sylvie winced when she put pressure on her hands to push herself up off the ground.

"What hurts?"

"My wrist. It's not broken. Just sore." She held it out in front of her.

Holding my hand above her wrist, I reached for it but waited till she looked at me. "Okay if I touch your arm?" I asked, and she nodded.

Her skin was red and raw, but she pulled her wrist from my hand gently before I could get a good look. She rolled it. "Like I said, just sore."

"How old are you, Sylvie?"

"Fifteen. Almost sixteen."

"Was anyone else involved tonight? Do you have brothers or sisters at home?"

"No, ma'am. My brother's grown. He's married now, and I'm pretty sure he wouldn't have helped anyway."

Looking at her busted lip, the tiny trickle of blood below it, and at the welt starting to swell on the side of her face, I asked, "Your daddy do that to you?"

She shrugged.

"Is there anything you *can* tell me?"

"I'm fine," she said, looking at the ground again, trying to hide behind the strands of hair falling in front of her face.

Changing my tack 'cause I didn't want to push too hard too fast till I knew more about what had happened, I said, "Gimme a minute, Sylvie. I'll be right back."

I caught Theo's eye behind Sylvie, and he left Brady standing in the doorway when I nodded toward Sylvie. He could probably guess she needed a familiar face right about now.

Red stood next to Frank, still guarding his left arm, but they weren't talking. It looked like he might have been waiting for me.

"What the hell, Red?" I whispered. "What happened? She won't say."

"I dunno what the… protocol is. She told me, but ain't that breakin' the law if I tell you?"

"No. She's a minor."

"Yeah," he said, dragging his uninjured hand over his head, "but I don't wanna break her trust."

Frank's eyebrows did a little dance. He was just as surprised as I was.

"Wow, Red. Maybe this switcheroo has done you good. That's somethin' I never imagined you'd say about some 'punk' kid." Frank and I had heard him complain at one time or another about every teenager in town.

He didn't even acknowledge what I'd said. His eyes darted back and forth between my face and Sylvie's.

Finally, taking care to keep his voice low, he said, "I'll tell you 'cause I'm worried this will happen again if I don't." He took a deep breath. "Sylvie was here when I got here this mornin'. She was shook up, cryin'. Her father did that to her. He slapped and punched her. She said he knocked her to the ground. Her mother was there when it happened, but she didn't lift a finger to stop it. She watched it happen. And then he came here lookin' for Sylvie so he could hit her and yell at her some more." Red looked over at Sylvie standing with Theo and Brady now. They'd wrapped her up in a blanket, and it looked like Brady was trying to make her drink water from a plastic bottle. Red cringed and said, "She drove, but she doesn't have a license."

"Don't worry about that right now," Frank said. "She's not in trouble."

Closing my eyes, the anger rose up inside me. That feeling of betrayal all over again. The loss of the love you were supposed to be able to count on your whole life. *Goddammit. Some people shouldn't be allowed to have kids.*

"Do you know why he did this?" I asked.

Red nodded, but he didn't add anything.

"Red, it's kinda important. Do you know where they live? I recognize her from the center, but she doesn't live in Wisper, so I don't know her dad."

"David Locke's been comin' into my store for years. They live out west of Barton, right near the Idaho border. I can't believe he raised his hands to me. The rage in his eyes when I warned him to take his hands off her… That's when I noticed his gun. He was mad enough to use it."

Yeah. I'd noticed that, too, which was why David Locke now had a hole in his leg.

I'd heard his name before from some of the Game and Fish guys. If I remembered right, they'd caught David Locke hunting without tags and in places he shouldn't have been. Unfortunately, it wasn't an uncommon occurrence.

"You did the right thing, Red. Thank you."

As the adrenaline began to leave my body, I blew out a big breath. The last five minutes were like a tornado raging around inside me. A small part of my mind flipped through every move I'd made, like a slideshow, but I knew in my gut I'd done what I had to do. I'd give Ranger Summers a call. Maybe he could fill me in a little more about Mr. Locke. But it was done now. And the kid was safe. So was Red, and so was I. That was all that really mattered.

I turned to go back to Sylvie. I wanted to drive her over to see Doc Whitley so he could X-ray her shoulder and wrist while we waited for CPS to get here, but Red reached for my arm and locked the rough pads of his fingers around it to stop me.

"Her daddy did that to her 'cause she's—because she told him she's…"

"What?" I said, turning back to him. "She's what?"

Red looked at the building in the background, lifting his eyebrows, like I should understand from where we were.

"You're gonna have to say it, Red. I don't understand."

He whispered, "She's a… *lesbian*."

And suddenly, it all made sense. Red's unease, the reason David Locke had hunted his daughter down to dish out what he probably considered discipline, and why Red was whispering. He could barely say the word.

"Her parents found out she's gay, and her daddy hit her." I didn't ask it as a question. I already knew the answer. It wasn't the first time I'd heard this story. Parents beating or disowning their kids 'cause they identified as something other than "normal" wasn't an uncommon occurrence either.

And it hit closer to home than I wanted to think about.

"Yeah," said Red. "But his own daughter? I've known Dave a long time. I didn't know he was capable of this."

"It happens," I said, so *fucking* sorry that it did.

"She's just a kid," he said, getting angrier the more he thought about it. Apparently, Red really had learned a lesson here.

"Where was he tryin' to take her?" Frank asked.

"To his church. The preacher there says he can fix kids like… like Sylvie."

Pray the gay away, right? *Motherfucking* ignorant bullies!

I had to work hard to hide the shake in my voice. "I'm gonna drive her over to see Doc Whitley, just to check her out. You wanna catch a ride with us? Have Doc take a quick look at that arm?"

He shook his head. "I told you, I'm fine."

"Red," I said, spearing him with a look. "Don't argue."

"Fine. But it's just my damn shoulder. It'll hurt for a couple days. Ain't nothin' new."

Something occurred to me then. "Why were you here by yourself so early?"

He looked down at his boots. For someone usually so full of piss and vinegar, he was awfully quiet.

"Red?"

"I'm glad I was here," he said. "She asked me not to wake Theo. She was scared. I wanted to help set up for the day. Start the coffee. I just… wanted to help." He shrugged but didn't look up. "Maybe I like it here."

"You do?" What the hell? Prepare a press release: Red Graves has a heart?

"Don't you go makin' anything out of it," he grumbled, finally looking at me. "I've been alone a long time. My house is so *damn* quiet, and I don't sleep so well. It's… nice to be around young people. Nice to feel needed."

"Yeah," I said, agreeing. Frank nodded silently.

What else was there to say?

"Mr. Graves?" Sylvie's soft voice interrupted us, and Red cleared his throat gruffly. She stepped next to him. Tears filled her eyes again, and in a small voice, she said, "Thank you for tryin' to help me," and then she threw her good arm around him and held onto him tight.

Red grunted at the pain, but he didn't move. He let Sylvie hug him and cry silently all over his shirt. He patted her back awkwardly for a moment with his uninjured arm, and finally, he hugged her back.

CHAPTER SEVENTEEN

DEVO

LYING in the bed I used to share with my sister, Lola, in the tiny bedroom I'd had to share with both my brother and sister, I gazed up at the flower stickers I'd dotted along the ceiling the day we moved in.

All I could think about was Abey.

Against my better judgment, I'd left the window open all night, because if I'd closed it, I would've suffocated. My mom said she couldn't sleep with the sound of the fancy new air conditioner running. The thing was nearly silent! It was one of the reasons I'd picked out the model I had. Paid extra for it too.

Whatever. I hadn't slept well anyway, and it had nothing to do with the heat.

Theo had filled me in about the situation with Sylvie Locke. God, that poor girl. I ached for her. He said Abey had taken her to the doctor and she was okay physically, but everything else in that kid's life had gone up in smoke. She couldn't go home. Even if Sylvie had reported what her father had done, which she refused to do, her mother was of the same mind. If Sylvie wasn't willing to be someone else entirely than who she was born to be, then she wasn't welcome in her own home.

And Red had tried to deal with it by himself? Theo said that Red and Sylvie had bonded in some way, so he wasn't upset with Red for keeping quiet and not waking him when Sylvie showed up at the center.

It wasn't the first time we'd dealt with that kind of situation at Ace's House, and it wouldn't be the last. Wyoming Family Services would look into it, but I didn't have much hope that they would make much of a difference.

In the meantime, thankfully, Sylvie had an aunt on her mother's side who had been horrified to hear how her sister and brother-in-law had treated their own daughter, so she'd driven over from Laramie last night to pick up Sylvie and take her somewhere she could feel safe. Her mother hadn't even fought it. She let Sylvie go, but Laramie was a college town, so I knew she would find like-minded people her age there. She could thrive there. I hoped.

The whole thing had me thinking about my dad. The good memories I had of him were fuzzy. My mom never talked about him or about why he'd been so miserable, why he'd made my mom's life miserable.

She grieved when he died, but I didn't think I was wrong as I remembered her breathing easier after he was gone. Remembering his reaction to my coming out and all the other times he hadn't been there for his family left me feeling indifferent.

His absence from my life, even though he had been sitting right there, made it easy to let the memories fade away. Still, I felt like I should feel *something* about him being so dismissive of me, but I didn't.

Relief, just like my mom had felt, was all I knew about the man who had provided half my DNA. Relief that he was gone. I wondered if he'd have an opinion about my job if he were still alive. Maybe I liked helping people because he never had. If he wasn't trying to help himself in some way, then he didn't help anyone. He'd never seemed to care about anything enough to hold an opinion about it at all.

I wondered what Abey's dad had been like. Had he been like mine—apathetic? Had her dad known about her? Had he hurt her, too, like Sylvie's dad? Was it the reason for all the awkward, hushed silences when her family made the mistake of bringing him up?

I wanted to call her.

Abey was busy though. She'd taken the sheriff promotion, and I hadn't seen much of her the last couple days. Today would be my last day at The Red Wild Outdoors. I couldn't say I'd learned much from my time there, at least not about Red's way of life, but from everything Theo had said, the arrangement had turned out to be good for Red.

I was glad of that. I mean, not that I thought his entire belief system could've changed in the span of a few days, but at least now he had an understanding of what we did at Ace's House, how we were simply a soft place for people like Sylvie to land when they didn't even know they'd been falling.

Rolling onto my side, the box springs beneath me creaked as I looked at my phone on my rickety pressboard bedside table. I reached for it and clicked till I saw Abey's contact info on the screen. The heart emojis on both sides of her name made me blush. If she ever saw them, I'd die of embarrassment. I thought about changing it just in case that ever happened, but I liked the little yellow hearts. They reminded me of her hair when the sun shone down it.

If she was busy, she wouldn't answer. Maybe she'd call

me back on her lunch break, but at least she'd know I'd been thinking about her.

I hit the "Dial" button and waited.

"Hi," she said when she answered on the second ring.

"Hi."

A minute of silence passed between us.

"Did you call just to listen to me breathe?"

I laughed. No one had ever made me laugh the way Abey did. There was just something in the tone of her voice. A teasing. I loved the sound of it.

"No. I… I was thinkin' about you. About how you're doin' after the thing with Sylvie."

"Oh. You were? Why?"

I shrugged even though she couldn't see me. "Your mom…"

"Yeah—my ol' mama. But y'know, as awful as she can be, she'd never lay a hand on me. She never kicked me out of my own home. Sometimes, I think she says the things she does 'cause it's all she knows to do. Like, maybe she just thinks she can't relate to me. And maybe that scares her."

"What about your dad? Did he know you're gay?"

She didn't say anything for a minute. "He knew." Two little words, but somehow, from them I understood that my suspicions were right on, and Abey's dad hadn't been supportive.

It made me want to run into my mom's room, jump into her bed, and hug her. I was so lucky to have been given the gift of acceptance, of true, unconditional love. A lot of people weren't so lucky.

Abey wasn't.

"Where are you right now? I wish I could see you." I wanted to wrap my arms around her, wanted to rest my head against her chest and breathe with her. How funny that, only two months ago, if I'd thought about her, besides subconsciously registering how beautiful she was, I probably would've wanted to yell at her.

She smiled. I heard it in her voice when she said, "I'm sittin' in my truck, takin' a nonscheduled break. Needed a minute."

"You okay?"

"Yeah. It's just… Yesterday was hard. And there's a lot to this sheriff thing. It's only, what, eight a.m., and there's paperwork up the wazoo already, and everybody wants my attention, and everybody thinks their problem is more important than anybody else's." She paused. "Not to say I don't like it. I do. I wasn't sure if I would, but I do, at least parts of it. I like bein' the one who decides how things are gonna go down, y'know?

"So many times in the past, I had ideas about how we should handle a call or a problem, and Carey was always good about hearin' me out, but ultimately, it was his decision. Now it's mine. It's kinda cool." She laughed. "As long as what I decide works. If it doesn't, I'll probably find myself in a shitstorm of epic proportions.

"Teton County is *big*. I stay near Wisper usually, but we get called out to other places sometimes, if we need to help another officer. Carey put me up to this to focus on Wisper and Barton mostly, and the surrounding areas, while he's away, but those are enough. I don't know if I could handle the *entire* county. Part of Yellowstone? I mean, we work with the rangers there, and the National Park Service guys, but still. It's a lot."

"I can't even imagine," I said. "I've never even been to Yellowstone."

"What? Girl, that's nuts. You live right here!"

I giggled at her outrage. I loved when she called me

"girl." I'd never admit it to anyone, but when Abey said it, it felt like she meant *her* girl. Like I was hers. Like she'd claimed me too.

I wanted to be claimed by Abey Lee.

"I know, but it's always busy with tourists, and honestly, it's expensive. Until I got the job at the center, I never had extra money to spend on a day at the park. I bet a hot dog costs twenty bucks there."

She huffed a laugh. "You ain't far off. But it's beautiful. There's so much to see, and most of the tourists don't know about any of the good backcountry spots."

Rolling onto my back and kicking my sheet down to my feet, I breathed deeply, trying to picture it: spending a day out in the mountains with Abey, having a picnic lunch, and playing in a waterfall somewhere in Yellowstone. Just listening to her voice relaxed me. I wished I could snuggle up to her while she talked. "I've seen pictures."

"It's not the same thing. Not even close."

I smiled at the wistfulness in her voice and wished I could see her eyes, blue as the sky over Wyoming. "Maybe we can go sometime."

"I'll take you," she said. "I'd love to take you. Plus, I don't have to pay. Got me a shiny law enforcement pass, but I'll save my pennies and buy you *two* hot dogs."

"A Yellowstone date?" I asked, noticing how my voice had gone from sleepy and raspy to a high-pitched swoony sound when I thought about going on a date with her, just the two of us.

"Yeah. By the way, you know what I like to do, but what do you do when you get a day off?"

"Mm, dunno. I mean, usually I run errands or help my mom around the house. That kinda thing. But… Well, do you promise not to laugh?"

In her most serious voice, she said, "Not on your life."

"Gee, thanks," I teased, smiling to myself because I knew she wouldn't laugh. "I like to… garden."

"Why would I laugh at that?"

"I'm not very good at it. If I can keep a plant alive longer than a month, it's a miracle. Actually, they usually do okay outside, but it's when I bring them indoors that shit goes sideways."

She laughed then. "What kinda plants?"

"I like growing food. Vegetables and herbs and stuff like that. I worked in fast food for a little while at this *awful* chicken place, and it made me insane to see how much food is thrown away and wasted when there are people literally starving right here in our backyard. Ugh!"

I took a deep breath, trying to calm Devo the Devil. "But it's so satisfyin' when I eat somethin' I've grown myself. I've been thinkin' I'd like to… I dunno. I'd like to learn more about it. Maybe start a small farm. I could grow food for the community. There's this one farm I found when I gave a kid a ride home from the center. He lives out here, past Barton in the sticks. Anyway, the place is beautiful, and they do this CSA program where they grow the veggies and then they box it all up and give 'em out. People pledge money to the farm, then you grow the food, and the donors benefit, but there's a portion of the food that goes to the community. Everybody wins."

"Wow," Abey said. "That's really cool. Sounds like a lot of work though."

"Yeah," I admitted. It would be a ton of work. Not that I couldn't put in the hours, but by myself? "And I have my job at the center." But the more I read and thought about it, I really wanted to try it. "It was just a thought."

"It's a good one, and I think you'd be a pretty hot farmer."

I chuckled at that, then she said, "Ah, well, a dream for another day?"

"Yeah," I said. Man, the way she thought all my ideas were amazing made me want to kiss her. She accepted me as is. "When's your next day off?"

"Probably next year." I didn't need to see her to know she'd rolled her eyes. "Speaking of, I gotta go."

"Really?"

"Yes, *really*. But thanks for callin'. You made this whole 'park my truck down an alley and avoid my responsibilities' thing fun."

"When can I see you? I want to see you."

"Are you back at Ace's House today?"

"No." I sighed. "One more day."

"If I get a minute, I'll stop in."

"Promise?"

"I can't, but I'll try my damnedest."

Pulling into the alley next to Red Wild early, I'd been hoping to catch a glimpse of Abey around town. Yeah, yeah, she was busy, but that didn't mean I couldn't get a gander of her ass and legs in her fine-fitting uniform. A girl could only hope.

As I parked behind the store, I heard the beeping of a delivery truck backing up at a nearby business, probably the flower shop a few doors down. Rye had already arrived, and he stood talking to his uncle beside the loading dock.

The morning was hazy with heat already but quiet. The weather was expected to break soon. We'd go from eighties and humid to sixties and dry. I couldn't wait. Sweater weather had always been my favorite weather.

"Good mornin', guys. Red." I nodded and offered a smile. Maybe I could start this day off on a positive foot.

"Mornin', Devo. Ready for your last day?" Rye asked.

"I think so."

Red turned to face me carefully. Afraid to poke his least favorite bear? But he was trying. I had to give him that. "Mornin'," he said.

The old fury I felt toward him tried to build up inside me. It really chuffed my bunny that I had to look up at him. Being short really sucked sometimes, but then I reminded myself to take a breath. Red Graves and I would probably never be friends, but I was trying my hardest to see him as someone other than the villain in my mind.

"Thank you for helpin' Sylvie," I said.

"Don't mention it."

"Are you okay?"

He grumbled, "Why wouldn't I be?"

Shrugging one shoulder, I said, "I've dealt with almost that exact situation before. It's hard."

"You think I can't handle your job?" He was trying, but he was still Red.

Lifting my hands up in front of my chest, I hurried to say, "No. That's not what I meant. I meant it's heartbreakin'. It's a hard thing to witness, that's all."

"Oh. Well, I'm fine. Don't worry about me," he mumbled, but then he looked behind me, and his face changed. His expression went from grumpy dickwad to enchanted idiot. What the hell was he looking at?

"Devona!"

Mom?

I turned to see my mom hurrying up the alley, her worn work sneakers crunching over the gravel. She held a brown-bag lunch in one hand and my phone in the other.

She shook it in the air. "Where's your head this mornin', Devona? You forgot your lunch and your phone. I'm surprised you remembered to put on shoes."

"Oh! My phone. I need it." After talking to Abey, I'd been in a daydream all morning, picturing us tending rows of green peppers and sweet corn hand in hand, feeding the birds and packing boxes of brightly colored vegetables to offer to people at the food bank at Ace's House.

"Which is why I followed you all the way here and why I'm gonna be late to work. We're supposed to start prep for the new school year, but they've called a meetin' this mornin'. Everybody has to be there."

"I'm sorry, Mom. Thank you."

She didn't reply. She was too busy looking up at Red.

"Um, Mom, this is Red Graves. He owns the store, and this is his nephew, Rye. This is my mom, Liluye."

"Nice to meet you, Rye" she said, but she was still staring up at Red. We were the same height, but it didn't seem to chuff anything of hers to have to gaze up at the man.

"Ma'am," Red said. He offered his hand, and she shook it. "Pleasure to meet you."

"So, you're him, the devil himself," she said, and my cheeks got hot. *Whoops. I should probably stop saying things like that.*

But Red laughed. He laughed! "Oh no, ma'am. I ain't the devil. I'm an angel."

Rye choked on the coffee he'd just taken a big gulp of while we both watched this bizarre meet-cute go down. Really? My mom was charmed by Red? Red *Graves*?

Ugh!

Stepping closer to Rye, I patted him hard enough on his back to leave a bruise, and he coughed out the coffee stuck in his windpipe, but neither Red nor my mom paid him any attention.

"Liluye? Did I get that right?" Red asked, and my mom's eyes lit up when he said her name correctly. People usually didn't—but they were still holding hands. "It's a beautiful name."

My mom blushed. She flippin' blushed! "Thank you," she said. "It's Western Apache. It means Singing Hawk While Soaring."

"It's lovely. I'm a bit of a birder myself," Red said. "But my true love is photography. If you can spare a minute, I'll show you. I have a whole photo album inside filled with hawk pictures." He let go of her hand, but he seemed reluctant. My mom nodded and followed him up the loading ramp into the storeroom. Hadn't she just said she was late for work?

"What the fuck just happened?" Rye said.

I had no clue. I couldn't even speak.

CHAPTER EIGHTEEN

DEVO

RED HELPED my mom into her car, and I watched from the front doors of The Red Wild Outdoors, still dumbfounded.

I couldn't seem to take my eyes away from the scene outside. Theo watched it go down from the stoop in front of Ace's House too. Finally, he looked at me and I at him. I shrugged with a seriously confused sneer on my face, and he shook his head. When my mom drove off, Red jogged across the street, and there was a little bit of a pep in his step.

"Well, ain't that the finger in your pie?" Rye said, pulling me out of my grossed-out confusion. What a visual!

I turned and slumped back against the doors behind me when I closed them.

He said, "If they get married, does that mean we'll be cousins?"

"Uhh…"

He laughed at me. "Look at it this way. If they date, Red will be much nicer. At least, I hope he would be."

I shuddered. My face was blank. I could feel it, but I couldn't seem to rearrange my muscles.

He laughed again. "I told you his bark is worse than his bite. But I don't think I've ever seen him react to a woman that way, and I'm damn sure he's never been more charmin'. Your mama must be special."

He did have a point there. "She is."

"Alright then," he said. "What's the plan for your last day?"

Right. The reason I was stuck here. "I guess we should finish the display we started yesterday. Did Red say anything about it this mornin'?"

"No. He didn't come into this part of the store. He was diggin' through some boxes in the back room when I got here. He pulled a bunch of merchandise and said he needed to get over to the post office. I think maybe he wants to send a care package to that girl from the other day. He didn't say that, but I can't figure any other reason. He keeps talkin' about her."

"Okay, good." If Red wanted to do something nice for Sylvie, then I was kind of excited to surprise him, to thank him.

So maybe I had learned a little something from this whole thing. I didn't have to agree with someone personally to help them. I surrounded myself with issues I felt passionate about or issues that directly affected me, but that was pretty small-minded of me. There were plenty of other issues in the world that I knew nothing about because I hadn't wanted to know about them. I ignored them or avoided them because they didn't fit into my world view.

I still didn't agree with hunting, but I had never really realized or thought about how many people hunted for their food. In this day and age, I guess I'd just assumed everyone went to the grocery store. But as I'd learned from being at

Red Wild over the last week, that wasn't true at all. And some people, whether it was how they'd been raised or out of financial necessity or a need from within, lived differently than I did.

The whole thing had the farm idea churning in my mind. Maybe we could do it through Ace's House. Maybe Theo would be into it. In fact, I bet he would. He'd do anything to help people.

"I'm gonna grab some breakfast," Rye said. "Think I'll walk up to the café. You want anything?"

"Thanks, no," I said as I turned to check our progress on the camping display we'd started setting up the day before. Making the displays had turned out to be fun. "I'm not hungry, and I wanna get started."

The cowbell on the door clanked when Rye left, and I ran to the back room to grab the T-shirts that had started this whole thing. I hung them up on a rack in the new clothing area, but just 'cause I could, next to them, I hung shirts that said "God Created Us All." It had a picture of mountains with bears and deer in the background and people in the fore-ground. If a customer wanted to buy the homophobic shirt, at least they'd have to look at the other shirt too. Maybe it would make them think.

I tapped my finger on my chin, looking at the camping display, trying to decide if I should set up a really comfy-looking inflatable couch to display with the other cool camping accessories we'd found still in their boxes in the back room. I'd already set up this amazing tent thing that was like an instant bathroom, complete with a portable toilet, sink, and shower. I could definitely be persuaded to camp if I was armed with a pop-up bathroom.

I stood there, envisioning it: setting up camp with Abey, hiking over beautiful golden plains and rugged trails through the Tetons, grilling fish we'd caught in a stream for dinner, and then laughing with her and snuggling up together in a big, heated sleeping bag… But then the clunky cowbell on the door jingled again.

"Forget your wallet?" I asked Rye without turning around. I'd learned quickly that if his head wasn't screwed onto his neck, he'd forget it.

"Nope," Abey said. When I jerked my head around to the sound of her voice, she was coming straight for me. She looked official and sexy as hell in her uniform, but she wasn't wearing her hat. Her hair was pulled tight into a bun. "Anybody here? I saw Rye leave."

"No. We're alone."

"Good."

When she reached me, she steered me backward with her hands on my hips, and my feet shuffled as she moved us behind the murder curtain.

Her breath caressed lightly over my lips, and then her mouth was warm on them, her tongue hot as it slid over mine. I reached up and tugged gently at the bobby pins holding her hair in place. I stuck them in my front pocket as long blond tendrils fell around her face and over her shoulders, and I ran my fingers through them. I loved how it looked, light against dark, as the static between our bodies drew her hair to my black "Hike it Red Wild style" T-shirt.

She moaned as my fingernails scratched lightly over her scalp. "That feels so good. I swear I hold my stress in my hair follicles."

I laughed and kissed her harder.

"I only have a minute," she whispered, "but I couldn't think of anything I wanted to do more with that minute than kiss you." She looked at me in the dark of the storeroom, a little V forming between her eyebrows. "What're we doin' here, Devo?"

"Makin' out," I said, grinning, and pulled at her bottom lip gently with my teeth.

"No, I mean"—she gripped my hips over my jeans and pulled me closer—"between you and me. Where's this goin'?"

"Dunno," I said, peppering little kisses below her mouth, nuzzling my lips against her neck as her hand slid up the back of my shirt slowly. "We're gettin' to know each other, aren't we?"

"Yeah, but I mean, is it only sex? Is it just casual?"

"I don't want just casual," I said, moving lower and feeling the warmth of her chest with my lips as far down as her uniform shirt would allow.

"Me neither."

Untucking one side of her shirt from her pants, I slid my hand up her stomach. My goal was always her breasts. They were so full and soft, her nipples perfect, round disks that had become the stars of my dreams. "Okay, so then we're datin'."

Before I could reach them, though, she pulled away.

I leaned back, looking up into her eyes. "We're not datin'?" I said, confused. "I thought you wanted to take me to Yellowstone?"

"I do, but…"

The look on her face, the hesitation and fear—it was enough to tell me what I needed to know.

No matter how good it felt to be with her, no matter that we were doing absolutely nothing wrong, weren't hurting anyone, all of that was just a lucky benefit of a bigger disease.

She wasn't willing to be in a relationship with a woman,

not out loud in the world where the men in her job could see. Where the residents of Wisper could see.

We'd both been kidding ourselves.

How had I not realized it before this moment? Now, it was a glaring truth right in front of my face. Maybe the thing with Sylvie had brought it too close to home for Abey.

I wanted to deny what I was seeing on her face, the fear I could feel coming from her. It was like an electric forcefield all around her, but there was a resolute feeling winding its way around the fear, like barbed wire.

She took one step away from me, and all I could do was nod. I finally understood, and my heart shattered into tiny little shards that stabbed at me. Her beautiful blue eyes were arresting, even in the dark, but there was still fear in them.

"You want to take me on a date, but only if no one sees us on that date." It wasn't a question. I already knew the answer.

She whispered, "Devo."

I backed away and tripped on a box behind my feet. Abey reached for me.

But I wasn't going to depend on her. "No," I said, and I caught myself from falling backward. "I don't get how we went from kissin' to this, but am I right? How did I not see it?" I hadn't really expected an answer. I adjusted my shirt and pulled it back into place. "You took me out to your brother's place, which is miles from town, and then we went even further off the grid to eat lunch. If lunch had been at José's Diner, would you have invited me?"

She opened her mouth, but no sound came out.

"I see." I turned away. What more was there to say? My voice sounded paper thin when I mumbled, "Okay, well, I have to get back to work."

"I'm sorry, Devo." She pressed her fist hard against her stomach, below her breasts. "I want things to be different, but… I-I wanna be with you. God, I can't even tell you how much—"

I shrugged into the darkness and wrapped my arms around stomach. "But you can't. Or you won't. We're in different places in our lives. I thought I'd be okay with it. I *really* did. I understand where you're comin' from. Truly, I do, Abey, but I can't hide who I am. I'm sorry. I'm not tryin' to make you feel bad about where you're at, but the kids I work with—it would feel dishonest to me to be an advocate for them and not be honest with them. I thought I could be okay with it." I stood tall and took a deep breath. "But I just can't."

"I'm sorry," she whispered. "I don't know what the fuck I'm doin'."

And she left. The curtain fell back into place behind her, the bell on the door clamoring loudly when she opened then closed it, and I wanted to cry.

In fact, I did.

I stood there, staring at the back of the murder curtain as tears dripped from my chin, breathing deeply, trying to understand my reaction to Abey's rejection. She wasn't rejecting me as a person. She liked me—maybe more than liked me— but all I felt was shame when I thought about being her dirty little secret.

I couldn't be anyone's secret. I couldn't advocate for LGBTQ youth and, at the same time, hide my own relationship. That wouldn't be right, and it didn't feel good.

But not being with Abey again, not touching her again or kissing her, hearing her soft voice or the musical lilt of her laugh, the thought of that didn't feel good either.

It hurt.

The goddamn bell jingled again. The sound grated inside my head, and a gruff man's voice demanding service cut through my confusion. Great. One more man to look down on me.

I flicked away my tears, took a deep breath, and went out front to sell guns or fanny packs or whatever else, as the woman starring in the future I'd stupidly let myself envision climbed into her truck outside and drove away.

CHAPTER NINETEEN

ABEY

"Why're you sittin' out here?" Frank asked when he walked into the station after lunch.

"Where else would I sit?" I asked, annoyed. "This is my desk, ain't it?"

"In the sheriff's office," he said, like *duh, Abey*.

"This is my desk, dammit. Why's everything gotta change?"

He stopped in front of me with his hands on his hips. I didn't have to look up to know it. I could feel it. "What's wrong with you?"

I didn't look at him. I couldn't. I'd never shared my feelings with Frank before, not about this. It just wasn't me to talk about that kind of shit. I wanted to laugh when I realized the old grouch was more in tune with his inner self than I was. "Nothin'."

Walking behind me, Frank rested his big hands on the back of my chair and then spun me to face him. He pulled his own chair away from his desk and sat two feet in front of me.

Arching an eyebrow, he waited for me to explain my bad mood.

"Things have to change, don't they?"

"Seems like they do."

"I'm gay, Frank. I'm a lesbian. I fuck women."

He nodded. "Mmhm. And?"

Really? That was all he had to say on the matter?

"And I'm also the sheriff, for all intents and purposes. I can't be seen galavantin' around town with a woman. And now that I've found the one I want, it's even more important that people respect me. I just can't. It's not the right time."

God, just saying the words hurt. My chest ached so goddamn bad, I had to hold back tears.

I wasn't fooling Frank. He pursed his lips and crossed his arms over his chest, leaning back in his chair.

Looking at him, with his big biceps trying to split the sleeves of his uniform, I hated how angry it made me that he was free to love whomever he wanted to. He and Sam didn't get the disgusted looks Devo and I would if we were seen together. No one talked badly about them behind their backs, even though Frank was nearly twenty years older than Sam. But he was a man and she was a woman.

I loved my friends. I didn't want them to have to face strife, but at the same time, I wanted to scream at the top of my lungs, "It's not fair!"

"You can't beg peoples' respect, Abey. You gotta earn it. And you know what feels even better than earnin' respect?"

I shook my head and sighed out a breath. I wasn't really in the mood for a pep talk or whatever the hell this was.

"When you earn it from someone who really doesn't wanna give it. So, live your life the way you want and need to. You're a good person. People *do* respect you. They will continue to do so no matter who you love, and those who don't will either learn to or they won't, but you'll still deserve it."

Dammit. Why did he have to be so… right? "You make it sound easy."

Shrugging, he said, "You do you. There ain't nothin' wrong with you, except that you're a slob"—his perceptive gray eyes flicked to the carefully disorganized piles of papers on my desk—"but as long as the general public's kept in the dark about that fact, I think you'll be just fine. No one cares about your life more than you do." He waited for me to look him in the eye again. When I did, he said, "So fuck 'em."

I wanted to laugh at his joke about me being a slob, although I wasn't entirely sure he had been joking, but I couldn't because everything he'd just said was right. I knew it was, but it didn't make it any easier. And as far as I knew, no one had published a book about how to be a good lesbian, how to live my life out in the open, and how to deal with assholes.

No one could tell me how to get over my own prejudices. Internalized homophobia. I'd read about it. It was the reason the word "lesbian" grated my nerves.

I was afraid of what people might say because I was scared shitless myself.

The door opened behind us, interrupting my need to scream and rail at general injustice. Frank sat forward, rolling his eyes.

When I turned my chair, Roxanne and Dan stood silently on the other side of my desk, Dan with something pink dripping onto his uniform from his head. His sunglasses were covered in the stuff.

"Sorry," Roxanne said in a tight voice, trying hard not to laugh out loud, "but it wasn't me. He tried to tell one of the ladies at the farmers market that she couldn't park her truck on the sidewalk to load her stuff, and she dumped her smoothie over his head."

"Sissy Melton?" Frank asked, fluttering his hands around his head. "Long gray hair, big hat?"

Roxanne was ready to burst. "Yep. That'd be her." She lost the fight and bent over, cackling and sucking in air, trying to catch her breath.

"I'm changin' my shirt," Dan said, ignoring Roxanne. "Then I'm gonna go arrest her."

"No, you're not," I said and stood from my chair. "You're lucky blended fruit all over your head's all you got for your efforts."

Dan stomped his foot, and pink smoothie spattered around the station. He yanked his sunglasses from his face, and the frothy liquid slipped down his crooked nose, welling above his lip. "She attacked an officer of the law!"

I flicked a drop off my forearm. "All Sissy did was put you in your place, and it'll go better for you if you learn where that is. Nobody tells that woman what to do, and she's earned the right."

"Seriously?" He was outraged. He pegged Frank with a glare. "Even you?"

Frank stood too. "Even me what?"

Dan looked almost a foot shorter than Frank and probably half his body mass. He shrank back a step, his angry tone faltering under Frank's glare. "Y-you're ex-military. I thought you'd have my back. This place is backwards. I feel like I've stepped into a fifties sitcom. All anybody cares about around here is gossip."

I nodded. "That's the job."

"You've all gone soft." Dan stomped away. He slammed the locker room door in the hall, and Frank laughed so hard, he snorted.

Roxanne had collected what little decorum she could, hiccupping between giggles. "I knew Sissy wasn't someone we wanted to piss off. I could tell just by lookin' at her. I warned him." She wiped tears from under her eyes as I walked around my former desk.

"I'll talk to Sissy," I said, grabbing my hat from the hook by the door. "And Roxanne, that's your desk now." I pointed to the little bit of brown wood peeking out from my mess. Okay, so maybe I was a slob. I winced when I remembered the pile of empty chili cups and Ho-Ho wrappers in the back seat of my truck. Maybe if I stopped eating so many of them, I could quit with the fucking burpees every morning. "I'll clean it off before I head home tonight. Guess I'm movin' into the big guy's office."

"Thanks," she said, looking toward the hallway. "But what about Pink Hair back there?"

"I was plannin' on settin' up a desk for him over there." I nodded toward the corner of the room, where we kept a round fluffy bed for Frank's dog, Grum. "But if he doesn't figure out how to relax around here, he's gonna find himself out on the street sooner rather than later."

We had an extra desk back in the conference room, but before I dragged it out to the bullpen, Dan and I needed to have a conversation about a couple things.

Reading the room was one, and respect was the other.

I texted Devo on my lunch break in my truck, parked half a block away from Red Wild. My eyes flicked back and forth every few seconds from my phone to the two doors and the sidewalk between Devo and me.

The feeling inside me, knowing I'd hurt her, knowing that the fear I couldn't help but feel had made me act a fool... It was unbearable.

> I'm sorry. I'm so fucking sorry. Will you give me a chance to fix it?

She hadn't replied yet, but my phone told me she'd seen the message.

> If you come to my house tonight, I'll apologize properly, and I have something I want to ask you.

She'd read the second text, too, but still wouldn't respond. Dammit. *C'mon, Devo. Give me a chance.* I wasn't sure I deserved one, but I was desperate for her to text me back.

> This isn't about sex. Sorry, I kind of made it sound like it was.

I waited, holding my breath, like if I let it out, the possibility of her responding would be carried away with the wind.

Three dots appeared, then disappeared for thirty seconds.

. . .

I was about to storm into Red Wild to demand her attention. All I wanted was her eyes on me, and maybe I wanted to hold her heart in my hand and protect it and love it and watch it grow.

But then the three dots reappeared.

. . .

What time?

Yes!

> Unless there's an emergency, I should be home by 9.

. . .

Do you PROMISE not to hurt me???

> I'm doing everything I can think not to.

That's not a promise, Abey.

> I promise.

And I hoped like hell I could keep it.

It was the slowest day on freakin' record.

There had been an hour in the afternoon when Roxanne, Frank, and I sat around the break room in front of an oscillating fan, sweating through our uniforms and staring at the walls. Shelley sat at the desk out front with a cold pack slung over the back of her neck and a little plastic table fan aimed right at her face.

Dan was still pissed, so he ate his lunch in his cruiser out back. At least he had good air conditioning. The sheriff's station felt like a swamp in the dregs of summer in fucking Louisiana. Even my ears were sweating.

After I texted Devo and she granted me the chance I'd been hoping for, I'd gone over to the farmers market to talk to Sissy. She promised not to dump any more beverages on Dan's head as long as he loosened up a bit.

I couldn't guarantee he would. There were a lot of promises I wanted to make but couldn't, and I didn't like how it felt. I wanted to be someone who could make them, and more than that, I wanted to be someone who could keep her promises, someone who could be *counted on* to keep them.

It applied in my job, and it applied to Devo.

If I could have, I would've promised her the world. She deserved it.

And there it was.

I'd never felt that way about anyone before, had never imagined how bad it would feel to break a promise to a woman like her before.

I'd never wanted to offer so much of myself to another person, to have them depend on me, to have the things in their life rely on the things in mine.

I'd never wanted someone to love me the way I wanted Devo to love me. Down to my soul. To my bones.

It didn't matter what I looked like, if my hair was a mess or my house was. I wanted her to love me because I was me. Because I was worthy of her love. I knew I could be.

Devo was more than worthy. I loved her conviction for everything she believed in. I loved how she fought tooth and nail for things that were important to her and how she cared so much for people she'd never even met, the way she cared for the people who came to Ace's House, the way she loved Theo and Vern, the way she loved her mama—because of what was inside them.

And I loved the way she made me feel, like with just a look, I'd been wrapped up tight in her arms.

I loved how I felt when she looked in my eyes and found good there. And strength.

Frank had been right that I could be myself, and Devo deserved someone who was brave.

When I spoke to her, Sissy had some advice on the subject, though I couldn't imagine how she'd even known I was struggling, but it was Sissy. She was like the unofficial grandma of Wisper. She knew everything there was to know about everyone in this damn town.

She'd said life is full of things that "ain't fair" and things we wish we could change, but if I let an opportunity for happiness pass me up because I couldn't drag myself out of my own wallowing, if I couldn't rise above my own fear, then she would dump a smoothie over my head too.

And Sissy had been right. Devo made me feel one hundred feet tall and like the richest person in the world. She made me believe I could accomplish anything, even though I didn't have faith in myself sometimes. I acted like I did, but it wasn't always true.

Devo believed. So I could too. Was I really willing to walk away from that?

From her?

CHAPTER TWENTY

ABEY

At 9:05 P.M., a tinny knock on my aluminum screen door wiped the cheesy smile off my face, and I sprang up from my spot on the couch, where I'd been thinking about Devo and waiting for her.

Suddenly, my hands began to sweat, my heart pounded, and everything I wanted to say to her became a swirling jumble of spit in my mouth.

She pushed open the door, peeking her head in before I could get to it. "Abey? Is this okay?"

"Yes," I said. "Please come in."

She stepped over the threshold, pulling the screen shut behind her and dropping her big messenger bag by my work boots on the floor.

I walked behind her silently and shut the big door, then locked it. I needed privacy and security for the things I wanted to tell her. All my windows were open though. It had become habit 'cause my little apartment didn't have air conditioning, and this summer had been a constant heat-wave. I'd never been so ready for fall to kick in, but already, tonight, the temperature had begun to drop. Today was the last day forecasted to be hot. Just imagining the crisp breeze that would soon be whipping down from the Tetons made me feel cooler, and soon they'd be topped with snow again too. Seeing the snow always made the shivers set in.

"Hi," she said when I stood in front of her.

I felt my soul light up as I looked at her. She was a vision, still wearing a black "Hike it Red Wild Style" shirt with khaki shorts and black flip-flops. Her toenails had been painted black too. But under her clothes, she was a strong woman. Even the way she stood was powerful, with her hand fixed on her hip. She knew what she wanted and what she didn't, and she wouldn't accept anything less than total honesty.

"Hi."

The side of her mouth lifted a little, but she cocked her head. "So…?"

Oh, right. She was waiting for me to do more than stare at her. I flung my arm toward my couch. "Sit with me?"

"Okay." She wasn't sure about me yet, was probably doubting me, wondering what I could possibly say to make up for everything I hadn't said earlier. And I had no doubt she'd walk away if I didn't say it now.

"C'mere." I patted the cushion next to me when I sat on the couch, tucking my bare foot under my thigh and turning toward her as she sat two feet away. She smelled like fresh honeydew, sweet and earthy, so I breathed her deep into my lungs. It had to be her lip gloss. Her lips glistened while her brown eyes searched mine. I wanted to be the reason they lit up, and I suddenly heard myself asking, "Will you go to the dance with me?"

So much for all the things I'd planned to say, things that made sense.

Her face scrunched up in confusion, eyebrows dipping down in doubt. "Huh?"

"Oh, wait, sorry," I said, laughing at myself. "I meant to say some other stuff first and then ask you, but guess I got a little ahead of myself."

She smiled, but it felt guarded. She had come, though, and she seemed open to hearing what I had to say, but she was still wary. She didn't plan to get invested if anything I said even had the possibility to cause her pain. I understood that, and I didn't blame her. I hadn't exactly given her anything steady to hold onto.

"I've never had a girlfriend. I told you that," I said, and she blinked. "I guess I tried to convince myself it was a necessary fact of workin' the job I do, that I needed to be discreet so I didn't ruffle anybody's feathers, but that's not true. I mean, yes, the whole gay thing does factor in. Obviously. Look where we live. And in my job, it's… Well, you can imagine. But plenty of people live their lives out in the open. Like you."

She nodded.

"Theo and Brady do. Shit, there's even some cowboys who do. That's pretty brave around here. So, I guess I'm thinkin', why can't I?"

She blinked once. "So… you're askin' me out? Like, officially? *Out* out? Out in the open?"

"Yes."

Her hesitation hung thick in the air between us. A lot of it. Had I screwed up too badly already?

"I'm scared," she said.

"Me too." That was the biggest understatement I'd ever made.

"Yeah, but I'm scared for a different reason than you."

I reached for her hand and held it. "Why're you scared?"

"Because if you change your mind, if it's too hard or people react badly, then you're gonna hurt me. I can already feel the rip wantin' to start." She touched her chest with her free hand, right where her heart would be if I could've seen inside her. If she'd let me. "Can you promise you won't?"

How could I promise that if I couldn't promise myself the same thing?

Whatever she saw in my eyes pissed her off. She pulled her hand out of my grasp and leaned away from me. "What the hell happened to you? Why does the word 'promise' make you squeamish?"

Of course she'd noticed.

I sighed, and my heart broke as I admitted the truth. "People break promises too easily. They don't mean anything. They're just words."

"They mean somethin' if—" She cleared her throat. "If the person makin' the promise cares for you, they can mean the world."

I hoped she did, but I had to ask, "You care about me?" I needed to hear her say it.

"'Course I do." She lowered her eyes, playing with a rip in the knee of my jeans, pulling at the frayed edges. "Do you care about me?" There was a mountain of vulnerability in that one small question.

Lifting her chin with a touch of my fingertip, when she finally looked in my eyes, I said, "More than I know how to say."

She beamed, lighting up my whole house with her smile while I worked out the rest of what I needed to say.

"You've been in love before." It wasn't a question. I'd known since that first night, when she told me some ex had broken her heart.

"Yeah," she said, "but it was that stupid first love, where

all you see is the good stuff while all the bad is buildin' up in the background, gettin' ready to take you down."

"Like what bad stuff?"

Devo shrugged. "She decided she wasn't gay after all. Or maybe she's bi now. I don't know, but after three years together, all of a sudden, she wanted some dickhead over in Idaho. Some farm boy."

"What was her name?"

"Bella."

"Hm. I don't like it," I said with a smirk. "Sounds like that chick from the vampire book everyone wants me to read."

"Sam's makin' you read *Twilight*?"

"No, she refuses to assign it for book club, but Aislinn and Cal keep pushin' for it, which makes no sense. Cal DuBois readin' about sparkly vampires? As if."

Devo giggled. Just the sound of it resurrected something inside me.

"I'm sorry she did that to you," I said, sobering the moment again. I tucked her hair back behind her ear for the thousandth time, and she grabbed my wrist and held it to her cheek.

"Abey, I want this. I like you. A lot. But I'm scared you don't know what you want. How can I trust this?" She motioned between us. "I don't wanna get hurt again. How can I trust you not to break my heart?"

I dropped my hand back into my lap and nodded, taking the deepest breath I could. How could she know me and trust me if I didn't show her all the parts of me, even the bad ones? Even the ones that hurt so much to say.

It was time.

"When I was little, my daddy was my whole world. My hero. The biggest, strongest, most wonderful person in my universe. He loved me to the ends of the earth, told everyone I was the apple of his eye, that I was his angel.

"No matter what I did, in his eyes, it couldn't be wrong. My brothers got in trouble all the time, but not me. I was daddy's little girl. I can't even tell you how many times he said he'd love me forever. And I'd say, 'You promise?' and we'd pinky swear to love each other till the end of time.

"Then I grew up. I realized I was *not* the same as everyone around me. I couldn't have cared less about the cute boys my friends were always goin' on about. They were gross and sweaty, and when my friends would talk about kissin' or makin' out with guys, it just felt wrong. Finally, I figured it out because, when I thought about those things with other girls, I had an entirely different reaction." Cocking my head, I raised my eyebrows, and Devo nodded. She understood.

"One day, my friend Paula came to my house. It was my fifteenth birthday, and we were out in the barn. We had this game where we named the sheep when my daddy would round 'em up for vaccines or vet checks, and then, whoever remembered the most names next time she came over, they won.

"There were hundreds of sheep." I laughed. "No one could remember that many, and every time we played the game, the names changed, but Paula won that day. She remembered twenty sheep's names. We didn't actually keep track, but we were just bein' silly, jumpin' up and down, squealin' and laughin', and I kissed her. I didn't mean to. It just happened. I loved her, had loved her since we were six. But we were growin' up. Things were changin'."

I took a deep breath. Here was the hard part. The painful part.

"My daddy walked in right then. He saw me kissin' her. She kissed me back, too, which surprised the fuck outta me, but he was irate. It was the only time my daddy ever laid hands on me. He slapped me across the face, and he took his love away after that. He never tried to talk to me about it, and everything changed. He forbade Paula from ever comin' over again.

"He'd promised to love me forever, but the day he found out I would never be the daughter he wanted—a *normal* daughter—he broke that promise, and he broke it again every day after till the day he died. He said he didn't even want me at the hospital. My mama and my brothers were all there at the end of my daddy's life, but he was so ashamed of me, he didn't even want to say goodbye."

Devo placed the pad of her thumb right over the pulse of my blood beneath my skin on my wrist. "I'm so *fucking* sorry he did that to you."

It still cut like a knife, still felt like it might rip my heart to shreds. But I still missed him.

"It hurts to know the person I adored most in the world couldn't even look at me. But now, all I can think about is, what if I promise somethin' to you, and then I break my promise because… I dunno. Because of work or life or whatever. If I hurt you the same way he hurt me, I couldn't take that, Devo. What if you hurt me like that?"

"Abey, I would *never*. I'm so sorry." She reached for my hands and held them between us. "You didn't deserve that."

Still trying to cling to denial, I mumbled, "It's not like what happened to Sylvie. He only slapped me across the face the one time. He didn't beat me or even kick me out."

"Maybe not," Devo said, "but once is enough, and withholding love is just as bad, just as painful, in a different way."

"Yeah. Guess you're right."

I'd never thought it was that bad. Parents swatted their

kids all the time, or they used to. But Devo was right that it was different.

Before that day in our barn, I'd never seen the kind of anger and disgust like I saw on my daddy's face.

I hadn't even known that kind of hate existed.

I'd heard about it, of course, but I'd never really *known* it. And it had never even crossed my mind that he could be capable of it.

"He made me ashamed of what I was. He made me want to hide my sexuality, 'cause if my own father couldn't love me for who I truly was, who else would?"

Tilting her head, Devo gripped my wrist harder. "But Abey, don't you see? There are so many people who love you for who you truly are. This whole town loves you."

"Sure. Maybe they do, and I work hard to appear love-able. But they also don't really *know* me, and what if once they know the truth, when it's out there for all to see, what if they take their love back? Right now? Right when I'm step-pin' into this new job, right when their lives depend on them respectin' me and knowin' I've got their backs?"

"Have you ever thought that maybe if you're honest with 'em, they might trust you more?"

I snorted. "Right. That'll happen."

Devo sighed, but she didn't let go of my wrist. She rubbed her thumb over it. "I can't tell you what to do. All I can tell you is that I will support whatever decision you make, but I can't live in the dark. I want to see where this can go between you and me, but it hurt too much the first time. I can't be your secret. I just can't. It's not who I am."

"I don't want that either. That's why I'm askin' you on a date."

"To the fall dance," she said flatly. "To the place literally everyone who lives in Wisper will be… at the same time?"

When she put it like that, my heart raced inside my chest. I thought I might puke. But I said, "Yes."

I said it 'cause I could picture it: laughing while we line danced together, tripping over our feet, holding her hand while I paraded her around, showing off my beautiful girl-friend. It was everything I'd ever wanted in my life.

Someone to call my own.

And Devo could be my own. I'd be scared, but I'd be damn proud to have her on my arm. No one else would do.

She was it for me.

"Can I think about it?"

Shit. That wasn't the response I'd been hoping for. "Y-yeah. Of course. Take as much time as you need."

She pushed my chin up with a nudge from her finger this time when I stared down at my lap. I didn't know what else to say. "I want to, Abey. I really do."

I nodded, trying to smile, but I was doubting everything now. If she cared about me the way I did her, wouldn't she have screamed yes from the rooftops?

"C'mon." She slid from the couch and stood, dragging me toward the back of my apartment by my hand.

"Where we goin'?"

"You said you had a bed, right?"

CHAPTER TWENTY-ONE

DEVO

ABEY LOOKED relieved as I led her to her bedroom.

Everything she'd said was "right."

With everything I had inside me, I wanted to believe in her—in us, in what we could be together—but if Abey hurt me, I'd never recover. I knew it now.

Love was all light and sunshine. It felt so good… until it didn't anymore.

That light could betray you. Lull you into a false sense of security.

Who was I kidding? I had already fallen in love with her. Her light had begun to settle under my skin the night I picked her up with my pizza.

Watching her closely over the summer and getting to really know her had shown me just how beautiful she was and how good and how loving she was to everyone around her. She even cared about cranky old Red Graves, and he barely deserved it. His status as a human being was the only thing that made him halfway worthy, at least that was what I'd thought a week ago. Maybe my opinion was changing.

Maybe what he'd gone through with his wife wasn't so different than what I'd gone through with my ex.

But Abey hadn't judged Red for his bad attitude. She gave her love and protection anyway, just like my mom gave hers to every living being on the planet. Until they proved themselves undeserving, they loved everyone. Was that why I was so drawn to Abey?

I had been the one going around claiming to love and accept every sexual identity—every single identity, period— but I hadn't accepted or loved Red. I hadn't even thought he had even been deserving of *other* people's love, let alone mine.

But none of it mattered if Abey wasn't sure. I *needed* her to be sure before we went public with this. Before the reality of it in the public eye stressed us both out and cracked all that was good between us.

We had to know if we could patch it back up or if everything would just fall apart.

Sex wouldn't make her sure, but I wanted her just as much as I could see in her eyes that she wanted me, and I wanted to show her what we could be. I wanted her to know in her bones that I accepted whoever she was, and I wanted to make her come so hard she'd scream, so she'd never forget tonight.

So that no matter what happened between us, she'd never forget how it felt when she truly shined her light on the world.

I knew the passion was there inside her. She was always so careful, so steady and level-headed, but I wanted to be the reason Abey screamed. I wanted her to throw a brick through a window for once.

Envisioning a future when I looked in her blue eyes, I

could see a life. A house. A family maybe someday. I pictured kissing her in the morning and again at night before bed, where I'd cuddle up next to her watching trash TV while she read her romance books.

I knew she could see it, too, as I led her to her bed. "What're we doin'?"

When I didn't answer right away, she tugged on my hand, and I turned to face her. "I wanna make you scream."

An eyebrow arched, but her eyes slid to the open window next to her bed.

"No one's home," I said. "There are no cars parked downstairs."

She dipped her head, her eyes flashed midnight, and she licked her lips.

I had been about to pull her mouth to mine when we stepped over the threshold into her bedroom, but my eyes landed on something on the wall behind her shoulder next to her dresser. "Who is that? Abey, is there somethin' you need to tell me?"

"Huh?" She turned her head, her eyes going to where mine were. "Oh shit. I should've taken that down. Oh my God, I'm so embarrassed."

She pulled away from me and turned to rip the Taylor Swift poster from her wall. Her fingers lifted the edge of the shiny paper away from her bedroom wall, but she froze in place.

"You, Abey Lee, Deputy Sheriff of Wisper, Wyoming, are a *Swiftie*?"

"I can't do it," she said in mock-despair, slapping a hand to her chest. "I can't rip it."

"I cannot believe you like Taylor Swift." I crossed my arms over my chest as she turned back to me, chagrin and laughter in her eyes. Her cheeks had turned bright pink with embarrassment.

"Hey now, she's a wordsmith. I don't get why it's a bad thing to like her music. Tell me your head doesn't bop along to the beat when you hear it."

I couldn't deny it, and it fit that Abey liked her music. They were both such uplifting people. They always saw the good in others. At least, that was the vibe I'd picked up about good ol' Tay-Tay.

That hopefulness made me want Abey more.

"Forget about her," I said breathlessly, and she leaned into me, walking forward, and our feet shuffled to the bed behind us.

We hit the mattress and became a tangle of legs and arms then. Lips, tongues, and fingers too.

I kicked off my flip-flops, breathing, "Wait," as she reached for my shorts, trying to unhook the button.

"What?" she asked uncertainly, her blond brows bunching together. God, I'd never seen anyone more beautiful.

"Will you get my bag?"

Her eyes grew big and round, like a cartoon character. "Why?"

"I brought somethin'."

She stopped moving, and when she spoke, the sound of her voice hummed deep inside me. "'Somethin'?"

Reaching between our bodies, I popped my fly for her. "Yeah. Somethin'. Go get it?"

She dashed from her bedroom, and I couldn't help but look for more incriminating evidence.

There wasn't much. A tall black metal gun safe stood in one corner, and a little unease settled in my chest as I looked at it. I'd never really been around guns, other than the last week working at Red Wild, but I knew they were necessary in Abey's work. My apprehension of them had more to do with the sadness I felt about the necessity of guns as tools for law enforcement than it did my dislike of them. Knowing she carried them and might have to use them on someone like she had not so long ago on Sylvie's father made me worry for her. But it was also a little hot that she had the knowledge and capability to wield a gun. I couldn't lie to myself about that.

Her sheets were crisp white, and her bedspread was blue, like her cerulean eyes. Besides the picture of Tay-Tay holding a microphone and dressed in black booty shorts with her signature red lips, there were only two other pieces of art hanging on the walls—two square paintings she'd hung next to each other that looked like they might've been painted by a kid. Maybe Athena had painted them, or possibly Abey's partner's foster daughter, Nic, had painted them. I thought I remembered hearing Murph say his little sister liked art.

The only possibly incriminating things I could find were stacked on top of her small dark-wood desk in the corner: three piles of colorful books lined against the wall. I wanted to investigate further, to see what she'd been reading in her kinky book club, but then she was back, and she dropped my gigantic bag next to me on the bed.

"C'mon," I said, and I scooted up and over, patting the bed beside me. "Lie here."

"Okay...?" She looked unsure, but I had plans for Abey Lee.

"Just do it."

"I'm a little scared," she said, eyeing my bag as she sat and then scooted back to her headboard. "What's in that thing?"

"You'll see." The object I was looking for was right there,

ready for me to pull it out when the right moment presented itself. "Lie down."

She did, and I straddled her legs as I unbuttoned her jeans. She filled them out so well. It really was a shame to slide them down her long legs, but what hid underneath tempted me even more. She reached for my hips as I leaned forward, and she lifted up and met me in the middle to steal a kiss.

"I like kissin' you," she whispered. "I love your mouth. 'Specially when you're smart-mouthin' me."

Breathing a laugh, I said, "I'm about to wipe that smirk right off those sexy lips."

"Oh yeah? How?"

Sliding my hand beneath her undies, I found what I wanted, wet and hot and ready. She bucked her hips, rubbing her pussy against my fingers, coating them in her silky wetness.

I worked her slowly. "Take off your shirt."

"Yes, ma'am."

She moaned softly as I scooted lower to remove her jeans fully, and her light-blue cotton underwear went next. She pulled her T-shirt over her head and then unhooked her bra and tossed it across the room, and her full, heavy breasts spread apart above her ribcage as she lay back. Her nipples had already hardened into rigid peaks for me, and I hadn't even touched them yet.

They distracted me from my mission.

"Your breasts are—" I groaned, diving between them, licking and nipping the warm mounds gently with my teeth, my head going back and forth between them as I dipped my fingers inside her body and pumped.

She moaned and reached for my shirt, trying to lift it by the hem, but we became a jumble of limbs again.

"Stop," she said, laughing. "This ain't gonna work."

Suddenly, my hips were pinned between her knees, and she flipped us. She knelt above me, but the laughing stopped and was replaced with a look full of lust so intense that butterflies flitted in my stomach. They marched lower to the quick pace of my heartbeat until I felt my thighs get wet.

She slid my shorts down my legs, catching my underwear with them, and stared at my body as I lifted my tank top over my head. I threw it somewhere, but I didn't know where it landed because my eyes couldn't move from hers.

"I'm overwhelmed by you," she whispered.

Swallowing hard, she lowered herself above my body, resting her weight on one hip beside me, raising a hand to tuck a lock of hair behind my ear.

Leaning closer, she kissed me, but her eyes stayed open. So did mine, but only for a second, because then the slow, warm glide of her tongue against mine made me crazy. I wrapped my arms around her neck, tangling my fingers in her hair while she kissed me stupid.

Abey's kisses were like nothing I'd ever felt. They were the main attraction, and my whole body felt like a live wire, humming and buzzing deep inside from just her lips on mine, her tongue sweeping inside, smoothing over mine. The repetitive motion lulled me into some deep place, like I was being dragged under the sea, but if this was what drowning felt like, I'd die willingly for one more taste of Abey Lee.

I pulled her closer, breathing her in and feeling every press of her fingertips as they glided over my skin so carefully, like I was precious to her.

She lowered her head, leaving me breathless as she licked my nipple once, twice, a third time, and then she groaned and sucked it into her mouth. Her fingers slid between my legs, and she rubbed slowly.

It felt good to be with her like this, naked and bared to her. *With* her.

My legs opened wider, and she moved between them, focusing all her attention on my other breast, fingering me and swirling her thumb over my wet clit in tight circles.

"Abey."

Her voice was the softest hum. "Hmm?"

What had I wanted to say? To do? I knew there was something.

She slid lower, kissing each rib as she passed, dipping her tongue in my navel, licking a path down my low belly and kissing the annoying pat of fat there. She nipped it, growling softly in the back of her throat, and lowered even further as she wrapped her hands around the backs of my thighs. She pulled them open as far as they could go and nestled her face between them.

She whispered, her warm breath rushing against my most private place, and it made me shiver. "Forget what you wanted to say?"

"Yeah," I breathed as she blew on my pussy, making the wet wetter, making me gush for her.

She licked once, lapping my cum onto her tongue.

I looked down between my legs as she drew it into her mouth and swallowed. Her eyes rolled shut.

"Oh God. Do that again."

She repeated the motion, this time dragging the tip of her tongue to my clit and flicking it quickly, pumping inside me with three fingers.

My whole body arched, my legs shook, and it made her moan.

This wasn't going how I'd planned. "M-my bag. In my bag."

I heard my keys jingle when she slipped a hand in there,

and then the buzz of the clitoral stimulator I'd brought to use on her filled the room, and I opened my eyes as she pressed it to my clit.

I gasped.

The smile on her face was the sexiest I'd ever seen. "Devo, you naughty, *naughty* woman."

CHAPTER TWENTY-TWO

ABEY

"I BROUGHT it to use on *you*," she said and yelped when I pressed the handy "women's little helper" harder against her clit.

It was a handheld stimulator, its sole purpose to deliver tiny bursts of air right where a woman needed it most, but every time Devo squirmed and undulated to the pulsing, her moans growing louder and huskier, I felt the vibrations deep inside *my* body.

It was a buzzing. A yearning that set me on fire for her.

"You like toys?" I asked, completely unabashed, surprising myself.

I'd never talked about sex toys or masturbation with anyone, which was stupid. It wasn't like everyone on the planet and their grandma didn't do it. But I wanted to share this with her, wanted her to know this part of me. A woman's personal satisfaction was not an unimportant part of her life.

Also, I wanted her to know what I liked. Logically, I knew I shouldn't feel shame about it, but I felt more vulnerable than I ever had.

Apparently, she did too. She pressed her teeth into her

bottom lip, and I watched how they indented the soft skin. "Sometimes."

I lifted off her, her risqué little toy quickly forgotten, and she followed me with her eyes as I rolled off the bed and lunged toward my dresser. Pulling open the top drawer, I dug through it.

When I turned back, her mouth popped open as soon as she saw the harness I was stepping into. I dragged the leather straps slowly up my thighs, and she almost choked on the words, "Abey, that's a…"

Finally, I had rendered Devo speechless. If you'd asked me yesterday, I wouldn't have thought it possible.

"A strap-on. I've always wanted to use it. Is it okay?" Nerves and uncertainty were carving out a hole in my stomach, but I so desperately wanted her to say yes.

She nodded quickly, pressing her legs together and moaning softly in what I hoped was anticipation. The sound was so quiet, I didn't think I was supposed to hear it.

"Just lookin' at you in that thing is makin' me wet. The way it hugs your hips…" Her legs fell open, and she let them drop to the mattress.

"What?" I looked down at myself, then at her. Did I look ridiculous? But if I imagined the black leather harness strapped around *her* body, I practically came right then and there, standing in the middle of my bedroom.

"You are the *sexiest* woman I've ever seen," she said, and the side of her mouth tipped up, her eyes traveling up to mine. "Get over here before I come without you." Her chest rose and fell faster and faster, and I was having a hard time not staring at what the movement did to her little tits.

My responding smile felt dirty. *Oh!* But I forgot the most important part.

Turning back to my dresser, I removed the sky-blue dildo

from its case. I'd ordered it online months ago for just this kind of occasion, but back then, I could've only hoped it would be with Devo.

Attaching the dildo to the harness, I turned toward her and instantly felt ridiculous. I had a blue dick attached to my body, for shit's sake, like one of those dudes from the alien romance Ace had brought to book club.

But Devo didn't seem to think I looked silly. Her chocolate eyes flashed with lust, and she reached for my body with her grabby fingers as I turned back to my dresser for the little bottle of lubricant I kept with the dildo.

I crawled over her again and kneeled between her legs, running my hands up and down the insides of her thighs, feeling how perfectly soft they were, and then I dipped a finger in her slick and dragged it up to her clit. I grabbed the lube and coated the dildo, then wiped the excess on my discarded T-shirt, dropped it to the floor, and leaned over her, sliding my legs between hers.

She gulped. "It's huge."

"It feels good," I whispered, and she reached up to nip at my chin with her teeth.

As my body hovered above hers, she watched me from behind her long eyelashes, and her eyes tracked my every move. The hunger I saw in those dark, heavy-lidded pools made me brave.

"You can take it," I said. "I wanna make you come. *Hard*."

She nodded her permission, and I lowered back onto my knees and rubbed that long, hard shaft of silicone along her slit.

Pushing in slowly, I watched her face. She gasped and I slowed. I planted my elbows next to her head on the pillow, never taking my eyes off hers. The length of her body below mine, anchored beneath me, felt like heaven.

She had never been more beautiful than she was in this moment, turning into liquid lust below me, her black hair the sexiest contrast to my white sheets.

She accepted me fully. I probably shouldn't have been so surprised, but I'd truly never imagined finding someone who would.

I'd bought the harness thinking I'd never get to use it. This was my first time fucking anyone like this. "You okay?"

"Yes," she breathed. "Your pillow smells like you. Like honey. You smell sweet."

She trapped my body between her knees as she bent them, and I moved my hips in a slow and steady push and pull. I grazed my lips over hers, nipping her bottom lip with my teeth. "I'm not thinkin' sweet things right now, Devo."

"This isn't goin' how I planned," she said, but she writhed against me, rolling her hips up to meet mine while she looked down to watch me move against her.

Everything was hot and slick between us. She moaned again and again, beads of sweat forming quickly on her chest and belly, and I felt it wetting the back of my neck. She grew silent, but she breathed harder with every glide.

Her body began to tighten, every muscle beginning to shake. "Oh," she begged over and over. "Oh yeah, Abey. Faster."

I smiled and adjusted the little nub attached to the dildo so it hit her right where she needed it. Depressing the invisible button near the base, the attachment began to buzz as I increased my pace, just like her tiny stimulator, the thing she'd brought with her tonight, thinking she'd shock me.

But I was the one doing the shocking.

I felt the buzzing, too, and I could already see her release taking root inside her. There was an electricity building on her skin. It pulled me closer, made me move even faster. My hips worked out their own rhythm, a roll and soft push each time I stroked the dildo inside her, and her eyes rolled shut in pleasure.

Her mouth popped open, more sexy gasps spilling out. I swallowed them down and kissed her as she came closer and closer to release.

Our bodies moved together, sliding against each other in the quickly cooling September night air floating in through my bedroom window, and it surrounded us in its gentle embrace as the season seemed to change from summer to fall in a second.

I wanted to remember this night forever, our connection and the way her body fit together with mine, the heat of her skin, the sounds she made, and the taste of her need on my tongue. I would always remember the sweet taste of her mouth and the feel of her breath on my skin.

Nothing had ever felt so good. No woman had ever given me anything like what Devo had given me tonight. I wanted her so much, I felt like I would cease to exist if I couldn't touch her.

Working hard to make her feel good was the sexiest thing I'd ever known, and I felt happy and at peace in a way I'd never experienced before. Maybe it was because I'd never felt so much like myself.

This was who I was born to be—someone who wanted women, loved women, and found pleasure in them. With them.

With *her*.

She gasped in a breath when I slowed my body, gliding the dildo out of her slowly, watching what it was doing to her between her legs. What *I* was doing to her. "Abey, I've never —this is—"

"I know," I whispered.

She patted the bed beside my knee in the mess of covers bunching up around us till she found her forgotten toy. She held the button down for a few seconds to turn it on and then searched between our bodies. When she found it, she pushed the stimulator against my clit.

I groaned when the air pulsed hard and fast, and my ass cheeks tightened under her legs wrapped around them. The harness bit hard into my hips, but I couldn't have cared less. I was so thankful I'd ordered the crotchless model so she could touch me while I fucked her.

My breasts smashed against hers, connecting our bodies together as I pushed inside her again. We were fused together so deliciously that the vibrator stayed right where I needed it, despite the slick sweat covering us both. She tucked the handle beneath the harness strap where it crisscrossed low over my hips, then wrapped her arms around my neck, reaching to capture my lips with hers as her fingers dug into my hair.

I kissed her, fucking and rubbing, both of us moaning, rocking together, getting lost inside each other as my hair fell around her face, shielding us from everything.

It was Devo and me against the world.

"Come like you mean it," she whispered. "Scream for me."

"Devo. I… I—"

Electricity seemed to rise from her skin, and it transferred from every part of her to me. My core pulsed hard with it, and the sound breaking free from my mouth sounded foreign.

It felt so fucking good, the delicious coiling and tightening deep inside me.

I moved faster as she reached between us again, applying as much pressure as she could to the little device nestled against my clit. Buzzing, buzzing, buzzing until…

My whole body stiffened against hers. My toes curled as I rushed the dildo in once more. I needed her to come like it was a biological imperative. I needed to give her back what she was giving me.

She locked her lips onto mine, and I came, letting loose a cry into her mouth so primal, it set free something inside me.

It was awe and desire, love and reverence for this person who accepted the real me, who let me love her the way I'd been longing to love, who didn't judge me for wanting something no one else thought I should.

It was release.

It was permission and guidance.

It was *everything*.

"Yes, Abey," she whispered, matching the slow roll of her hips to mine while I fell slowly down from my high, her mouth still on mine, her breath in my lungs and her arms wrapped tight around me.

My hair whispered across her breasts as my head fell to the middle of her chest. Goosechills rose all over her, and the rest of me settled onto Devo while she came apart beneath me, crying out for us both, 'cause we had come home.

I had always belonged here with her. I just hadn't known it till now.

CHAPTER TWENTY-THREE

DEVO

"THESE TWO FRECKLES look like an ice cream cone," Abey said, tracing her index finger over my inner thigh and kissing where two freckles had always been. One almost looked like an upside down triangle, and the other was a perfect circle above it.

After literally the most mind-blowing sexual experience I'd ever had, she pulled me to her tiny shower in her itty-bitty bathroom in the hall, and we'd washed each other's bodies. She made me come again with her mouth on mine and her fingers inside me, and then she knelt in front of me on the hard shower floor, dragging her hands all over my soapy body, eating me out while I writhed and thrashed against the tile wall.

Something was different about her now as we lay in her bed, replete and boneless. She seemed looser, more open, silly, like the sex had freed her somehow, but for me, it was the opposite.

Not in a bad way, but what we'd done felt serious to me. Heavy. Impactful. But I didn't know why. I knew what it meant for Abey. At least, I thought I did. She'd never had that kind of connection with another woman before. But I had.

I was comfortable with my sexuality, had never viewed it through a negative or doubtful lens. It never made sense to me when people like Red Graves acted so negatively about someone else's private thoughts, identity, or who a stranger invited into their bed. Who they held hands with or kissed. What did it matter to them? Who did it hurt?

But maybe with Red, it was more of a personal thing.

I couldn't know for sure, but it made me hurt for Abey, because she'd never felt like she could show her true self to the world. She hadn't felt like she would be respected if she came completely out.

"What're you thinkin' about?" she asked, drawing a line from my ice cream cone, up my belly, to my breast. She lowered her head, sucking my nipple slowly into her warm mouth. With the heel of her hand pressing hard on my hip bone, she flicked her tongue lazily over the stiff peak. Her fingers reached around to dig into my ass cheek, like she was branding me with her handprint, leaving a mark, claiming me again.

"I was just thinkin' that you're insatiable."

"Mm. Now I've got you in my bed, I may never let you go."

Releasing my breast, she lifted up and straddled me. Her lips were wet and rosy, matching the blush of her cheeks. The flush of color made her look younger than thirty-two, but when she settled her body over mine, her soft pubic hair rubbed against my belly, and there was no innocence left lingering in her gaze. "But now tell me what you're *really* thinkin'."

I took a deep breath, filling my lungs with her honey scent. "I was thinkin' about what we just did."

"Was it... Was that okay for you?"

"Okay?" I breathed a laugh. "Abey, it was..." I was at a loss for words. How could I explain to her how it had felt? The physical feelings were easy, but the other stuff, not so much. Sliding out from under her, I sat up, and she kneeled in front of me on the bed, sitting back on her heels. "It was beautiful."

"Yeah, but was it, I dunno, too much? The harness and the..."

"No."

She looked down at the bedspread, plucking at the fabric. "I always kinda felt ashamed." She looked up, pegging me with her gorgeous eyes, blue like the endless clear sky over our little mountain town. "I know what you're thinkin'. But I meant I was embarrassed about the dildo."

"Oh?"

"I don't know much about that kinda thing. I mean, I've never watched porn. I was always too afraid of who might know, like maybe there are internet bots who keep track of that shit, and somehow it'll get out to the public." She laughed. "But I saw this TV show once where two women used a strap-on. I think it was on Netflix. The minute I knew somethin' like that existed, I wanted it. But does that make me... Does it say somethin' about me? About the kind of lesbian I must be if I like that?"

I could feel my brows furrowing. "I don't understand."

"Remember that date you picked me up from a while back?"

Seriously? Did I remember the first time she'd touched her lips to mine? Of course I did. I could *never* forget that night. "Yes."

"Well, my date—cute Kayla was her name." I laughed,

but she said, "I don't wanna talk about her. Her eyelashes traumatized me."

I giggled, reaching out for her, drawing my fingertips slowly over her collarbones.

"I'm tryin' to be serious here," she said with a smirk. "Anyway, cute Kayla asked if I was butch. And she asked what kind of women I liked. So, does usin' a dildo mean I'm butch? That I think of myself as a man or that I want to be like a man?" She blinked fast, uncertainty making her nervous, and it all made more sense now, her question about the definition of butch in my truck that first night. "'Cause I don't. Not that I'm sayin' there's anything wrong with butch lesbians. I dunno why I can't get this outta my head, but I mean, I guess I don't know what I am, but that's not why I like what we did."

I climbed up on my knees, too, facing her. "Why did you like what we did?"

As she breathed deeply, thinking about what she wanted to say, I reached for her hand and twined my fingers between hers, then did the same with her other hand. The vulnerability in her smile made me want to reach forward to kiss her, so I did. A light kiss on her mouth, then little baby kisses down her jaw.

Squeezing my fingers gently, she said, "Because it was with you. Because I made you feel good. And if you want to, you can wear it. You can do that to me too. It's not a power thing. I wasn't tryin' to dominate you or anything like that."

My voice hummed softly against her neck. "It'd be okay if it *was* a power thing. I might like you to dominate me."

She bit the inside of her cheek, her lip dipping down with the movement, when I leaned back a little to look at her.

"Really?"

I shrugged. "Maybe. But if you don't feel butch, you

don't have to be butch. You don't have to *be* anything. Just be you."

She smiled. Her face lit up like there was a sixty-watt bulb behind it. "Thank you."

She wrapped me up in her arms and turned, pulling me down on top of her as she fell back to the bed.

I straddled her this time, loving her warmth beneath me, loving the way her shiny, freshly washed blond curls spread out over her pillow, how the pink in her cheeks deepened and how her smile felt like it was just for me. Like I was the only person on the planet lucky enough to see her shine.

A light glinted in her eye as she spread her arms out wide across her bed. "C'mon now. Smear that ice cream cone all over me, baby. Do your worst."

———

Abey went to work, and I hurried home early the next morning to shower and change my clothes.

I'd almost made it to my bedroom before my mom stopped me. "You didn't text me last night," she said. "You do remember promisin' me you'd always text if you weren't comin' home, right? I don't need to know what you get up to or where you are, but it would be nice to know my daughter hasn't become roadkill out on Route 20."

"Ah, shit," I breathed, freezing mid-step as she surprised me in the hallway. "I'm sorry, Mom. I totally forgot."

I could feel her eyes on me. I had always been able to.

"I'm glad to see you're in one piece."

Turning in my bedroom door, I couldn't wipe the smile off my face for all the money in the world. I hid my arms behind my back and stepped forward to kiss her cheek, feeling all kinds of guilty. It seemed weird to reach out to hug her with the hands I'd had inside Abey's body all night long.

She uncrossed her arms, the long sleeves of the teal and coral floral cashmere robe I'd given her for Christmas last year falling over her hands at her sides. That thing had cost a pretty penny, but working at Ace's House, I could afford it, and she was worth the expense. And she loved her robe. She said she wished she could wear it to work, it was so soft.

"Well, you gonna tell me who she is?"

Twisting my lips, trying to hide my perma-smile, I said, "Remember the deputy who arrested me? The one I said was annoyin'?"

"Devona!"

"Oh, Mom, relax. It's not like I traded sexual favors for my freedom."

She cocked her head, her kind eyes inspecting my face, and the long braid she wore to sleep every night slipped over her shoulder and fell down her back. I wasn't sure what she saw when she looked at me, but the annoyance she'd felt over worrying about me disappeared.

"I haven't seen you smile like this in a long time, at least not about anything outside of your work at the center. It warms my heart, Devil. Is it serious?"

"Mm. I don't know. I-I'm not sure."

"C'mon," she said. "I've got the coffee brewin' already. We can have a cup, and you can tell me."

While she fixed our coffee, I watched her, even more grateful for her now. To know—to take for granted, really— that she'd always been there for me, that I could talk to her about sex, that she supported me in whatever I wanted to do had been such a freeing thing in my life.

My mom gave me confidence and strength, and I realized as I listened to her humming an old Chiricahua song that she was the reason I felt like I could make a difference in the world. That I could fight it. And when the lilting sounds she made settled inside me, like the notes of the music had inked themselves on my bones because the song had been such a solid part of my childhood, I realized that maybe I could try to be more like my mom.

Maybe she had been right the eight thousand times she'd tried to tell me that I could fight injustice much harder with my heart than I could with my mouth or my fist.

She was a wise woman, and I respected her more than anyone else in the world.

"I love you, Mom," I said when she set my coffee in front of me. She'd even added a little frothed milk on top, just like I liked. She'd bought a ten-dollar battery-operated frother just so she could spoil me a little 'cause she knew how much I loved the silky taste of cappuccinos.

"'*Sil n'zhoo*," she said with a warm smile as she patted my hand on the counter. *I love you* in our native Apache language. It was beautiful, and the softness of her voice warmed me. Made me feel safe and loved.

She sat across from me at the long kitchen island. "I have somethin' I need to say before you tell me all about your new love—"

"Wait, I didn't say—" My heart almost burst out of my chest when she used the word "love." How could she know that already?

"I lost my job, Devona."

"What?" I stood, all thoughts of love and sex pushed to the back of mind. My mom loved that job, and we'd depended on her income from the school for as long as I could remember. "They fired you? They can't do that!"

"Sit down. Please."

But I couldn't sit. Not at a time like this. What did this mean?

"It's not just me. They're closin' the elementary school. There just aren't enough kids enrolled this year. It doesn't make sense to spend all that money to run a building for seventeen kids. They'll all get bussed to nearby schools like the older kids. So there's no need for a lunch lady anymore. I already looked into it, and they're already fully staffed in Corner Junction."

She sighed, a look of heartbreak on her face as she stirred the coconut milk in her coffee with her spoon. "We'll have to depend on your income for a while. I don't make enough from my crafts to cover all the bills."

I was already nodding. "That's okay. I can cover it. I've been tryin' to pay for stuff, but you keep pushin' my money away."

She reached out to pat my hand on the countertop again. "You need to save your money."

"I am, Mom, but I can help. Maybe I could even get a second—"

She interrupted me. "I already have a plan. I've been talkin' with a friend about maybe… maybe openin' up my own store in downtown Wisper. What would you think about that?"

"Which *friend*?" My eyes narrowed all by themselves. I just knew she was going to say Red's name. It was too much of a coincidence that they'd just met. She didn't know anybody else who owned and ran a store.

"Well now, don't go gettin' yourself in a huff, but Mr. Graves told me there's an empty space next to his store. He owns it, and he said it's all fitted out already with nice floors. It gets good light and could easily be turned into a little shop. I could even have my own studio there, could sell my Native crafts. I could even take on bigger projects. The space is pretty small, but there's room for multiple workspaces, and it's right off the alley, so customers can see it when they walk by, and there's good parking. And it's got huge front windows where we could make displays and put up a big sign."

Huh. It wasn't the worst idea in the world.

I'd wondered about the space next to Red's store. It was barely a hole in the wall, but there were two floors, just like the store. All the old brick buildings had at least two floors, so she could have her shop on the bottom floor and her studio up above. Rye said Red used his second floor for storage, but I hadn't been up there. Theo and Brady lived on the third floor above Ace's House across the street, and it was a really cool apartment that had a kind of urban vibe. I was already picturing my mom's crafts and the clothing she made in a place like that. And with the increased tourism and commerce settling into town lately, I bet she could sell the hell out of her crafts.

But there remained one huge red flag. Redder than red. Blood red. *Ugh. Freaking Red Graves.* Yeah, so maybe he and I had more in common than I wanted to admit, but could we trust him?

"Yeah, but, Mom, I don't know if we can—"

"Devil, when are you gonna grow up?" She stood and carried her mug to the sink and dumped it out. She was really irritated with me if she was dumping her coffee. I winced. "He may not be your favorite person, and I understand why, but that man has been a successful business owner for years. Decades. He's a respected—" She stopped the lie about to fall from her lips. "His store is a staple in that town. I could learn a thing or two from him, and so could you."

"What do you want me to learn from him? He's awful. He's mean!"

"Devo, people are more complicated than you're givin' 'em credit for. Red Graves has been through a lot."

"Seriously?"

"Yes. He's well aware of how badly he's treated people, and he's already thinkin' of ways to make amends. You don't know his history. And frankly, I'm disappointed in you for not tryin' to get to know him better so you might understand him. That's what you were s'posed to have been doin' this last week, but it doesn't sound to me like you learned a thing."

Well. That was just… I scoffed. It was a load of fucking malarkey! And it scared me to trust the man who'd been giving me hell for years. She was my mom! My responsibility. What if he hurt her? What if…

What if?

"I don't know what kinda Kool-Aid you been drinkin', Mom, but you better watch out, 'cause it might just choke you."

CHAPTER TWENTY-FOUR

ABEY

SHOP OWNERS HAD COME out to gear up and get ready for the first of many start-of-fall sales days in Wisper. Windows had been cleaned and seasonal displays decorated every storefront on Main Street.

Decorative hay bales, red leaves, and pumpkins littered the store windows and sidewalks. Walt over at Coffee Shot was having an "I hate pumpkin spice" promotion. If a customer ordered a drink without it, he gave them a discount. Some people needed a kick in the butt to get their mindset out of the long, blue-sky days of summer and into the cooler, sweater-wearing days of autumn. The fresh dusting of snow on the tallest mountain peaks would help. Any day now.

But Red Graves didn't seem to need assistance getting into the fall mood. For once. When I walked up behind him in front of Red Wild to check on him and see how he was doing now that he was back to working in his own store, he was whistling a cheery tune as he swept the dirt off his front stoop.

Whistling? Red?

"Mornin'," I said, and he spun to face me.

"Oh, good mornin'. It's a fine day already."

He smiled, and I felt my eyebrows dipping down and bushing together like a long caterpillar under the brown brim of my hat. "A fine day?"

"Yeah," he said, a peaceful look plastered across his face as he gazed down Main Street, surveying the slow morning foot traffic. He looked up at the cloudless blue sky and closed his eyes for a few seconds, breathed deeply, then opened them again, and they landed back on me. "The sun's shinin', the birds are singin'. A *fine* day."

"You feelin' alright?" I asked, completely caught off guard. Thinking back over the entirety of my life, I couldn't remember the man ever saying "good morning" or that any day was a "fine day."

"Fit as a fiddle. Actually," he said thoughtfully, "I haven't felt this good in a long time. Must've gotten good sleep last night."

O-o-okay? Red acting like a nice person had to be the weirdest thing I'd encountered in a while, but I didn't plan to argue or complain about it. If he'd decided to be a decent human being all of a sudden, I could definitely get behind that.

"Y'know," I said, "I think you're right. It is a fine day." And hopefully I'd get to see Devo again soon, so then it would be a fabulous day.

It had certainly been a *fine* evening, night, and morning.

I'd never had such a happy morning. Waking up to Devo's face next to mine on my pillow was the perfect way to start my day. Her unruly hair had flipped out around her face while she'd slept, and when she woke, she kissed me and my heart soared.

After her long, drawn-out process of waking up—even the way she stretched was fine, back arched, lips pursed in a sleepy smile, hands in fists pushed up above her head as she flexed every inch of the soft and sexy body God had granted her—she lay there, watching me dress for work, making undeniably appreciative noises in the back of her throat as she got a good look at my ass in my work pants. And when I strapped my holster onto my hip and fitted my Glock in there, she growled at me and crawled toward the end of my bed to kneel in front of me so she could pull me down for another kiss.

The girl couldn't keep her lips off me. I swore she'd kissed literally every inch of my body, even my dang toes, which had made me gag, but she just wiggled her eyebrows and kissed another one.

Her lips were fire. They were warm and soft, and the naturally darkened line around her bottom one was the most sensual thing I'd ever seen. I'd found myself leaning in to trace it with my tongue or nip it with my teeth. God, those plump pillows of sin were fucking magic on my cl—

"I owe you an apology," Red said, snagging my attention and focusing it back on his weirdness.

"Oh? You do? An apology for what?"

"Yes, I do. For a lot of things." He sighed. "I haven't been kind to you. I'm sorry for that. I've been an ass, and not just to you. I'll be makin' my rounds to apologize to many people, but it's lucky you stopped by so I can tell you right off the bat that I'm sorry for bein' rude, for insultin' you and sayin' you weren't capable of doin' your job."

"Uh, Red, you didn't say that to me."

He smirked. "Not to your face."

Oh. Well then. Good to know. I tried not to roll my eyes. "Okay. Thanks. I accept your apology." I'd never been one to hold grudges, and truthfully, it was nice to hear. I'd never imagined I'd get to hear him apologize to anyone for anything.

"Thank you. I appreciate that. Oh, hey, can you come inside a minute?"

"Sure," I said, holding the door when he opened it and following him into his store.

The place looked good, and I could see Devo's influences here and there. It was in the tidy way the shelves had been reorganized, the way every surface shined because she had washed and dusted each one, and in the flow of the product displays.

The Red Wild Outdoors wasn't such a clusterfuck anymore. Now there was a clear path from the door to the register, and each sport or activity had its own area in the big, open space. Hunting, gun racks, and the ammunition case had been moved to one corner, hiking and fishing products and poles to another, but camping took up the front and biggest area. Devo and Rye had even set up a tent and made a whole campout display, complete with a faux cardboard fire, which they'd encircled with stones, a blow-up bed and couch in the tent, and a decked-out campfire stove.

I laughed to myself, realizing how much she'd been up to over the last week. Red would definitely benefit from Devo's presence in his store. There was no doubt about that.

As I looked around, he disappeared into the back room but quickly returned with a box in his hands. He hefted it on the counter. "Here. Take these." Reaching around the box, he placed an open bubble mailer in front of it.

"What's this?" I asked, stepping closer to have a look.

"I want you to take this box and these stickers and set 'em on fire. Burn them, bury them, or rip them up and use them for cleanin' rags. I don't care."

Lifting the mailer carefully, I peeked inside. In it was four shrink-wrapped stacks of the LGBT stickers plus the loose ones I was guessing had been on display on his checkout counter a week ago.

I looked up. "Red, what's gotten into you? What's goin' on? Not that I'm complainin'. These stickers are rude, but why the change of heart? I assume the T-shirts to match these stickers are in the box?"

"Yup," he said. "I guess I've been realizin' some things lately. I never had a problem with Ace's House. It was more personal than that, but when I saw how Sylvie's dad treated her, I realized I would never hurt my kid like that. I never want to hurt *anyone* like that, no matter who they love.

"And I suppose I can tell you. It's a small town. I'm sure you'll hear it on the grapevine soon enough anyway, but I've met a lady."

"Uh, you mean Devo's mama? Liluye? Didn't you just meet her? Devo told me—" I had been about to say that Devo had told me Red and her mama met—and that it was weird—last night while we'd lay in my bed.

But even though Red seemed to have turned over some kind of monumental new leaf, I still felt my heart racing in the pit of my stomach at the thought of him knowing about me.

"Yes," he said cheerfully. "Turns out, we have a lot in common. She's a beautiful woman with a beautiful soul. Did you know she's an artist? She makes all kinds of clothing and accessories in the traditional ways of the Mescalero-Chiricahua Apache tribe. I offered to sell them here, but then an even better idea came to me. I told her she oughta open up her own store, and I offered her the use of the space next door."

Looking at the wall to the left of the checkout counter, as if I could see through it to the space he was talking about, I was trying to patch together words to express how shocked I was at the stuff coming out of his mouth, but I had become a stuttering, blubbering idiot. All that came out of my mouth was, "Soul? Traditional—huh?"

Red chuckled, and I took a step back. Turned my head from side to side, looking around the store, trying to find the evidence. This was some kind of body-snatching thing, right? The dude in front of me looked like Red. Sounded like Red. But come on. Where the fuck was the *real* Red? *Come on down. Show yourself!*

"Um, Red," I said slowly, still waiting for him to jump at me and holler, "Just kiddin', I'm still a dick. Now get outta my store, little missy." "I-I, well I guess I'm glad that you've, uh, taken an interest in life again?"

He nodded. "That I have."

"But are you sure you should be… I mean, it's pretty fast. I guess I'm just surprised to see such a change in such a short amount of time."

"It's been a long time comin', don'tcha think?"

"Well… yeah. Yeah, I do."

"Good. Hey, whatcha know about that big dance comin' up? You goin'?"

"I… Yeah. I mean, I invited someone just last night, actually. But they haven't given me an answer yet."

"Oh, well, I'm plannin' to ask Liluye to go with me, and you're welcome to tag along, if you'd like, Sheriff Lee. I'd be happy to escort ya."

Sheriff Lee? *Was this the fucking twilight zone?*

"Thanks, Red. That's real kind, but no, thank you." I laughed. I had no clue what else I should be doing or how to respond. That would be the weirdest date ever. With the town jackhole and the mother of the woman I was hoping to perform cunnilingus on every night from here on out?

Yeah, no thanks.

Plus, he hadn't even asked Devo's mama yet, and she might say no. She probably *should* say no.

But Red shrugged, like the possibility of being shot down hadn't even occurred to him, and he turned to lift a feather duster from the far end of the counter, humming and dusting perfectly clean shelves on the wall behind the register.

It occurred to me that I'd stumbled on the perfect opportunity to test the waters. I could tell Red about Devo. As bizarre as he was this morning, Red seemed as receptive as he'd probably ever be.

And Devo was definitely worth the risk.

So was I.

And it was the perfect way to find out just how committed Red was to his new attitude.

I stepped a little closer to the counter. It felt weird, but I stood my ground and shook out my hands, then let them hang by my sides. "Actually," I said, "I invited Devo to the dance."

Red turned slowly but didn't say anything. I had his attention, though, as he looked right at me and waited for me to say more.

"I'm a lesbian, Red. I'm gay."

Someone could've knocked me over with that feather duster when he walked around the long length of the counter, stopped right in front of me, and wrapped me in a heartfelt hug.

"Then I owe you another apology," he said. "I'm sorry I've been disrespectful. You didn't deserve it, and I'm ashamed of the comments and dirty looks I've given people over the years. I was angry. Lord, I've lost *so much time* bein' angry." He hugged me tighter. "I lost the love of my child. I've lost a lifetime. But no more. I just… Somethin' just clicked inside me. Has that ever happened to you?"

He stepped back. I didn't answer his question because I couldn't. I couldn't talk, and when he saw the tear fall from the corner of my eye, he nodded. He understood the emotion clogging my throat, and he said, "I should've been someone you could depend on. A friend. At the very least, I should've been tolerable and *tolerant*, and I wasn't. I hope someday I can earn your forgiveness."

CHAPTER TWENTY-FIVE

DEVO

MY MOM STEPPED into my bedroom, planted her feet, and crossed her arms. "Devil, I'm gonna say this to you one more time, and I say it with love, but it's time for you to grow up."

"What?" I turned to face her, leaning against my tall, wooden dresser, one sock on, the other one still in my hand. "How can you say that to me? I've been bustin' my ass. I've never worked harder than I do at the center. And where are Lola and Avi?" Looking around my bedroom dramatically, I flung my arms out around me, like she needed to be reminded that my brother and sister were gone, off living their lives elsewhere. *Barely bothering to call to check up on you, I might add.* "I've always looked out for you, haven't I? I feel like all I do is take care of other people. Of you. But *I* need to 'grow up'? What does that even mean, Mom?"

"You're right. You have taken care of me. You stayed. They left. Everybody knows Devo carries the weight of the whole world on her shoulders. But who asked you to?"

My jaw hit the floor. "Wh-what? Who asked me to? You're sayin' I *shouldn't* take care of you? I shouldn't fight for the people I love? I shouldn't work hard to make sure you have the things you need? That you're safe and healthy and happy?"

"Oh, my courageous fighter, 'course you should, if that's what makes you happy. But it can't be *all* you do. And my happiness isn't your responsibility. It never has been. Not before your dad died, and not after. I love you so much for tryin', and I'm proud of every single thing you do. Every *legal* thing," she amended. "But aren't you tired? You've been runnin' like this since you were a teenager. I thought your tank would be empty by now, and you'd get on with life like the rest of us, but you're still standin' in the middle of the ring, ready to box. Haven't you noticed you're the only one there?"

I backed away from my open sock drawer and sat on the end of my bed. "What are you even sayin' right now?"

"I guess it's the curse of the oldest child." She knelt in front of me and took my hands in one of hers, brushing my hair away from my face with the other. "I'm sayin' the whole world is not your responsibility. You can let the rest of us carry it sometimes."

"I know that."

But why did it feel like the opposite was true? She was right though. I had been walking around with my fists up for a long time. My three visits to the holding cell at the sheriff's station were proof of that, and maybe the look of exhaustion I'd seen on Theo's face that day during my last "time out" was too.

Doubt clouded my mom's eyes. I didn't see pity or anger. All I saw was that she loved me. "Do you though?"

"Yes. I... I do."

"Sometimes, I wonder," she said, shaking her head. "Now, I understand you're mad, and I get why, but don't I deserve for you to trust my choices?"

"Mom, of course you do, but not Red Graves."

"Well, fortunately for me, you do not get a say in who I spend my time with."

"I just don't understand. He's the exact opposite of you. He's everything we don't believe in. So what? All of a sudden, you don't care about kindness and—"

"Devil, haven't I *always* cared about that? Just 'cause you can't see what I see, that means I'm supposed to give up on a person? I should just walk away from what my heart's tellin' me 'cause you say so?"

"Your *heart*?"

"Yes, Devona, my heart. I am the matriarch of this family. I'm a grown-ass woman. You may think the world will stop spinnin' if you aren't there to turn it, but it's just not true. I can make my own decisions and come to my own conclusions. I don't need you to do it for me. I didn't ask you to, and I don't want you to. Is that understood?"

"But, Mom—"

"But *nothin'*. This is all I'll say on the matter. The subject is closed. You don't have to like it or try to understand it if you choose not to."

Breathing deeply, recognizing the finality in her tone, I gave up. It was rare for her to shut me down like this, but I knew when she'd made up her mind. For some mysterious reason, she had decided to dig her heels in over Red freaking Graves.

I didn't want to say something I'd really regret, so I closed my eyes and sighed. "Yes, ma'am."

"Good. Now check your texts. I want you to click the link I sent and have a look around the website it leads to. You look at it, and then you tell me there isn't more to that man. There has to be good in Red somewhere for him to have created the beauty he did."

Huh? What good had Red Graves created?

"And I wanna know more. Maybe I'm wrong, and he is who you think he is, but that's my problem to discover. Not yours."

She stood and left my room quietly, and I felt completely… empty.

If she didn't want me fighting for her, if she thought I had been immature when all I'd ever wanted to do was advocate for people who couldn't do it for themselves, then what the hell had I been doing with my life?

But since when had I decided she needed my help with anything? She didn't. She was the strongest person I'd ever known.

And as I thought about what she said, it occurred to me that I remembered the exact moment I had vowed to always help and care for her, above and beyond what any child should have to do for their parent that they loved.

I remembered the rough house we'd lived in in New Mexico, the one without air conditioning or a heater that could be counted on to work all winter. It didn't have a lot of things, and one day, the washing machine broke down. When I got off the school bus in second grade, I ran home to show my mom the picture I'd painted in art class, and I found her out back, sweating and trying to wash five peoples' clothes in a bucket. The water was dirty and barely soapy, and there were articles of clothing draped over every surface they could be draped, set out to dry in the hot desert sun.

She had been at her wit's end that day, and when I asked why she didn't just go get a new washer because I had been too young to understand the complexities of adult financial responsibilities, she began to cry, and I thought, *When it's up to me, you'll never cry again.*

Apparently, the sentiment had translated to my adult life.

I'd been prancing around, thinking I had been doing all this good in the world, thinking everyone needed me to sort out their shit for them, to protect them and fight their battles, but did they all agree with my own mother? Was I a nuisance who couldn't keep her nose out of other people's business? Was I doing more harm than good?

What in the fuck was I even doing at all?

Falling back on the bed, I pressed up on my toes, lifting my butt to reach my phone in my back pocket. I needed to talk to Theo. He'd back me up. He'd tell me everything I'd been working for wasn't a waste.

Wouldn't he?

But when my phone blinked to life, I saw the text notification from my mom.

I opened it. Clicked her stupid link.

And when the website she wanted me to see popped up on my phone's screen, I gasped out loud.

She'd found the photographer!

The same image that had been the focal point of our home —the focal point of my mom's entire life—for as long as I could remember was right there in front of my eyes.

I sat up, crisscrossing my legs and scrolling down the page until I came to a description of the picture. The website had been made by an art collective as a place where different artists could share and sell their work. There was a disclaimer at the top of the site's home page stating that some of the artwork was old and no longer for sale, but that the website owner didn't have the heart to take any of the artists' work down even if they were no longer active on her site.

The site itself looked dated, but there was no denying the photograph in front of my eyes was the same one hanging on my mom's bedroom wall.

The description read:

River of Dreams

*Taken with a Nikon F5, using 35mm film, this image was captured near Mount St. John in the Bridger-Teton National Forest on the Holly Lake Trail, approximately half a mile from the southeastern-most point of Holly Lake. The image was taken in late August on a camping trip I took with my wife and my son, Junior. We saw moose that day, but Junior scared them off when he jumped in the water, laughing and dancing because he was so excited. He cried when they ran away, and I captured this image of the creek as his soft, heartbroken sounds filled the air. We saw other animals later that day, though, so he wasn't sad for too long. But I will never forget this spot in the mountains, a place I hope to take him back to every year. **Disclaimer:** I am not a professional photographer, just a hobbyist, but I hope you can see the love I have for my son in this picture, and how much I love these mountains. Everybody's talking about digital cameras these days, but for my part, I will always love film best.*
–Redmond Graves, Wisper, WYO

Red Graves was the mysterious photographer? The same one who took the picture my mom loved almost as much as she loved her children?

The owner of The Red Wild Outdoors *Red Graves*?

Shut the fucking fuck up!

But then I remembered the boxes of photo albums in the back room at Red Wild and the tripod I'd tripped over and broken. Well, shit. Now I would have to replace it.

When I clicked on the highlighted "See More From This Artist," a grid of photos appeared, seemingly all taken by Red. The pictures were all similar in tone and subject matter, and my mom's favorite picture popped up at the end of the first row.

None of the photos were clickable, so I assumed that meant they were no longer for sale, or maybe they never had been and the website was just a way for Red to display his hobby. Was that what people did pre-Facebook? Weird.

I saw images of mountains, trees, and lakes, camping tents and evening fires under the stars. There were a few animal pics, some of moose and river otters, their sleek bodies slipping through the water on whatever merry task they had been on their way to do, and there were photos of eagles and hawks, too, but there were also pictures of people.

Four people to be exact.

In one photo, an old-school selfie because I could see Red's arm holding the camera up above their faces, I saw a much younger Red. He used to be really handsome, tall with a full head of brown hair, and his other arm rested easily around the shoulders of a beautiful woman with long, poufy, ash-blond curls. Both were smiling. Both seeming to be enjoying their time together. It was clear that hiking and camping had been things Red enjoyed with his family.

A little boy featured in many of the pictures, with the same color hair as the woman. He looked to be five or six years old.

Red's little family looked happy, but as I continued to scroll, another woman began to appear.

At first, she seemed to be a third wheel to the family—she was included with the family, but always off to the side or separate somehow—but as time went on, the new woman was almost always photographed with Red's wife. At least, that was who I assumed the blonde had been.

The second woman looked eerily like me. Same dark hair, cut similarly like mine in a sharp bob to her chin. She was short, and she laughed a lot.

The little boy always seemed to be captured in pictures

taken away from the women, playing in the mud at the edge of a lake or with a plastic bucket and shovel near their campsite. "Digging up 'clams,'" one picture had been captioned. His smile grew less and less frequent, until, in the second-to-last picture, his eyes looked tired and vacant, like he wished he was anywhere else. Like he had been a witness to his mom falling in love with someone who was not his dad, and it had emptied him.

The very last picture was of the two women embracing. It looked intimate, and it felt as if the photographer was on the outside of a small group of friends, looking in and wondering how he'd gotten stuck out in the cold.

And that was it. I searched the rest of the site but only found that one page of photographs. There was a definite retro vibe to them, like they'd been scanned and then uploaded to the site. They definitely weren't digital pics, and they'd all been posted years ago at the dawn of the internet, if the dates below each image were correct. Nothing before. Nothing after.

Even I could see the heartbreak in those pictures.

I could practically taste it.

CHAPTER TWENTY-SIX

ABEY

WHEN I RETURNED to the station with the box of T-shirts, I set it on a chair in the reception area and went to check the morning call sheet Shelley had printed out for Roxanne and me. I really was planning to rip the T-shirts up and maybe clean my boots with them or a toilet. I'd give some to Devo too. She'd get a kick out of that.

There wasn't too much happening around Wisper yet, but with all the sales and local markets going on and more and more tourists finding their way to us, especially with the festival and dance right around the corner, there was bound to be some kind of drama.

Planning to make a dent in some of the annoying paperwork I'd inherited when I'd accepted the acting sheriff gig, I settled into the fancy office chair I'd also inherited when I took over Carey's office. In my mind, it was still his office. A name plate had been delivered that read "Deputy Sheriff Lee," but I knew it'd come from Carey and not from any official transfer of power situation. There wasn't actually an "official" position. You were either the sheriff of a county or you weren't.

But that sat fine with me. I had no hopes or aspirations to run for Carey's office. My friend had a lot on his shoulders, and I had no desire to carry all that. I liked my job. Liked working with the townsfolk, liked protecting them and checking up on them, keeping the peace. It was a great job, and it fit me perfectly.

Somebody had to do it, and I was good at it. I felt a lot of pride when the fact that I was a woman turned out to be helpful to someone in need, someone who was scared or in trouble. Screw those fucktwats at Headquarters. And screw assholes like David Locke. This "girl" cop had shot a hole clean through his leg without batting an eye. And at the same time, I'd shown his daughter that she didn't have to take his intolerant shit.

Served him right.

And who said I needed to be sheriff to make a difference? Maybe I'd been making a difference all along. Carey had done a great job by hiring me, and now Roxanne, and there was a third female deputy who'd been working at the Jackson station for a couple years.

Carey had forced the male deputies to become more tolerant because they had been made to work side by side with women, and we even had an openly gay deputy who'd worked up in Yellowstone with Roxanne. She'd told me all about him and how he'd been the one to introduce her to MM romance. We still had a lot of serious issues facing us in the law enforcement field. I couldn't hope to fix all that on my own. I didn't have all those answers, but I'd made my small mark, and that was a good thing.

The people of Wisper and Teton County knew they could depend on me, that I would protect them and treat them fairly, no matter who they were, the color of their skin, where they lived, or who they loved.

I thought about Devo and about all her causes and crusades. I'd never really considered us alike in that way. But now, as I remembered when I'd had to bring her in for protesting without a permit, the thing I respected the hell out of her for, despite her having not quite figured out how to do it peacefully, was that she was a believer. Of many different things, that was for sure, but they all boiled down to right and wrong. Devo fought every day for equality, for tolerance and acceptance. She fought for kindness and education and every other good thing in this messed-up world.

And it was sexy as hell.

But wasn't it the same thing I did every day? She was the one who'd told Athena that I believed in right and wrong. Fought for it and worked hard to protect it.

Huh.

Yeah, it was what I'd been doing, pretty much since the first day I became a deputy. And I was really proud of myself for that.

So, I decided that, as long as Carey didn't have any plans to add an official title to my new position, I'd keep the job, and I'd do it justice. Every damn day.

Speaking of, I heard boots marching down the long hallway in what I'd quickly come to know was Dan's usual stiff way. He was probably headed back to the locker room to change before going back to the one-room rental he was staying in over at Mrs. Ellison's boarding house after he'd worked the night shift.

In my mind, since I'd met him, he had come to represent the bad kind of officer people were becoming more and more scared of every day. Someone who would've tear-gassed Devo at her little protest instead of trying to help her and Red work things out.

Placing that assumption on Dan hadn't been fair of me.

He hadn't done anything to warrant such an assessment, so I called him into my office and asked him to have a seat in the chair across from mine. He didn't sit and continued to stand with his hands clasped rigidly behind his back. His uniform was still buttoned up to his chin even though he'd been off the clock for a good thirty minutes.

Usually, he wore a cowboy hat like I did when he was out working the streets, except his was black. It was a pretty common thing for law enforcement in these parts, but today, covering his tight crop of a haircut was a Teton County Sheriff's Department ball cap with his sunglasses perched on top of the bill.

"There's a chair behind you," I hinted.

"I'm good, thanks."

"Okay." Was he really that big of an asshole, or was there something else going on? "Actually, no, sit. That's not a request."

A muscle pinched in his cheek. "Yes, ma'am."

"So," I began as he lowered himself into the hardback chair, "how do you think things are goin' for you here in Wisper?"

"Ma'am?" he said, eyebrows pinching togcther as he removed his hat and sunglasses, then rested them over his leg. "I don't understand the question. Am I not meetin' the requirements expected of the job?"

"No. Technically, you're doin' what you're s'posed to. What I mean is, whatcha think? How're you fittin' in? Do you like the job?"

He nodded. "It's fine."

Jeez! Could this guy emote? Like, did he even know how?

Studying his face, I looked for any kind of connection I could come up with to bond in some way with the guy. I tried to remember what I'd read in his personnel file before he arrived in Wisper. He was only five or six years older than me, but as I studied him, I saw a long lifetime in his eyes. I got the feeling it hadn't been an easy one.

When all else failed, I gave him the "full Abey experience." A smile and a laugh. Maybe it was a self-preservation thing, and I used it when things felt awkward and uncomfortable, but that might mean it'd work with Dan. "You know, I heard once that 'fine' stands for freaked out, insecure, neurotic, and emotional."

He didn't say anything, and I had to work to resist the urge to cross my eyes and groan out loud. The guy was something else.

He should've learned by now that you had to find the fun where you could in this job, 'cause sometimes it got hard. It could be heartbreak and hard shit every day, and we needed the laughter and crack-ups for when it was. At least, I did.

Leaning back in my chair, I figured it was time to go the direct and earnest route with him. I rested my elbows on my desk and steepled my fingers together. "Dan, what do you want from this job? I mean, what do you hope will come of it?" All of a sudden, I felt downright sheriff-y.

"I'd like to be the sheriff someday. This job is my first step in that direction."

Hm. Okay. I could work with that.

"Good. That's a great goal. But the problem is, you got some big shoes to fill. Sheriff Michaels does a damn good job, but it's not just a title. He works hard every day to know the people he's workin' for. The people who *elected* him. Those same people will have a choice to make someday when it's your name on the ballot. Don't you think you might use this time to get to know them? To help them, be kind to them, and learn what their lives are like? If you show an interest, you might just win 'em over before you ever even need their votes."

I could see the wheels turning in his head.

"I s'pose you're right, ma'am."

"Okay. Good." I nodded, happy to at least be having a conversation with him, one in which he participated. "Glad we agree. First things first, though. Every time you call me ma'am, I wanna throat punch you. It's not the word itself, it's the way you say it. So let's unpack that. Do you have a problem with women in positions of power? Does it piss you off that I'm your boss? Is that what I'm detectin'"—I waved my hand in the direction of his scowl—"by that look on your face?"

"No." He shook his head quickly. "Not at all, m—" He stopped mid-sentence, unsure what to call me if he couldn't call me ma'am.

Lifting my hand off the desk, I splayed my fingers wide in frustration, resisting the urge to throttle him. "My name is Abey! Please just call me Abey."

"Abey," he said, wincing a little, possibly realizing he'd just narrowly avoided being jaw-socked by a girl. "No, Abey, I don't have a problem with a woman as my boss. I'm sorry I haven't been very personable. I don't talk about myself often. It's not somethin' I usually do. It's just not…" He thought about what he wanted to say, lips pursing to the side. "I guess it's just not easy for me to open up. I was in the military a long time, and before that, I was a military brat. We moved a lot. Never stayed in one place long enough to get to know people"

Aaand now we were getting somewhere.

"I understand completely. No need to apologize. And you're in luck. You just landed yourself in the friendliest place on the planet. This town and the surrounding areas are filled with some of the kindest, most helpful and lovin' people in the world. If you can find it within yourself to open up to 'em just a little bit, they'll welcome you into the fold. They'll come when you call, and when it's time, they'll vote for you."

He actually smiled. It looked kind of weird on his face.

But I went on. "I don't have plans to take over the sheriff's office officially. At least not right now. Carey's still in his prime. But maybe in the future. Maybe not. I dunno, but if I do decide to run, you'll be a formidable opponent. But first, you're gonna have to prove you're worthy. Think you can do it?"

He stood, fumbling quickly to catch his hat and glasses before they hit the floor. "Yeah. Yeah, Abey, I know I can."

I stood, too, and held out my hand for a shake. He took it and grasped it tight.

"Good. You can start by comin' with me on some of the calls on this list if you don't have plans this mornin'?" I handed him the call printout.

"I'm happy to come along," he said.

"One of the things we do here is work with some of the elderly residents who live out in the sticks. We do small jobs for 'em when they can't do it for themselves anymore. We check in, make sure they have what they need. I think that's a good place for you to start. I'll go with you this first time to make introductions, and you can start to get to know the area and its people and history better."

He looked over the list. "Okay."

"Alright then. That's step one. By the way, you like pie?"

"Yes, m—" He caught himself before he called me ma'am again and looked up from the paper in his hands. Seriously, as soon as the word began to spill out of his mouth, my hand balled into a fist, and my eyes inevitably found their way to his Adam's apple. "Yeah, *Abey*, I love pie."

"Good," I said, relaxing, "'cause you're gonna get a lot of it. Just don't let it go to your waistband. Trust me. It's hard to run down perps with too much pie under your belt."

CHAPTER TWENTY-SEVEN

ABEY

DAN PROVED to be a natural when he loosened up just a smidge.

The old folks on our route got him talking about all the places he'd been with the military, and then it seemed like he *was* an old folk. The guy could talk for days about cars, and I'd learned quickly, when one of the elders couldn't get his truck started, that Dan knew how to make them run too. He fixed Mr. Quimbly's twenty-year-old Ford right up and got the engine revving in no time flat, which earned him points with the cranky old goat and all his neighbors.

When we returned to the station, I checked in with Shelley and then made my way over to Ace's House, hoping to see Devo back in action before the end of her workday.

My stomach felt like it had a whole nest of caterpillars crawling around in there. My heartbeat thudded in my throat. I didn't know what last night meant for us. She'd never answered about going to the dance with me.

But the sex we'd had wasn't only that. It hadn't been *just* sex.

It had been... transcendent. Something more than a hookup. It had been a hell of a lot more than just fucking.

It was a belonging.

Had she felt it too?

Theo smiled when I jumped up the few steps leading to the center's front doors. I crossed the threshold, and his face turned into a big ol' smirk while he stood there, watching me.

What the fuck was that about? He wasn't usually such a smiley guy.

"What?" I said, and I looked down at my uniform to make sure I hadn't spilled any of José's chili on my shirt.

"Nothing. Can't a guy smile when he's having a good day?"

"Sure. Why's it such a good day?"

The center seemed chill and quiet. There weren't any kids throwing tantrums today. Everybody was probably preparing to wind down for the weekend, and I knew Devo and Theo would be busy making last-minute preparations for the Fall Festival.

"Well," he said, "for one, Red has made a complete turn-around in his attitude. He just took a break from his store to pop over here to ask if he could sign up to volunteer. Apparently, he liked it here."

"He did," I said with a nod, and I took off my hat. I could feel the rat's nest tangled on top of my head since I'd fallen asleep in Devo's arms last night with wet hair, but there wasn't much I could do about it at the moment, and besides, my workday wasn't over yet, so it'd just get messed again later. I ran my fingers through it anyway. "Red told me as much."

"Well." Theo laughed. "Isn't that just..."

"It's nuts," I said, finishing his sentence, "but I'm not

gonna complain. I'll take weird-but-happy Red over grumpy Red any day."

"Me too." He shuffled the stack of papers in his hands, tidying them into a nicer pile and switching them into the crook of his arm. "Devo's in her office, by the way."

"Oh." I looked around, trying not to seem too interested. And then I realized that was dumb. A new era had been settling in all around me. It had come time for me to get with the program.

"I'll leave you to it," he said. He was too polite to call me out about a relationship with his assistant director, even though, of all the buildings in Wisper, this one was the most welcoming no matter who you were. No matter who you loved. "Unless you need me for anything?"

"Nope. Just came to talk to Devo."

"Okay," he said. "Have a good evening, Abey." And he turned to make his way to the staircase at the back of the hallway. He climbed the stairs two at a time and disappeared.

When I peeked my head around the door to Devo's office, she was standing behind her desk, talking on the phone.

She waved me in with a sexy smile, and I plopped down into the chair across from her, getting a good eyeful of a mess of decorations and what looked like fun activities for kids she'd been working on for the festival.

A box full of miniature Halloween candy bars sat by my boots on the floor, next to it another box filled to the brim with toy bracelets, rings, and trinkets of all shapes and sizes, and resting against the wall behind her, there was a life-sized tic-tac-toe board someone had made out of a huge piece of cardboard and black felt, with red felt X's and blue felt O's stuck around the sides.

I smiled, thinking of all the kids who would get a kick out of it at the festival, playing the game, dunking for apples, and getting their faces painted, plus a whole host of other games and rides.

"Yeah, Calysta, you got it," Devo said into her phone. "And again, I'm sorry about Vern. He really does mean well, he's just not… um—" She hesitated, her brown eyes drifting to the side as she tried to come up with a way to describe Vern Wexler to this Calysta on the end of the line. I held in a chuckle. I doubted there was a good way to sum the guy up. He was one of a kind. "He's never really worked a job where he had to be professional, but in the future, it'll be me or Theo who calls to make the orders. We could always do it online, but you know I love gabbin' with ya."

Scrunching her cute little nose, she flashed me a grin, listening to whatever Calysta had said before they ended the call. "Absolutely," Devo said. "And thanks again. Have a great weekend."

She hung up the phone, setting it back in its cradle on her desk, and her smile grew till her teeth gleamed in the overhead office lights.

I placed my hand flat on my stomach, trying without success to quiet the bite of the ache I felt when I looked at her. I'd never seen anyone so beautiful.

"Hi," she said in a breathy voice that had my mind digging down through all kinds of dirty memories, making the ache worse.

"Hey."

"What's up?" she asked. "You're not here in an official capacity, are you?"

I shook my head, looking her over. I felt relieved to lay my eyes on her again, felt happy to see her thriving in her job, looking sexy as all get-out in a lilac-colored and silky-looking business kind of shirt above some seriously tight-fitting black pants. Her outfit seemed different than the T-shirts and jeans she usually wore to work, and the color of her shirt made the brown of her eyes almost glow. I cocked my head, wondering why the change.

"No. I just wanted to check in. Say hi."

"Hi," she said again. There was peace in her expression and, at the same time, an excitement, like looking at me lit up her whole world.

Did it? She lit mine on fire.

"So," I said, leaning toward her while she lowered herself into the chair behind her desk, "about that question I asked you. You never did answer."

She lifted her hands from the desk, elbows resting on top, and pointed both her index fingers to her mouth, tapping them lightly on the edges of her lips. "I didn't, did I?"

"Nope." I uncrossed and re-crossed my ankles. I held my breath, feeling like I might chuck my lunch all over the papers and files on her desk and the cute little brown and white horse-shaped paperweight she kept on top as I waited for her answer.

Although I couldn't help but notice the slow way her eyes traveled down my shirt and back up. They landed on my neck, and she cocked her head a little as her eyes finally found mine again. "Yes."

"Yes?"

"Yes, I'll go to the dance with you."

My whole face cracked into the biggest grin. "Well, hot damn, girl."

Her smile grew impossibly bigger, she giggled, and I about died and went to Heaven.

CHAPTER TWENTY-EIGHT

ABEY

THINGS WERE ALL WELL and good. Red Graves's miraculous turnaround had wound its way through the rumor mill. There'd been a little bit of talk.

"Maybe he's lyin'."

"Maybe he's dyin'!"

"Maybe the judge told him to change his attitude or he'd send Red to prison."

None of it was true.

Red had learned a hard lesson, and then he fell in love in an instant. "Insta-love" was what we romance connoisseurs called it, and Devo's mama put her new suitor in his place. She'd no doubt gotten an earful of all the despicable things Red had said and done since she lived with Devo. So, Liluye Mescal told him he needed to get his shit together 'cause she wouldn't be with any man who treated her daughter or anybody else that way.

But it didn't feel to me like Red was whistling a new tune just because Liluye told him to. If that had been the case, he wouldn't have hired one of the kids from Ace's House—a *gay* kid—to work at his store part-time so he would have more time to take up photography again. He'd wanted to offer the job to Sylvie, but we'd learned that she would be living with her aunt in Laramie permanently. Her father was still in jail, serving out the rest of his punishment, but Sylvie's mama still held her father's line and wouldn't allow Sylvie to go home.

She was better off with her aunt. Even Red agreed with that.

Red also wouldn't have volunteered to take the daycare kids to the park once a week or offered to teach an outdoor survival and safety class for teens once a month if his new attitude hadn't gone soul deep, and he sure as hell wouldn't have hung a sign in his front window that said "EVERYONE is welcome in The Red Wild Outdoors—ALL colors, genders, orientations, religions, cultures, abilities, beliefs, sizes, and ages. Even grumps and vegetarians!" The sign looked more country than it did rainbow-y, with pictures of cartoon chickens, cows, and horses, but the meaning was the same.

It was a peace offering.

And it felt genuine to me. Red smiled and laughed all the time now.

And all it had taken was friendship and the possibility of love.

Now, there was one last person I needed to set straight.

I called my mama on my way home from the station a few days before the dance and told her to stay put, that I would be on her doorstep in a few minutes.

It had come time for us to have a conversation.

Pulling into the drive in front of her trailer ten minutes later, I shut off my truck and sat still for a moment, watching the sun fall behind the mountains to the west. The purple and strawberry-colored sunset filled my chest with this feeling that I couldn't put a name to.

I didn't know how to say what I wanted to say to my mama. And I had no clue how to stop her from trying to run from the subject of my sexuality this time, but I needed it to be over. I needed everything to finally be out in the open.

It was time for her to listen to me and time for her to finally *hear* me.

If she and I were going to have any kind of relationship going forward, I wanted it to be a real one. An open one. I needed it to be because I'd spent my life always wondering where I stood, never knowing where I fit in, so I'd tried to fit in everywhere.

My daddy had all but disowned me. He fed me and clothed me, but I'd always thought that had been only out of his own sense of responsibility—he knew his parents would've rolled in their graves if he'd kicked his own child out—and Mama had done what had been expected of her by keeping quiet and not talking to me when he was around, but she'd always held onto me. Kept me in her life.

She'd tried to keep me part of the family, even when Daddy had worked hard to make me feel separate, like when he'd bought my brothers new cowboy boots and hats for Christmas, and I'd been given new work gloves 'cause that was the only use he had for me after he knew I was gay—a ranch hand. He tried to distance himself from me so the shame he felt about me didn't choke him. His shame made me feel like I was never good enough.

But I was. And I fit just fine now. I fit with my friends, my brothers, my niece, my co-workers. My community.

And I fit with Devo.

It was time for my mama to accept it.

She could like it. She could not. But she needed to come

to terms with her only daughter. She needed to make a decision. Daddy died a long time ago, so it was time for her to choose me or live her life without me.

It took a few more minutes of breathing deeply and evenly, but I finally gathered my courage, climbed out of the truck, and ascended the four stairs leading up to her front door. I knocked twice on the weathered, cheap-as-shit wooden screen door, then pushed it open.

It clattered shut behind me, and I jumped at the noise, then turned to find Mama waiting for me at her small square oak dining table. The TV wasn't on in the living room. No music played. The only sounds I could hear were a couple of magpies out back, squawking and squabbling at each other on her back fence. Apparently, she knew it was high noon too.

"So," I said as I sat across from her. I rested my hands on the table, then folded them, locking my fingers together.

"So what?"

She looked nervous, but she wasn't puffing away on a cigarette for once. In fact, her trailer didn't smell like an ashtray like it usually did, and I could tell she'd washed her curtains and had been in the middle of a major house cleaning when I called. A broom leaned against the kitchen wall, and the vacuum cleaner I'd bought her stood in the living room, waiting to be used.

Maybe she had finally realized she couldn't avoid life any longer, couldn't hole herself away in her trailer anymore, chain smoking and avoiding all the things in her life that were too painful for her to face.

She couldn't avoid me any longer, that was for sure.

"You quit smokin' or somethin'?"

"I did," she said.

"Good. Proud of you."

"Thanks," she whispered.

"I love you, Mama."

She smiled a little, but "I know" was all she said.

"I'd like to talk to you about Devo and me. About your opinion on the subject of my sexuality."

Her eyes became glued to the table beneath her hands, and she smoothed her right index finger back and forth over a long grain in the wood. The arthritis had gotten worse. Her hands looked mangled and swollen, like knotty wood. I wondered how long it would be until she couldn't even change the channel on the TV with the remote.

She pursed her lips but then released them, blew out a breath, and tried to relax her face, as if she knew that this time, her usual responses wouldn't work with me. "What about it?"

"We've never talked about it. After Daddy… After you became aware that I was a lesbian, I expected you to talk to me about it, but you never did. Daddy certainly didn't."

She looked at my hands clasped together on the table. "What was it you wanted me to say?"

"Anything?"

I stared hard at her hair, noticing how gray it had gotten. My brothers all had brown hair like our dad, but I'd gotten Mama's blond, so it was hard to tell she had been going gray, but suddenly, it was easy to see.

She had been a knockout in her day, beautiful beyond what people probably knew to do with back then. My whole life, all the pictures lining the walls of the house out at the farm showed a long-haired beauty who laughed a lot.

My daddy had known what to do with that beauty. He locked that shit down, put a ring on it, and knocked her up right quick. But now I wondered what she had been like before that, before she became someone's wife, someone's maid and cook. Before she had been expected to come to heel when her husband put his foot down.

Had she been wild and free? A romantic? Or a pessimist like she was now? I realized I didn't really know my own mama.

But while I registered that fact, I tried to will her into looking into my eyes and having an open conversation with me for once.

It occurred to me that a few weeks ago, I would've given anything to have her look at me and not be disappointed. I wasn't kidding myself—I still wanted that. I wanted it badly, but now I knew I could live without it.

I might *have* to live without it.

It felt like an hour had passed, but finally, she said, "Well, maybe I didn't know *what* to say."

"Okay. I can understand that. It wasn't like we had experience or knowledge of that kinda thing back then. It wasn't somethin' we dealt with in our sheltered lives. But what about now?"

"You think you were sheltered?"

"Well, yeah. I'm not sayin' it was always a bad thing, but there were a lot of things I knew nothin' about until I grew up and moved out. Until that day, the day Daddy… the day Daddy caught me kissin' Paula—until that day, I truly thought if I didn't go to church at least twice a week, I'd be struck down by God. Obviously, that's not true." I held my arms out to my sides, proving no lightning bolts had come for me yet.

"That's a different conversation for another time," I said, "but I don't know who God is. I don't know who it is you believe in, 'cause I could never believe in a God who hates me, who thinks I shouldn't have been born or that there's somethin' wrong with me. That's not *my* God, Mama."

She peeked at me, but mostly her eyes stayed on the table.

"I'm your daughter," I whispered, but then I made my voice louder. "Didn't you see me cryin'? Didn't you see the way Daddy talked to me, hear the awful things he said to me? Didn't you know how it made me feel? How it broke me? How I dreamed about runnin' away so I wouldn't have to feel like every breath I took let you down?"

I wondered if she could feel the desperation finally exploding out of me, the feeling inside my body that filled every cell, every thought, every memory. The sadness and hurt that I wasn't enough for her. That soul-deep rejection I felt every time she wished I was someone else.

That was too scary to confront. Much scarier than the fact that I was gay, but it was all a byproduct of it.

"Maybe I was afraid to make your daddy mad."

"What?"

Finally, she looked up, biting the inside of her lip for a minute. "I was brought up to obey my husband, Abey. If I had spoken to you about any of this, that would've been disobedient. It's not an excuse, but it's the reason."

"Daddy forbade you to discuss it with me?" I'd figured as much, but still, it hurt to hear.

"More than once. I begged him."

"Why?" Did she even know? Had my daddy even known why he hated me?

She scoffed softly. "Because you scared him, and it's a pretty well-known fact that big, strong men who think they rule the world and that women are here just to do for them, well, they don't take well to things they don't know or can't control."

"What was so scary about a fifteen-year-old girl kissin' another girl? It was just a peck on the lips."

She sighed. "Our church told us that if a man lay with another man, or a woman with another woman, they were p—

that it wasn't… right. It wasn't what God wanted, and it was unnatural."

She stopped herself from calling me a child molester, and my hands began to shake. I was terrified of the answer to the question I was about to ask, and hearing her say it out loud would break me in two.

"Do you think that? Truly? That I could hurt a child?" She didn't answer, and it looked like it might physically hurt her to look in my eyes. "Look at me, please, Mama."

She did finally. She lifted her head, and her blue eyes landed on my matching ones. There was a lifetime of sadness and regret in hers. "I don't know what I think," she said. "But no. I don't think you'd hurt anyone. But I didn't know the first thing about that stuff back then, only what I'd been told, what we were made to believe. How would anything I said back then have been helpful or made a difference?"

I hadn't known the relief I'd feel when she said it. I couldn't have accepted any kind of relationship she tried to have with me if she'd truly thought I would ever hurt a child like that. I'd never realized how much the possibility of her believing such disgusting things about me had become a disease inside me.

I breathed a little easier now, and the pinch in my chest lessened from a raging fire to a throbbing ache, but we weren't done yet.

"Maybe it wouldn't have made a difference, but Mama, I needed you to talk to me. I just… I *needed* you. You're my *mom*. It wasn't about what you might've said. It was about me knowin' I didn't disgust you too. That you could love me even if I wasn't what you wanted me to be."

A strangled sob bubbled out of her, but she didn't cry. "Don't you know how bad I struggle, Abey?" she said, looking in my eyes, seeing the tears welling up in the corners.

My bottom lip wouldn't stay still. She shook her head and looked down again, and I tried hard not to let the pain on her face break me. Her struggle was clear, and I felt ashamed that I'd never noticed how hard this had been for her too. I hadn't forgiven her, not even close, but I could see the pain inside her plain as day.

"What I learned in church tells me it's not right. It's what my parents thought. It's what your daddy thought, and it's what most everybody around here thinks." She pushed away from the table and stood from her chair, and I hung my head, expecting that, like she had always done in the past, she would walk away from this conversation. From me.

I couldn't force her to accept me. What else was there to say?

This was it. This was all I would get from her. And it would have to be enough for me.

Sure, I'd go on with my life. I'd take Devo to the dance. Maybe we'd get married someday, have a family. Maybe I'd get everything I'd ever wanted in Devo.

I already loved her.

But my mama wouldn't be a part of that if she couldn't truly accept me.

She'd walk away from her disgusting lesbian daughter, and she'd never look back.

And I'd have to figure out how to not have my mama in my life. To not see her grouchy face when I brought her groceries. To not allow myself to worry if she was taking her medicine the way the doctor had prescribed. To never feel her fingers glide softly through my hair as she separated it before pulling it into braids, even though her hands had to ache.

I'd never see her face again on Christmas morning when Athena opened all the presents Mama had bought for her by saving as much of her social security checks as she could throughout the year, even though she hadn't bought new clothes for herself in as long as I could remember. And still, she lived in this god-awful trailer in the winter, when I suspected she had to wear two layers of thermals to bed to stay warm when the winds from the tops of the Tetons carried the dry, frigid cold down into the valley, even though there was a perfectly warm bedroom out at the farm, sitting empty, waiting for her to get over her own stubbornness.

She wanted to continue to avoid the truth, and it meant that I'd have to say goodbye.

But that wasn't what happened.

Mama came to stand in front of me, and when I lifted my head and the tears finally dripped free and fell down my cheeks, she cradled my face in her hands.

I couldn't stop crying. I tried hard 'cause I wanted to be able to hold my head high when I walked out of her life.

But she was looking at me. *Really* looking.

Was she finally seeing… me?

"But I *love* my only daughter," she said solemnly. "I have loved you since the day I found out I was pregnant with you. I loved you the day you were born. I loved you when you were a ten-year-old brat and you couldn't leave your brothers be. Even when you ripped out the braids I'd spent an hour on when they weren't the kind the girls at school wore. I loved you the day Daddy saw you kissin' that girl in the barn, and I love you still.

"You will *always* be my daughter, Abey. Even if we don't agree. Even if you decide you don't want me in your life because I disagree, I'll still love you."

Oh God.

The relief was immediate, like the sadness, fear, and weight of seventeen years had been traveling through my bloodstream, settling down into the very fibers of my veins, heavy like sediment, but finally, it had been washed free.

I felt weightless again but, this time, for an entirely different reason.

"And if I take Devo to the Fall Festival dance?"

She brushed the hair away from my temple, looking at it lovingly, but then her eyes moved back to mine. "I'll love you even then."

"Even if people talk? Even if they say nasty, mean things about me? Even if they say it's my parents' fault that I'm a lesbian and that God hates me?"

She swallowed loudly, but she said, "Even then, baby. My sweet little girl." Her words made me *feel* like a little girl, like I used to before everything went to pot. "I love you. How could I not?"

CHAPTER TWENTY-NINE

DEVO

"For me?"

Red stood outside my front door, on the empty concrete-slab porch, holding out a bouquet of daisies and pink roses with one hand.

My mums were long dead, probably petrified by now, and I'd already tossed the early-girl tomato plants I'd kept out there 'cause they liked full sun. At least this year, we'd gotten a few to use on BLTs before the things died a sad, crunchy-leafed death. Thankfully, my green pepper plant was still thriving out back. It stopped bearing fruit a month ago, but I wasn't about to complain, because the pride I felt at simply keeping that damn plant alive was flowing through me still.

Red's weathered, old face was shadowed on one side by the night but lit by the light of the moon on the other. Chagrin descended over the whole thing. "Yes."

He'd worn dark jeans, shiny brown cowboy boots, and a crisp white shirt under a brown suit jacket with suede patches on the shoulders and elbows. He looked properly Western. I had to give it to him—he looked good.

"But I'm not your date."

I'd spent all day at the festival. Abey patrolled it with Frank. Thankfully, there hadn't been any major issues. I'd seen her a handful of times throughout the long day, but now, it was almost time for the dance to start. All the parents had taken their kids home, and I had just enough time to run home to change.

"No," Red said, thrusting the flowers into my hands, "but it's the least I can do to apologize again for all the trouble I've caused you. For all the times I sassed you and cussed at you behind your back. I made you think I didn't support what you're doin' over at the center."

He'd apologized to me already, had explained that he'd noticed the physical traits I had in common with the woman who he'd blamed all these years for stealing his family.

It happened the first day I'd gone into his store to ask him if I could hang a flyer for Ace's House in his front window, before the center had even opened.

But then he went on to explain that he'd known all this time that it wasn't her fault. He and his ex-wife had had issues from the day they married, and instead of placing blame where it had belonged, on his wife *and* himself, he'd blamed the person who had been the easiest to target, because then he didn't have to look too closely at how he'd failed his marriage and, more importantly, his son and himself.

My mom told me that Red had tried to reach out to his son, who was only a few years older than me, but that he hadn't responded. Red had hope that he would, but I had to wonder. If it was my dad trying to reach out to me after so long a time with no communication, I probably wouldn't pick up the phone either.

At least, the old me wouldn't have. My mom would probably kick my ass for it though. So maybe I would respond. The new, more open and accepting Devo would.

But from that first day on, Red had seen me as his enemy. It had never been about "gay this" or "lesbian that." It was just about him and me. But it really had nothing to do with me at all, other than the color of my hair.

It was some kind of karma or weird alignment of the universe that my mom had found his photograph all the way down in Solo, New Mexico over twenty-five years ago. Red said he'd never sold them, but he suspected the picture had ended up there because he'd had a friend back in the day, another photographer who lived in New Mexico and spent his time traveling through the state, capturing images of the local cultures and people. Red had given his friend a few of his favorite shots he'd developed and printed. Maybe this friend had given the photo to someone or traded it for something else and that was how it ended up in a booth for sale at a dusty desert flea market.

Who knew? However it had gotten there, my mom seemed to think she was meant to find it. That it was meant to lead us here, to the Tetons. She believed Abey and I had been destined to meet, and so had she and Red, that she and Red working together had been written in the stars.

Which was exactly what was happening. They were talking about and planning to open a gallery next to Red Wild so they could showcase and sell all the art they planned to make together.

Dating was another thing entirely. My mom hadn't let Red right off the hook for the way he had behaved around me and the rest of Wisper, but I could already tell his charms had begun to work their magic on her. And after his apology, and especially after seeing him open up to everyone in town, I wasn't planning to get in their way.

I could accept Red if he could accept me. If he couldn't, I

knew for certain Mom would kick his butt to the curb quicker than a jackrabbit hopped.

The idea of them together still creeped me out, but I didn't have to agree with it. My mom had made it clear she didn't need my permission or blessing to work with Red, or do anything else with him, for that matter. All I could do was continue to love and support her, which was easy to do since she was just about the most loveable person who'd ever existed.

"Okay. Thank you." Stepping back from the door, I motioned for him to come in with a swing of my free arm.

When he entered the living room, he pulled another bouquet from behind his back that was equally as pretty as the one he'd given me. The roses meant for my mom weren't pink though. They were deep red and long stemmed.

She appeared at the end of the hallway, dressed to kill, in a deep purple number that hugged her hips enough to embarrass me. She smiled shyly at Red and accepted the flowers when he walked to her and held them out. She took them from his hands and lifted the bunch to her nose, drawing the fresh perfume of its petals into her lungs.

She was blushing hard-core. "Thank you, Red. They're lovely."

"You're welcome. Thank you for bein' my date to the dance. You look exquisite."

I didn't think her cheeks could get any redder without all the capillaries in her face rupturing, but she said, "You better be on your best behavior tonight."

He paled a little but nodded with a wry smile.

"So, um, have her home by ten," I joked, 'cause somebody had to say something, but nothing was coming to mind and no one else offered up anything else. They just stood there, staring at each other. "And don't do anything I wouldn't do."

Red turned, offering my mom his arm, and she slid her hand beneath his elbow, then rested it on his forearm. She grabbed the sweater that matched her dress off the back of the couch, and Red took it from her to drape it over her shoulders, then hooked her arm back through his.

"You drive a hard bargain," he told me with a nod. "But we'll be good."

My mom smiled. "Devo, what time will you be there?" She held her flowers out to me, and I took them and tucked them into the crook of my arm next to my flowers. "Put those in water, will you, please? But trim the stems first."

"Sure."

She winked at me. "Thanks, Devil."

"Welcome. I'm leaving in ten minutes," I said. "Just need to change."

"Are you sure you don't wanna ride with us? It's silly for everybody to take separate cars."

"Thanks, but no. I'm not sure what time I'll be home or if I'll make it back tonight." Now I was blushing. My mom wouldn't have batted an eye at me making a reference to staying out all night, but it was weird to say it in front of Red. "I'd rather take my truck."

Mom nodded, and Red did his best not to look uncomfortable. "Drive safely then," she said, "and we'll see you there."

"Have fun," Red said as he pushed out the door, leading my mom on their first… date?

What was the world coming to?

When they weren't talking on the phone about the new studio, they texted like teenagers. It was bizarro land, but my mom hadn't been this excited about anything, even her Etsy store, in… well, I'd *never* seen her like this. It was a side of her I'd never expected. And shame on me for that. But my dad had certainly never inspired the kind of spark I saw in her eyes now.

I was marking the whole thing down as weird shit that worked. What else could I do?

But I couldn't think about my mom and Red right now. If I didn't get a move on, I'd be late for my own date.

I ran to the kitchen, trimmed the stems of both bouquets with the kitchen scissors, and set each bunch in its own clear vase with water. I added a little flat 7-Up from the fridge 'cause my mom always said the flowers liked it—whatever that meant—and then skipped to my room.

My hair looked as good as it was going to. It refused to behave no matter what I did to it. Even the hottest flat iron wouldn't tame the stupid wave that couldn't seem to stay tucked behind my ear, even if I'd shellacked it with Elmer's glue.

Oh well. No time to worry about it now.

Abey knew what I looked like. She liked me no matter how bedheaded I appeared, but I still wanted to dress up for her, for our first extremely public date. She'd said she had a surprise for me, and I would get it when I met her at the station so we could walk through town together to the dance.

What could it be?

My favorite black, wide-leg, pinstriped trousers hung from my closet door on a hanger in front of a few new shirts I'd ordered for work.

It was a new day. Devo the Devil wouldn't strike again, 'cause she'd grown up. She would no longer fight everyone about everything. Instead, I would work hard to help the people I could, and I would build a life I could be proud of. Which meant no more trips to lock-up, even if it guaranteed getting strip-searched by the hottest cop I'd ever seen. She could strip me when we got home at night.

Yanking the trousers from the hanger, I pulled them on. I grabbed a white tank from my drawer and pulled it over my head without a bra 'cause I knew it drove Abey crazy when I didn't wear one. Since we had officially begun dating, her head had disappeared beneath my shirt more than once while we watched catty housewives or naked survivor shows on her couch so she could assault my bare breasts with kisses. Abey hated my trash TV shows, but she watched them with me because she said she loved the sound of my laugh.

I covered the tank with a fitted, white button-down. It had long sleeves, but the fabric was light, so I wouldn't get too hot, but my nipples wouldn't show through either. Only Abey had permission to obsess over them.

The September nights were cool already, but the nervousness running through my body would definitely make me sweat. Hopefully, it wouldn't rain like the weather dude from Jackson had predicted and everyone at the dance wouldn't get a show if my white shirts got soaked and didn't do a good enough job of covering me up, but I had a sweatshirt in my truck just in case.

Finally, I stepped into my deep-whiskey–colored patent leather boots. They were punk-rockfully clunky and had three-inch platform soles. If I was going to be dancing with my girl, I wanted to be as close to face-to-face as I could get. Having my eyes stuck at boob level all night was not a good idea. Already, I couldn't wait for the dance to be over so I could strip her bare back at her apartment.

"Okay. I think you're ready," I said to my empty bedroom, and I grabbed my wallet and lip gloss out of my bag. I headed to the bathroom for one more face check. I never wore makeup, besides gloss occasionally, so I wasn't sure what I was looking for, but I studied my face in the mirror anyway.

I looked good. I felt good.

My eyelashes looked kind of sexy and dark in the low yellow light, and I turned, eyeing the line of my body and pushing my butt out. Patting the pooch on my stomach, I tried to smooth it away, but Abey loved it, so I smiled at myself, noticing how the anticipation of seeing her made my cheeks pink all by itself.

Taking one last deep breath, I stood tall, pushed out my tits, and nodded.

Here we go!

———

Traffic downtown was a bitch!

Luckily, I had an in with a certain sheriff, so I got to park behind the station. I skipped around to the front sidewalk, excited like a teenager for my date, and when I pulled open the glass door and walked into the reception area, a whole cluster of faces turned my way.

Abey's partner, Frank, and his two foster kids, Murph and Nic, were there. Murph helped me out at the center some-times because he'd spent a lot of time there when he was homeless, after his mom abandoned him. We did movie nights for the center kids, and he was in charge of the popcorn. He reached out to high-five me.

Nic smiled, then sat at her dad's desk to draw on a piece of paper with a pencil. She was a lot more shy than Murph. I assumed Frank's wife, the town librarian and Abey's best friend, Sam, was in the locker room with Abey. I didn't see them anywhere.

Sheriff Michaels walked in from the back hallway, and

when he saw me, he nodded, his face shaded by his brown hat. "She's almost ready."

I let loose all the anxiety in my chest in one long breath. "'Kay," I breathed. "Thanks."

Shelley, the station's receptionist, sat at her tall desk, smacking a piece of gum in her mouth and twirling a lock of her hair around her finger. She kept looking at me, and I couldn't understand her expression. She looked almost angry, but every time her eyes traveled down the hallway toward where Abey most likely was, she couldn't help smiling. The people who worked at the station were like a little family, so maybe Shelley felt protective of Abey, but I was still glad she had the opinionated woman in her life.

The new female deputy was preparing to leave, probably to patrol the dance and festival on foot. Standing behind the desk that used to belong to Abey, she patted her vest, making sure she had all the tools she needed: handcuffs, pepper spray, a small handheld flashlight. She turned the knob on her shoulder radio and then set out.

When she passed me on her way to the door, she said, "Hi. I'm Roxanne. You look real nice."

"Thanks. Nice to meet you. Abey's told me all about you."

She raised an eyebrow. "Treat her well, y'hear?"

"I will," I said, and she tossed me a smile and a nod and left.

And then I heard a door at the end of the hallway open and close. Quiet whispers preceded them before Abey's mom and Sam walked out to the waiting room. Sam was grinning hard, and Abey's mom held a sweater in one hand while she argued with Sam. She kept lifting the sweater, but Sam wasn't paying attention. She was watching my face.

It wasn't that big of a room, and suddenly, I felt cramped and stuffed in there like a sardine.

Merv looked seriously uncomfortable. I would've laughed at how she kept lifting the sweater, trying to make Sam look at it, if I hadn't known how hard this probably was for her, but that was the only thought I could spare for her, because then Abey appeared.

Holy shit.

Like an ethereal blond goddess, Abey seemed to materialize in front of my eyes. She stepped into the room, and everything else, all the people I'd just felt so crowded by, faded into nothingness.

Abey was all I could see.

My surprise had to be apparent as my jaw dropped open. And Merv's insistence on Abey wearing a sweater finally made sense.

Abey had worn a dress! It was a sleeveless, red and black buffalo plaid body-con with a square-cut neckline. It fell to her calves, but it hugged her gorgeous curves like a dream. I could see every dip, swell, and hollow.

Her bare, toned arms were sexy as hell, her hips flared out below her waist enough to make me lick my lips, and her ass in that scrap of fabric was sure to bring grown men and women to their knees.

But she was with *me*.

Her hair had been braided into an intricate and sexy plait, but curly tendrils framed her face. The end of the braid cascaded over her breasts, which filled out the top of the dress. And I mean, it was *full*. I couldn't look at them though. Drool didn't go with my outfit.

I stared hard into Abey's eyes, watching the deep blue color and the way light flickered and lit up behind them when she saw me. She smiled, knowing full well she'd shocked me into speechlessness, and I stumbled back a step, knocking the backs of my knees into the chair behind me. I fell into it and just sat there.

I had no words, no thoughts, except that I wanted my hands on her. My hands, my lips, my tongue, my fingers. I wanted to jump her and have her carry me away.

I wanted to rip my heart out of my chest and hand it to her. She owned it anyway.

I stood, and she stopped in front of me. She whispered, "Well, ain't you gonna say anything?"

CHAPTER THIRTY

ABEY

"Mama did my hair," I said, patting the elegant, loose fishtail braid at the back of my neck. I pulled the end, twisting the hair between two fingers, taking out the edge of my nerves on the poor thing. Mama stood behind me, and she reached around and swatted my hand away. She'd kill me if I messed up the braid she'd worked on for almost an hour.

Devo smiled at her. "My mom's already at the dance," she said. "She'd love to meet you, if you'd like. Her name is Liluye. She's wearing a purple dress and sweater. She has long, black hair. You can't miss her."

I felt grateful to her for offering an opportunity for Mama to get out of the station. She was trying to be supportive, but I knew she'd probably never been more uncomfortable and didn't know what to say.

"We'll see you there," Frank said, trying to help move things along. He waved his hand in a circle above his head, giving everyone a "get the fuck outta here" look.

Sam, Murph, and little Nic followed him to the door, and my mama went next. But before she left, she stopped and turned back to me. She smiled softly and looked me over. Bet she never thought she'd see me in a dress again. I hadn't worn one since I was fifteen. She would be pissed all night that I wouldn't wear the sweater she'd brought to cover me up. She held the ridiculous angora thing out toward me again, but I shook my head "no" for the fiftieth time, and she finally gave up. She rolled her eyes and pushed out the front door.

Carey came to stand beside me. He clapped me on the back like he always did, like the fact that I was a woman didn't even matter. It never had to him, no matter who I kissed.

"I'm meetin' Frannie over there. Better get goin'. You kids have fun." He smiled at Devo, winked at me, and was gone. Technically, he was on duty tonight, along with Dan and Roxi, but he'd never pass up a chance to dance with his wife, not after they'd found their way back to each other after years apart.

When the room was empty except for Devo and me, and Shelley, who promptly excused herself and disappeared down the hall, Devo finally blinked.

"You are more beautiful than I know how to put into words." She stepped closer and anchored her hands on my hips, looking up at me. The boots she'd worn must've had some good heels, because the distance between our lips was less.

"Thank you. You look amazin'. So sexy."

She blushed, and I found myself having a hard time looking away from her shiny pink lips. The color was subtle, but it was there, and I marveled at how it matched the rosy hue of her cheeks.

She didn't seem to be able to move her gaze away from my cleavage, of which there was ample. I was kind of embarrassed, having the girls out there for all to notice, but it felt good too. I felt powerful and disarming.

I'd certainly disarmed Devo tonight, which had been my plan.

She lifted up on her tiptoes to press a kiss to my lips, and I closed my eyes and inhaled, breathing in the berry scent of her lip gloss and then tasting it when I licked my lips.

"I think I'm fallin' in love with you," she said.

My heart skipped five beats. The smile on my face couldn't have been bigger, and my cheeks cramped. "I don't just *think* I love you." I'd been so nervous to say the words, but now they flowed out of me easily, and Devo stood a little taller when she heard them.

She kissed me again, but this time, it wasn't quick or innocent. It was the single most intimate kiss I'd ever shared with anyone.

Our eyes closed, and she moaned, and then I did, too, as her tongue swept into my mouth. The sounds of our kiss filled the station, and I felt free in a way I'd never experienced. There wasn't anyone else there, but still, I'd never have risked a kiss like this before.

Her hands slid upward, her palms cupping the sides of my breasts in my dress, and I wound my arms around her back, my fingers reaching up to play with the ends of her shiny black hair, fingering the little duck tail she hated. I tugged on it, and she shivered at the now familiar way goosechills danced down her neck.

"I'm not sure if this dance is a good idea," she said. A smirk began taking over her lips, and she pursed them, trying not to smile any bigger.

"What? Why not?" I looked down at myself, letting go of her and sweeping my arms out dramatically, but I knew where her thoughts had been headed. "I wore a dress for you! Do you know what it took to get me in this thing? Think Crisco."

She laughed, then followed my gaze from my shoulders to my toes. "It's a shame," she said, "'cause all I can think about is gettin' you *out* of it."

"Mm. Well then," I whispered, then bumped her nose with mine and peppered those rosy lips with tiny kisses, winding my arms around her again, "we better get this show on the road."

She spun on her foot, turning toward the front door, but her eyes never left mine. She held out her hand, and I took it and tucked it under my arm.

"Yes," she said, "we'd better."

Standing on the stoop outside, we looked up and down the street. People milled about everywhere. Some shops hadn't yet closed for the night, their owners hoping to cash in on the infusion of tourists who'd come into town looking for a little bit of country-mountain fun.

The lights and displays in the windows lit Main Street with a subtle glow. The white twinkle lights hanging all through town from lamppost to lamppost helped, and the warm chatter of conversation and laughter in the air gave a homey and comforting feeling.

No one bothered us. Some people tossed smiles our way as they passed us on the sidewalk. My dress got a few double takes from a couple of the cowboys who'd wandered into town from the ranches surrounding Wisper, but they all knew me, so they knew better than to make any lewd comments. I'd thrown a few of them behind bars at one time or another over the years, so they probably didn't want to risk it.

And I looked damn good. There wasn't anything they could've said to ruin my night.

Holding the hand of the person who was quickly becoming my home felt perfect. It felt right in a way I couldn't describe, like there was a song inside me. It was cheesy but true.

Really, the sound had come from the dance a couple blocks up the street, but then a flash of lightning above us made my heart beat faster while the notes of the music danced and played in the air around Devo and me, frolicking and following as we walked silently toward the very center of town.

But even rain couldn't ruin this night, if it ever fell. It wouldn't matter if it did. We'd still dance and laugh and rush home to make love later and fall asleep to the sounds of its quiet tapping on the windows.

"You okay?" she asked me, lacing her fingers through mine as we walked.

"Yeah. I'm more okay right now than I've ever been. You?"

The smile on her lips said it all. "Never better."

"Good. Although I think I maybe shouldn't have worn these shoes." I looked down at the pain-inducing leather cowboy booties currently squeezing my toes. "They're cute, but they hurt like a bitch."

"Take 'em off," Devo said.

"What, and just go barefoot?"

"Why not? Nothin' should ever cause you pain."

She stopped walking, pulling me to the stoop outside Your Local Bookie. In the window, Aubrey stood behind the counter, ringing up her last customer of the night, and she smiled and waved, then wiggled her eyebrows in a bawdy way. I shook my head and rolled my eyes at her, then sat when Devo pulled me down with her.

The cold of the concrete step seeped through my dress, sending a shiver through me as she crouched in front of me and unzipped my boots, then pulled them off slowly, like I was Cinderella and she the prince.

I wiggled my toes and flexed my feet. "Thank you. Feels better already."

"Does your uniform come in a dress option?" she asked, eyeing my rack again. "'Cause a girl could really get used to seein' you like this more often."

"Yeah, they do. Skirts for desk duty, but they're brown and awful. I ain't wearin' that shit. Ever."

Devo laughed. "Fair enough." She stood, gripping the ankles of my boots in one hand as she reached for me with the other. "Ready?"

The celebration in full swing down the road lured us again, and we could see people dancing around the edges of the dance floor, men twirling women around, some teenagers swaying to the rhythm awkwardly, but before I looked back at Devo to take her hand again, two women caught my eye.

They danced the two-step together and held onto each other as if the rest of the world didn't matter.

My heart swelled, and I had to hold back tears as I watched them.

This was for me. Cal and Phil wouldn't be dancing and showing their relationship to the rest of our small town if it hadn't been for the struggle I'd been going through. I knew it had to have been Cal's idea. Phil never would've been able to talk Cal into it if she hadn't wanted to do it.

Finally, I took Devo's hand and let her pull me up. "Look," I said lifting my chin in their direction.

Devo turned and squinted. "What? I don't see any—" Her mouth popped open. "Is that... Is that Phil Beasley and Cal DuBois? Holy shit!" She turned to look at me, her eyes wide. "Is that who you meant when you said you knew of two other lesbians in Wisper?"

I just smiled. It hadn't been my secret to tell, but I figured it was a secret no longer.

"How the hell did *that* happen?"

"Love is love," I said, shrugging. "Sometimes, you think you know what it is, what it means, and sometimes you don't. Friends can turn into lovers for lots of reasons. In Phil and Cal's case, I think it had somethin' to do with soup."

Devo laughed, and we held hands again as we sprinted toward our first real date.

More lightning flashed above us, lighting the way, and as soon as we stepped under the safety of the tent, Devo stashed my boots behind the wooden stage someone had built for the occasion. Finn and Evvie Cade were up there, surrounded by slow-pulsing stage lights, Evvie crooning away as Finn strummed his guitar.

He gave us a wink as we looked out at all the couples dancing. I saw an open space, so I led Devo there and turned to face her. As we merged into traffic, I noticed Theo and Brady on the sidelines, Theo with his arm around Brady's shoulders while Brady's hand snaked around Theo's back. They gave me courage.

"I don't actually know how to do the two-step," Devo said nervously. "But I watched a YouTube video."

I chuckled and placed my hand in hers when she held it out. We came together, face to face, and she reached up, resting her other hand on my shoulder as mine wrapped around her waist.

"Nothin' to it," I said, taking the first step backward. She followed my lead, stepping with her left foot when I stepped backward with mine. "One two, one two. Fast fast, slow slow. Fast fast, slow slow. There ya go. You got it."

"Is this really dancing though? Isn't this just walkin'?"

"I s'pose it is walkin', but we're doin' it together and to a rhythm. Isn't the waltz the same thing?"

She nodded, watching our feet. "You're not scared I'll crush your toes?"

"Nah." She hadn't stepped on my feet yet, and she had swagger. She could move. Her hips were sultry little attention grabbers.

"How do you know how to do this?"

"My daddy taught me when I was a girl," I said, smiling at the memory flashing in my head from when I was thirteen or fourteen, dancing with the man who had been my favorite person back then, in a place much like the fall festival.

Devo looked up. "Your mom did a good job with your hair. You're like a red plaid angel tonight. Sometimes, I look at you, and it hurts"—she lifted her hand from my shoulder and placed it over her heart—"in here."

I nodded and rested my hand over hers. "I know what you mean."

We danced then, ignoring the rest of the world and looking only at each other. Devo's eyes stayed on mine, and her lips held the most brilliant smile, her teeth gleaming in the glow from the thousands of tiny lights twinkling under the massive black tent.

I would have to remember to thank Aislinn for making this night unforgettable. She couldn't see for herself the ambiance she'd helped to create all over downtown Wisper, but I'd do my best to describe it to her at book club.

"Who did all this work?" I asked, motioning with a bob of my head around the dance floor. "Aislinn told me she was in charge of the dance, and she and I planned out all the road closures, but she had to have help with all the decorations."

"Vern," Devo said simply.

"Huh. Who woulda thunk it?" I joked, remembering the delinquent the guy used to be.

Carey had made it a career goal to arrest Vern as many times as he could before he started working at Ace's House and turned his life around. I still remembered when Vern had lived in our jail cell for a week 'cause his mama wouldn't let him come back home after he'd gotten drunk with his friends and crashed her car in a ditch.

Devo rushed forward a step to kiss me unexpectedly and then moved back into our rhythm just as quickly, right before Carey tapped her on the shoulder.

His wife, Frannie, held his hat at the edge of the dance floor, and she waved. He rarely went without his hat, so he always had hat hair. He ran his hand through the rusty red tresses, trying to fluff them. "May I cut in?"

"Sure," Devo said, transferring my hand into his, but she leaned closer to me, whispering, "I'll get a better look at your ass in this dress from the sidelines anyway."

I giggled. I couldn't help myself as Carey stepped in, leading me backward, and I watched Devo go over his shoulder.

"You look like a million bucks tonight, my friend," he said, grinning at me. "Frannie says that dress should be illegal."

"Tell her I said thanks."

We'd barely gone twenty steps when Frank cut in next. And then it was a long line of people cutting in every few minutes. Sam cut in, too, and then Phil, Carly, and Juneau each took a turn. Even Roxanne popped into the dance tent for a minute.

They all wanted to support me, just in case there was anyone watching who thought it wrong that I was with a woman. My friends were all there to make sure any naysayers would keep their cake holes shut.

Finally, Red stepped forward. He'd been talking and dancing with Liluye all night, but when she went to get a drink, he came straight for me, tapping Cal on her dainty, lace-covered shoulder. She looked positively lovely tonight, dressed in an ivory and lavender skirt and jacket set.

"May I cut in?" he asked her.

"Of course," she said. She stopped our movement and looked at me. "Proud of you."

"Proud of you too," I said with a shy smile. Cal wasn't one to broadcast her feelings or opinions, but her actions tonight spoke louder than words ever could have.

When she was safely surrounded by the group of book club ladies, they all crowded around Devo next to an old red Ford truck that had been backed up to the dance floor. The bed was decorated with hay and pumpkins. It was a cute spot to take photos.

As all my friends and my extremely beautiful date watched from afar, Red held out his hand. He spun me so he walked backward, and we fell into the "fast fast, slow slow" steps.

"Never thought I'd be dancin' with you," I told him, brushing a loose string off of his jacket's lapel. "You clean up pretty good."

"So do you," he said earnestly.

"You havin' fun?"

He nodded. "More fun than I've had in a very long time."

"I'm glad."

"You know," he said, "in another life, I could've been your dad."

A bark of laughter escaped me. "You couldn't handle my mama."

"No." He chuckled, looking over his shoulder at where the woman in question stood with Liluye, drinking orange punch from clear plastic teacups and chatting. I could tell from her body language Mama was enjoying herself, but she still had a scowl on her face. "You're probably right about that. But you're a good kid. Thanks for always lookin' out for me. I never woulda admitted this before, but sometimes, you stoppin' in the store was the only thing to get me through a hard day. Sometimes, you were the only person I held a conversation with in a week's time. You were the only one who could tolerate me. I appreciated that, even if I didn't say so."

"You're welcome, but I'm glad you've got more people to talk to now."

"That I do," he said, glancing toward Liluye again. "It's funny, ain't it? All this time, they've been here. You and I were just too stubborn to see it."

"*You* were definitely stubborn," I said. "For me, it was about somethin' else."

Red nodded. "I understand that."

"Maybe a little bit of stubbornness," I admitted with a sly grin.

"I hope you know I got your back. You ever need anything, you let me know. Okay, kiddo?"

"Thanks, Red."

He stopped moving when Devo tapped his shoulder. She almost had to tiptoe to reach it.

"Well, guess I'll give you back your dance partner," he said to her. And to me, he said, "Thanks for the dance."

I saluted him before grabbing my date and pulling her to me.

"You sure are a popular woman tonight," she said as she

urged us back into the dance. The crowd moved clockwise around the floor, and we joined back in the shuffle.

"You 'bout ready to head out?" I asked while visions of dirty deeds danced in my head.

"Head out? You wanna leave already? We just got here."

I shrugged. "We came, we saw, we danced, but I've got other plans for you tonight."

"Oh really?"

"Yes, *really*. Plans that don't include anyone but you and me."

"Do these plans involve clothes?"

"Yes," I said, and her face fell into a frown. But I leaned in closer and whispered, "Only so I can rip 'em off and ravish you till the sun comes up."

That got her smiling again. Both her hands wrapped around my hips, and she squeezed, reaching up on her toes to kiss me. We stopped in the middle of the dance floor, and for a moment, I could hear people noticing, coughing and chuckling, but then it all faded away.

The only thing that mattered was Devo's mouth on mine, her tongue dueling with mine, and the warmth beneath her hands as they slid slowly up my back. Finally, she pulled away, and we both gasped for breath.

Twisting the end of my braid between her fingers, she peered up at me from beneath her eyelashes as a pink flush spread over her cheeks and neck. "Let's go," she said, and she pulled her truck key from her pocket.

I snatched it from her fingers. "I'm drivin'. Don't wanna have to arrest you for speedin' or gettin' reckless."

"Oh, we're *definitely* gettin' reckless tonight."

I looked for Frank. When I spotted him on the edge of the dance floor, twirling Nic around in a circle by her hand, I caught his eye and nodded to my mama. He nodded back.

He'd drive her home. What a good dad he'd become. It filled me with joy to see how happy that little girl made Frank.

I caught a quick glimpse of Rye in a dark corner. His eyes were glued to the area all the book club ladies had just been congregating, but when he noticed me looking, he threw me a smile and a nod and then backed out of the tent.

Thunder boomed and lightning cracked in the dark sky outside, and as the rain began to fall, people scrambled from the edges of the dance floor for the cover of the tent. Devo held my hand tighter. She led me toward the exit, swiping my boots from behind the stage as we went.

I waved to my friends huddled up together near the drink table to ward off the sudden drop in temperature. Everyone looked around for their belongings or for their dates so they could all make a mad dash to their vehicles, hoping to avoid the worst of the rain.

Taking the first step into the onslaught, I turned as it soaked my dress and hair. The rough Main Street concrete beneath my feet felt grounding, and I pulled the elastic band from the end of my braid, dragging my free hand through my wet hair, letting it loose.

Devo gasped behind me, and I turned, still holding her hand as I squinted against the whipping wind and stinging rain. "Baby, you comin'?"

There were stars in her eyes and dreams splashed across her beautiful face, etched into the tilt of her smile. "With you? Always."

EPILOGUE
DEVO

"Murph, I don't think *Die Hard* is the best movie for movie night," I said, laughing under my breath.

He plopped into the chair in front of my desk. "Aw, man. Why not?"

"Well, 'cause your dad would probably arrest me if I let you watch it."

"Nuh uh," he said. "My dad's the one who showed it to me. Besides, 'tis the season. It's practically a Christmas movie, so November is the perfect time to watch it."

Abey snorted. "Sound logic. And that sounds like Frank, though I'm not sure we should tell Sam. She'd probably arrest Frank."

Murph sighed, his teenage angst on full display. "Alright, well, what movie do *you* wanna do?"

"I dunno," I said as I scrolled down the search on my computer's screen that listed every "family friendly" movie since 1980. "Somethin' family friendly. That's all I got. If you ask me about TV shows, I got you covered, but movies… not so much"

"Like what?" he argued. "*The Lego Movie*? Lame."

"How 'bout *The Goonies*," Abey offered, leaning against the door frame inside my office at Ace's House, looking delicious in her uniform, her boobs pushed up front and center. *Mm mm mmm*. Gone were her days of sports bras. Now that she knew how in love with her breasts I was, she'd gone shopping. Demi cups, lace, black, strappy bras every day, all day.

Next, my hungry eyes went to the crotch of her brown pants as I remembered her kneeling naked over my mouth last night. I bit my lip when an image of her leaned over a dining chair, rolling her hips above my face as I ate her out on her living room floor threatened to make me moan.

Oh my God, the way she'd screamed as she came.

Shit. Not with the kid here. Get your mind out of the gutter, Devo! But it was such a nice gutter.

"You ever seen that one?" Abey asked Murph innocently, not having any clue to the whereabouts of my thoughts.

"Never heard of it," Murph said, playing with the paperclips stuck to the magnetic horse on my desk.

"My mama was just talkin' about it the other day. She used to play it for me and my brothers when we were kids. They loved it."

"Fine," Murph relented. "But it better be good."

"It is," Abey said, nudging his shoulder on his way out the door.

"See you tomorrow night," he called behind him.

Abey looked at me, straightening from her perch against the door. "Kid's a hard sell."

"You ain't lyin'."

She unleashed the full Abey experience on me. Her smile was the stuff of legends. "You ready then?"

"Am I ready to go check out the land my girlfriend wants to build me a house on?"

"Yep. That about sums it up."

"And you're sure Bax has no problem with this plan? And he doesn't mind us usin' the land for a small CSA farm?"

"I'm positive. He finally admitted he hates sheep." She laughed. "He's ready to move on to the next stage of his life. He even wants to talk to you about gettin' the resort guests involved. Maybe they can help with plantin' and harvestin'. Athena's over the moon about it. She wants to plant water-melons. So, in the spring, Brand will—"

She stopped mid-sentence, scrunching up her face, looking off into space.

"What?"

"It just occurred to me. That movie. *The Goonies.* One of the character's names is Brand. And my mama loved that movie. And my brother's name is Brand... Huh. Never caught it before."

I chuckled. "Then we should invite her to movie night."

Abey sighed. "She's bein' more supportive, but I wouldn't expect any miracles where she's concerned. She still goes to the same church, the one that told her that her daughter is the spawn of Satan himself. Although the other night, she mentioned to Athena that she might try a new church. I hope the people at her old church aren't givin' her a hard time about me, but at any rate, I doubt she'd be up for hangin' out with a bunch of gay teens to watch a movie."

"You never know," Devo said. She shrugged. "But we can still invite her. Maybe one of these times she'll say yes."

"Maybe. Anyway, Brand will be here next spring to start buildin' the cabins for Bax's new business plan. And he said it won't be too much for him to throw up a house for us on the back of the property, too, as long as we can put up the money for the supplies he doesn't already have, which we can. It'll have a mother-in-law's quarters for your mama, just in case she and Red ever break up."

She laughed 'cause she knew how in love they were. Fat chance I'd ever get Red out of my life now.

"And he's buildin' another house for my mama and Dixon near the main house." She rolled her eyes. "We'll all be a happy family."

Stepping around my desk, I stood in front of her and pushed up on my tiptoes into her space, winding my arms around her waist. "You sure that's what you want? I mean, to live on the farm where your dad treated you like shit?"

She wrapped her arms around my shoulders. "Yeah. It's all I've ever wanted, to be close with my family again. And Daddy's gone. When the sheep are gone, his influence won't be there anymore. We can all have a fresh start.

"Plus, where the hell we gonna get land like that for a better price? In the Tetons?" She shook her head. "Never gonna happen. All we gotta do is help Bax and Mama get the Lee Family Mountain Resort started. I don't mind washin' a few loads of sheets every week to help out. We'll get to see Athena more, and we can teach her everything we learn about farmin'."

"That makes it worth it for sure."

I locked up my office, and she led me to her truck parked out along the curb in front of the center. Her blue and white plastic cooler sat in the bed.

"What's that for?"

"You didn't think I'd take you to the place we're gonna live together without a picnic, did ya?"

I looked in the back seat of her truck and saw blankets, a pillow, and more food.

She winked at me through the truck's windows. "I might also have *other* plans."

The mid-November day was chilly, the blue, cloudless afternoon sky as beautiful as it could only be in Wyoming, and the sun warmed everything up.

"But it'll be cold out there under the shade of the trees."

She wiggled her eyebrows. "We've never gotten it on in my truck."

I gasped and clutched at my neck playfully. "Deputy Sheriff Lee, I'm appalled. That's dangerous behavior. It's probably against the law to have sex in a county vehicle."

"Oh, didn't I tell you?" she mocked, arching an eyebrow as she opened her door. When we were both seated inside, she waited for me to click my seatbelt into place, then said, "I'm an outlaw. I play by my own rules."

She started the truck, and Tay-Tay's loud voice spilled out of the speakers.

"Oops!" She turned it down as a lovely pink blush spread across her cheeks, and I watched it travel down her neck.

"You play this song a lot. What is it?"

She turned her head, gazing at me as she hit the button on her dash to start the song over. "It's my favorite. It's called 'I'm Only Me When I'm With You.'"

I leaned over to kiss her lips. "Who would've ever guessed Abey Lee was a romantic?"

"Seriously? The fact that I sit through an hour every week with a bunch of ladies swoonin' over imaginary book boyfriends didn't clue you in? And I actually *read* the books. Sam's finally forcin' us to read *Pride and Prejudice*. Do you know how old that book is?"

"I thought you just did it because of your friendship with Sam."

"Well, yeah. I mean, that's part of it. She's my best friend. But that wasn't why I went originally."

"Why'd you go?"

"Because I found out that there's such a thing as gay and lesbian romance books. I had to believe that kind of love existed for me. Y'know?"

"Believe it now?"

"Mm." She smiled at me, her face taking on a dreamy fairy-tale quality as she leaned back against her seat. Her head lolled in my direction, and loose blond tendrils of her hair fell over her shoulders. "I believe."

"Alright then. Let's get this show on the road. Let's go make our lesbian dreams come true."

"You got it."

She put the truck in gear, and we headed off.

"Isn't that Dan?" I asked, watching Deputy Draven as he looked at a display in the front bookstore window before he moved down the sidewalk toward an outdoor sale table.

"Huh," Abey said. "He told me he wasn't a reader."

"Maybe he wants to join book club too."

She snorted. "He'd have to fight Cal DuBois to gain entry. She wouldn't stand for a man in book club."

"That could be fun to watch," I said, laughing.

"Oh God. She'd kill him." She rolled down her window, tapping her horn and waving to Dan and Aubrey when she stepped out of her store.

Rye rounded the corner of Washington and Main, and he stopped dead in his tracks when he saw Aubrey swatting a hand in our truck's direction. She blushed, but when she turned, she caught sight of Rye, and all the color drained from her face.

Aubrey stood in the middle of the sidewalk between a frozen Rye and a clueless Dan. Both men looked at her, but no one said a word.

"What was *that* about?"

"Uh. I have no idea, but you better believe I'm gonna

bring it up at book club." Abey snorted. "I'm freakin' excited I finally have some gossip and somethin' to poke fun at her about! You think it's a love triangle?"

"I don't know," I said, shaking my head, but I turned in my seat to look out the back window as Aubrey fiddled nervously with books on the outdoor display in front of the bookstore. I'd walked by the display earlier in the day on my way from Coffee Shot to my mom's studio next to Red Wild, so I knew exactly what was on that table, and it was all romance. Pink, swoony, cartoony romance. I couldn't picture Dan getting into that. Like at all.

I'd only met him a couple times, but I was fairly certain he wouldn't be caught dead reading that kind of book. I knew Rye a bit better. We'd never talked about books, but I would've bet money if he were reading one, the title would be something like *Monster Trucks: A Way of Life* or *Building 4-Wheelers for Dummies*.

When Dan finally noticed the invisible tension between Aubrey and Rye, he straightened and stiffened, then tipped his hat toward Aubrey and walked away quickly. Rye fled in the opposite direction, leaving Aubrey standing in front of her store alone. She threw her hands up in the air, rolled her eyes dramatically, and stomped back inside.

"Oh my God!"

Abey's head ping-ponged back and forth from the road in front of her to my face. "What! What'd you see?"

"I'm not sure," I said, giggling. "But whatever it was, it was weird."

"Whatcha think?" Abey asked, standing behind me with her arms wrapped around my middle as we looked out at the mountains in the distance. She tucked her chin into the crook of my neck.

Snow had already fallen on the tallest of the Tetons' peaks, and it made the dark rock all the more rugged and stark-looking.

The spot she'd chosen on her family's land was beautiful. Surrounded by evergreen trees and tall field grasses, it was less than half a mile to the lake she'd taken me to on our ATV date but set back into the rise of a small hill. There was plenty of room for a two-stall barn and a small CSA garden.

"I think we're lucky to get to look at that view." I turned in her arms. "But I like *this* view better." I kissed her chin. "You sure though? I mean, I know technically I'm homeless since my mom shacked up with Red, but that doesn't mean *you* have to house me. I could get an apartment in town."

She tucked her favorite lock of my hair behind my ear, watching my face as she spoke. "I told ya, the Carringtons are sellin' their house in the spring, so I'd probably have to move anyway. But Devo," she whispered, "to be able to wake up to your face every mornin'? That's all I've ever wanted. I can't wait to live with you."

"Okay. Me too." I nodded, trying not to look like the giddiest idiot on the planet, but my smile just kept growing. I tried to look serious. "But only if you're sure."

She laughed softly. "I am. Are you?"

"Well, I mean, we're goin' in on the costs together, but you own the land. So…"

"So what?"

"So if you ever dump me, I guess I'll be homeless again."

"What's mine is already yours." She kissed me quickly, leaving the taste of her lips on mine. "So why don'tcha marry me then, and we can make it official?"

I choked on the spit in my mouth. "Wh-what? Did you just ask me to m—"

"Yes," she said resolutely. "I asked you to marry me. Want me to get on my knee?"

"No. But Abey? A-are you sure?"

Since we'd started dating, there hadn't been any major issues with the people in town. A few snide comments, even more disgusted looks when we held hands or kissed in public, but no one had said anything. Abey'd heard about a few comments some of her fellow deputies at the station in Corner Junction had made, but in Wisper, things had been pretty copacetic for the most part.

"I'm so damn sure. I've wanted to ask you for, like, a month."

"But…"

Her cheeks turned pink. "But what? I thought lesbians liked to stake their claim on their women."

I chuckled. She wasn't wrong.

"And no one says we have to rush it. I mean, we could get engaged and then wait till the house is done and we're settled to start plannin' things. But I want you to feel secure about where you live. I need you to know every day that I want you and that our home is where we both belong. I want us to choose our life together."

Reaching up, I took her face gently between my hands. "Yes," I whispered. "Yes. I'll marry you. I want that for you too."

She blushed and looked at the ground between us. "I don't have a ring."

I pushed my thumbs beneath her jaw so she'd look at me again. When she did, I said, "We can get them together."

"Yeah?"

"Yeah. You can pick out my ring, and I'll pick out yours. I

already have an idea about the one I wanna get you." I wrapped my arms around her neck, imagining a sapphire-banded wedding ring. "I love you, you know? Wherever you are, it's where I'll always call home."

This time, the full Abey experience nearly knocked me on my ass. Her smile was brilliant. "I'm gonna love you till the end of time," she said, and she kissed me.

Into her mouth, I breathed, "Feels like my heart's gonna pound right outta my chest."

"I got you," she said, pulling me tighter against her body. "I *promise*."

If you liked Abey & Devo's story (or loved it, I hope), **please consider leaving a review—even just a few words would help—wherever you buy your books, Goodreads**, or **Bookbub**. Self-published indie authors rely heavily upon reviews to get our stories out to the masses. And thank you. I know it takes time to do this. I appreciate the time out of your day and the effort.

If you'd like to stay up to date with my book releases and news, please sign up for my newsletter on my website, gretarosewest.com. I promise not to spam you. I usually only send out one newsletter a month, sometimes two if I have a new release or a big free book promo, but that helps you, cuz **FREE BOOKS!!**

DEAR READER,

Thank you for reading this book!

I had a lot of fun writing it and letting free my Devo tendencies a little. Being in her point of view takes me back to high school, when I told my dad I'd move out of the house and never speak to him again if he didn't remove from our living room the bear-hide rug he'd brought home from a hunting trip. Spoiler alert: he did remove it. He put it in his bedroom, and I never ran away from home. Lol. It was a compromise that I still can't believe he made for his socially conscientious know-it-all teenager. He'd gone all the way to Canada for that bear, and he was so proud because it was some kind of record-breaking kill. The hunting camp people even put him on their brochure for the next season. But he was a great dad. He raised three girls all by himself, and he knew how badly it hurt my heart every time I looked at that bear rug.

Abey and Devo's love story led me to some naughty internet searches. You should see some of the stuff that still pops up in my search results! That'll teach me not to use an incognito tab. But writing and researching the book also introduced me to some really cool people, and I'll forever be grateful to Abey and Devo for that.

There's an odd place I go sometimes, where the characters take shape and come to life in my head, and this book was born and lived in that place. I met Abey in the first book I ever wrote, *Burned*. She was only mentioned in passing, I think in only one sentence, but somehow, I already knew her. She's been biding her time in my imagination, waiting for her turn, and when I finally sat down to write her story, the words flowed easily. She may be silly and blunt, but she's beauty personified on the inside, and I cherish her like a sister. And Devo just stomped right into the mix during the writing of *Storms Inside Us.* She's bossy, but I adore her for it.

People have said that it's stupid for me to try to bridge the gap between one side of a political line to the other. And while I know a romance book will never accomplish world peace, I sometimes feel like I live on that line. A lot of people in my life are on one side, and even more are on the other. What's so wrong with wishing the two sides could blend and live together in some kind of weird, sexy Western harmony? That's my hope for our world, foolish as it may be, and if my book allowed you to imagine that world, even for just a moment, then it was worth it. Romance should let you escape and allow you to feel love for the characters and imagine how being loved by them would feel. Romance should allow you to dream, and a world where hate doesn't exist is my dream.

love always,

greta

greta@gretarosewest.com

gretarosewest.com

From small-town Western romance author, Greta Rose West, preorder this angst-filled love story, the fifth book in the Wisper Dreams Series, Midnight Surrounds Us. You'll swoon, probably cry, and you will 100% fall in love...

Ryder Graves dreams about taking the reins to his family's farm, but one thing stands in his way: his dad. As the baby of the family, Rye's never been taken seriously. He never went to college, and he can't even keep a good woman; his last girlfriend proved that when she dumped him in front of his entire family with a fistful of potato salad to his face. But he's desperate to show everyone what he can do.

And he just might have a trick up his flannel sleeve.

Rye's had an eye for his brother's best friend's widow since high school. She was off limits back then, but things are different now, and he just heard a rumor that might provide him the perfect opportunity to show his dad he's not a failure. If he can convince her to go along with his plan, maybe his devilish good looks and his overflowing bank account will help him win more than his dad's approval.

Aubrey George thinks all men suck. Swipe right? No thank you. She's a leftie.

When her husband passed overseas, Aubrey found herself middle-aged and alone with twin boys who couldn't stay out of trouble if she hog-tied them to her bumper, but they're grown now and somebody else's problem, so it's finally time for her to focus on what makes her happy: her bookstore. Unfortunately, nobody's buying books, not from her anyway, and she's in danger of losing the only thing in her life she's good at. She can't deny Rye Graves looks damn good in jeans and a cowboy hat, or that his cocky smirk makes her heart race faster than it has in years, but he's arrogant, young, and thinks he can solve all his problems with money, but when he offers to pay off the back taxes she owes and help her build her business, she laughs in his face—but then she says yes. What's she got to lose?

Her panties, if she's not careful. And her heart, if she can find it.

The fifth book in the Wisper Dreams series, *Midnight Surrounds Us*, is a steamy fake-dating farce, but it's hot and funny, and it's the small-town romance you never knew you needed till now, about finding your piece in this world, standing your ground, and letting love sweep you

**off your feet when it shows up wearing jeans and a
cowboy hat.**

Coming January 2025
PREORDER *Midnight Surrounds Us* NOW!

EXTRA CONTENT

Join my newsletter for a FREE short story, *Wild Heart: Welcome to Wisper*, Wisper news, and The Cade Ranch Sexcapades—naughty little interludes for my subscribers ONLY!

Jack and Evvie's wedding scenes are there!

Sign up on my website: gretarosewest.com

LETS CONNECT!

You can also join me in my Facebook group, Wisperites Unite. We get up to a lot of fun there. Mostly we drool over sexy cowboys, but we do other things there too, I promise, like giveaways and fun games, and my Wisperites always get new book news first, teasers, and we chat about life. We'd love to have you!

Go to: https://www.facebook.com/groups/wisperitesunite

I would love to hear from you. Email me at greta@gretarosewest.com. I'll reply. You can find me on the usual social sites, but I mostly hang out on Facebook and Instagram.

@gretarosewest

ABOUT THE AUTHOR

Greta Rose West was a floundering artsy flake until cowboy Jack Cade showed up, knocking on the door of her brain, pounding on it, and then he just plain kicked it down. She's a boy mom to a grown freakin' man, and she lives in NW Indiana with her husband and her two precocious kitties, Geoff Trouble and Sally Mae Midnight. When she's not writing, she's reading and devouring music. She enjoys indie films no one else likes, and her favorite food is Aver's Veggie Revival pizza.

You can find her on Instagram @gretarosewest, in her Facebook group, Wisperites Unite, or on her website.

gretarosewest.com

Printed in Great Britain
by Amazon